Praise for Iain Stewart's
Knights of the Air, Book 1: Rage!

***BookView Review*, Gold Award Winner**
"A remarkable historical novel... A sharp and effective blend of WWI aviation action and adventure, a hefty dose of emotion and human drama, plus a dash of romance, keep the pages flying. Finely written and vividly imagined, this is a complex, gritty novel delving into the brutalities of war. Stewart is an author to watch."

Independent Book Review
"*Rage!*, the first book in Iain Stewart's *Knights of the Air* series, is about as realistic and loyal to history as they come... If *Rage!* is any indicator for the rest of the series, military history buffs better be making some room on their bookshelves now."

Historical Fiction Company
"Highly recommended... Splendid tale of aerial warfare in WWI... Book 1 of what promises to be a highly enjoyable series, and this reviewer, for one, is looking forward to the sequel."

Kirkus Reviews
"A rousing yarn that deftly delivers both a wartime adventure and a character study."

Kristina Stanley, bestselling and award-winning author of the *Stone Mountain Mystery* series
"Stewart weaves drama, integrity, and conflicting emotions through a captivating story of human spirit."

Midwest Book Review,
D. Donovan, Senior Reviewer
"A thriller story replete with nonstop action."

Feathered Quill
"Iain Stewart has created a cinematic viewpoint as seen through the career of a dedicated, determined, vengeful loner."

IAIN STEWART

knights of the air

BOOK ONE

RAGE

atmosphere press

© 2022 Iain Stewart

Published by Atmosphere Press

Cover design by Matthew Fielder

No part of this book may be reproduced without permission from the author except in brief quotations and in reviews. This is a work of fiction, and any resemblance to real places, persons, or events is entirely coincidental.

atmospherepress.com

To my mother, for inculcating a love of good stories. To my father, for encouraging and funding my early flying. And to Cassia, for her understanding that sometimes my body was present but my mind was cavorting in the skies of the Western Front.

Fury!
Rage!
Sing to me Goddess; sing through me, of Achilles' rage and fury,
Black and bloody-minded, that hurled a host of heroes' souls into Hades' dark.
And left their bodies as carrion,
A feast for the jackals and vultures.
    —Opening lines of Homer's *Iliad*

~

The closest modern equivalent to the Homeric hero is the ace fighter pilot.
    —W. H. Auden

~

The young airmen…of the First World War were unique in the history of mankind, for they were the first mortals ever to give battle in the vast spaces of the sky… They were the airborne warriors who engaged in single combat, like the knights of mediaeval chivalry, but wielding a winged machine gun in place of lance and sword.
    —Group Captain Arthur Gould Lee, ace of WW1 and author of *No Parachute*.

1
Digging Two Graves

August 1914.
German East Africa, Moshi Town, near Mt. Kilimanjaro

A shame. A crying shame. Lance Fitch lifted his hands and twisted them around to examine them from different angles. But whatever he did, he could not hide the fact that these hands were not the hands of an artist.

They could turn a page readily enough. Ma had bequeathed him a love of the written word, so he wasn't uncultured in all aspects. They were strong hands, strong enough to handle the tomes that Pa gave him, like *The Rise and Fall of the Roman Empire*, the legends of King Arthur and his knights of the Round Table, and Robin Hood and his merry men. All of them adventure tales long enough to help whittle away evenings during a long safari. Mind you, there were limits. Lance had once packed a battered version of the complete works of William Shakespeare for a six week-hunting trip. Pa said nothing, just cocked an eyebrow. Its bulk strained Lance's saddlebags until a strap broke after a week. Pa just smirked, he believed you learned through your own mistakes.

Maybe in an earlier century, a much earlier one, Lance could have been a wandering bard. He knew all the legends and myths, plays and poems. Carry a tune? That was another matter. Not the hands of a musician either. Besides not a lot of call for a bard or minstrel in British East Africa these days.

They looked like a worker's hands, nicked and calloused, strong for an axe and cutting fence posts for the farm. But they were capable of sensitivity. He could strip his rifle in the darkest night and assemble it by touch. That wasn't a skill to be sneezed at. But a brush and paint? He had tried, but the mystical connection between eyes and hands didn't work. His brother Francis called his best efforts blobs and blotches, and it was hard to argue—no matter how hard you squinted.

Which was a shame. A crying shame. Not for art's sake, but because he ached to capture the view in front of him. Perhaps if he froze it on canvas, he could seize forever these moments of pure happiness?

For how lucky could a man get?

A cold drink in his hand, the glass beaded with condensation in the burgeoning warmth of an African morning. Five yards away, a lissome lass posing her tanned limbs on the verandah wall and favouring him with a dazzling smile. Behind her, the towering, snow-capped caldera of Mount Kilimanjaro, glistening in the morning sun under the azure sky.

"A jug of wine, a loaf of bread—and Thou...were Paradise enough." Lance toasted Heidi as he lounged in the wicker chair on the shady porch. He took a sip of her bittersweet lemonade, made with stream water from the melted snow of Africa's highest peak, and almost choked as she eased into a languid stretch. His fiancée held the pose longer than necessary and finished with a wiggle of her bare toes and a mischievous grin.

"I can't believe Germany and Britain will go to war over Serbia," Pa said, "but if they do, I'm afraid they will drag us settlers into their idiotic rivalry."

Lance started guiltily. He'd forgotten their fathers were seated deeper in the shade of the veranda. A quick glance reassured him. They were too distracted by their own conversation to notice the flirting.

"Nonsense." Herr Schumacher waved his pipe in a dismissive arc that trailed acrid clouds of smoke. "Governor Schnee himself told me he'd agreed with your man Conway-Belfield. If war starts in Europe, they will invoke the Congo Treaty of 1885 and keep us East African colonies out of it."

"I hope so," Pa muttered.

"More lemonade, Lance?" Heidi asked as she materialised beside him, smelling of fresh soap. Her dress gaped as she leaned over to refill his glass from an earthenware jug, unveiling a tantalising glimpse of the creamy curve of her cleavage. Lance's eyes lingered too long, and her eyes widened. As she straightened, she tossed her blond ponytail in mock indignation.

Lance blushed and looked away. Herr Schumacher pointed his pipe at Pa.

"People like you and me, Stan, we've carved livelihoods from this harsh land side by side. None of us settlers, German or British, want war. I will never forget how, when my Heidi became ill, you rode to Mtito Andei through the night to fetch the best doctor, a Britisher who saved her life."

"And I will always remember how you and Bertha helped care for my three boys when my wife died."

Herr Schumacher's voice was gruff. "Ach so, who are these men in Europe to tell us to fight our friends?"

"I agree," Pa raised his glass. "*Prost!*"

News from Europe took an age to filter through to this sparsely populated area, but Herr Schumacher played poker every day with the garrulous German officer who ran Moshi garrison's military telegraph. Whoever ran that telegraph was invariably the best-informed man in the region. Herr Schumacher used those poker sessions to make sure he was the second best informed. Such things were good for trade. So, if Anton Schumacher wasn't worried, that was good enough for Lance.

But Pa did not look so convinced. "Thanks for your hospitality, Anton. We must go. I have to meet a hunting client back at the farm this afternoon, so I will ride there now with Will. Lance, you're in charge of the wagon, and take Francis with you. Promise me you'll look after your brother, get a good price for the skins in Moshi, buy the supplies, and get back home by sunset. Manage that and I'll let you lead the next small hunting safari."

Lance could not repress a huge smile. "I promise, Pa."

By the standards of Pa's usual challenges, this promised to be a doddle. Moshi was the inland terminus of the German railway that stretched two hundred miles to the port of Tanga. As a result, the town ruled as the trading mecca for colonial settlers from both sides of the nearby border. Skins were always in demand. Heck, even Francis could haggle a good price in Moshi. Meanwhile Hamisi would barter supplies from Bal Singh. Now that was a tough ask. If Lance bargained with Bal Singh, he'd lose both thumbs and four fingers and leave the *Many Wonders Emporium* thanking the slippery beggar. Which is why Lance would leave that to Hamisi, who was no mean huckster himself. Then an easy five-hour ride home to Taveta Ranch.

Lance found Francis in a hammock on the side porch, alone with a book. "Time to go, bookworm."

Francis pushed his glasses up his nose and frowned. "But D'Artagnan has just met Milady, and I want—"

"If you don't come now, I'll tell you the ending."

Lance chuckled as Francis almost fell out of the hammock in his haste.

It took longer to find Will who was hunting mousebirds with a catapult. When Lance passed on the message from Pa, Will's face fell. "Why can't I go to Moshi? I'd be more use to you than Francis."

"True," Lance allowed. His younger brothers, Will and Francis, were as alike as chilli peppers and peas. Will sported the brawn and red hair of a hell-raiser and thought of books only as useful projectiles, but he was tough and competent in the bush. Unlike Francis.

"But," Lance added, "Pa won't allow you near Moshi until the Mother Superior forgives you. Pa is convinced she has a price on your head for a good beating."

"Aw, come on! She wouldn't do that."

"No?" Lance raised an eyebrow. "You weren't there when she promised Pa she would geld you with blunt scissors. When Pa said you'd marry Kathy and that would be the end of it, the Mother Superior offered to geld Pa first."

Will winced. "That bad, huh?"

"At least it pushed Pa onto your side. Nobody threatens his family. Or his balls! But I'll never know what possessed you to screw a nun."

"*Trainee* nun. Kathy wanted it as bad as me. Besides, being a nun was her mother's idea. This was her way out. Neither of us figured on her getting pregnant."

Lance snorted. "Like Pa says, actions have consequences. The Mother Superior says you are hell-bound."

Will uncorked his trademark guffaw. "Definitely worth it! Kathy is out of the nunnery and we're married, so she's happy. I'm happy. The hag Mother Superior is the only killjoy around here."

"That's as maybe, but you aren't going to Moshi. Better saddle up before Pa comes looking for you."

As the Fitch family left, Heidi tried to sneak a goodbye kiss with Lance, but Herr Schumacher kept a proprietary eye on his eighteen-year-old daughter. Lance was only a year older than Heidi, and Lance knew they would marry one day. But until that day, Herr Schumacher made it clear that any Lothario-esque behaviour would be as welcome as a hyena in his henhouse. He used a 12-bore shotgun on those occasions. Heidi's kisses were the sweetest in the world, but buckshot was a powerful counter argument.

Lance swung into his saddle and blew Heidi a kiss. But she was looking behind him and giggling at his brother's attempt to mount. Francis had one foot in a stirrup and was hopping after his horse as it sidled away. Lance sighed. He manoeuvred his horse until he could grab Francis by the collar and yank him into the saddle like a sack of coffee beans.

The spectacle provoked peals of laughter from the road where the supply wagon waited. Hamisi—the cook and major domo of the Fitch household—sat in the driver's seat with his habitual smile splitting his black face like a half moon. Beside him sat his son, Thomas, the same age as Lance. They'd grown up almost as siblings. When Lance tested a curry by dipping his finger in the sauce, Hamisi walloped him with the ladle just as hard as he hit Thomas for helping himself to a handful of groundnuts from the kitchen.

"You look like a stork chasing the horse, Bwana Francis," Hamisi yelled in Swahili.

"Thomas," Francis retorted red-faced, "Make sure old man mzee here does not fall asleep and drive our wagon into a ditch."

"I will try," Thomas grinned, "but he is *mzee sana* now."

Hamisi cuffed the back of his son's head. "Not too old to beat respect into a cub." Thomas chortled with glee at getting a rise from his father.

"*Twende!*" Lance said. Hamisi cracked his whip over the mules, and the wagon jolted towards Moshi.

~

Six hours later Lance hummed as he led them eastwards, skirting the southern foothills of Kilimanjaro. Waves of pale straw grass rippled in the wind, stretching into the distance like a limitless ocean, dotted with islands of green flat-topped acacia trees and streaked with reefs of rust-coloured termite mounds. The occasional zebra or gazelle cantered away from them. God, but it was beautiful. Lance would never grow tired of this land. It lifted his soul.

Despite the idyll, Lance kept his rifle slung over his back, and Thomas had a shotgun under his feet. Best to be cautious with Africa: you might startle a lioness protecting her cubs, or a black mamba might spook your horse. Yes, Africa was beautiful, but she was also dangerous to the unwary.

Pa would be delighted. German silver rupees for the skins jangled in Lance's pocket, and he would be home before sunset. In an hour, they would cross the invisible border near Taveta, where settlers and tribesmen crossed as freely as the wild game. No fences, flags, or men marked the frontier, only a few acacia thornbushes whose hollow-holed bulbs moaned a lonely dirge when the wind blew.

Lance drifted into daydreams of Heidi. Francis said that her face was strong rather than beautiful, but Lance could bask for hours in those cornflower-blue eyes and her quirky half-smile with the crooked eye-tooth. Yesterday evening, she had taken his hand and led him behind a scarlet bougainvillea tree that hid them from the house. There, she lifted her face for a kiss. He obliged, nibbling on the entrancing softness of her ripe lips. She murmured as she pressed against his hardness with a wanton thrust of her hips. His hand slipped under her blouse. "No, no," she protested, but after more passionate kisses she—

The whiplash crack of a bullet snapping inches past his head stunned him.

An instant later the deep boom of rifles followed. Lance jerked with shock. Black gun-smoke billowed from bushes on his left. Time slowed, a dream happening to someone else. Thomas grabbed for the shotgun under his feet, but another volley of gunfire boomed from the bushes. Bullets hammered Thomas from the wagon seat. He pitched headfirst to the ground, twisted and broken, his shirt blossoming red.

Lance gaped. Then the tumblers in his mind clicked into place. He yanked his rifle off his shoulder. "Run, Francis!" he shouted, and slammed his heels into his horse's ribs. The startled animal, already spooked by the gunfire, leapt forwards.

A black man in khaki uniform stepped from the bush and swung his rifle muzzle towards Lance. Lance yanked the reins and smashed his horse into the man, sending him spinning. Another attacker leapt for the bridle. Lance kicked him in the teeth with a stirrup iron. A satisfying crunch and the man fell away. Ahead was open space and Lance yelled with savage glee. His horse's hooves drummed on the hard earth, pulling Lance clear of the ambush.

But more soldiers emerged from the tall grass. Lance swore as they swung their rifles towards him, and he hunched low over the horse's withers. Black smoke blossomed. He ducked. Bullets struck his horse with the sound of sticks beating a wet carpet. Her legs folded and she ploughed nose-first into the dust. Lance catapulted over her head and crashed onto his left shoulder, grunting with pain as the rifle jolted from his grasp.

Winded, he staggered to his feet, hunched over in pain, and cradling his useless left arm. The hard-baked earth had scraped his left cheek raw, the weeping flesh stinging under its coat of grit. Two soldiers pricked his belly with their fastened bayonets—eight inches of sinister steel glinting in the bright sunlight. They prodded him back towards the wagon, their bayonets drawing pricks of blood with each prod.

Francis remained frozen on his horse, still open-mouthed as a soldier held his horse's bridle. Hamisi sat on the wagon, looking down, ashen-faced and wide eyed, at his son who lay curled in a pool of congealed blood. Fat tears tracked down the cook's cheeks, leaving rivulets of black skin between the layers of red dust.

Lance's head throbbed, and his shoulder sent bolts of pain with every move. He stared round his captors, all askaris—the black soldiers who fought in the colonial armies. Their khaki uniforms and the eagle heads on their belt buckles proclaimed they were German Schutztruppe,the most notorious colonial army in Africa. But brutal as they were, the *Schutztruppen* had never attacked whites in East Africa.What the hell was happening? "*Unafanya nini?*" he croaked.

A German officer thrust his way through the crowd of askaris. Lance stared—the man stood at least six and a half feet tall with a gargantuan belly. Under a white field cap, hard eyes perched above a pockmarked nose and a blond handlebar moustache. The voice was incongruously high-pitched, accented but fluent. "Our first Englander prisoners. What are your names?"

Lance spoke through waves of agony: "What do you mean by shooting at us? I demand—"

The officer backhanded Lance across the mouth. The casual swing pulped Lance's lips and sent him staggering backwards into the arms of the soldiers behind him, flecking their uniforms with blood. They propped Lance up and chuckled as the German moved towards Lance with a menacing smile. "Perhaps you have not heard, English puppy? Germany and England are at war now. Your names?"

"Murderers!" Francis shouted. He jerked his reins to break free and kicked at the soldier holding his bridle. The askari sidestepped the clumsy blow and punched Francis' horse hard on the nose. It reared up, throwing Francis off balance, and the askari pulled the boy headfirst into the dust. Two askaris seized Francis by his arms and legs. To a roar of acclaim from the others, they swung him high into the air and threw him as far as they could. He flew six feet before screaming in high-pitched agony as his right leg snapped when he hit the hard-baked earth. As Francis writhed in the dust, his knee mangled at an angle that made Lance blanch, the German officer walked over and kicked the knee with deliberate precision. Francis' back arched off the ground in shock, and mercifully he lost consciousness.

"Bastard!" Lance tried to lunge at the officer. A thick arm circled his neck from behind and choked him, and a bayonet sliced a shallow line of red across his belly. Lance heaved against the bunched muscles, but his vision clouded as the arm tightened. He stopped struggling and the arm relaxed a fraction, allowing him to breathe. Whooping for air, he gasped, "Animals! What the hell are you doing?"

The soldiers laughed as the officer walked over and peered into Lance's face. "Look at me, pup. So the next time you see me, you remember your manners with Captain Otto Peters."

Peters braced Lance's face with his meaty left hand and feigned a punch with his right. Lance dropped his head downwards, but the German kneed him in the balls. As Lance doubled over in agony, Peters brought his knee up again. At the last second Lance twisted his face, and the knee drove like a pile driver into his left cheek. The bone shattered, and a flash of intense whiteness exploded into Lance's brain, before darkness took him.

~

When Lance regained consciousness, he wished he hadn't.

Ropes dug into his chest and bound him to a fence post, seated upright with legs splayed in front and hands tied behind his back, so tightly his shoulder joints shrieked a protest. Each breath bubbled with coppery tasting blood, and a dagger stabbed up his cheek into his eye socket with every movement. Swelling jammed his left eye shut. He squinted through the prism of his concussion and dusk's lengthening shadows, at what appeared to be a ramshackle fort. Its wooden stockade walls enclosed a dusty parade ground, barracks ran along one wall, and a corral for horses along another. Lance was tied to one of the posts of the empty corral. The black-white-red tricolour of Germany fluttered in a desultory fashion from a flagpole at the centre of the parade ground. Francis' crumpled body lay motionless ten feet away, and with Lance's hazy vision he could not tell whether his brother was dead or alive. *This is my fault. Pa put me in charge, and I was too busy daydreaming about Heidi.* The guilt that seared his soul hurt worse than the agony of his shattered face.

Captain Peters sat thirty yards away under the shade of a temporary canvas awning, his massive bulk incongruous on a three-legged stool. Beyond him, in the centre of the parade ground, stood a large slatted wooden cage. Two soldiers dragged a black man in native dress towards the officer. A desiccated askari sergeant with tribal scars on his face interrogated the terrified man, then translated to his Captain. Peters raised a dismissive hand, and the soldiers hustled their victim into the cage, which they chained shut. The askaris hauled another prisoner in front of Peters for a brief interrogation. Again, Peters' verdict was peremptory, and the victim joined the other man in the cage. The same scene repeated with a half-dozen more prisoners dragged screaming to the cage.

The last prisoner was Hamisi. Lance hoped that Hamisi's easy style with powerful white men would help him with Peters, for Lance had never seen Hamisi at a loss. But despite the cook's obsequious bowing and pleading, Peters raised his hand, and the guards threw the screaming Hamisi into the cage. Dully, Lance wondered how the German generated such terror, and why he took such pleasure in that fear. In Lance's concussed state, emotions seemed alien to him. His world was only pulsing pain.

Peters took off his cap and ran his fingers through his damp thinning hair. The askari sergeant pointed towards Lance, and then strode over to untie his hands and drag him to the awning.

Peters peered at Lance. "Not so cocky now, pup?"

Lance stared through his one open eye, fascinated by the double head and wobbling chins of the concussion-induced vision in front of him.

"No smart answer? Perhaps you have learnt respect? But perhaps not. Just in case, I will teach you a lesson. Sergeant Keino here will make sure you have a grandstand seat."

Peters' lips twisted into a parody of a smile. He walked away to supervise his troops, who were unloading bundles of dried grass from a wagon. They stacked the grass around the wooden cage, now jammed tight with screaming prisoners. Keino gripped Lance by both arms to keep him upright. "A treat for you!" he gloated in Swahili, baring his tobacco-stained teeth.

The askaris backed away from the cage as Peters threw a flaming brand into the dried grass. Hungry flames soon licked at the wooden walls of the cage. Screams from the prisoners turned into high-pitched shrieks of pure terror as evil red flames danced. The captives kicked at the flames with their bare feet, trying to prevent the fire from taking hold.

"For God's sake—" Lance tried to wriggle free from Sergeant Keino, who kidney-punched him and let him drop sideways into the dust, writhing in agony. Several askaris carrying jerry cans danced around the prison, throwing petrol into the cage and over the prisoners. With a dull 'whomp', the jail turned into an inferno as the dried timber caught fire.

Bile rose in Lance's throat and tears rolled down his face as the screams escalated in volume and pitch. One of the jail walls fell inwards with a crash, and human torches escaped, lurching onto the dusty parade ground.

A figure flecked with blue-edged flames staggered through the choking smoke. The askaris laughed and fell back to give the burning man room to stumble forwards, until he collapsed twenty feet from the horrified Lance. Despite the melting of his flesh, Lance recognised Hamisi.

"Help your friend, English pup!" Peters said. Hamisi howled inhuman agony from between the white teeth of his lipless skull. Lance clamped his hands over his ears but could not tear his eyes away.

Peters nudged Lance with his foot. "Why aren't you helping him?" Lance vomited. The human pyre reached out to beseech Lance with fingers burned to crooked claws. Lance scrabbled away on his knees, gibbering with horror. Peters kicked him again, and Lance curled into a whimpering foetal ball.

When Lance looked up again, strings of vomit dribbling from his lips, there was no Hamisi left, just a twitching, smoking corpse. The sickening stench of burned human coated the inside of Lance's mouth and nose. Peters wagged a thick finger at Lance.

"Ach pup, I expected more of you. You talk so big, but you are nothing but a *Hosenscheisser*, a trouser shitter to you English. Sergeant Keino, bring him to my table."

The askari yanked Lance to his feet, winning a grunt of pain. A sudden breeze fluttered the German Imperial flag and wafted across more of the sickly-sweet smell. Lance glared at Peters with all the searing hatred in his soul. The fat man laughed at Lance's helpless rage.

"*Ja*, you have learned respect, I think! Now you will do what I want. On this table is your confession. You are British spies, sent here to gather intelligence so your Army can attack across the border. When the authorities see this, even that peace-loving puppet, Governor Schnee, will have no choice but to declare war." Peters held out a pen. "Sign it!"

Lance leant on the table for support, head hanging. Bloody drool dripped from his mouth onto the table next to the paper. Slowly he raised his eyes. "Lies," he mumbled.

"Ach so! The heroic Englishman. You would rather burn?"

Lance spat blood. Words came with difficulty around the swollen sausage of his tongue. "You wouldn't dare."

Peters chuckled and shook his head. "Because you are white? Or because you are English? No matter. English are hard for themselves but soft for others. Sergeant Keino, burn the brother."

Yellow teeth gleamed. "*Ndio Bwana!*" The big askari dragged Francis's unconscious body towards them, dropping it two yards away. He picked up a nearby can, twisted open the top, and sloshed petrol over Francis. The foul fumes washed over Lance, followed by a horror that raised gooseflesh. He'd thought he was beyond terror, that he had plumbed the absolute depths, that hell went no deeper.

But Peters proved him wrong.

Lance lunged for the German. A rifle butt smashed into his back and his face smacked into the ground. Bolts of agony jagged through his cheekbone. He sobbed with rage and pain, hands beseeching Peters. "No! You can't!" Tears ran down his cheeks. He struggled to his knees and pleaded, but he might as well have begged a slavering hyena for mercy.

"*Kommen sie...* It is simple. Sign or your brother burns." Peters' lips twisted and his eyes gleamed. "I show you how simple." He lit a match and held it in his right hand, which hovered over Francis. Peters offered a pen in his left and waved the flaming match and the pen closer then apart. "Choose *Hosenscheisser! Schnell,* before the match burns my fingers and you are too late!"

Something inside Lance's mind fractured, and malevolent ancestral urges uncoiled, venomous in their intensity. "I... will...kill...you," he mumbled past his bloated tongue.

Peters frowned, uncertain for a second.

Hooves beat on the hard-packed earth. A Schutztruppe officer galloped towards the fort, drawing up in a flurry of dust in front of Peters. The rider stood in his stirrups, shouting and pointing outside the compound.

Peters blew out the match with an oath and swung into a frenzied bellowing. Keino grabbed Lance and ruthlessly bound his arms, kicked his feet away, and trussed his ankles, ignoring his moans.

Around them, the askaris poured into ranks with well-drilled precision. Minutes later they marched double-time out of the fort with shouldered rifles. Peters followed on a mule, his long legs dangling to the ground.

All was quiet except for Lance's rasping breaths. Smoke from the smouldering cage drifted upwards, black against bloody streaks of sunset. Lance tried to roll onto his knees, but with his hands tied behind his back and his battered muscles weak as a child's, he could only flop in the dirt like a stranded fish. His head dropped back into the dust, and he sobbed with frustration. Nothing in his life had remotely prepared him for the evil he had just experienced. Despair and self-pity crashed over him, drowning his will to fight with their inexorable weight.

"Lance. Lance! Can you move?"

Lance shook his head to get rid of the nagging voice.

"Christ! They brutalised him. Get Mebeke over here to lift him to the wagon. Then do the same with Francis. But get me a knife first."

I'm delirious. It sounds like Erwin Bohme. A voice that belonged in the gilded life Lance had once enjoyed an aeon ago. It couldn't be. Erwin was one of Germany's most famous Alpine climbers and Moshi's most glamorous bachelor. He often visited the Schumacher's farm, and, as Moshi's railway engineer, he'd arranged Lance's first steam railway ride. No connection could exist between that idyllic life and this world of pulsing pain and barbaric brutality. *Only a nightmare could mix the two...it's just a nightmare.*

A knife sawed at the ropes tying his hands behind his back. The hands, the knife, they were real. Lance groggily accepted he was not hallucinating.

Erwin's voice grounded him further. "Steady, Lance. We'll have you out of here in a minute."

Strong hands lifted and carried Lance into a wagon. Erwin propped him up and trickled warm water between his torn lips. "Francis is unconscious, but he will live. But you must go now. We told the Schutztruppe there was a British raiding column threatening Moshi, but they will soon find it was a lie. Then they will come back in a hurry. My man Kipchoge will get you over the border while Anton and I cover your tracks and lay a false trail. Do you understand?"

Lance nodded. The wagon rocked as someone climbed up to join them. He heard another voice in the darkening gloom—Herr Schumacher, sounding low and strained. "Lance, I must get a message to the British, and I can't trust it on paper. Can you pass on a message?"

Lance swallowed more water and gave a minuscule nod.

"*Gut.* Listen carefully. War was declared in Europe between Germany and Britain a few days ago, but the news only reached us today. Peters and other brutes are carrying out provocative acts to suck us colonies into this war. We must not allow that. We German settlers will ensure Peters is court-martialled for what he has done today, but we need you to tell your father, and the other British, that we will work with them to keep peace. Our Governors will help us. Do you understand?"

Lance raised his agonised face, swallowed, and looked at Schumacher with his one open eye. "I will kill Peters," he slurred, not caring that the motion of his jaw sent new shock waves of pain stabbing up his cheek. "Court-martial...not enough."

"You are young, Lance. Peace is the most important thing. Take my message to your father, and I promise you we will deliver Peters to justice. God knows we have no use for that animal."

Rage boiled through Lance. *I don't want "justice"—I want to send Peters into the hottest part of hell, screaming in agony.* The German's brutality had unleashed a demon, the strength of which shocked even Lance. Yet the demon was cunning. It knew survival must come before revenge, and survival required Schumacher and Bohme's help. So Lance nodded as he hooded his eyes to hide his hate, and made a silent vow to Francis, Thomas, and Hamisi that he would avenge them.

~

Four weeks later – September 1914.
British East Africa, near Taveta Farm.

Lance had waited for this day with wolfish hunger for five weeks. The last of the stars still pricked through the black shroud of night, but the orange glow on the horizon signalled the new day—a killing day.

Savage glee flared inside him as he caressed his rifle, its metal cold and purposeful. He lay on his stomach in the long grass, shivering in the pre-dawn chill as dew soaked through his hunting jacket.

Pa lay on Lance's left, his jaws grinding as he worked on a stubborn piece of biltong. They had inserted into the ambush site an hour before dawn, long enough for the wildlife to grow used to them. When men and other predators moved in the African bush, a chorus of alarms from birds and other animals preceded them. For this ambush site the loudest alarms would come from the vervet monkeys clustered in the fever trees on either side of the riverbed. Vervets possessed a plethora of alarm calls: a low-pitched twittering for snakes, guttural repetitive grunts for eagles, and urgent high-pitched screeches for mammal predators like man. But for now they cavorted in the trees on the far side of the ravine, ignoring the patient men who had not moved since dawn.

Pa fumbled in his pockets for his customary morning cigar but that was just habit, he would never be so stupid. A whiff of tobacco in the morning air would alert the dullest scout as surely as if Pa stood up and flapped his arms. And the *Schutztruppen* were not dullards. These days it wasn't easy to hold the title as Africa's most brutal army. God knows the Belgians in the Congo had made a serious run at infamy, but the *Schutztruppen* were still the undisputed heavyweight champions. When the Maji-Maji rebels killed fifteen Europeans and four hundred askaris in German East Africa in 1905, the Schutztrupperetaliation littered the plains with more than 75,000 native corpses. But they were efficient too. Take away their brutality, and they were still the most battle-hardened colonial Army in Africa.

But Pa was no slouch when it came to war in the bush. Even before rising to the rank of captain while fighting the Boers in South Africa, his father had served as the chief scout for the British army in the Second Matabele War. There he became friends with Frederick Selous, the legendary explorer, naturalist, and war hero. The American president Theodore Roosevelt had once called Selous "the last of the great white hunters". More important to Lance, Selous was his godfather and had imparted his guiding philosophy as a hunter: "When you hunt dangerous animals, think like a leopard. Leopards lack the speed of the cheetah, the muscles of lions, the vicious horns of the buffalo, the bulk of the elephant, or the armour plating of the rhino. The leopards' greatest weapon is their cunning. Yet they are the most dangerous of all." Pa and Lance lived by those words when hunting. Man-eating lions and canny Boer commandoes made vicious teachers, and both had left scars on Pa. But he learned fast, remembered long and taught well. Pa could still teach the Schutztruppe a lesson or two in the bush.

Lance raised his binoculars, but Pa stretched out his hand and pressed them to the earth. "We're facing the sun," he whispered. "The rays will sparkle on the lens and give us away. Be patient."

Lance nodded and packed away the binoculars, annoyed by his own foolishness. He settled to wait once again, trying to ignore the ever-present ache in his left jaw and cheek.

Old Doctor McCulloch, a once talented surgeon turned partial soak, had done a good job restoring Lance's shattered cheekbone, now almost healed. Lance did not enjoy the memory. Pa had made sure the Doc sobered up for the operation, but also promised a post-operative reward of a premium bottle of Scotch if the surgery was successful. McCulloch had no anaesthetic, and excruciating jolts of pain skewered through Lance's cheek, teeth, and eye socket as the doc's shaky fingertips slid together the shattered pieces of bone under the skin, like a blind man completing a jigsaw.

"Hold still, laddie," McCulloch demanded. Pa cradled Lance's face in his strong hands to hold it steady as the needles of pain stabbed and stabbed. Lance sobbed—the pain was too much.

His father tightened his grip. "Be a man," he grunted.

The hate saved Lance. It came roaring like a mighty river in flash flood, scouring his mind clean. Lance floated from his body, away from the harsh breathing of the doctor, the sickening reek of disinfectant, the lightning bolts of agony. In this new place he heard only the mesmerising message of revenge in the drumbeats of his heart.

The bone was only half knitted three weeks later, but the only visible damage lay in the two-inch scar a finger's width below his left eye, and a permanently damaged tear duct that leaked single teardrops intermittently. Lance never wiped the tears away, refusing to even acknowledge them. When he grew angry, those teardrops multiplied and chased down his cheek.

The night the *Schutztruppen* burnt Taveta Ranch those tears of rage had flowed like scalding lava. Warmongers on both sides had quickly gained the ascendancy and swamped all attempts to keep the African colonies out of the war. No message came from Anton Schumacher, or Heidi. Pa reckoned they must be too carefully watched. Von Lettow, the *Schutztruppen* commander, cast the die when he ignored Governor Schnee and invaded Taveta with two hundred men. The twenty men of the British East African Police force fired one volley and fled to Voi, pausing only to warn the British settlers to run.

Pa had already sent Will to Nairobi to look after the crippled Francis, so Lance knelt with his father in the darkness and watched as the askaris made a towering inferno of the only home he had ever known. The next morning, with the grey ash flakes of their home still on their skin, Lance and Pa planned revenge as they watched the distinctive figure of Peters riding his mule around the Schutztruppe temporary camp in Taveta.

When the swelling on Lance's cheekbone began to diminish, Pa and he returned to haunt the Riata Hills, waiting for an opening to spring an ambush. So Lance could kill Captain Otto Peters.

At last, they saw a chance—a slim one, but a chance.

Every morning Peters would take a column of about a hundred men out on a raiding mission, with advance scouts on both flanks to prevent any surprise attack. Peters rode in the middle of the column, the safest place if an enemy ambushed them. Such a formation made it impossible to kill Peters and escape alive. But when the *Schutzruppen* first left their camp, Peters rode at the head of the column to avoid the dust kicked up by marching boots. So the ambush must be in that first mile, close to the German camp, before Peters deployed the scouts.

Pa and Lance agreed there was only one possible ambush site in that first mile. The *Schutztruppen* habitually took the old Arab slavers' trail eastwards out of Taveta, which wound down a slight slope towards a belt of fever trees and heavy bush, then dropped out of sight from Taveta as it crossed a ravine. The *Schutztruppen* would be an easy target as they crossed the riverbed, and the ambushers in the long grass on the far bank would be out of the sight of the soldiers left in Taveta. Behind the ambush site, a long gully snaked away for two-hundred yards before fading into a narrow belt of brush. The gully was deep enough for the ambushers to escape unseen, and the brush behind provided cover for tethered horses.

"All ambush plans need to be simple," Pa had said. "The simpler the better, because in war Sullivan's Law applies."

"You mean Murphy's Law?" Lance asked. "Anything that can go wrong will go wrong?"

"Close, but no. Sullivan's Law says Murphy is an optimist."

And so, Pa's ambush plan was simple: "Shoot Peters in the heart. Lay down two minutes of rapid fire at the askaris to convince them we are a large force and dissuade any immediate pursuit. Then run like hell along the gully, jump on the horses, and ride like the wind. Got it?"

Lance had nodded, though he had one big variation in mind. One Pa would not enjoy.

Now they were putting Pa's plan into action. The rising sun slipped the horizon's embrace, a perfect yellow sphere of flame illuminating the grass in its golden glow. This was Africa, land of extremes, so having shivered for the first hour soon they would drip sweat. Ahead of them, the ravine yawned fifty yards wide and ten feet deep. The locals called these ravines *donga*. During the rainy season mighty flash-floods carved out riverbeds with a deadly maelstrom of water and debris; in the dry season they lay dormant. Now, with the short rains just finished, a narrow crystalline stream chuckled down the slope towards Taveta.

Time crawled as they waited, and Lance worried that the raiding column wouldn't come. The molten sun burned higher into the cloudless sky, a fiery hammer beating Lance against the anvil of the baked earth. Despite his wide-brimmed hat, sweat beaded on his eyebrows, and he tilted his head, so the drips fell onto the earth instead of stinging his eyes. He pulled his hat brim lower against the glare and lifted the collar of his hunting jacket to protect his neck against the pitiless sun.

They waited with the stamina of experienced hunters. The still air shimmered in a heat haze, and a thousand feet above them a lone vulture turned in a widening gyre.

Lance wondered what Heidi was doing and his guts flopped inside out. He could still see her face as clearly as if she were in front of him, taste her kisses, hear her call his name, his heart flipping at the slight German intonation she gave his name. It wasn't just the kisses, the satin smooth skin, the warm softness of her and the flower fresh waft of her hair. Other girls had those things too, but only Heidi lit his whole world. She made the sunsets more vivid, laughter easier, music more stirring, food more mouth-watering, and when she looked at him with those cornflower blue eyes, he was both wise and invincible. He treasured the quiet times too. Her head resting on his shoulders as they silently watched iridescent kingfishers dart over a sun-dappled stream. Surreptitiously holding hands in the dark as their families gathered around a crackling fire, the tang of woodsmoke strong and shadows cavorting. Or sipping coffee, alone together on the veranda rocking chairs as the rain hissed off the roof and ran down the eaves in rivulets, releasing the pungent scent of the thirsty red soil.

But Pa had been blunt. "Best put her out of your mind. You won't see her until the war is finished, and even then, war changes a lot of things." That assessment had knelled like the bell of doom to Lance, but he could not fault the wisdom. He must become a warrior, hard of heart and purpose. Such a man did not pine for love. Or so Lance told himself, but his heart ached more fiercely than his broken cheek. And his cheek ached something fearsome.

Another good reason to extract revenge. Peters had broken Lance's bones, his heart, his faith in humanity, and his pride. Killing him wouldn't mend all that, but Lance knew with certainty that justice was a necessary first step in the healing process.

The screech of a vervet monkey interrupted his thoughts. Pa touched Lance's shoulder. Lance nodded without turning his head, proud he had picked up the alarm as fast as Pa, the experienced white hunter. He eased his rifle forward through the grass, so he had a clear field of fire across the *donga*. Between the treetops came a faint pall of dust.

Lance forced himself to breathe. Would Peters protect himself in the middle of the column with flanking scouts deployed? If so, the ambushers would have to kill the first scouts in the ravine, then run for their lives. As Pa had said, "As a Plan B it isn't the best, but it's a darn sight better than suicide."

Lance agreed—much as he lusted to kill Peters, throwing his life away in a futile attempt would only give Peters the satisfaction of killing him.

The monkeys on the far bank jumped up and down on their branches, their cries shriller and more urgent. Lance's pulse beat faster, his hearing became more acute, and his vision sharpened.

He tensed as an askari broke through the brush on the far bank, and then another. Lance swore, sighted on the left man's khaki chest, and his trigger finger tightened.

Pa made a low soft "sic, sic" noise between his teeth, and Lance eased pressure off the trigger. Pa had noticed what Lance had missed—the askaris were not on alert. They had slung their rifles over their shoulders as they hacked at the branches and brush along the path. They were clearing the way for Peters, who with magical abruptness materialised on the far bank.

Lance took a deep breath. In his nightmares Peters ruled as a chilling ogre, but the officer in front of him appeared comical. He sat astride a mule that sagged under his massive weight. The German's uniform was a patchwork of dark sweat stains, large crescents from his armpits merging with the spreading stain from the belly that strained against the brass-buttoned uniform. That belly wobbled as the mule shuffled its way down the bank into the shallow riverbed, its front legs quivering with each step as the full load of the gargantuan German fell on the mule's front haunches.

Lance laid his sights between those eyes—eyes that still haunted many a night.

"Thou shalt not kill." The unwanted commandment forced itself into Lance's mind as he squinted through the sights. His rifle barrel wavered, and his trigger finger hesitated.

Images flashed into his mind. Thomas lying crumpled in the dust, his scattered brains grey and red against the brown earth. Hamisi beseeching Lance with his wide lidless eyes and skeletal claws. Lance took a deep breath and shifted his sights a fraction. "An eye for an eye…" he whispered. And fired.

Dust jumped from Peters' jacket as the bullet bisected the first and second brass buttons above his belt.

"Belly shot, by God!" Pa growled. "How in hell's name did you miss the heart from fifty yards?"

Peters clutched his stomach and toppled from the saddle. The scouts scattered back into the brush on the far side of the river. Pa fired as fast as he could work the bolt action, not aiming but firing fast to prevent the troopers realising that the ambush was only two men. The plan called for Lance to do the same, but he just stared at Peters.

The German sat upright in the shallow stream with his legs straight, mewling with pain. Bewilderment filled his coarse features and both hands clutched at the growing stain that darkened his khaki uniform. The river flowed red downstream.

"Finish the bloody job," Pa snarled, still firing as fast as he could.

Lance did not reply. His youth and innocence seeped away with the crimson stain blossoming in the once clear stream. He fixed the scene in his mind—the long stalks of golden grass swaying either side of his glistening gun barrel, the stench of gunpowder, Peters whimpering, and the river running red. Lance had crossed his Rubicon.

"Lance! What are you playing at? Finish the bastard and let's go!"

Lance ignored Pa as the bullets whipped past him into the long grass. "Suffer you bastard!" he whispered, staring at Peters.

Pa swore and swung his rifle onto Peters. Before he could squeeze the trigger, Lance fired for the second time. This bullet took the German between his eyes, sending his peaked cap flying and knocking the hulking figure onto its back.

Pa emptied the rest of his magazine at the askaris crouching in the bush. "*Twende!* Now!" The two men turned and elbow-crawled the ten yards through the long grass to the gulley. Once in the gulley, they ran crouching low for another fifty yards. Then the cover doglegged to the left and grew deep enough so they could run upright at full pace to the horses. Behind them they heard the bellowing of the Schutztruppesergeants as the askaris realised the ambush had ended. The two panting men, hunters turned prey, slipped the horses' tethers and vaulted into the saddles.

The riders bolted out of the brush onto the plain. They rode low, their weight over their horse's haunches as they galloped, swerving between the low thorn bushes dotting the dun-coloured grass. The hooves drummed on the hard earth and dust plumed behind them.

After a mile, Pa slowed them to a fast trot so the horses did not blow themselves out. Further on they slowed to a walk. Father and son rode in silence, alert to their surroundings. When they reached Kiboko Springs, Pa dismounted, and they led the horses to the cool water. Then they grabbed their rifles and binoculars and climbed the rocks above the spring to search their back trail. No sign of pursuit, no plume of dust, just the hot windswept plain.

Pa unscrewed his canteen and offered it to Lance, who shook his head. His father took several deep swigs, poured a little onto his neckerchief, and wiped his face. Anger flushed Pa's face under the tanned skin, but he kept his tone measured. "Care to tell me what happened back there?"

Lance looked at him without speaking.

"Lance, you can hit a charging buffalo in the heart at fifty yards. You didn't gut shoot Peters by mistake. You put us in danger by not sticking to our plan—in, kill, out. Why, man?"

"I wanted him to suffer like Hamisi, Francis, and the others," Lance said in a low voice. "A bullet in the heart was too good for that animal."

"I understand the sentiment, but revenge is dangerous. There's an old saying that when you start on the road for revenge, you had better dig two graves—the second being your own. Hate distorts your judgement. Peters was evil, but if you descend to his level, victory over him has no meaning. We were putting down a rabid dog, not indulging in an act of revenge."

"If you say so." Lance's voice was toneless.

Pa grunted in disgust. "Well, if today was revenge for you—how did it feel?"

"Good, it felt good."

"I doubt that, son. When I killed my first man in battle, I had an empty feeling in my guts for days. Killing a man should not come easily, whatever the righteousness of it. But enough talk, we need to ride. We've done what we came to do." Pa clapped Lance on the shoulder and walked back to the horses.

Lance hung back, detouring to vomit behind a thorn bush. Whatever he had said to Pa, the killing did not sit well on his stomach. He wiped away the drool with the back of his hand and took a long swig from his water bottle. The tepid fluid wet his parched mouth but failed to flush away the sour taste.

2
Vultures in France

*Seven months later — April 1915.
Western Front, Belgium, Ypres. "C" Company,
Royal Fusiliers.*

*I don't want to join the army
I don't want to go to war
I'd rather hang around Piccadilly underground
Livin' orf the earnings of a high-born lady.*

Artillery thudded near their destination, the ruined town of Ypres, as Lance's platoon of thirty men bellowed their raunchy marching song.

*I don't want a bayonet in my belly
I don't want my bollocks shot away
I'd rather stay in England, in merry merry England
And fornicate my bleedin' life away!*

They had been marching all day towards the front lines, to the battlefields. The morning had been yet another cold and wet Flanders spring day, with the low clouds weeping a bone-chilling drizzle, and Lance's men had marched through the mud in silence with shoulders drooping. But the clouds cleared by midday to reveal a pale blue sky and a watery sun. Now the platoon was closer to the battleground, closer to danger, but with the sun on their backs they sang and swung their arms as they marched. It might have been the forced bravado of men who had not yet bloodied their bayonets, but Lance took pride in having earned the right to lead such men into battle. They were ready to show the Huns a thing or two.

It had been a long road from Africa to the Western Front, seven months to be precise. Lance's execution of Peters had ended nothing. German and British East Africa had been dragged into the inexorable conflagration between their homeland masters.

That suited Lance well enough. The papers told of Germany bragging they would soon be the supreme *Weltmacht*, or world power. The reports of Huns pillaging Belgium and raping nuns rang true to Lance after his own experience of Schutztruppe savagery. Germany, dominated by the ruthless and militaristic Junker culture, would rule a brutal new world order where steel and strength rode roughshod over rights and decency. Lance knew bullies. If you didn't give them a bloody nose, they grew bolder. On that, Pa and Lance agreed. But not on much else.

"Stay and fight here Lance. What's happening in Europe isn't our battle."

Lance shook his head. "We're a sideshow Pa. If we win here and Germany wins there, the politicians will carve up the colonies as the spoils of war. We'll become part of German East Africa, and we'll lose everything. We need to beat the bastards in Europe, take German East Africa and make it British. Only then will we sleep soundly at night without worrying about *Schutztruppen* rampaging across the border to kill and burn."

Pa couldn't deny the logic, but Will's wife, Kathy, fought harder than Pa. To everyone's surprise, Will and Kathy had settled into a happy marriage as they waited for the baby. Now she tried everything to keep her man. She screamed at Will, then smothered him with kisses. She tried the silent treatment, then made him listen to the tiny heartbeat inside her. Nothing worked. Will was adamant. So, Lance and Will had booked a sea passage to England to join the British Army and fight in France.

When the time came for the brothers' departure to England, Kathy wept as she clung to Will as best she could with her big belly. "Don't go. The baby needs a father."

"I'll be back, and with a fistful of medals for the baby to play with!" Will laughed.

Kathy turned to Lance. "Promise you'll bring him back to me."

"I'll defend him with my life, Kathy."

She'd looked up into Lance's face and hit him on the chest. "Don't think you'll ever be welcome here again if you come home without him."

Will ushered her away with surprising tact and gentleness.

Lance was astonished to see moistness in Pa's eyes, but his father's handshake was firm and his gaze direct.

"Bye Pa. Let me know if you hear anything about Heidi and the Schumacher family."

"I will," Pa's voice was gruff, "but I'm not hopeful. I haven't received a sniff of news about them. I don't know if the German Army found out Herr Schumacher helped you escape and imprisoned them, or the family was caught by the typhoid epidemic, or it's just the fog of war. There's no working mail left in our part of Africa, and even the tribal grapevine is silent about them."

He ran a hand down his face. "Africa has always been a dangerous place, but the war has added chaos, famine, disease and breakdowns in transportation and law and order. A lot of folks are missing."

Lance grimaced. Revenge had replaced romance as the driving force in his life, but still, the only way he coped was to accept that Heidi was dead to him for the duration of the war. When the war finished, whenever that might be, he could search for her and find if she was still alive, and if the magic remained. Until then, he must erase Heidi from his mind, for his own sanity.

Lance was new to war, but already he'd learned hope was dangerous when carnage ruled. Despair pitched you into a valley and left you there to mope. But hope could take you to the top of the mountain, and then kick you off to tumble thousands of feet into the void. You ended up in the same place, but in far worse agony.

Pa held out a hand. "Here, take these."

Lance took the two thick battered heavy books. "Heck, Pa, they're monsters, they weigh a tonne."

Pa shrugged. "You'll find that most of war is waiting, and you'll need big books to help pass the time. *Bulfinch's Mythology* was your mother's favourite book and contains timeless lessons. Remember she used to read it to you in bed?"

Lance's own eyes misted at that thought. Before Ma had died, every dawn the boys had clambered into the big bed for early morning tea. Then Ma regaled them with stories of heroes and dragons, maidens and monsters, feckless gods and fickle goddesses, all told in her soft Celtic lilt. Those magical dawns were full of the thunder of Thor and the lightning of Mars. Helen's beauty launched a thousand ships against Troy and Salome danced for John the Baptist's head. Macbeth washed his bloody hands in vain and Henry exhorted his band of brothers on Saint Crispin's Day. Legend, myth, history, religion—they were all grist for Ma's storytelling mill, as spellbinding as Odysseus' tales of old.

Lance shook away the past and squinted at the faded gold title embossed on the spine of the pale blue cover of the second book. "*Moby-Dick*? I tried to read that once, but it's impossible. Daft book all about mad Captain Ahab who wants revenge on a whale. Not very subtle, Pa."

His father shrugged. "Even if you've read it before, war will change your view. God knows I'll never understand all of it, but after the Boer War I understood a lot more." Pa's face split into a teasing smile. "*And* it's a great cure for insomnia!"

Lance still carried those books in his backpack, together with a new and glossy King James Bible that Francis had given him. His brother, who would forever walk with two crutches and in constant pain from his wrecked knee, had inscribed the flyleaf in his immaculate forward sloping script: "Hosea 8:7. For they have sown the wind and they shall reap the whirlwind."

After landing in England, Lance and Will joined the hastily trained Infantry Battalion of the Royal Fusiliers. Lance won a commission as a 2nd Lieutenant and was given command of a platoon. Will, who early in his army career had exhibited his mutinous attitude to authority, was a private and lucky to be that. "Just as it should be," Lance had said. "Me giving the orders, and you obeying." Will saluted his superior officer in an unmilitary manner with two fingers.

Now as they marched towards the front in France, Lance smiled as he listened to Will and the other enlisted men singing of the girls they had left behind. Lance's grizzled old company sergeant looked more worried. As the youngsters sang, he scanned the skies.

"What are you looking for, Sergeant Moss?" Lance asked. The battle-hardened Moss was Lance's worry barometer. If Moss was worried, Lance should be very concerned.

The older man spat into the mud. "Bloody vultures."

"Vultures?" Lance asked. "Didn't think you had any left in Northern Europe."

The sergeant smiled without humour. "Not birds, Hun vultures. When you see German airplanes hanging in the sky, them's the eyes of the Hun artillery. They call in targets to the Hun's big guns, the ones that can reach far behind our lines."

The sergeant raised his voice. "A nice big batch of you useless bastards, that's just the plum target the Hun guns are looking for." The youngsters jeered at his warnings but cast pensive looks at the sky as the long march towards the front lines continued.

So twenty minutes later, when a rushing moan split the skies, they were ready. To a man the new recruits dived for cover into the churned-up mud. But the shells whistled overhead into the distance. One by one heads looked up from the mud like turtleheads in a pond at feeding time. Only Lance and the sergeant stood upright, the latter grinning in sardonic satisfaction.

"Look at you sorry lot, covered in mud. No one loves Mother Earth like a soldier when he thinks shells are coming. Use yer ears, you clots. That big noise, them's the huge shells, the coal scuttles, passing over to the rear. They won't use that on us. Keep yer ears open for a shrill piping, them's the daisy cutters, *then* you eat mud in a hurry!"

The sergeant laughed as the troops stood up shamefaced, brushed off the clinging mud as best they could, and pretended they had lost no dignity.

Thirty minutes later the battalion stopped at an unmarked crossroads. The senior officers pointed at maps, argued, and looked disgusted. Plainly the maps and the terrain differed. The men were allowed out of ranks while the officers debated. As the soldiers chattered and lit cigarettes, Sergeant Moss approached Lance and steered him a few discrete paces from the platoon.

"Don't make it bleedin' obvious, sir, but look up there." Moss pointed to the sky in the east. Lance saw nothing at first.

"Black dot like a cross, hanging in the sky by that big white cloud." This time Lance saw it and nodded.

"Hun aircraft, sir, close enough to see us. And we are stopped on a crossroads the Hun artillery will've marked on their maps and ranged their guns on. We're a sittin' duck, sir. The longer we effing sit here, the more likely it'll be raining Hun shells."

"What do you want me to do, Sergeant? It's not up to me where the battalion stops."

"Just point it out to the effin' major, sir, or whoever yer can, and get us off these damn crossroads. If we get off the road, the guns may still shell us, but the bastards won't have the coordinates ranged in."

"How do you know for sure they'll shell us if we stay here?"

"Experience, sir," said the NCO bitterly, "way too much experience. Them vultures are up there for a reason."

"Don't our senior officers have the same experience as you?"

"No, sir. Most of these officers are like you, sir—they've never been on the front lines."

The correct thing to do, the army thing to do—if the British army ever considered that advice could flow uphill—was for Lance to approach his direct superior, Captain Lawes. But Lawes was an upper-class twit who disdained all colonials in general and the "Blackie" colonials from Africa in particular. And even if Lance made a direct appeal to the major, he wasn't likely to get a sympathetic hearing. The chain of command was sacred in the British army, and Major Moyes had no more use for Blackies than Captain Lawes.

"Please, sir," the sergeant pressed. Lance had never seen the man so agitated. He was shifting from foot to foot as though he were standing on hot coals.

"Here's what I'll do, Sergeant. If we don't move in five minutes, I will approach Captain Walters and pass on your suggestion. He's got sense and the major likes him, so maybe he can be more persuasive. In the meantime, let's move the men to the side of the road."

Moss looked at Lance, the craggy folded lines of his face etched with anger. "Effing Hun pilots know which crossroads we're at because the effing plane observers can read their maps. How come our effing officers can't?"

Lance had no answer to that. Sergeant Moss stared at him, implying without a stitch of punishable insubordination, the complete contempt of the British NCO for untested officers. Then Moss stomped off, calling to the men. "Listen yer sorry lot, stop clogging up the road and get into the fields. Move!"

"Aw, Sarge, just got the weight of our feet…"

"Fuck your feet, soldier! Get your flabby arse off this road. Now!"

Lance watched as the soldiers straggled off the road. No sooner had Sergeant Moss chivvied them into the fields than Captain Lawes materialised in a fury. "Lieutenant Fitch! What the dickens do you think you are doing? Get your men back onto the road. At once!"

"Sir, there's an enemy observation plane above us. I'm just trying to disperse my men, sir, in case the Huns have ranged their artillery on this crossroads and fire on us."

Lawes thrust his face so close that spittles of his rage flecked Lance's face. "Do you think you know better than the major? Of course the Huns might fire at us. We are at war. I've told you before that I don't want you using your so-called 'initiative'. Just do as you are sodding ordered and get those men on the road again!"

Lance stared at the bulging eyes and fought the impulse to punch Lawes.

"Do you understand me, Fitch?"

Lance took a step towards his superior officer, but Will grabbed him from behind. "Lance!"

Lawes realised Lance's intent, his eyes widened and his mouth opened. But no words ever emerged.

Lance's head jerked upwards at the violent ripping sound, as though the entire sky was a giant canvas ripping asunder in a giant's hands. The tearing stopped.

A half second of utter silence stretched into eternity. Broken by Moss's despairing wail, "Oh, fuck!"

A brilliant white flash. The explosion sledgehammered Lance's eardrums and flung him through the air. He slammed into the ground and lay helpless, whooping for air, unable to move except for his eyes. An incessant rolling percussion reverberated in his bones, yet he could hear nothing. Fountains of leaping soil sprouted around him in eerie silence. The earth quaked, and broken men and severed limbs cartwheeled through the air. Lance tried to melt into the heaving ground, willing the earth to enclose him in its loving womb. Clouds of smoke writhed with phantoms, a sulphuric inferno without end.

After a lifetime the explosions stopped. The pulverised earth ceased heaving and lay still as the earth should. Smoke hung over the blasted crossroads. Lance lay paralysed, his mind stunned and his bones liquefied by the percussive maelstrom.

Above Lance, through the drifting smoke, he saw the harbinger of this carnage. The dark cross of the Hun observation aircraft floated in the blue sky, impervious and implacable—Moss' vulture.

A face appeared through the haze. The lips moved but Lance heard only the loud ringing in his ears. A strong arm pulled him upright, but Lance staggered and fell over again like a punch-drunk prize-fighter. The face jabbered at him, and Lance shook his head to show he did not understand. The man sat him upright against a pile of backpacks and left him. Men wandered amidst the slaughter, splashed with blood like butchers in an abattoir. Lance shivered as though he was burning from a fever. He wiped his face, and his fingers came away strung with human viscera. He vomited between his knees.

Captain Lawes lay five yards away. Shrapnel had shredded his chest. Bloody bubbles blew from his lungs with each breath, yet his face was unmarked. Lance crawled over to him, wanting to pulp his superior's white face, to apportion his own sense of blame onto the other man. Lawes watched him crawl closer. His mouth shaped to speak, then his eyes glazed and his bowels voided. Lance retched once again, over the corpse of his captain.

Lance staggered to his feet, remembering his brother. Torn and shattered bodies lay hurled at random, some in isolation, some flung together in heaps. Men were cursing and crying and pleading. The dead were more eloquent in their muteness. Blood, so much blood, pools and puddles of red stuff glistened everywhere. And the smell of it, God—the awful smell of it.

Checking for Will, Lance tripped over a facedown corpse. The shell-torn carcase was barely recognisable as the body of a man. Only the remnants of the sergeant's chevrons on the sleeves showed it had been Moss. He'd been wrong about the Germans using only daisy cutters.

Still on his knees, Lance turned away in revulsion. And looked into Will's eyes.

Will appeared untouched by the surrounding mayhem, lying on his back, his eyes open, his face puzzled. Lance shook him. Will's head lolled to one side, and a mush of grey brains slithered onto the mud. A splinter had severed the rear of his skull as neatly as a surgeon's saw.

Lance hugged his brother and rocked him from side to side. Tears flooded down Lance's cheeks. Once he started nothing could stop the outpouring, and the tears grew into convulsive sobs and an incoherent keening. They were tears of shock and self-pity, but most of all they were tears of loss—the loss of his brother, and of the world he had known. His cries were those of a new-born child ripped from the protection of a womb and about to be cast into a furnace, a furnace that would forge him into a warrior or consume him.

When the tears ceased, Lance felt desiccated. Most of his platoon, and his brother, lay dead. Because Lance hadn't had the guts to do as Sergeant Moss suggested. His soul was as arid as a desert, and a great wind hungered and howled around him as he knelt by his brother, alone in a dark and bitter place.

~

Lance had no memory of how he reached the front lines.

That night, in a waterlogged trench amongst the chittering of rats and other survivors crying out their nightmares, the balm of sleep eluded him. In a twilight world, he floated as an invulnerable phantom through a misty forest of shell bursts. The trees flowered and fell in slow motion, awesome in their beauty, their random dance macabre. Jagged metal slivers wafted past him, so slow he could see their razor-sharp torn edges and drops of blood spraying in geometrical arcs. Kathy's spectral voice echoed and re-echoed. "Promise you'll bring him back to me. The baby needs a father." Culpability coiled in his belly and guilt coursed through his thoughts like venom.

A roar rose in his head like the heavy Mombasa surf. Crashing rollers tumbled his mind and senses. Then a blanketing fog descended, deadening all sound. He floated from his body and looked down on himself. Tears rolled down his cheeks, his hands and legs twitched, and sobs wracked his lungs. Yet he felt nothing. Except in a far distant corner of his mind, something shrieked defiance against surrender. Then that small voice faded too, and the fog stole his mind.

~

His eyes opened to white walls, people dressed in white and hushed murmurings. Heaven? A pretty face swam into view and smiled, blue eyes dancing and their surrounding skin crinkling with real delight. Suffused light made a halo around blond hair. Definitely Heaven then.

"You're back?" she asked.

"Back where?" he croaked, his voice shaky with disuse.

"With us, silly! We're a hospital behind the front lines. You've been absent for three days!"

"If you say so." He didn't have the energy to work it all out.

"That's what we call it when you're, um, not all here. Absent. I'll tell the doctor."

Heaven slid downhill from there.

"Shell-shock," the doctor told him. "But you're better now."

"What's shell-shock?"

"Nobody really knows. But it seems like a combination of physical symptoms—you have symptoms of concussion as though you had a heavy blow to the head—and a mental breakdown. Not everyone recovers, and, although you seem better now, the symptoms often re-occur under fire at the front." The doctor sat back and looked at him. "I believe it is a real disease. However, be warned. Some doctors and senior officers believe men with these symptoms are fakers, cowards trying to avoid being sent back to the fighting."

That didn't sound good. Either Lance was a nutcase or a coward. He felt more like a nutcase, but that wasn't reassuring. Or maybe it was. They shot cowards. He couldn't think straight and his head ached, so he lay there and stared at the ceiling—all white of course. That made the headache worse.

An hour later, a captain stomped in with a clipboard. He possessed a big moustache, a big belly, and little sympathy. "Come on Finch, you're needed at the front. A truck leaves for your regiment in two hours." An ostentatious tick with the pen and the man vanished.

Lance spent the hours and minutes and seconds until departure staring at the white walls and white ceiling.

Terrified. Would another episode break his fragile sanity forever?

~

Ten months later – February 1916.
Western Front, Belgium, Ypres.

Toe or brain? Lance watched as Private Anderson unlaced his right boot with slow deliberation. Last night's rain had frozen, and a man removing his boot in this icy weather and this close to an attack meant one of two things—either he would blow off a toe or blow out his brains. Shooting off a toe was the most common way to earn a "Blighty" wound, one that wouldn't kill you but would get you shipped out of France for good. The subsequent court martial would disgrace you, and you'd limp for life, but live you would. Anderson would leave his sock on if he wanted a "Blighty," but if he took off his sock, then he would put the muzzle of his rifle in his mouth and use his big toe to press the trigger. That angle guaranteed a bullet in the brain and was best done with a bare toe so it didn't slip off the trigger.

Once Lance would have spat at entertaining such a thought himself. No longer. On his return to the trenches, days blurred into each other. Horrors that once seemed seismic didn't even register in his memory. Summer had passed into autumn, and then into winter's iron grip as 1915 died. A new year tottered into the world, but precious little changed.

For ten months, attacks and counterattacks flowed into each other as seamlessly as the rainstorms. Around him the mud grew ever deeper and more glutinous, and the damp chilled his weary bones to the marrow. The only thing Lance knew for certain was that tomorrow would bring more of the same.

And that death would be a release.

Lance wasn't the only one watching Anderson. Troops packed the trench, their breath steaming in the frigid February air. The generals had delayed the planned dawn attack twice already, the interminable wait leaching fear into the troops' bones as a murky dawn puddled across the horizon in the east.

Where the Huns' massed machine guns and rolls of razor-barbed wire waited for them.

Every time they went over the top, the Grim Reaper's bony claws squeezed Lance's heart. The relentless rattle of machine guns signalled the Reaper's scythe—that wet fast *slap-slap-slap* as bullets tore into soft flesh, a merciless man-mincing hell. Today's dawn attack would be no different. So far, the Reaper had left Lance alone. In one attack, a burst of machine gun fire scythed down the man on his left and on his right and left Lance standing. Who knew why?

Their trench was dug deep to keep the troops safe from snipers, and wooden-planked firing platforms every few yards allowed the men to step up so they could fire at the enemy through horizontal slits in the sandbagged trench lip. Now the men clustered in the bottom of the trench, sitting on the muddy duckboards or leaning against the earthen trench walls. The stink of funk, stale sweat, and damp wool mixed with the smoke of cheap cigarettes.

Anderson eased off the boot with a sigh and peeled off the sock. A small strip of rotten flesh came with the wool, making Anderson wince. Trench foot. A man leaned over to Anderson, offered him a cigarette, and murmured something. Anderson shook his head. Sergeant Finn caught Lance's eye, and they both looked away.

Lance struggled to his feet, his frozen limbs aching and his boots slipping on the icy duckboards. He limped away, avoiding Sergeant Finn's accusing gaze.

It was an officer's duty to prevent suicides or "Blighty" wounds by the men in his company, but Lance sympathised with Anderson's likely choice. Lance had once seen an African tribesman squatting for days outside the Taveta sanatorium, unseeing as he stared into the distance. "He is a dead man busy dying," the doctor had said when Lance asked what was wrong with the man. "A local witch doctor has cursed him. Now he is a dead man in his own mind. It will take his body time to catch up, but there is nothing I can do for him." The answer made no sense to Lance at the time, but it did now.

Since Will died, Lance had suffered his breakdown several times. Rather than send him to the sanatorium, Lance's fellow officers had rallied around and protected him until he recovered. That led to friendships. When Lance re-surfaced and found himself wrapped in a grubby blanket and surrounded by concerned faces and grins of delight, warmth flooded through him. You could sit on cold nights and hug that precious, life-affirming warmth around you.

Until those friends died. That was never very life-affirming. Now Lance knew the Great Truth. Friendship was a weakness. Friends led to madness. Each of their gruesome deaths prodded you closer to the edge of the precipice.

Peyton reacted too slowly to the ominous cloud of chlorine gas and coughed out his lungs in bloody lumps before dying in Lance's arms. It took several hours before Lance could complete a sentence.

Ashton and Burrows were buried alive when their bunker collapsed under a storm of shells. A broken beam smashed Lance across the head but covered his face from the fallen earth. He lay entombed in total darkness, unable to move his arms and legs, surrounded by the dead and the smell of their voided bowels. A lifetime of quivering terror followed as the earth raged and shook, every explosion sending soil trickling into his tiny pocket of air. After the barrage ceased, ragged breaths came harder and harder as precious oxygen ran out, each gasp as demanding as lifting a boulder, all the while praying that the chipping and thunking of pickaxe and shovel would move closer. Please God!

Doc Simpson said they took three hours to dig Lance out, and when he emerged he was catatonic. The doc stitched up his head and dribbled a half a bottle of rum into him through his slack lips. Forty-eight hours later, Lance could talk and walk. Sort of. His limbs and lips moved, but neither obeyed him too well. The doc joked he wasn't sure what was shell-shock and what was a hangover. Simpson always had a lousy sense of humour, but he was a good doc.

Barrett died with cloth and skin snagged on barbed wire, jerking like a marionette as a machine gun nailed him. When Lance dragged him free and into a shell-hole, Barrett was miraculously still alive. He clutched Lance's hand. "Get my body…back for Christian burial," he whispered. Then he gurgled blood and his eyes opened wide. Under the mantle of darkness, the survivors of that doomed attack crawled back towards their trenches. Lance dragged Barrett's body back across No-Man's-Land, pursued by vindictive shellfire and hunting machine guns. It took him too long. At dawn a sniper found them. He put two bullets into Barrett's corpse and one into Lance. It didn't take much acting ability for Lance to play dead. He lay there all day, semi-conscious, not daring to twitch a muscle. A day where his thirsty throat grated like he'd swallowed gravel and his shoulder throbbed as the devil stabbed him with a red-hot poker on every heartbeat.

They sent him to a hospital in England. The bullet had passed through his shoulder without hitting anything vital and it recovered quickly, although it would remain stiff. But his mind took longer. Every ten days the hospital rounded up their shell-shocked zombies and sent them to a special mental asylum. Lance saw the routine after he'd recovered. You could tell the victims by that blank stare. The same tell-tale sign he'd seen on the tribesman's face back in Africa, and now on Private Anderson.

Lance had been a day away from being moved to the asylum when he surfaced. A damned close-run thing. Lance shuddered at the thought of being caged in a soulless mental sanitorium. Death would be preferable. After that narrow escape, Lance vowed he was finished with friendship. Since then, he'd made no friends, shared no intimacies, and never laughed.

So now, facing the hell of another day's attack, he understood Private Anderson only too well.

Lance stepped onto a firing platform and wrapped his arms around himself, hugging his soaked greatcoat in a vain search for warmth. He flinched as a rifle cracked behind him, and he said a short prayer for Anderson.

His head slumped against the sandbags, ice searing his forehead as a flood of envy surged through him. Through the horizontal firing slit the stark fingers of shattered tree stumps pointed heavenwards from the blasted morass of no-man's land. Why wait? Why not cheat the Huns or insanity of their victory and take control of his destiny like Anderson?

His fingers fumbled at the snap fastening on his revolver holster, almost of their own volition. He wondered at the haste of his hands, and a wry shock of recognition hit him. "If it were done," Macbeth said, "then 'twere well it were done quickly."

He lifted the gun to his temple but stopped as rainbow colours glinted off the barrel. Puzzled, he looked through the narrow firing slit and saw the orange disc of the sun rising in the east. Small stalactites of ice jagged downwards from the top of the firing slit and caught the sun's rays in imperfect prisms. The rainbow-tinted stalactites were, to his febrile and fragile mind, a portcullis to the gates of heaven. He had almost forgotten what the sun looked like, and he drank in its rays, a lover staring at the matchless face of his beloved.

He frowned as puffs of white blossomed high in the dawn sky, creating a trail of tiny white clouds. Then he saw it, a dark shape like a cross. A Hun artillery-spotting plane, a bloody vulture, gliding past the anti-aircraft fire. No sounds from above reached Lance, no engine noise, no thud of distant explosions—the life and death struggle played as a silent ballet. His eyes fixed on the airplane with fanatical hunger, and his jittery mind focused on a simple epiphany.

Revenge.

The brilliance of the sun and the compulsion of his new-found crusade began to mend his mind. Lance had failed to protect Will and the platoon, but at least he could wrench retribution from the vultures responsible for those deaths.

HQ cancelled the regiment's planned attack for that morning, and Lance requested a transfer to an anti-aircraft battery that same day.

~

Two days later the path of his new crusade took an unforeseen twist. Lance was summoned to the major's command dugout to meet a dapperly dressed captain. The slim dandy wore a sardonic expression, a pencil-thin moustache with slicked-back brown hair, and a pair of pristine riding boots.

Lance's commanding officer was brusque. "Fitch, this is Captain Clayton of the Royal Flying Corps. He wants volunteers to join the RFC to fly as gunners. I am ordered to assist him in that process, even though I think it a ridiculous errand. Take him around each company. Anybody wanting to volunteer must sign his name. Remind the men that whatever blandishments Captain Clayton offers, the Royal Flying Corps is taking part in an unnatural and dangerous activity, and the life expectancy of these fools is far shorter than in the infantry."

The major glared at Clayton as though flying was a perversion that the captain had invented. Clayton stroked his thin moustache and looked as angelic as his sardonic face allowed.

Lance led him from the dugout and through the communication trenches towards his own company. The captain limped after him, and a light smur of rain caused Clayton's gleaming boots to slide on the muddy duckboards. The RFC officer swore in disgust as he grew wetter and muddier.

To Lance, Clayton's appearance seemed a favourable omen for his crusade. He asked three questions.

"If I join up as a gunner, do I get to shoot down those observation airplanes that fly over our lines?"

"It is one of our raisons d'être, old boy," Clayton replied, kicking a rat carcass off the duckboards into the shallow river running at the bottom of the trench.

"Does the RFC shoot down more of those aircraft than our anti-aircraft guns?"

"Ha! No contest. The ground guns, British or German, seldom shoot anything down. In fact, the pilots call it 'Archie' as in that music hall song, 'Archibald, certainly not!'"

"Do you see the sun when you fly?"

"Absolutely, old chap—when you earthbound mortals are enjoying your daily French showers, our brave aviators are gallivanting like gods above the clouds in glorious sunlight. Are you a good shot?"

Lance laughed for the first time since Will died. His throat was out of practice, and the laugh sounded more like a rusty hinge. But his shooting skill was the one thing he never doubted.

Clayton looked at him askance. "I'll take that as a yes. You should sign up, m'boy."

That was sufficient for Lance. Better to perish in the sunlit heavens than in the glutinous mud under the perpetual grey murk of drizzling clouds.

Clayton dried the ink on Lance's signature by flourishing the paper in the air. He thrust out his hand. "As adjutant," he proclaimed, "it is my pleasure to welcome you to 13 Squadron, which will turn you into a bold and daring aviator."

Lance lifted his head and searched the sky with hungry eyes. "And they shall reap the whirlwind," he murmured.

3
A Tale for the Ages

March 1916.
Western Front, France, Arras Sector, Bruay Airfield.
Royal Flying Corps, 13 Squadron.

Clayton was not aware of any template for recognising those who might excel in the air war—the science was too new—but his intuition tingled over his latest recruit.

The 13 Squadron adjutant had been a professional soldier for almost half of his thirty-five years, and that included time spent in the British Empire's eternal attempts to pacify the wild and wily mountain tribesman on India's north-west frontier. So Fitch's eyes intrigued him. He had seen similar eyes among the Pathan tribesman high in the rugged mountains—the same green iris flecked with bronze, the same disconcerting watchfulness. If Lance Fitch were half as cunning and ferocious as those tribesmen, he would be some warrior.

Otherwise, Fitch looked nondescript—early twenties, lean, medium height, with brown hair flopping over a slightly battered face.

On Clayton's return to his squadron, he found his commanding officer, Major Lord Arthur Wolsey, standing outside his office smoking a large cigar. Clayton shook his head at the unfairness of life. Not only was the man one of England's most powerful and rich aristocrats, he looked like a recruiting poster for the RFC with his blond hair, blue eyes and open face.

Arthur greeted his adjutant with a perfect smoke ring and a smile. "What ho! The wanderer returns. Any luck recruiting from the PBI?"

"Those poor bloody infantry seem to think they are better off with the rats and mud than cavorting in the heavens," Clayton grumbled. "But I press-ganged one wild colonial lieutenant. His CO says he is the best shot in the regiment but his manners in the officers' Mess are shocking. Apparently, he is first rate with a shotgun and ducks on the wing, but not so hot with the regimental cutlery and duck à l'orange. Notwithstanding these peccadilloes, I think we may have a rough diamond here."

"Only one recruit? He had better be the Cullinan diamond, or I am firing you as my recruiting officer."

In fact, over the next month, the diamond proved too rough for the squadron. The adjutant watched with concern as Fitch ostracised himself. He trained like a fanatic to be a gunner and talked like a zealot about killing Hun two-seaters. His fellow officers in the officers' Mess did not enjoy his frank bloodthirstiness. The upper-class British pilots preferred to pretend war flying was a sport. When Fitch spoke about his war, it seemed a grim and premeditated sort of murder, one requiring psychopathic tendencies.

13 Squadron had only one hut, split in two, for the officers' Mess and anteroom areas. In the evenings or on rainy days the pilots had nowhere else to go. Theirs was a claustrophobic social world where flying crews rubbed shoulders with each other whether they wanted to or not. For most officers the noisy camaraderie of the mess was the closest thing to a home they possessed in this war. But Fitch regarded it as a cage. When circumstances trapped him there, he sipped lemonade while the other officers played their laddish drinking games, and he never joined their raucous singing.

Once Fitch qualified as a gunner and started patrols, he spent most of his non-flying time in the hangars, checking his ammunition belts for the following day's flight. The upper-class officers mocked him for being an uncouth

Blackie more at home with the working-class mechanics than his fellow officers. They ridiculed his lack of English social graces and parodied his colonial accent and vocabulary.

Clayton had a soft spot for non-conformists, and 13 Squadron's only colonial became his protégé. The adjutant was vocal in his support for the newcomer, but his efforts accomplished little. However much Clayton socialised with the pilots, there would always be an inseparable gulf between those who risked death in the air and the non-combatants. Clayton was thirty-five, ten to seventeen years older than the pilots. He possessed his own bullet wounds from earlier wars, and his dress uniform showed Britain's second highest award for valour, the Distinguished Service Order, but none of this counted for much with the young pilots in this Great War.

Clayton admired how Fitch refused to allow the mockery to deflect him from his habits, however pointed the jibes became. He continued to spend his evenings in the hangars under the hissing hurricane lamps, checking his guns and cartridges. To the best of Clayton's knowledge, Fitch checked every round he fired. And though the machine gun stoppages that plagued other gunners did not happen to Fitch, that did not make him more popular. Neither did the hours he spent honing his shooting skills with the Lewis machine guns.

Frank Winterbottom, the self-appointed wit of the squadron, voiced the mess opinion while stroking his moustache. "Y'know, Blackie, you'll wear out the gun barrels."

Lance said nothing but gazed at Winterbottom with those disconcerting green eyes. Most antagonists ceased their banter under that stare, but Winterbottom continued. "It makes a frightful racket, and I'm sure Major Wolsey has already heard you are gagging to murder Huns."

Lance's expression did not alter, but tears began to drip across the faint scar across his left cheekbone. The tears and the hard glitter in Lance's eyes, put Clayton in mind of a volcano: a lava flow hinting at a subterranean rage that could blow with ferocious force. Winterbottom must have received the same impression, for he faltered to a stop. After that, the harassment was more subdued.

Fitch queried Clayton later. "For Christ's sake, don't they want to win the war? Why is it 'bad form, old boy' to practice things to kill Huns and help you stay alive?"

"To them, every burst is your way of saying, 'Look at me, I'm showing I'm keen.' I don't agree with them one iota. I'm only passing on their thoughts to help you understand."

"It's bloody hard to practice machine gunnery silently."

"It isn't so much the keenness that is bad form, Lance, it is the being seen to be keen. Public school teaches them that a gentleman should be a duck swimming against the current, serene and unruffled above the surface but paddling like hell beneath the water."

Lance snorted. "That may work in peace time, but these boys need to adapt. Ducks don't sneak up behind you and riddle you in the back with a Spandau machine gun."

"Don't worry, when they see you having success they will come around to your way of thinking."

But Clayton's predicted success never materialised.

In early 1916 the RFC was suffering crippling losses and 13 Squadron was no exception. The German air force had made technological and tactical breakthroughs in late 1915. Antony Fokker, the greatest aircraft designer of the age, had designed the slim and deadly Fokker monoplane. Then he bolted a Spandau machine gun in front of the pilot and synchronised it to fire through the propeller—the first ever such device. Now the machine gun became a true extension of the plane, and pilots pointed the aircraft to shoot. The "Fokker Menace" had arrived, and with it, a new level of slaughter in the skies above France.

By winter in late 1916, British planes were falling in flames like moths around a lit hurricane lamp. German papers boasted of their daring new aces, Max Immelman and Oswald Boelcke. Immelman invented new flying manoeuvres that enabled him to surprise Allied pilots and shoot them down with a terrifying élan. Boelcke pioneered new tactics that allowed the Fokkers to fight as irresistible teams. Together the two of them inspired the Germans into ruthless ascendancy above the Western Front. The British sought to blunt German technical superiority with the tenacity of the British bulldog spirit, and a relentless willingness to offer the blood sacrifice of their aircrews.

13 Squadron flew FE2bs, a pusher biplane design with an open fuselage shaped like a big bathtub. Not even the FE2b's designer would have called it elegant. The gunner sat in the front of the tub with the pilot behind him, the latter on a raised seat so he could see over the gunner. Behind the crew lay forty-seven-foot-long biplane wings, a huge engine, and four wooden struts that tapered back to a tailplane that looked like an afterthought. The ten-foot propellers at the rear pushed the contraption forwards, hence the name "pusher". Some wag had christened FE2s as 'prehistoric packing cases'. Lance reckoned they were being unkind. They reminded him of Chinese box kites, modern technology circa 200 BC.

The gunner handled two machine guns, one in front of him to fire forwards, and another behind him to fire backwards. Both guns swivelled so the gunners could fire in wide arcs. Firing the forward gun was easy, but to fire backwards over the head of the pilot and the engine was a nightmare. The gunner had to stand upright in the shallow bathtub, the lip reaching just to his calves, in a ninety-miles-an-hour gale. Only a vice-like grip on the machine gun handles would prevent him being hurled into the void by any unexpected movement. A thin canvas safety harness around the waist provided little reassurance. A gunner needed strong hands, iron nerves, and a trust that his pilot would not jolt him out of the cockpit to fall shrieking to the earth below.

The trust needed to flow both ways. Hun pilots soon learned to attack from behind the clumsy aircraft and hide behind the huge engine. So FE2 pilots often sat trapped in a shooting gallery, with enemy tracers flashing past from behind while their own gunners returned fire over the pilot's head in the opposite direction.

Some pilots froze with fear, leaving the Fokkers free to hide behind the engine and shoot without resistance. More flinched at their own gunners' flickering muzzle flashes a foot from their faces, disrupting the gunners' aim. Yet others tried to hurl their clumsy pusher aircraft around the sky in vain attempts to outmanoeuvre the Fokkers, with the gunners clutching for their lives at whatever handles they could find.

Lance was passed from pilot to pilot like a hot bullet casing. When Clayton asked the pilots if there was a problem with Fitch, they never gave a military answer. They would glance away and mumble something like, "He makes me uneasy," or, "I just don't like to fly with him." When the adjutant asked Fitch what the problem was, the answer was always the same. "Silly bastards won't fly straight and steady to let me get a good shot at the Huns. When I tell them that, they get annoyed with me."

Clayton gave Lance more than a month, but as March 1916 limped towards its end, even the adjutant wondered if it might be best to post Fitch out of the squadron. He spoke to Arthur Wolsey about his conundrum. "Fitch is one hell of a shot, but he's so intense and so desperate to shoot down Huns that none of the pilots want him as a shipmate. They think his demand to fly straight will kill them, and besides they don't like the cut of his jib."

Arthur put his pen down, ran his fingers through his thick blond hair, and leaned back in his chair. "Why are you even asking me? Sounds an easy choice. If he will not be part of a team, his shooting skill is irrelevant. Post him out of here."

"It seems such a waste of a crack shot who is itching to have a go at the Huns. If we reject him as a gunner, he'll end up sweeping floors for the RFC somewhere back in England." Clayton's voice tailed off, sounding lame and hesitant even to himself.

"I will not force a gunner on anyone. It is their lives at stake. If no one wants to fly with him, get rid of him."

Clayton delivered the bad news that night in the cold hangars, where he found his quarry checking ammunition belts under the hissing hurricane lamps. Fitch flinched at the news as though Clayton had struck him with a whip. In the gloom his eyes seemed to sink even further into their sockets. He stared at the adjutant for long moments. When he finally spoke, his voice quavered.

"The pilots are in the wrong."

Clayton shrugged. "Maybe. But it's all of them against you. If no pilot wants to fly with you, there is no point in staying here. Besides, Major Wolsey has decided—you're to go."

"How can he judge? He's never seen me in a plane. Aristocratic bastard. Bet he's like all the rest, thinks I'm a colonial scumbag."

Clayton said nothing.

"If I'm posted out of here," Fitch asked, "will I go to another squadron as a gunner?"

"I'll do my best," Clayton said without conviction. "But if you flunk one squadron, the others tend not to want you."

Fitch grabbed Clayton by both arms, and his eyes burned with intensity in the yellow cast of the hurricane lamp. "I have to shoot down those Hun planes. I won't take anything else!"

"This is the army," Clayton said. "You take what you get." He levered himself free from Fitch's grasp and walked out of the hangar.

~

Next Day

The damaged FE2b vibrated as if it would fall apart at any second. Arthur Wolsey's right thigh trembled with fatigue as he pressed down on full right rudder, nursing the crippled plane home. If he eased a fraction off the rudder pedal the nose would lurch downwards into a deadly spin.

In front of him, his lung-shot gunner gasped for oxygen, his mouth opening and closing convulsively like a fish out of water. Pink bubbles frothed from Broad's lips, and his eyes bulged. The airspeed blew the bloody bubbles over Arthur, filming his goggles with a red mist.

Arthur could not reach the injured man without releasing the controls and unbuckling his own safety harness. Despite the full right rudder, the FE2b flew left wing low as though hunched in pain. They would both die if Arthur lifted his foot off the rudder, so he flew on as Broad watched him with bulging eyes, gasping unheard against the roar of the engine and the howling wind.

Never knew there was so much blood in a man. God knows why the Fokkers left us. They must have run out of ammunition.

Bracing wires in both wings fluttered in the wind and the wooden spars flexed alarmingly with each bump of turbulence. He had visions of the wings folding and his screaming body hurtling earthwards.

Broad stopped flopping. His head slumped back, mouth slack, eyes closed, but the blood still flowed from his torn flesh. He was a good man, cheerful and even-tempered. But a hopeless gunner, God knew.

During their previous flights together, Broad hosed bullets around the sky with the generosity of a drunk let loose in the distillery. When Arthur suggested it might be more effective to fire at the enemy aircraft, the gunner had protested. "You bloody well try it, sir. It's like shooting jinking partridges from the back of a galloping horse with someone else controlling the reins."

For a while the tactics worked, but not today. A white and black Fokker, the colour scheme of the legendary Boelcke, ignored Broad's wild tracers, closed to within fifty feet, and riddled Broad and the FE2b. How the plane was still flying God only knew.

The ground below crawled past. Arthur had reached the British side of the lines now, but he refused the safety of an immediate landing. If he could reach his airfield at Bruay, Broad would be in the nearby military hospital inside fifteen minutes and his chance of survival would be much higher. Or perhaps the gunner was already dead, and Arthur was risking his life for nothing? He closed his mind to the risks and his cramping leg and focused on keeping the nose level.

By the time the airfield slid into view, the cramp was knotting Arthur's leg. Just before landing his right leg cramped and gave way, and the nose of the plane pitched downwards. He grunted and grimaced and locked his knee, using his hip and heel to push all his body weight onto the rudder pedal. The nose lifted. *More, you bitch, more! That's it! Yes, girl, more!*

The left wing hit and splintered, spinning the plane in circles as it careened across the grass. Arthur's world blurred into cracking wood, snapping wires, and rending canvas. His harness broke and his nose crunched against the cockpit coaming. The top wing collapsed on his head, shunting him lower into the cockpit and pinning him against the joystick. He prayed, jammed and helpless, as the world whirled.

When at last the spinning, snapping, ripping and crunching stopped, Arthur exhaled a prayer of thanks. But the collapsed top wing trapped him inside the cockpit, curled up like a foetus, unable to move. The clanging bell of the emergency wagon came closer. He closed his eyes and sagged against the joystick.

A loud hiss of petrol dropping on the hot engine punctured his relief. Arthur screamed and thrust his back against the wing that pinned him. The aircraft shook but did not yield. Another hiss, and another. The pungent petrol smell galvanised him. He heaved upwards again and again. The plane rocked but still the wing entombed him.

"Don't move!" The bellowed order brought Arthur back to sanity. He recoiled as an axe head plunged through the tangled wood a foot from his face. Axes hacked everywhere, and the plane lurched from the rescuers' efforts. Sand cascaded into the cockpit as someone poured it over the engine. Canvas ripped and daylight glittered above as strong arms seized Arthur from behind, lifted him from the cockpit, and tried to lay him flat on the ground.

He struggled. "No, I can stand."

"You've lost a lot of blood, sir, best lie down."

"It is Broad's, not mine. I am fine."

Clayton's concerned face swam in front of Arthur. When the arms let go, Arthur's knees sagged and he clutched at his adjutant. "Not wounded," he insisted. "Just my knees knocking like a music hall act." Then he laughed. It started weakly but grew and grew. Arthur heard the hysteria in it but could not stop. It poured from him in torrents, convulsing his body.

"I was afraid," he gasped, "I would be the first Lord Wolsey to be killed by an axe since the Tudor days!"

Clayton thrust a flask between Arthur's lips. "This'll help the shock."

The brandy didn't, but seeing Broad's limp body being rolled into a canvas shroud killed his laughter.

"Dead?" Arthur asked.

The fitters nodded as they carted the body away. One of Broad's arms escaped the canvas and dragged along the grass in mute appeal.

"Do me a bloody favour, Clayton," Arthur said. "Find me a blasted gunner who can damned well hit the bloody Huns."

The adjutant blinked at the unaccustomed profanity. Arthur knew that Clayton could handle his CO's self-indulgent vent, but he felt guilty all the same. Not only was Clayton indispensable for the smooth running of the squadron, but he'd also become a friend who helped Arthur carry the lonely burden of command. Not that Arthur would admit either fact to Clayton.

"Sorry, it was a tough trip. Is that awkward colonial still here—the one who can shoot?"

"Yes," Clayton muttered, apparently not inclined towards rapid forgiveness.

"Tell him he flies with me tomorrow."

~

At noon the following day, Arthur stood in front of a new FE2b, dressed to fly. His hands shook and his guts churned. Every cell in his body shrieked at him to never, ever, set foot in a plane again.

Most majors did not fly on patrols; in fact, Boom Trenchard discouraged it. And Arthur was old for a combat pilot at thirty-five. Air warfare might be a recent invention, but one thing was already clear—it was a young man's game. No one would blame him for becoming a desk jockey, but an aristocratic belief that he had been born to lead was bred into his bones and schooled into his psyche.

And leaders did not hide behind desks. They led from the front.

Yet the devil tempted him. The ground crew had counted more than two hundred bullet holes in his wrecked plane—a record for any plane that made it home.

"It's a miracle, sir," his fitter had told him. "So many bullets, and they hit nothing vital."

"Except Broad," Arthur said, and the rigger looked shamefaced.

Arthur had tossed and turned all night as the memories of his gunner's last bloody breaths jittered his nerves. In the darkness, he allowed himself to imagine he had done his fair share and could end his self-imposed duty of air fighting with good conscience. Then self-contempt scalded him. "Gutless," he mouthed at himself in the darkness.

Now, faced with the reality of another sortie against the Huns, his body was betraying him with the shakes. But if he didn't fly over the lines today, he would never have the guts to do so again.

He stroked the wingtips of his new FE2b and inhaled the whiff of dope resin fresh on the linen. It smelled brand new, as did his goggles, gloves, and flying coat. Their leather crackled with every movement. His batman had scrubbed and scrubbed his old flying gear but could not banish the stain and stench of blood, so Arthur had told him to burn the stinking stuff.

A throat cleared, startling him. Arthur turned to find Clayton and another man standing next to him.

"Lieutenant Lance Fitch, sir, your new gunner."

Fitch stood impassive, appraising Arthur as Arthur appraised him. The unblinking intensity of the green and tawny eyes startled Arthur. Those eyes locked on his, yet they seemed focused far beyond him, so much so that Arthur had to resist an inclination to turn and look behind himself.

"I remember you now," Arthur said. "The colonial who is good with a shotgun at duck on the wing but not so hot with the duck à l'orange. But can you shoot Huns?"

"If you hold the plane steady enough," Fitch said.

Clayton interjected. "That should be 'steady enough, sir'."

"Steady?" Arthur's eyebrows rose. "You want me to hold this flying bathtub steady while the Fokkers shoot us. Really?"

"If you hold it steady, I'll shoot them before they shoot us—sir." The gunner's voice was rocklike in its certainty.

"Remind me, if this man is so darned good," Arthur asked Clayton, "why was he being posted out of the squadron?"

Before Clayton could answer, Fitch replied. "Because none of the other pilots had the guts to hold her steady so I could shoot."

In light of his recent experience, every fibre of Arthur's body recoiled at the thought of flying straight while the Fokkers machine gunned him at the rate of five hundred bullets a minute. But he prided himself on his judgement of men, and Fitch did not seem to be a braggart. "Well, if the Huns cannot bring me down with two hundred bullets," he muttered, "we may as well try your way." Arthur pulled on his thick flying gloves and banged them together. "After all, it is only our lives at stake, eh, Fitch?"

"Wait," Fitch said. "If the Huns get on our tail and hide behind the engine so I can't shoot them, I'll tap you on the shoulder of the direction I want you to turn. Always turn towards the arm I hit you on. Turn thirty degrees then hold her steady unless I bash you again."

"Who is in charge of this aircraft, Lieutenant, me or you?"

"You are in charge of flying it, Major, but when the shooting starts I am the only one who can see every direction, and the only one with machine guns, so that puts me in charge while the shooting is happening…sir."

Arthur looked at his new gunner. "If you shoot as well as you talk, we might just live. Come on Fitch. Let us go fly." Arthur turned towards his new FE2b, finding his nerves reassured by Fitch's utter certainty.

Clayton demolished that reassurance. "Happy April Fool's Day."

~

"Christ! Not again," Arthur said.

The two Fokkers materialised from the thin haze, their slim monoplane silhouettes elegant and deadly against the soft blue sky. The pair curved apart to attack from opposite sides, forcing a gunner to choose which enemy to engage and leaving the other a free shot. "Bastards!" Arthur swore, recognising the dilemma Fitch faced.

The enemy bore closer, one from each beam. Arthur watched Fitch stand to grab the spade grips of his front Lewis gun. The gunner braced himself against the slipstream and swayed easily at the knees as the FE2b dipped in the air currents. He kept the machine gun pointed forwards, refusing to show his hand to the Fokkers.

Fire flickered from the port Fokker. Tracer streaked past the FE2b, but still Fitch did not move. Arthur gritted his teeth. Had his gunner frozen with fear? Bitterly he heard his own joke—"It is only our lives at stake."

At last Fitch swung his gun towards the left-hand Fokker and fired in staccato bursts. The tracers speared at the Fokker, which swerved away. Fitch gracefully swung the Lewis gun 180 degrees, his body leaning far out of the nacelle, held only by the thin harness, and fired at the other Fokker. For long seconds the two planes hammered at each other. Fabric tore and jagged holes sprouted in the FE2b's wings. With a deep breath and firm resolution Arthur held the plane steady. The black and white Fokker flashed past. Arthur cursed. Boelcke, again! The test of his new gunner would be the sternest possible, and death the price of failure.

For the next attack the Fokkers arced behind the FE2b, out of Arthur's vision. Seconds ticked like minutes as he hunched his shoulders and waited for their attack. Fitch stood on the firing step, clutching the rear gun and staring over Arthur's head, his expression giving no clues as to the events behind Arthur. Only the green eyes, slitted in concentration, showed any emotion.

Arthur twitched as tracer slashed past, so close he smelt the burning phosphorus.

Fitch clapped Arthur's right shoulder, and Arthur skidded the plane thirty degrees to the right. At once the Lewis gun hammered and its tracers speared a foot over Arthur's head. A hot spent cartridge flicked Arthur's cheek. He flinched, and the plane jerked in sympathy. Fitch's mouth opened, shouting unheard abuse. Arthur steadied the plane. The harsh stink of cordite filled his nostrils.

The first Fokker roared overhead, trailing a banner of red flame. Arthur gaped in surprise. The plane rolled onto its back as the pilot jumped into the void and tumbled over and over toward his death. Arthur grimaced in empathic horror.

Fitch was still firing backwards at the second Fokker. Arthur kept his eyes forward, blinking as the Lewis gun pounded tracers just above his head. Enemy tracer flashed in the other direction, splintering the central struts. Fitch flinched as blood streaked his cheek but he never stopped firing short bursts. The second Fokker flashed past, black and white, fast as a swallow.

Arthur watched with disbelief as it continued ahead. It circled the pillar of black smoke left by its vanquished comrade then turned away and vanished into the haze. Arthur sagged with relief. They had survived.

As they crossed the front lines into safety, Arthur eased off a glove, leaned forward, and offered a heartfelt handshake to his gunner. "Our first kill!" he bellowed against the slipstream. "And we saw off the great Boelcke. A tale for the ages!"

Fitch grinned at him. He looked years younger with his face cracked in a smile and his green eyes less grim. Arthur found himself smiling back like an idiot.

~

From that day Arthur flew only with Lance Fitch. The odd configuration of the FE2b, with the crew often facing each other in the nacelle while fighting for their lives thousands of feet in the air, gave them a unique intimacy. Every time they fought the Huns they saw, from a yard away, each other's looks of naked fear, grimacing fury, and sagging relief.

Over the weeks and months, they developed their own rituals. Each time they crossed the lines into German territory, they took off their leather gauntlets and shook hands, eyes locked together, faces stern. There were no words, just the unspoken mutual pledge that if this flight was their last, it had been an honour and a privilege to fly together.

Each time they survived and crossed back over their own lines to safety, they shook hands again. This homeward bound handshake was sometimes joyous and jubilant, and other times weary and relieved. Either way, it commemorated another flight in which they had spat in the eye of the Grim Reaper.

In this crucible of fire Arthur and Lance first forged trust, then mutual respect, and finally iron bonds of friendship that Arthur treasured.

4
No Man Is an Island

> Six months later – Autumn 1916.
> Western Front, France, Arras Sector, Bruay Airfield.
> Royal Flying Corps, 13 Squadron.

"Told you Lance Fitch was a diamond," Clayton gloated, as he read the letter from the King.

Arthur rocked back in his chair and scowled. Clayton crossed his arms and waited. Conceding errors never was Arthur's forte, but this time he would have to admit he was wrong.

As 1916 had slunk from a soaked spring into a wet summer, the tide turned for the RFC and 13 Squadron. More powerful engines for the FE2b and better tactics showed the limitations of the Fokker Eindeckers. Arthur and Lance knocked four more Hun planes out of the sky, and both won a Military Cross. Confirmation of the award and attendant congratulations from King George V lay in the letter Arthur had just opened.

"I suppose," Arthur conceded, "that even you must get something right every now and then."

"Ha! If I hadn't found him for you as a gunner, you'd probably be dead now, instead of basking in His Majesty's pleasure."

"My skill as a pilot might have something to do with that."

Clayton snorted. "I'll grant you some skill as a pilot if you, just this once, concede you were wrong to tell me to post Fitch out of the squadron."

"All right!" Arthur stood. "I owe you for finding me Lance as my gunner. Satisfied? Now I have to meet Major Baring at HQ."

Clayton basked in the glow of Arthur's rare admission that he might not have been entirely right. Arthur was the best commanding officer Clayton had served under but prising the concession of a mistake was harder than shucking pearls from an oyster. Still, as faults went, it was more of a foible.

Truth was, even Clayton was surprised how Arthur and Lance had gelled, considering that ostensibly they were such an ill-matched pair. Arthur could pass as an archetypal Anglo-Saxon hero—tall, fair, and self-possessed. Whereas Lance put Clayton in mind of a musketeer, slim and dark with a swordsman's lithe movements. The horizontal scar two finger's-widths below the left eye contributed to that image.

Arthur's uniform was one of Savile Row's finest and their artistry showed. The buttons gleamed like gold and his epaulettes shone with silk threads, and the bespoke tailoring showed off the wearer's broad shoulders and slim waist. But even the cheapest tailor on Savile Row would have sniffed disdain at Fitch's neatly kept but drab and threadbare uniform. Sartorial it wasn't.

Their differences extended beyond just the physical. Arthur extended a warm smile and kind words to all, even the lowest in rank. Angry or worried pilots stormed into his office and exited with a light step. In his fifteen years in the army, Clayton had seen no one so adept at smoothing troubled minds. Unlike Lance, who used those penetrating green eyes and battered face as a mask to repel intimacy and possessed a rare gift for raising hackles. On the few occasions Clayton saw a pilot try a friendly chat with Lance, they returned spitting tacks. If the pilots perceived the aristocratic Arthur as having the common touch, they regarded Fitch as a bumptious colonial lacking respect for his betters.

Yet despite the lack of obvious common ground between Arthur and Lance, Clayton knew they shared a burning desire to win the war by shooting down Huns. For sure, they had different motives. Lance worshipped the dark gods of revenge while Arthur fought for the more admired motives of King and Country. Yet whatever the differing inspiration, their joined quest and shared dangers made these unlikeliest of partners into cast iron comrades.

But now that partnership was about to be broken.

13 Squadron was converting from the two-seater FE2b to the new Sopwith Pup, an agile single-seater fighter with a Vickers machine gun synchronised to fire forwards through the propeller. The pilots were ecstatic—the Pup was the latest and best fighter in the RFC, and faster and more manoeuvrable than the Fokker. But the gunners were now redundant and would be posted elsewhere.

Arthur posted Lance to flight school in return for a promise that he would return to 13 Squadron as soon as he qualified as a pilot. Clayton had no doubt the maverick would shine as a pilot, but how would he fare on his return to the squadron once he was no longer under the protective embrace of being the squadron commander's gunner?

~

On Christmas Eve the pilots celebrated with carols. Clayton's foot was tapping of its own volition as he sang along to one of his favourite hymns.

Hark! The Herald Angels sing,
Glory to the new-born King!

Christmas sprinkled its magic even in wartime, and nature was playing its part. Fresh-fallen snow lay pristine outside the officers' Mess and gleamed under the moonlit sky. For once the artillery guns were silent, and the horizon did not flare with explosions. Memories flooded Clayton; the smell of fir from the tree as he tied baubles to branches, the taste of plum pudding doused with rum, shrieks of joy as presents were opened. Happy times.

Peace on Earth, and Mercy mild,
God and Sinners reconcil'd.

Arthur shattered Clayton's mood by grabbing him and marching him outside into the cold.

"Lance is such an idiot!" Arthur said. "He told the mess officer he would not attend the squadron Christmas dinner tomorrow, and as a result the other officers have voted to expel him from the officers' Mess."

"God," Clayton said, hugging himself to stay warm, "it's like running a kindergarten."

"There are rules even in kindergartens. It's Christmas dinner for the squadron. Attendance is mandatory although it should not need saying. Go find the idiot and tell him I am ordering him to attend."

"Aye-aye, sir. I expect he'll be in the hangars." Clayton went into the officers' Mess to collect his greatcoat and cap. Happy times didn't last long these days.

His feet squeaked on the fresh snow. Voices sang *Silent Night* as snowflakes drifted down from the windless night, pattering chill droplets on his upturned face. He stopped outside the hangars and stood for a while, enjoying the peaceful scene under the moonlight.

The drone of a passing Hun night bomber broke the idyll. Star-shells burst—*crump! crump!*—as anti-aircraft gunners tracked the intruder. A white flare sizzled skywards, and the snowflakes reflected a dazzling white in the glare.

All of Clayton's premonitions, good and bad, had come true. After six weeks of pilot training Lance had returned to the squadron. Soon he became an ace with five kills of his own.

The speed and agility of the biplane Pup and the French Nieuport 17 gave the Allies technical superiority over the Fokker monoplanes, and Lance and other pilots took full revenge against their one-time persecutors. The Eagle of Lille, Max Immelman, the Fokker ace with seventeen kills, plummeted six thousand feet to his death. A few months later his rival, Oswald Boelcke, the *Luftstreitkräfte's* driving inspiration and the highest-scoring ace for any nation, joined his comrade six feet under the French mud.

By December Lance was one of the top echelon of aces in the RFC and had won Britain's second-highest decoration for bravery, the Distinguished Service Order. With his success the officers in 13 Squadron were ready to acclaim their oddball colonial as their very own hero, but they had no opportunity. Now that Lance was a pilot, he had an airframe and engine to obsess over as well as his guns. He spent even less time in the officers' Mess, something that Clayton had not thought possible.

Instead, Lance dedicated himself to experimenting with the rigging, tautening wires, and playing with trim tabs, throttle settings, and fuel mixtures. The mechanics and fitters enjoyed his bribes of wine and cigarettes to find a few extra miles per hour. On the occasions when Clayton found Lance in the hangars, he noticed the mutual respect between the ground crew and pilot. The hangars might be draughty and cold, but Clayton suspected Lance found warmer greetings there than in the officers' Mess.

The officers would see in Christmas 1916 in hard drinking style. In the past few weeks 13 Squadron's losses had increased again, to levels not seen since the Fokker Scourge. Several pilots returned with their planes riddled and reported a devastating new German biplane with twin machine guns and unbelievable climb. And as the losses rose, so too did the alcohol intake at the mess.

Clayton jumped as a voice spoke into his ear. "Dreaming of old girlfriends?"

"Christ, Lance, you shouldn't sneak up like that."

"You were a million miles away." Lance wagged an oil-stained finger at Clayton. "Has to be a woman on your mind."

"I wish, but nothing so pleasant. Have you seen this new supposed wonder aircraft of the Huns?"

Lance snorted. "No. I heard Winterbottom rabbiting on about it, but I don't trust that twit. Twin machine guns with ammunition would add a hundred pounds of weight, and still lightning fast with a climb like a monkey? Unlikely."

"Worrying, though."

"Only if it's true. Then I would have the screaming heebie-jeebies. Why are you standing in the snow wondering about Huns?"

"Because I was looking for you. Arthur has ordered you to attend the Christmas dinner in the officers' Mess."

"All right," Lance said mildly. "If it's an order."

Emboldened by Lance's sanguine response, Clayton tried for the extra mile. "Lance, it's Christmas. Don't abandon ship after the meal. Help the lads splice the main brace afterwards as well."

"The Huns won't cancel the war for Boxing Day. We'll have to fly tomorrow, so I'll have ammunition and my engine to check. Besides, the officers in the mess don't want me there."

As Lance turned away, Clayton grabbed his arm. "Y'know, Lance, it's not their fault. Now you're an ace they'll allow you to be eccentric, so long as you don't come across as a stuck-up git. Why not spend the occasional evenings with them? A few of them like Winterbottom are right plonkers, but most are pleasant chaps, as you might find out if you gave them a chance."

Lance turned an impassive look on Clayton. The gas lamps behind him in the hangars silhouetted his face into deep shadow, making it look like a skull. "There's no one in the officers' Mess working like blazes to repair the torn fabric on my Pup or risking frostbitten fingers to repair a broken fuel line, or oiling the guns to help me kill Huns. The men in the hangars do that. And if I don't show an interest in staying alive, why should they? If I don't check their work, they won't be so careful. Then one day it will be me roasting in hell because my fuel line frayed. So tell me, Stephen, why exactly would a sensible person spend more time getting drunk and singing than working with the men who keep him alive?"

Clayton sighed. "I sympathise with your central point, but you and I both know you could spend a little time in the officers' Mess, especially in winter when the weather is often bad and it's dark at 1600 hours. You don't make any effort."

"You're right, I don't."

"What's there to be afraid of? If you gave them a chance, you might make a few friends. Live a little, laugh a little."

"I learned in the trenches that it's pointless making friends. They die on you. Besides, I don't drink. I tell lousy jokes. I'm an awful singer. Why do they care if I join them or not? What can I contribute?"

"Yourself, Lance. They drink to forget their fears that they have no tomorrow. But your success, your hard certainty, your methods—if you were to share those things, they might not need to drink so much."

A piano started up the mess behind them, and the tune tinkled out to the two men standing in the moonlight. Then the rough male voices bayed.

Drunk last night
Drunk the night before
And we're going to get drunk again tonight
In case we never get drunk no more.

Lance cocked his head at the sound, and his laugh was more of a bark. His breath smoked in the frigid air. "They don'thave a tomorrow, Clayton. They are all dead men, and so am I. Only the manner and date are uncertain. I am fighting to stay alive for a little longer only so I can take as many bloody Huns with me as possible before I go. That's my certainty. You think they want that? They can't cope with the truth, that's why they drink."

"Fitch, I have to say that you make Captain Ahab look positively well adjusted. Sometimes you are an unmitigated, certifiable, mean-spirited son of a bitch."

"Only sometimes? I'll have to work on it until I am the completed article."

"If you went west tomorrow nobody would care, apart from Arthur and I. Doesn't that bother you?"

"All I care about is hunting down the two-seater buggers who murdered my brother. I want to send them to hell, win the war, and get back to Africa. Everything else is just noise." Lance stabbed Clayton in the chest with a forefinger. "All I want is a good plane, a gun that doesn't jam, and a clear sky to hunt the Huns. Winterbottom and the rest, I don't give a damn about them. Walk in there and the air is thick with cigarette smoke, the smell of booze and the stench of desperation. Out here…" Lance gestured grandly at the stars and the drifting flakes, "What more can a man want?"

Clayton stared after Lance as the pilot stalked back into the tomb-cold hangars. "You poor bastard, the trenches taught you the wrong lesson," he murmured. "Haven't you under-stood yet that Donne was right—no man is an island."

5
Good Riddance

Five months later – 4 May 1917.
France, Montreuil. General Haig's HQ.

As an accomplished raconteur and author, Colonel Maurice Baring enjoyed listening to interesting people with interesting things to say. Shame Field Marshall Haig wasn't one of them. So, Baring took a sip of tea and prepared himself for an hour of tedium as the Commander of the British Expeditionary Forces in France started his weekly briefing.

"Gentlemen, we are within a whisker of losing this war in the next two weeks."

Baring choked on his tea, sending a fine spray down his front and onto the massive, polished table. He dabbed his army blouse with his silk handkerchief, not that the khaki jacket would show the stains, and wiped the spots from the mirror-like surface of the table. Then he glanced apologetically at his boss, General Trenchard, commander of the Royal Flying Corps, or RFC, in France. But Trenchard hadn't even noticed Baring's gaffe. His mouth hung open as he stared at Haig. Clearly this was news to Trenchard. Baring looked around. The other generals displayed similar shock. *News to everyone.*

Haig gave a sardonic smile at the effect of his bombshell. "Our gallant French allies cocked up, and now they need us to pull their chestnuts out of the fire."

He paused to stroke his luxuriant moustache, apparently marshalling his thoughts. Baring pushed his teacup away. He'd lost the taste for it. The mood in the room was as sombre as the rain that splattered on the windowpanes, filling the silence with its relentless drumming.

"General Nivelle's attack was a much greater disaster than we were initially told. The French army suffered sixty per cent losses in some divisions. Worse, whole units have mutinied, thrown down their arms and refused to fight. In addition, they've expended almost their entire arsenal of artillery shells. In short, the French have depleted their manpower, morale, and munitions."

Baring rubbed his bald pate and looked past the rivulets running down the windows at the glowering clouds outside. Five minutes ago, the assembled room had been sanguine about the war effort. How had the situation deteriorated so rapidly?

"The French government," Haig continued, "has sacked Nivelle. His replacement, General Pétain, called me this morning and confessed the true state of affairs. He has begged me to attack the Germans, to draw their attention away from the French sector and give him time to sort out morale and to re-equip his army. Otherwise, he says the Germans will be in Paris within weeks."

"Huh!" grunted General Horne of the 1st Army. "Are you sure the French aren't exaggerating as usual?"

Haig shook his head, his expression bleak. "Pétain has executed over fifty soldiers for mutiny. That tells me he isn't exaggerating."

"The French Army has fought well so far despite tremendous losses, but if they collapse," murmured the lantern-jawed Allenby of the 3rd Army, "their government will surrender rather than let the Huns into Paris, just as they did in 1871. Then the Germans can cut us off from the coastal ports and trap us in France without petrol, food, or ammunition. We would have no choice but to surrender the largest army in the history of the British Empire."

Haig banged the table with a fist. "I do not want to hear talk of losing the war. We *must* launch a major attack as soon as possible to distract the German High Command."

Haig collapsed in his chair like a man exhausted by the pouring out of so much bad news. "To achieve that, we need to attack the Hindenburg Line. General Gough, can you launch a successful attack in your sector?"

Gough's long heavy nose, a gun barrel welded below gimlet eyes and a receding hairline, swivelled to face Trenchard. "I can do it, sir, but I need better help from the Royal Flying Corps than I am getting at the moment."

Baring winced at the insinuation. General Trenchard's nickname was "Boom" as much for his formidable temper as his loud voice. Trenchard's face darkened at the attack, and he opened his mouth to respond, but Haig signalled him to remain quiet. Haig was a strong supporter of Trenchard, and so his subordinate shut his mouth with a snap.

Gough continued, his tone lecturing: "Artillery is the king of the battlefield these days, but we need the RFC to use it to best effect. To succeed in this attack, we will need reconnaissance photos of the German trench systems, their machine gun nests, and their main artillery concentrations. Then once we know the targets, we will need spotting planes to report back to us where our shells drop in relation to the targets. But in April the reconnaissance photos dried up, and the spotting aircraft seem unable to remain over the targets. At the moment we are blind. If we attack blind into heavy concentrations of heavy guns and machine guns, they will massacre my men."

Trenchard scowled with his massive eyebrows. His dark hair flopped over his forehead, giving him a lugubrious look, but his stentorian voice rattled the windows as he ignored Gough and spoke to Haig. "Sir, none of this is for want of trying. The planes cannot fight their way through. We are sending them over in droves, but they are being shot down. The new German fighter, the Albatross, outclasses all our planes to a considerable degree."

Trenchard shuffled his papers and squinted at his notes through his reading glasses. "In January, when the Albatross first appeared in force, we had forty-seven casualties. As the Germans rolled out the Albatross across more units, our losses doubled every month: ninety-six in February, 188 in March, 421 in April—sixty per cent of our existing aircraft strength lost in that month alone. The pilots are calling it 'Bloody April'." Trenchard looked up and peered over his glasses. "If these trends continue in May, the RFC will cease to exist as a fighting force." Baring knew the figures by heart. He'd compiled them. But hearing them out loud like this made them more frightening. The heartbeat of the Royal Flying Corps, the experienced pilots, was growing fainter and fainter.

"You think four hundred casualties in a month is critical?" Gough scoffed. "Don't be such a milksop! I can lose ten thousand men in a day when I launch an attack. And I will likely lose double that if I attack without aircraft reconnaissance support. It is the RFC's job to give me what I need for a successful attack, not to give excuses! The size of your losses will be immaterial in a battle of this nature."

"That may be so, General Gough, in the context of your butcher bill. But you have two million men in the army in France. The RFC finished April with only 150 planes and fewer pilots."

"Less than 150 pilots?" Haig's voice rose. *You don't know the half of it. Many of those few are borderline competent.* The majority of faces that Baring saw in the squadrons he visited, were those of boys. In April those young faces turned haunted in a matter of weeks, like fruit ripening from fresh to rotten after a few days of blazing summer sun.

Boom Trenchard threw his papers onto the dark oak table. "There has been no slackening of the number of sorties over the front line. But these young men are just cannon fodder at present. And this will continue until we get better planes to take on the German Albatross. I promise the effort at reconnaissance and artillery support will continue—*whatever the cost*—but I cannot promise the results General Gough wants."

"It's not what I want man, it's what I need! The Royal Flying Corps is supposed to do the scouting job for the army like the cavalry used to do. I never heard any excuses from the cavalry about the enemy having better horses."

Trenchard's face darkened. "That is offensive, sir!"

"They got the job done. Those chaps at least had moral fibre."

Trenchard opened his mouth to snarl back, but somehow contained himself. Baring sensed his boss clenching and unclenching his fists under the table with the effort of unaccustomed restraint.

"General Gough," Trenchard said, a vein throbbing in his neck, "it is far easier to obtain horses than flying machines, and far easier to find men who can ride than men trained to fly. We are losing pilots at a rate we cannot replace. We are rushing in replacements before we can train them properly, and they kill themselves in crashes and wipe out aircraft we cannot afford to lose. Between the fourth and eighth of April alone we lost fifty-six planes to crashes. The Huns shot down seventy-five in the same four days. That's 134 planes *in four days!* If that happens again, we will have no RFC left. Then your attack will be truly blind."

Gough leaned forward in his chair and put his hands flat on the table. "Then the RFC will have helped lose the war."

The two generals bristled at each other like rutting bulls, but Haig interrupted before they could find more words. "Enough, gentlemen! I would remind you the Germans are the enemy. The splendid work of the RFC under very adverse weather conditions, and in the face of most determined opposition, has contributed largely to those successes we have managed, and calls for the highest praise. Nevertheless, we need to do something, for we cannot continue as we are."

In the silence that followed a stronger gust of wind rattled branches against the windows. Haig steepled his fingers. "Trenchard, I'm told that the Germans group their best pilots and planes under one man, and this one squadron is causing most of our losses."

"Yes sir, a man called Richthofen heads them, and they are very effective. His outfit causes half our losses on some days."

"Then why don't you do the same?" Gough interjected. "Get your best men and machines in one unit and hunt these Richthofen buggers down. Flush them out and chase them with the whole pack, like fox hunting. That's the ticket!"

Trenchard's voice quavered with the effort of sounding reasonable, even if the volume rose. "Because when you put the all the best men and the best machines together, the quality and morale of the rest plummet. I would rather have even quality across all the squadrons than throw all my eggs in one basket."

Gough smirked. "Well, obviously this chap Richthofen does not agree, and he does rather seem to be winning, doesn't he?"

Haig put a hand on Trenchard's arm. "I will speak to the prime minister and tell him we desperately need the new and better planes. But the war will not wait. We *must* aid the French, and we *must* do it now. I want you to form an elite wing to hunt down this Richthofen and his men. Let's see if that keeps the bastards busy enough so the rest of the RFC can get its job done."

Trenchard nodded. "Yes, sir. I will start right now." He packed his papers and strode out of the room, face down to hide his displeasure.

Baring scrambled after the general as he stalked out of the château towards their staff car. Trenchard ignored the umbrella offered by his waiting driver and stomped through the driving rain and puddles. Baring grimaced in sympathy at the driver and availed himself of the umbrella.

Once in the car, Trenchard cut loose. "I don't like it. I don't like it one bit, but we have no choice. So, the first question is—who can command this new elite wing?"

"Major Hawker might be the best choice, sir," Baring said. "He's well respected and popular across the RFC. Exceptional flyer and a real pilots' pilot. The generals and the press should like the appointment too. They'll know his name as the first pilot awarded the Victoria Cross for air combat between airplanes. He's got the guts, skill, and credibility needed for the role."

"Damn me, but you're right. He won't pussyfoot around Richthofen, that's for sure. Get him to my office as soon as possible."

~

Two days later – 6 May 1917.
France, Lille Sector, La Gorgue Airfield—RFC 13 Squadron.

"Ahoy there, Major." Clayton stuck his head around Arthur's office door. "There's a chicken here who says he's flown in to see you."

Arthur dashed off another signature on yet another requisition form. He'd lost count and his hand ached. Commanding officer? Ha! Just a slave to paperwork if he wanted to keep his squadron equipped with men, munitions, petrol, food and God knows what else.

Only then did he look up and scowl at his adjutant. "I do not have time for your infantile jokes."

"This chicken is a major in the RFC and I think you'll want to see him." Clayton smiled and ushered in the visitor, who wore a rough goatskin coat with a mink collar over a pair of thigh high, fur-lined sheepskin trousers. A woollen balaclava helmet completed the avian impression. Arthur stared at the outlandish figure for a second before recognising his friend, Lanoe Hawker.

"It's true, Hawker," Arthur said, "You look like a giant rooster, a very ruffled one!"

Hawker was unrepentant. "Looks damned silly, I know, but it does the job at fifteen thousand feet. If you ever get the chance to try it—which you won't since you've been so rude—you would beg to keep it. Keeps me warm as toast while you natty types freeze your balls."

Arthur slapped him on the back. "Well, none of us deny that you have the biggest balls of us all. And to what do we owe the pleasure of your company? Have a seat in my grand abode." Arthur waved his hand around the sparse office, which contained a desk made of packing cases, a plank of plywood and a large blotting pad. Three-legged wooden chairs sat scattered around the room. "Come to see how a real outfit operates?"

"Ha! No such luck for you, my man." Hawker sat gingerly on one of the chairs, which creaked and swayed. "In fact, I am here to purloin your best pilots and leave you in charge of the hopeless riffraff. Just the sort of squadron you deserve."

"In your dreams. Besides, last time we met you told me that you had all the world's best pilots in 24 Squadron already. How could you possibly find someone worthy in my humble 13 Squadron?"

Hawker scratched his temple. "That statement may have occurred as I was drinking with my pilots, so it might not be *entirely* true." The visitor rubbed his knee with a heartfelt sigh. "Oh, my aching bones. I'm getting old."

"Hawker, you're a fraud. How old are you now, twenty-six? I'm thirty-five, and I'm fit as a fiddle. Nothing like war flying to make you hale and hearty."

Hawker smiled faintly. "I'm carrying a few lead parts I was not designed for."

That was true. Arthur looked at him with concern. Britain's first ace, Hawker had been war flying since 1914 and suffered his share of wounds. In 1915 he had founded the RFC's first-ever fighter squadron, No. 24, which he led with the standing orders to "attack everything". During the battle for Ypres he had insisted on being carried to his plane every day after taking a bullet to the foot. Yet now his eyes had shrunk deep inside their sockets, which were themselves bruised dark with fatigue and strain. His cheeks had hollowed out, and his humorous mouth thinned into a taut line.

"Are you all right?"

Hawker shifted in his seat. "I'm not quite as well as I would wish."

The admission shocked Arthur. From the gung-ho Hawker this was a declaration of stunning depression. "Ask for a home posting if you're not well. You've more than done your bit."

"I might, Arthur, I might do that. Problem is that Boom Trenchard has decided that he wants to form an anti-Richthofen wing of three squadrons, and he has asked me to set it up. I can't let the side down now."

"Congratulations. No one better qualified. Tough job though, even if you were feeling great. Why not get this wing set up and working and then apply for a home posting? God knows you've invented enough stuff while war flying, you may even come up with something useful if you focus on it."

Hawker flicked Arthur a rude salute. Arthur grinned. Hawker was a trained engineer with a fertile mind who had designed many improvements for the RFC, from propellers to machine guns to flying clothes. Without exception his designs had been practical, which could seldom be said of the pen pushers in the government whose job it was to design these things.

"Anyway, Arthur, enough about me. Would you like to join me in this lark? I want you to be one of the squadron commanders. You're the best leader of men I know, and there's no one I'd rather have at my side in this rather hairy task. What do you say?"

"Count me in. You will need someone to ensure that your sorry backside does not get whipped by Baron Richthofen."

"Excellent. Do you have any pilots you'd recommend helping us take on the Richthofen gang? I only want the best."

"There is one. Lance Fitch, a colonial. He has big-game hunting experience, which he brings to air fighting. Good flyer and best shot I have seen. Keen as mustard. He already has twenty-one kills."

"Sounds perfect. Can I talk to him?"

"Be my guest. Your timing is good. He is due to lead out a flight in half an hour. I will get my orderly to fetch him."

A few minutes later, Lance strode into the office and turned a questioning gaze on Arthur. Those green and bronze eyes, with the surrounding skin crinkled from squinting into the bright glare of the African plains and the French skies, always mesmerised Arthur.

"Fitch," Arthur said, "Boom Trenchard has appointed Major Hawker to set up an elite wing to take on Richthofen's Circus. I have told him you are the best pilot in this squadron, and he is keen to recruit you."

"An honour to meet you, sir," Lance said with a small smile as he shook Hawker's proffered hand.

The new wing commander cleared his throat. "Enough of that guff. Will you join me?"

"Thank you, sir, but no. I'd rather stay here."

Arthur frowned at Lance, then at Hawker. The latter raised an eyebrow. The silence grew uncomfortable. Arthur often expressed orders as polite requests, but that did not mean he expected refusal. "Fitch," Arthur said, leaning on his words with emphasis, "this wing could be a vital step to winning the war in the air. We need our best against their best. I believe you have a duty to accept."

A stubborn look set on Lance's face, but Arthur tried once more. "I am joining Major Hawker. You and I have been together a long time, Lance. I'd like to keep our team together."

Lance blinked as he registered that Arthur was leaving, but after a pause, he shook his head.

The lash of the casual betrayal stung Arthur like a whip to the face.

"Please, Lance." Arthur pressed. It was humiliating to beg in front of Hawker, but the prize was worth it. Lance looked away and said nothing.Arthur turned his back and shrugged at Hawker.

Hawker scowled. "I only want volunteers, Fitch, so if you don't want to join, that's an end to it. But do you mind telling me why?"

"I am honoured by the invitation, sir," Lance replied, "but I have debts to pay off against Hun two-seaters. It sounds as though this new squadron will focus on fighting the Circus, who are all single-seater fighters."

"They're all Germans. We can't go around choosing who we fight. This war is not personal, you know."

"It is for me, sir. Besides, if I shoot down a two-seater, I double the number of dead Huns."

"Not scared of Richthofen, are you?" Hawker goaded.

Arthur grimaced at the clumsy ploy. Sure enough, Lance just stared at Hawker, with a set jaw and hard gaze. Arthur had seen mules that looked more tractable. He explained to Hawker: "Fitch was bombarded by Hun artillery, directed by two-seaters, when he was in the poor bloody infantry. He thinks the RFC was invented for his personal payback, and he's obsessed with shooting down two-seaters. Although he appears to enjoy killing all Huns to a disturbing degree."

"All I want is to win the war," Lance said. "Then go home to Africa where the sun shines, and there's space to breathe. The quickest way back to Africa is to kill enough Germans to win the war."

Hawker was unimpressed. "Not sure why you think you know better how to win the war than our senior officers, but if you won't volunteer then so be it."

Lance opened his mouth, but Arthur cut across him. "Thank you, Lieutenant Fitch. You are dismissed."

Lance closed his mouth with a snap. He looked hurt by the brusque dismissal but saluted and left.

"Awkward bugger," Hawker said. "I'm surprised you put up with him. Is he worth the trouble?"

"I used to think so," Arthur said. "In this day and age when you need warriors, he seemed worth his weight in gold. He could be a good man if he could get past being an antisocial, opinionated, stubborn, bloodthirsty psychopath."

"Lot of 'ifs' there. Good riddance, I'd say. We'll find other warriors."

6
Some Days...

Two days later – 8 May 1917.
Skies over France, Lille Sector. Luftstreikrafte, Jasta 11.

Leutnant Hans von Schmettow vomited the excess schnapps from the previous night into the cockpit of his Albatross. His boots skidded on the now slippery rudder bars, causing him to lose precious altitude and his close formation with his two illustrious *komrades*, the Richthofen brothers. Bastards, both of them.

Their leather-helmeted and glass-goggled heads turned impatiently. They throttled back so he could re-join their blood red Albatross fighters lurking four thousand metres above the muddy battlefields of Arras. The black Maltese crosses of the German air force, the *Luftstreikrafte,*stood out like tombstone markers against their scarlet wings and fuselages.

Stale schnapps pounded Hans' head with a cudgel. Despite the mind numbing cold, his face flamed as he imagined what Manfred Richthofen, his august leader, thought of the clumsy antics of the novice member of his flight.

Just as Hans caught up with the other planes, his stomach convulsed again. This time he forgot to duck his head below the cockpit fairing as he vomited. The 160 kilometre-per-hour slipstream hurled the acrid bile across his goggles and into the gap between his neck and silk scarf. For a few seconds he was almost grateful for the warmth of the vomit. Then it turned to ice. His Albatross wandered across the sky as he tried to smear his goggles clean with his leather gloves. No use. He removed a hand from the controls to pull down the goggles. Now the slipstream swept the stinging icy bile into his eyes. He grimaced with embarrassment and fought to bring his plane back into formation while peering through burning and blurred eyes. Two pairs of impersonal goggled eyes stared at him.

The first pair of eyes belonged to Manfred Richthofen, who apart from being a baron, also gloried in the title of hunting leader or *Rittmeister* of *Jasta* 11, commander of the most successful unit in the entire German air force. His personal tally of forty-eight kills was far higher than the great Immelman's, higher even than the incomparable Boelcke's—God rest their souls. Of course, his score dwarfed the feeble efforts of the Allied aces. Friend and foe alike recognised Manfred Richthofen's blood-red Albatross as the deadliest sight in the skies over the Western Front. Some said Richthofen painted his plane the colour of blood to inspire dread among his enemies, others that the red was a tribute to the colours of his original Uhlan Cavalry Regiment. Either way, Hans reckoned the arrogant prick had made his plane a giant bull's eye for the British.

The second pair of eyes belonged to Lothar Richthofen, Manfred's younger brother. Lothar had become a pilot later than Manfred but was scoring as fast as his brother these days. Together the Richthofens and *Jasta* 11 were a scourge laying waste to the British Royal Flying Corps.

It helped that they flew the latest Albatross DIII—the most advanced fighter plane in the skies. Sleek as a shark with a rounded fuselage and swept back wingtips, its snarling two hundred horsepower Mercedes engine left Allied planes wallowing in its wake. If the Mercedes engine was Teutonic engineering at its best, then close behind were the twin Spandau machine guns bolted on the nose above the engine. These beauties were synchronised to fire a thousand high-velocity bullets per minute between the propeller blades, double the rate of their Allied counterparts with their single machine gun.

The pilots of *Jasta* 11 copied Manfred Richthofen, adopting red as the predominant colour for their aircraft, but only Richthofen's plane was all red. Lothar Richthofen's plane flaunted a bright yellow tail that glistened in the sun as it rose and fell on the air currents. Hans' own Albatross sported a red fuselage with its white wings.

Hans suspected Manfred von Richthofen's invitation to join his flight this morning was punishment for Hans' indulgence the previous night. Yesterday the *Jasta* had set a record for kills in a day, and Richthofen's toast to his fliers launched a spontaneous party in the officers' Mess. Manfred Richthofen was fond of a glass of fine champagne himself, but the sanctimonious prick frowned on excess consumption. He insisted that hangovers blunted the split-second reactions required in fighter combat.

So, when Richthofen left the mess with a pointed "Good night, gentlemen, time for bed," the boisterous party subsided like a pricked balloon. But by then Hans had slipped five chilled and delightful glasses of champagne down his parched throat and into an empty stomach. The alcohol gave him the insight that Richthofen was only a jumped-up minor aristocrat. So Hans, alone of the pilots due to fly early the next day, remained at the bar to add a glass or two, or more, of delicious schnapps to the mix. No doubt a toadying sneak had ratted on him.

He jumped as the chatter of machine guns startled him from his musings. Manfred Richthofenhad fired to draw attention and now jabbed his gloved right hand downwards. Hans tilted his Albatross onto its right wing. There! Three black dots crabbing across the muddy brown landscape. Adrenalin surged through him, and he forgot his roiling guts. He loosened the vice of the icy cold by flexing his fingers, stomping his booted feet, and rolling his shoulders and neck like a prize-fighter. Richthofen's hand circled above his head, then chopped downwards. His plane half-rolled and plunged towards the enemy, a hawk swooping on its prey. Hans followed, his engine howling as the wind shrieked through the bracing wires.

He watched the three distant dots grow into recognisable shapes, SPAD VIIs. The new French-built aircraft were fast and agile, one of the Allies' main hopes of challenging the supremacy of the Albatross.

Hans licked his dry lips. The fight would be one on one.

The Frenchmen spotted the Albatross and climbed into steep turns to meet them. Hans hiccupped with the acrid taste of bile. He fought to keep the Albatross stable as it bucked against the airflow. His sights jittered over the small silhouette of the SPAD as they closed at over five hundred kph. The circular cowling of the enemy grew. Flame flickered from the SPAD's single gun. The tracer flashed past and Hans flinched. Still, he held his fire as Richthofen had drilled into him. At fifty metres he pressed his triggers.

The plane juddered with the twin Spandau machine guns. His tracers flew to the left. He corrected so his tracer lines stabbed into the SPAD. The enemy pilot sheered away, and Hans reefed into a tight climbing turn. His bilious stomach heaved with the centrifugal force. Vomit shot into his mouth. He swallowed as his head jerked from side to side to find his enemy.

The SPAD seemed untouched, and they jockeyed to get on each other's tail. Lothar's red and yellow Albatross banked in a similar deadly duet close by. A greasy pillar of smoke showed Manfred Richthofen had struck on the first pass.

Hans sweated as he manhandled the heavy fighter around the sky. He had more power, speed, and firepower, but the Frenchman was the better flier. And yet if the enemy made just one mistake and blundered across Hans' sights for an instant, that would be the end of him.

Tracer flashed past his cockpit. Hans kicked at the rudder. His boots slipped again. For fateful seconds his plane flew straight, the easiest target in the world. The Albatross shuddered from bullet strikes. Before Hans could react the SPAD dived past him. Manfred Richthofen flashed after it in pursuit. Hans followed, cursing his humiliation. The Richthofens had rescued him before he could show his shooting skills—they would think he was a clown.

SPADs were sturdy divers, fast and strong, and the Albatross chased the Frenchman to ground level before they caught him. Richthofen hammered bullets into the engine block from twenty metres. The SPAD's propeller slowed, and the Germans had to pull up hard to clear the gliding aeroplane. Hans circled back and saw the Frenchman land, well behind German lines and certain to be a prisoner. The SPAD's wheels caught in a muddy patch, and the plane tipped onto its nose.

Spiteful after his embarrassment, Hans dived on the enemy pilot as the Frenchman clambered from his wrecked plane. The pilot saw him coming and lurched into a panic-stricken run across the field. His cumbersome flying gear, the glutinous mud, and the man's unbridled panic combined to make his frantic progress comic. Hans smiled with satisfaction at avenging the humiliation this pilot had caused him. *Ja, run rabbit, run!* He touched the triggers. Bullets hammered the fleeing man into the mud, a broken rag doll.

The killing glow sent excitement singing through Hans' body, banishing his hangover. He had not covered himself with glory in the air fight, and Richthofen's patience was as thin as the troops' gruel back in the trenches. But now Hans felt ready for the challenge.

He hummed Wagner's "Ride of the Valkyries" as they turned towards Lille and clawed back to the height they had lost in the pursuit of the destroyed SPADs. If he wanted the great Manfred Richthofen to show him a little respect, he needed some kills for *Jasta* 11.

~

Lance stalked his chosen victim at twelve thousand feet, lurking in the sun's eye-watering glare. He eased his Sopwith Pup onto the tail of his prey with the practised ease of a master assassin sliding a stiletto from his sleeve. The Roland two-seater biplane droned onwards, oblivious to the threat behind it.

Lance's hands and feet, his ailerons and rudder, moved in easy harmony. As the Pup's gunsight framed the rear gunner, a deep atavistic instinct seemed to warn the German. He glanced up, and under the goggles his mouth gaped at the apparition only fifty feet away. Lance thumbed the trigger as the German scrabbled for the handle of his machine gun. The Pup juddered under the powerful pounding of his single Vickers machine gun, and Lance's nostrils flared at the familiar stink of gunpowder.

The gunner jerked like a marionette under the storm of steel-jacketed bullets. Lance fired again. Tracers speared the pilot. The Roland jerked upwards, stalled, and twisted into a full dive. Its wings crumpled and tore away. The fuselage coffin drilled towards the muddy earth ten thousand feet below. Four broken wings, iridescent in their mottled purple-green camouflage, glinted as they tumbled over and over in the sunshine.

Exultation sang through Lance's veins, warming him from the arctic temperatures at twelve thousand feet. He was alone and too far into Hun territory for any British to confirm the kill, but he didn't care. The Germans would suffer until Lance assuaged his guilt—a guilt nailed to his soul—for his part in the death or crippling of his brothers, friends, and comrades.

He stroked the firing button and whispered:
From Hell's heart, I'll stab at you.
For hate's sake, I'll spit my last breath at you…
I'll chase you through Perdition's flames.

The pledge had become his ritual since his first kill in a single seater. Now he repeated it after every kill, a reminder of his debts to be paid. These days, Captain Ahab's vow of vengeance against the great white whale seemed less like the ravings of a lunatic and more like the oaths of a soulmate. Nothing like your own quenchless feud to bring you cranky companions.

He swung his plane homewards. The sky remained empty except for the black plumes from the Lille smokestacks in the distance. But twelve miles of hostile skies separated him from the safety of the British lines. Twelve slow miles with the strong prevailing winds pushing against him. Twelve dangerous miles with Huns hunting for him. He checked the fuel gauge and grimaced. He tapped the glass, hoping the needle would move, but it remained low.

He'd waited too long for prey. A lust for revenge had gained him his kill, but now it might cost him his life. What was the saying? There are old pilots and bold pilots but no old bold pilots?

Last year the Pup had reigned supreme in the skies, but by 1917 the Huns had unveiled a raft of improved aircraft, including the unparalleled Albatross. Now Pups were cannon fodder. The latest Hun two-seaters flew too high or too fast, or both, for his obsolete Pup. Kills that had once fallen to his guns twice or more a week had become as rare as rain on the Tsavo plains. As the days without a kill stretched into weeks, Lance's thirst for revenge became a parched desperation.

He'd decided on a new risky strategy—to lurk deep over the German side of the lines, hoping to surprise two-seaters as their crews relaxed over their own airfields. So he flew past Lille towards Tournai, twenty miles behind German lines, and then swung back to hunt for prey with the dazzling morning sun behind him. Also, if the Germans saw him, they would assume he was friendly. No Allied pilot would be so daft as to go so deep into enemy territory alone.

Trouble was, a plan predicated on folk believing nobody would be that stupid, in a war full of bone-headed heroes, meant a plan that was off-the-scale imbecilic. Lance had succeeded in that at least. If this wasn't the dumbest thing he'd done, it was riding among the front-runners, with plenty of time for a late gallop into the winner's spot if anything went wrong.

He'd got his kill, so Lady Luck was smiling on him, but there again experience showed Lady Luck was a two-timing cow at the best of times. At the worst of times, she was plain vindictive. The worst of times was when you needed her most. He worked saliva around his dry mouth. He'd felt smart a few minutes ago. Why did he feel so dumb now? Satiated lust?

Past reason hunted: and no sooner had, past reason hated. The Bard always had the words.

But, so far, the strategy had paid off. Which made Lance's decision to stay in 13 Squadron the correct one. Lance's old nemesis in the mess, Bill Winterbottom, had inherited command when Arthur left. Much as Winterbottom disliked Lance, an ace in his squadron reflected well on the commander. So he allowed Lance to fly when and how he liked. A freedom Lance would never have enjoyed in Hawker's new wing.

The only downside was Arthur's absence. A sense of loss and regret, a curious ache deep in Lance's mind, was a constant, and that made him angry. Friends died and left you vulnerable, prey to useless emotions. When he flew as Arthur's gunner, their fates had been intertwined—they would live or die together. But now they flew apart, Arthur could die alone and become a millstone dragging Lance down into the cesspool of insanity. Better to crush any weakness now.

Lance checked his tail, his eyes watering against the blazing sun. He tapped his fuel gauge again. The strong headwind was chewing up his precious fuel.

The Pup vibrated under full power as Lance continued his run westwards for home and safety. He scanned the blue sky ahead through the blurred arc of his propeller. No enemy ahead, and the sky to the north was empty too, except for the smudge of Lille's smokestacks. He turned to check the south and cursed as he saw black dots emerge from the haze. Friends or foe?

The dots turned to intercept him, and he gaped at the speed with which they closed. Enemies, only the new Albatross DIII could be that fast. They would catch him long before he reached the lines. He hoped to God they were not Richthofen's crew.

British pilots, with their usual mordant humour, had christened Germany's most lethal and multi-coloured *Jasta* as "the Red Baron and his flying circus". Lance had heard they were operating in this sector but hadn't yet tangled with them himself. A tremor of premonition made his stomach clench, and the copper taste of fear coated his mouth. His lone Pup would be easy prey for any three DIII Albatross, never mind ones from the Circus.

He banged his gloved hand on the cockpit coaming, urging the Pup to find extra speed. But the gesture was futile—the Pup was already running for home like an old fox exhausted by whippet hounds. He searched the sky for any form of saviour but saw no sign of other Allied aircraft and no big cumulus cloud cover in which to disappear. That familiar wobble in his knees came to haunt him.

He loosened the seat harness straps so he could better turn and watch the pursuers over his tail. As the sleek Albatross devoured the distance between them, they spread into an arrow formation. Lance watched their tactics with a dispassionate, approving interest. Whether he turned left or right to evade the lead Hun, he would move into the sights of one of the other aircraft.

Still, he watched them as they closed to within three hundred feet. Lance would use their greater speed against them; it would push their turning circle wider. But that would benefit Lance only if he turned at the last possible moment.

He waited and waited…and forced himself to wait even longer. Each second stretched an eternity. The skin on the back of his neck prickled. Still the Germans did not fire, another sign of experienced pilots. Lance kicked the rudder bars to skid his plane from side to side, trading airspeed to offer a more difficult target.

When the Huns were a hundred feet away, Lance's nerve cracked. He hauled the Pup into a steep left turn. At the same instant he heard the lead Albatross open fire. Tracers streaked past his right wing. He had dodged the first attack.

Now he was in the sights of the Albatross on the left. Few pilots were skilful enough to hit such a fleeting full-deflection shot, but Lance hunched his shoulders, waiting, his life dependent on the gunnery skills of his foe. *Any second now…*

Machine guns stuttered, a terrifying ripping sound as holes stitched like magic through his lower left wing. Lance banked the Pup even harder, and she shuddered in protest. A second burst flashed wide.

He grinned mirthlessly. Now he was out of their sights and held the advantage. He quarter-rolled out of the turn and onto their tails. The leader was all red—Richthofen!Before Lance could fire, two of the Albatross poured on the power and soared upwards and away, leaving Lance gaping at their raw power.But the last of them, painted red with white wings, almost stalled as it tried to follow the Pup in the tight turn. It wallowed in the air, defenceless.

The familiar bloodlust surged through Lance as he curved his plane behind his hapless opponent. He had seconds to kill this one before the other two Huns would get on his tail. The Albatross' white elliptical rudder swung as the Hun tried to escape, but the plane, sluggish in the near stall, didn't respond fast enough.

Lance triggered a two-second burst that flashed a foot over the white wings. He corrected a fraction, fired again. Tracers punctured the Albatross engine cowling. Its propeller slowed. Lance laid his sights on the pilot's back, but before he could fire, pungent tracer slashed past his nose.

Raging, Lance flung his plane into a dive towards the Allied lines. *Out of time. I had the bastard!* He did not even bother to glance backwards. He knew the other two Albatross were snapping at his heels, competing to kill him.

His Pup could never outrun their pursuit, but he had no choice but to try. When it came to chances, slim beat none.

~

Hans shut his smoking engine. An ominous silence filled his ears as he glided gradually earthwards. He blew out a breath as the Richthofens swept after the Pup, hawks competing for the kill. He shook his head in disbelief at the speed with which the Pup had twisted onto his tail and the accuracy of the shooting. Without the Richthofens, Hans would be a corpse right now.

Hans watched as the pursuing Albatross caught the enemy plane with ease. Manfred fired a short burst, and the Englishman's head snapped back in agony, his plane jerking upwards in the characteristic sign of a back-shot pilot—a hand reflexively tightening on the joystick. The Pup zoomed upwards, stalled, and snapped into a fluttering spin towards the thin cirrus cloud layer two thousand metres feet below.

Hans spat into his cockpit. The Pup had disposed of Hans like a wolf and yet fallen prey to the *Rittmeister* like a lamb. That did not reflect well on Hans. *Hope the English bastard is alive and screaming when he hits the ground.*

Lothar's Albatross followed the spinning plane downwards. For a confirmed kill, German air force rules required ground troops or a non-claimant pilot to observe the aircraft crash. Ground troops were unreliable; sometimes they had better things to do than watch duels in the sky. A wingman confirming the kill was more reliable, and Lothar was a loyal lapdog in that regard.

Chattering machine gun fire startled Hans, but it was only the *Rittmeister* demanding his brother's attention and jabbing his fingers towards Hans's helpless plane. Hans blinked. Had Manfred Richthofen abandoned a victory confirmation just to protect Hans until he landed? *How fucking noble of the baron. Prussian duty before glory it seems. Must burn him up inside!* The thought made Hans feel better.

~

Three thousand feet below, the Pup spun through the clouds with Lance ricocheting around the cockpit. Idiot! He'd not re-tightened his harness after loosening it to watch the Huns behind him. He banged his left elbow.

Right on the funny bone. His eyes watered with pain. Then the machine gun handle headbutted him. Despite its padding, the stars still came.

Ironic if he escaped the enemy and got tossed out of the cockpit by his faithful Pup. He released the control stick to wedge his elbows under the cockpit rim, but his feet had no leverage on the rudder bars. No stick, no rudder bars, zero control. The plane was doing its own thing—spinning towards destruction.

A chequer board of green and brown fields revolved around Lance in a dizzying blur. He'd be digging his own grave six feet deep in that blur if he didn't do something soon.

The next revolution smashed him back into his seat, his coccyx taking a hammer blow. A jolt of pure agony up his spine made him grunt. Sod it! He let go off his safety holds and lunged for the stick, threw his weight on it.

The Pup's nose went almost vertically down. Lance fell forwards. The machine gun whacked him again, in the left eye this time. His knees scrunched bent against the instrument panel. He forced one leg under the wooden panel, scalping his shin, until he could kick the toe of his boot against the rudder. The sharp wooden edge wedged like a scalpel against his kneecap. His hip muscles screamed a protest. He gritted his teeth and kept his toes locked against the rudder bar. *Last chance!*

Like the beauty she was, the Pup eased out of the spin. Lance took a deep, long, grateful breath, and pulled gradually out of the dive. He fell back into his seat. Immediately he tightened the harness. Better late than never.

"Stick forward and opposite rudder and viola, the Pup will come out of any spin. Simple."

That's what instructors said. Never had simple been so difficult. Although, to be fair, it would have been easier if this fool had re-tightened his harness before deliberately manufacturing a spin.

A hasty scan of the sky showed it empty. Please God let it stay that way. He took stock inside the cockpit. The engine gauges showed all was well, but the Hun's last burst had mangled his altimeter. How had those bullets missed him? A cold chill went through him. They must have passed inches from his skull. He felt wetness on his right cheek and wiped it with the back of his leather gauntlet. A smear of blood stained the glove. Probably a cut from the altimeter glass. The Pup and him, both battered but still functioning.

The good news, hallelujah for good news, was that Lance's fake back-shot had worked. No Huns had followed him. The last time Lance had played dead to escape overwhelming odds, a Hun followed to check. Unfortunately for the German pilot, he did so without his mates. The unwary Hun paid for that mistake with his life when Lance ambushed him as they both broke out of heavy cloud. Afterwards, Lance studied the death throes of his back-shot victims to make his own theatrics more believable. Then he practised dramatically arching his back and head, at the same time jerking on the control stick so the plane reared upwards into a stall.

So far as Lance knew no one else tried such elaborate deceptions, but he did not ask the rest of his squadron. His colleagues would think it unworthy. Hell, they thought it bad form to flee when the odds were against them. Melodramatic death convulsions would be total anathema to their code of conduct. Bill Winterbottom, the chinless wonder, would drawl through his luxuriant moustache: "Cowardly amateur dramatics." Better to let them have their well-mannered deaths than invite more ridicule.

Hunters in Africa saw self-preservation tactics as basic common sense. Old Selous, the great white hunter and Lance's godfather, said it best: "Hunt lion and leopard often enough, and you will find yourself the hunted at some stage. In your own mind you can hang a label on yourself that says 'Big White Hunter', but the cat may just read the sign as 'Lunch'. There's a thrill in being a hunter, but be prepared for the fear of being the hunted. Finding the big cats is one necessary skill. Losing them when you need to, now that is quite another."

Once again Lance scanned the sky. It was clear, and he was now just six miles to the lines and safety. But the fuel gauge read close to empty.

The prospect of being caged like an animal in a prisoner of war camp twisted his guts. He'd seen Prussian hospitality first-hand, and God only knew how long the war would last. And all his own stupid fault for cutting his fuel safety-margin too fine.

Lance's burning desire for revenge had consumed common sense. Pa was right: "When you start on the road of revenge, you'd better dig two graves—the second being your own."

~

Hans licked his dry lips. This landing would be a bugger. He peered past his stationary propeller as he glided lower. Large flat fields littered France, until you needed one. The only possible location, a narrow grass field between a mud road and hedgerow, looked too short for comfort. He would have to come in high to avoid the trees at the near end, sideslip in, and hope the plane stopped before it ran headlong into the hedgerow.

The tall trees made him nervous, and he came in too high and too fast. He landed halfway along the field, bounced twice, and hurtled towards the hedgerow at the far end. At the last second Hans wrapped his arms around his head. Wires and wood snapped like gunshots. Whiplash jerked his neck. The harness snatched deep into his shoulders. Even so, his face smacked into the padded gun butts. His nose crunched. Savage pain flooded his eyes with tears. The plane's tail reared towards the sky, hung there for an agonising second, then fell back with a spine-jarring crash.

He coughed on dust thrown up from the cockpit floor. Steam hissed as water leaked from the radiator and dripped on the still hot engine. The reek of leaking benzene galvanised him. Fire! If the fuel and the hot metal met, the plane would go up like a bomb.

Hescrabbled at the harness release, fingers fat and clumsy with terror. Finally! He jumped from the cockpit and ran for his life. His heavy coat and boots hampered him. He cringed in his stumbling run, dreading the dull "whompf" that would cremate him.

Thirty lung-sucking yards later he slowed and looked back. No fire. Just the wrecked Albatross, its top wing sagging. Relief made his knees weak. He took two tottering steps, then his legs folded under him like an infant's, and he crumpled to the ground.

Everything ached, including his pride—especially his pride. That reminded him of the Richthofens above, who would be smirking at his fucked-up landing. Well, Lothar would. Manfred would lecture Hans over the loss of a valuable aircraft. Bastard. He stood up and waved at the circling red planes to signal that he was unharmed. The Richthofens waggled their wings and headed homewards. *Ja, bugger off, you've had your laughs.*

They would send a car. Hans sagged to the ground again and watched them go, no doubt pleased with the humiliation of the disobedient tyro. He shook his head. He didn'tbelong with these assholes in *Jasta* 11.

The German Press hailed *Jasta* 11 pilots as "Knights of the Air." Journalists waxed lyrical about these modern-day Teutonic Knights painting their planes with their own distinctive markings, like heraldry on shields from the days of chivalry. They wondered whether this was to enable *Jasta* pilots to recognise each other underneath their goggles and leather helmets or was a bold challenge to their enemies: "Know me. Fear me!"

As a result of this propaganda, all of Germany believed that every pilot in *Jasta* 11 must be, by definition, not only a supreme fighter pilot but also a chivalrous gentleman. Hans spat the bad taste out of his mouth and blood flecked his spit. He found a loose tooth and worried at it with his tongue. *I can't fly for shit, and I have the morals of an alley cat...or of the disowned and disgraced Prussian aristocrat that I am.*

Hans' plane might have worn the fabled colours of *Jasta* 11, but he'd crashed more of his own aircraft than he'd shot down enemy planes. His take-offs were fine, and he was an adequate pilot once in the air, although "adequate" was contemptible by *Jasta* 11 standards. But the real problem was his landings. No matter how much he practised, calculating the right moment to flare into his landing might as well have been Pythagorean trigonometry. Never let it be said that Manfred Richthofen made mistakes, but even Hans thought it an error that Hans had ended up in the elite *Jasta* 11.

On one of Richthofen's trawls for talent a few months ago, he had called on *Jasta* 7. The squadron's commander, Fritz Bronsart-Schellendorf, had recommended Hans Schmettow to the baron as the best deflection shooter he had ever seen. "Yourself excepted, Baron."

The pilots of *Jasta* 7 sportingly lined up to throw empty wine bottles into the air as fast as they could, and Hans blasted so many that the sky became a blizzard of green glass. Not with a shotgun, that would have been too easy, but with a rifle. Even Richthofen looked impressed. A talent for deflection shooting—marrying vectors of time, space, and distance so that bullets and a moving target intersected—was a rare commodity, perhaps the skill most prized by fighter pilots.

Bronsart-Schellendorf, with a shocking oversight most unlike a senior Prussian officer, neglected to tell Richthofen that the flying skills of the shooting paragon were somewhat deficient. No doubt Bronsart-Schellendorf hoped the hard driving *Jasta* 11 would take his *enfant terrible* down several hundred pegs, but to Hans the invitation to *Jasta* 11 meant he had crawled out of the shame of his birth. He saw himself lording it in Germany's most famous *Jasta* with the other legends of the *Luftstreikrafte*. The unwanted son cast out of the bosom of the noble von Schmettow family would become one of Germany's elite fliers, with all and sundry grovelling to him.

As he left *Jasta* 7, Hans believed he had escaped the slime of the gutter. He was on his way to fame and redemption.

The reality inside *Jasta* 11 shocked him. Instead of a court of fawning courtiers, he found a strict school dedicated to excellence and obedience. Pilots were trained and judged every minute of every day to ensure their maximum efficiency as predatory hunters and ruthless killers. The grim intensity of the daily routine dismayed Hans. In *Jasta* 7 Hans' three kills made him a hero for the Fatherland, but in *Jasta* 11 the old hands were quick to tell him that a mere three kills qualified him only as a short hair on sweaty balls, just another tyro with a lot to learn. Even worse, he no longer had time for the drinking and whoring that had been plentiful in his previous *Jasta*

In this, his first week with *Jasta* 11, Hans fought more air battles on each day than he usually fought in a week with *Jasta* 7. And yet he had failed to make a single kill with his new unit. At the end of each day he would crawl into his cot exhausted, the exhortations of his instructors ringing in his ears. The next day he would drag his sorry carcass out of bed to do it all over again, with little improvement. Several of Hans' landings left a trail of wreckage across the aerodrome.

His crude language and ill-judged practical jokes did much the same to his relations with the *Jasta's* snooty officers. Hans overheard their gossip that only the *Rittmeister's* reluctance to admit mistakes had spared Hans from being fired from *Jasta* 11. It rankled that the other pilots discussed this within his earshot, obviously hoping to drive him into submitting a transfer request. Hans determined to stay until they tossed him out on his rear. Who were they to judge him, even Richthofen? Resentment at the thousand insults, real and imagined, surged inside him as bitter and acrid as the bile in his stomach.

But, and it was a vital "but", *Jasta* 11's fourteen pilots wore more medals than any German regiment of a thousand men. Which other twenty-five-year-old besides Richthofen had the grace and favour of the Emperor and the adoration of the public? *Jasta* 11 was Hans' best shot at becoming an ace, and an ace would be a hero of the Fatherland. Only then could Hans savour his family's sour faces as they ate humble pie, relish the bitterness in their false smiles, and feel the rage in their sweaty welcoming handshakes. He would force them to lick his boots—after he had walked through pig-shit a foot deep.

For some people "Death or Glory" might be an empty slogan. Not for Hans von Schmettow.

~

Lance's guts twisted as the fuel gauge needle drifted to *Empty*. He was still three miles the wrong side of the front lines. The Pup droned onwards, fighting the strong prevailing winds. Below him a ribbon of glittering glass reflected the sun. The River Lys. If his fuel held out, Lance could follow the river west to his airfield at La Gorgue.

Lance's ears registered every change of beat, every timbre, some real, some imagined, as he waited for the engine's cough to signal an empty tank. If that cough happened now, it would be the sound of a prison cell door closing. Four grey walls. No sunlight.

A few minutes more was all he needed.

"Wuff!" Lance twitched as balls of red flame surrounded by black smoke exploded a few hundred feet to his right. The German 77 mm guns close to the front lines had begun their hunt.

"WUFF!" The plane bucked and kicked. Shrapnel rattled against the Pup, and the sharp pungent stink of explosive stung his eyes. Lance side-slipped off a thousand feet of altitude, and the next salvo burst far above him. He frowned at the fist-sized hole in his left lower wing. The German anti-aircraft fire wasn't usually so accurate. To avoid the next salvo of 'Archie', he'd—

The engine coughed. His heart skipped a beat. The engine coughed again, then died. He dropped the nose of the plane to find the best glide angle.

The mangled altimeter was useless, but he must have been around six thousand feet, high enough to reach his own side of the lines in ordinary weather. But this headwind was strong. How strong? He peered over the side and fixed on a bend in the river to judge his forward progress. He should make it.

"*Wuff!*

"Ha!" Lance exclaimed with glee. 'Archie' was way too high this time.

Things were looking up.

A string of yellow-green fireballs exploded on his left. He jerked, banged his sore knee. The twitch on the control stick saved him. Another fireball snaked past his cockpit, trailing long tails of fire. This one so close that the foul reek of phosphorus burned at the back of his throat. "Christ! Flaming onions!" He went into full evasion pattern, skidding and yawing the Pup. But every evasion cost him height.

So much for things looking up. *Seems like some days only go downhill.*

He must have dropped below 5,000 feet, inside the range of the 37mm anti-aircraft guns that fired so fast their shell-bursts appeared like a string of onions. Lance loathed them. The 77mm blew you to kingdom come if they hit. A flaming onion was more likely to ignite the plane's fabric and turn you into a burning comet. Nasty. Very nasty. If you had to go, better to go direct to the kingdom without going via Hell's flames. Damn keeping altitude, he wasn't going to be target practice for flaming onions.

He dived for the front lines, pursued by deadly streaks of phosphorus and a terror of burning. His eyes fixed on the brown scar that writhed between the two armies. Freedom and life on one side, capture or death on the other. The margins were small, the consequences...

Now the ground machine guns took up the hunt. With the Pup's engine silent, their staccato hate sounded worse than usual. The faint moan of wind through the wires sang a dirge. Sweat soaked his armpits, ran down his ribs. No-Man's-Land, festooned with barbed wire, inched closer, each foot a mile, each second an hour.

He stabbed at the rudder pedals incessantly, thighs quivering with the strain. Pin pricks of light flashed below as thousands of troops fired their rifles. His bum cheeks clenched. So many bullets from below. Simple logic said those bullets wouldn't hit his brain first. The Pup yawed from side to side as he tried to dodge the hailstorm of gunfire. Thank God no-one taught ground troops deflection shooting.

No sooner the thought than bullets thudded into the engine block. He winced. Still, every bullet in the metal was one less in his flesh.

No-Man's-Land loomed closer. But still the machine guns hammered. Still the fireflies sparkled. Each heartbeat gifted the next, every panted breath granted hope for another.

Until the last of the barbed wire slid under the nose.

And the fusillade ceased.

Khaki figures below jumped and waved in triumph at his escape. Lance felt his cracked lips grin. His sphincter relaxed too. He stretched out his glide, cleared the British reserve trenches, and found some flattish ground. Joystick back, he held the plane off the ground until the last possible moment, bleeding speed until even the wind in the wires ceased its song, and the wheels kissed the earth. They jolted and rattled in protest as they trundled over the rutted ground. Safe at last! He patted the faithful Pup.

The shell-hole loomed in front of him, out of nowhere. Lance snapped his jaw closed and ducked. The Pup's nose-dived into the hole. The tail somersaulted over the nose and crashed the other side. Lance's teeth rattled. The tightened harness held him upside down. He sneezed as dust from the cockpit drifted into his nose. Then silence.

I'm alive. The thought sang before another thought snuffed it out. The Huns would shell the wreck. They always did. Planes and pilots were valued targets.

He stretched a careful arm upwards above his neck. Or was it downwards? Damned confusing when you were upside down. Up or down, the important thing was the careful bit. Plenty of pilots had survived crashes and unbuckled while upside down, only to break their necks. Lance hadn't got this far to give the Grim Reaper a laugh.

He unfastened the harness but held onto it until he could work his feet under him. Then he splashed into the soggy shell-hole. He clambered out, moving fast despite the aches and pains. Shells were a powerful motivator.

Once out of the hole, he ran, stabs of pain with every pace from his injured knee. Direction didn't matter, only distance.

When he reckoned he had run far enough, he collapsed behind a ruined stone wall. He waited for the shellfire. Nothing. Minutes dragged past. Maybe the artillery had better things to do today? He put his back against the wall, took off his flying helmet, and straightened his legs. A cool spring breeze caressed his cheek. He turned his face to the sun and inhaled a deep breath. Alive felt good.

He ran his shaking fingers through his sweat-stained hair and shook his head at his own stupidity. The more he fed his urge for revenge, the stronger it became.

When he took his first step on the road of revenge back in Africa, it had seemed a simple journey. Yet every step since brought him only to crossroads with no good options. He'd crossed his Rubicon, killing Peters, with certainty in his heart. Now all was darkness and confusion.

He suffered no illusions; his death in this war was inevitable. English newspapers had reported the current life expectancy of an RFC pilot was a mere seventeen hours in the air. God granted a dragonfly a longer life. But Lance ached to die fulfilled, free of the crucifixion of guilt. When he fell to his destined doom and reached the other side, he wanted only to look his brothers and friends in the face and say with certainty: "I avenged you."

How many kills that would take, Lance did not know—thirty, fifty, one hundred?—before his guilt fell away from him like a lead cloak unfastened? Only one thing was certain—he wasn't there yet.

But what more could he do? He could not catch the new two-seaters when they were alert, and the speed and performance of the Albatross DIII now made the deep penetration over the German lines a suicidal tactic.

Could he add more speed to the Pup? No, his mechanics had already eked out every possible performance gain from the engine. He could lengthen the Pup's wing tips, which should allow him to climb higher, but that would also add drag and fragility. He might reach the high-flying reconnaissance planes, but he wouldn't be able to manoeuvre without ripping off the elongated wings. And God help him if an Albatross found him. Make himself invisible with better camouflage? Fly lower?

With bitter resignation he realised what he needed to do, and his mouth twisted in distaste.

A shell moaned overhead. He ducked. "Boom!" Shock waves punched his ears. Steel fragments whined over the wall. Clods of earth pattered downwards. That shell had been nearer to Lance than to the Pup. The one time you wanted the Huns to be accurate… Lance fell flat and cowered.

"Boom!" Once, twice, three times. The earth trembled. The shells settled into rolling percussion. Seemed the Huns weren't too busy after all. He pressed his face closer to the stone wall, damp moss cool against his cheek. And prayed.

7
Humble Pie

Two days later – 10–12 May 1917.
France, Lille Sector, La Gorgue Airfield. RFC, 13 Squadron.

"A man is allowed one mistake, isn't he?" Lance asked, hating the wheedling sound of his own voice. Humble pie wasn't his favourite dish, and it wedged in his craw. But sometimes it was the only thing on the menu.

"One mistake?" Arthur's voice rose, incredulous. Arthur had departed to join Hawker's outfit in such a rush that he took only a duffle bag of clothes. When Arthur came back to 13 Squadron to pick up the rest of his belongings, Lance waylaid him and begged for a second chance. Arthur dropped the suitcase he had been about to load into his racing-green, open-topped Bentley.

"Lance, I have been cutting you slack ever since we met. It's not one isolated mistake, it's a never-ending saga. But this was the worst. You as good as slapped Hawker in the face with his offer and spat on my friendship. Now you ask me to wangle you into the new Wing after that? After you put your self-imposed debts to the dead before your duty to your country, before your bonds to the living? I believed our friendship meant more."

"Of course it does," Lance said.

Caws of derision came from the poplar trees that lined the canal besides the aerodrome. Even the crows thought that was a feeble effort.

It appeared that Arthur did too. He snorted and turned his back on Lance to strap the suitcase into the car.

Lance stroked the Bentley's cool metalwork, a bit dented from its time in France, but still regal looking.

Beautiful design, fine workmanship, functional. This was a car that you could wear like a fine coat, just slip it on and drive, unaware of any degrees of separation.

His friendship with Arthur had been like that. Once upon a time.

Lance scratched his nose and stood helpless, bereft of words to heal the rift. With the new Albatross DIII ruling the skies he needed a better plane to achieve his revenge before the Huns killed him. Hawker's new elite outfit would be first to receive the latest fighters while the unglamorous 13 Squadron might be among the last. The new SE5 was said to be lightning fast, with a top speed of over 120 miles per hour. With that speed he would be the hunter, not the hunted. He could catch any Hun two-seaters, or run from Albatross if necessary.

"Not even for old time's sake?" Lance asked. Whatever pride he had left shrivelled and died with the question. The only rung lower than humble pie was the begging bowl. After that, you were finished.

"Forget it, Lance. Our friendship meant little to you when I pleaded with you to come with me and join Hawker. But when you almost get killed, then you realise you need a better plane, and now you come begging for another bite at the cherry. Honestly, I am surprised. I thought you would have the balls to stick with your original choice." Arthur tied down the last strap and stepped into the car.

Lance winced. When put like that it sounded bad. In his obsessional focus on his vendetta, he hadn't realised the hurt he'd inflicted on Arthur, who besides Clayton was his only friend in France. The shame of that sudden self-knowledge was ash in his mouth. He had magicked cinders from a golden friendship and had no one to blame but himself.

"You're right. I have no right to ask anything of you." The words came out soft. Unlike his begging, they were sincere. Unfortunately, they came out just as the Bentley roared into life and Arthur revved the engine. Lance turned away, defeated.

"Wait!" bellowed Arthur, "What did you say?"

Lance shuffled to the car door. "You're right," he said, "I have no right to ask anything of you. I'm sorry for the way I behaved. You deserved better. Thank you for everything." He touched Arthur's shoulder. "Look after yourself."

Arthur's eyes searched Lance's face as the engine burbled. "I'll speak to Hawker," he said after a moment, "though God knows he has little time for you. I'll do my best…for old time's sake." Arthur's expression was still hard and unforgiving as he drove away, leaving Lance eating exhaust fumes and dust. Which was pretty much what he deserved

To Lance's shame, he could not tell whether his relief came from the potential redemption of Arthur's friendship or from the prospect of escaping his obsolete Pup. Arthur's phrase rang through his head—debts to the dead or bonds to the living? The debts would never be extinguished, but maybe, just maybe, he could honour both. Never again did he want to go through such dark days as had followed Will's death. But for Arthur's friendship he'd take the risk. No-one else, mind. Only Arthur. He could manage one friend, couldn't he?

He walked back to the hangars with a spring in his step. Odd that. If friends made you weak, why did this decision feel so good?

~

As Arthur had predicted, Hawker did not dance a jig of joy when told Lance wanted another chance. Lance chewed his nails for two whole days before Arthur could persuade the new wing commander. When Hawker greeted Lance at the new wing's airfield at Le Hameau, his stare was hard and his handshake grudging. "Don't make me regret changing my mind, Finch."

Lance failed to hide his flash of anger as Hawker botched his name. "You won't regret it, sir," he replied through gritted teeth.

Too late, Lance noticed the glint of humour in Hawker's eyes. Hawker laughed. "That's quite a temper, lad!" He clapped Lance on the shoulder. "I'm glad the Huns didn't get you, Fitch, and I'm damned glad to have a Hun killer like you in this wing. You take that temper out on them, and we'll give the bastards a hiding." In that moment Lance realised why Hawker was such a legendary leader in the RFC.

Arthur was less forgiving. "I used a lot of credibility to get you here, Lance. Attempt to be friendly with the other officers, would you? We will have damn good men coming to the wing, and you might learn a thing or two. Albert Ball is joining."

Lance's eyes lit up at that. Ball was the top-scoring British ace, well ahead of Lance, and revered throughout the RFC for his kills, his bravery, and his modesty. An "elite wing" was an empty concept to Lance. But the presence of both Hawker and Ball, the two fighting legends of the RFC, would turn those words into reality.

~

Two days later – 14 May 1917.
England, Farnborough, Royal Aircraft Factory.

Lance fell in lust the moment he saw the SE5. "You beauty!" he breathed as he walked around the sleek new fighter. Its clean airframe oozed speed and menace. Like the Albatross, it looked right for a fighter. Unlike the Albatross, with its round fuselage and rounded wingtips, the British fighter was all hard angles with an angular lean fuselage and squared off wingtips. The long nose with the square radiator housed a monster engine that promised power galore. An upper wing sloped forward of the lower wing lent a rakish look of speed, and twin machine guns, one on the top wing and one in the cowling, completed the rugged and warlike fighter. Lance inhaled the brand-new smell of doped fabric and stroked the big exhausts that ran along the fuselage. His senses tingled with joy and anticipation. You didn't have to fly some planes to know they will be exceptional.

He climbed into the cockpit, dizzy with love, and promptly cracked his head on the Lewis machine gun grip mounted on the upper wing above the cockpit. Damn stupid, putting a drum-fed gun up there. It would be impossible to change a drum during combat. Why not have twin belt-fed guns like the Albatross? But when he caressed the twin triggers on the control column, he forgave everything. Two guns, however mounted, were twice as good as one.

The 150-horsepower Hispano-Suizsa engine exploded into life on the mechanic's first swing and throbbed with a sonorous rumble that resonated deep inside Lance's chest. When he opened the throttle, the big wooden propellers blurred into a brown haze and the thrusting acceleration caught him unawares. *Christ, she's like a runaway racehorse!* At fifty miles per hour Lance lifted her off the ground—and his lust turned into love.

When she climbed, he revelled in the seat pressure thrusting him upwards. She climbed like an angel up through the cloudless heavens at over eight hundred feet a minute, reaching ten thousand feet in twelve minutes—two whole minutes faster than the Pup. Two minutes did not sound much, but in air combat it meant life or death. And a top speed of 120 miles per hour in level flight would make her the cheetah of the sky. Even better, the engineers promised a new two-hundred horsepower engine soon that would add still more speed and high-altitude performance.

The controls were crisp and responsive. Turns either way were easy, with just a touch of adverse yaw requiring a firm balancing rudder. The SE5 wasn't as agile as the Pup but manoeuvrable enough to take on the Albatross. It dived faster than Lance had dived in his life. Wind screamed through the wires with a banshee's delight, but the plane felt strong and solid. He howled his joy into the raging slipstream that whipped his hair and tore at his cheeks. Even in a shallow dive it stayed stable, a rock-solid gun platform compared to the jittery Pup.

He held the control column between his knees and the plane tracked straight and true as he practised sliding the Lewis gun down its sliding and changing the ammunition drum above his head. Each drum held ninety-seven bullets, and they were a brute to change. By the time he'd done it three times, his arms ached.

Landing was a breeze. The plane whistled over the airfield fence at fifty-five mph and Lance held it off the ground until a stall approached at forty-five mph, and the wheels and tailskid touched down in a perfect three pointer. The SE5 designers had achieved the Holy Grail of fighter design: a stunningly well-balanced flying machine that would be deadly to the enemy but easy to fly.

As he clambered out of the machine his heart sang with the joy of owning such a beast, a weapon of war that surpassed his dreams

Then they took the aircraft away and kicked him out of the factory.

The chief test pilot was sympathetic but firm. "Buzz off, old boy, there's no point in hanging around here. We don't have an SE5 to give you. Count your blessings we allowed you to fly our only airworthy SE5. We only did that as a favour to Major Hawker. He's a friend of mine."

"He ordered me to fly back an SE5 today."

"That's because he wasn't aware of the strike."

"What strike?"

"Our workers are striking for more money."

"You mean while we fight and die in France, bastards who sleep safe in their own beds, cuddling their wives, refuse to build the weapons we need?" Even as he spoke the words Lance could not believe them. His voice had gone up an octave.

"Bingo."

"They...should...be...shot!" Lance squeezed the words through gritted teeth.

"A good solution," the chief wearily agreed. "But I'm told there are laws in England against shooting strikers."

"Bugger the laws. Men are dying over there every day because we're flying antiquated planes. Let's take a few workers over the lines and see what they say when the Huns are shooting holes in their rotten hides."

"Please don't shout at me, Lieutenant. I understand your point of view. Many of the pilots in France are my friends too. But it's more complicated than you realise. Just like we need skilled pilots to fly the planes, we need skilled labour to build them."

Lance clenched his fists; the urge to break something was overpowering. "Every time something stinks, the higher ups always say it's more complicated than we simpletons can understand. Perhaps those on the front lines should say attacking the Huns is more complicated than the higher ups think, and we can't do it."

"I wouldn't recommend that," the chief said. "No laws against shooting soldiers who refuse to attack the enemy. Listen, everyone from the prime minister downwards is working on it. Your wing will get your planes as soon as they're ready."

"When do you think that will that be?"

"Soon."

"When is 'soon'?"

"Sooner if you bugger off and let us get on with it, Lieutenant. Longer if you don't."

Lance's exit left the door of the Royal Aircraft Factory hanging off its bottom hinges.

When Lance joined Hawker's fledgling wing, he had been shocked to find it had no aircraft. Pilots were told to bring their own existing planes. But after Lance's forced landing last week, a Hun artillery barrage had obliterated his Pup before 13 Squadron mechanics could rescue it. When Lance went to the RFC depot at Saint-Omer to pick up a new plane, he found the losses of Bloody April had wiped out the stock of replacement Pups in France. So, Hawker had ordered him to take the boat from Dunkirk to England, collect an SE5 prototype from the Royal Aircraft Factory at Farnborough, and fly it back to the wing.

Lance cabled the wing with the bad news, hoping and expecting a blistering reply would force the factory to find him an SE5 to take back to France.

~

Lance woke energised the next morning, but Arthur's cabled reply doused him with cold water.

GO TO SOPWITH FACTORY STOP ORGANISE CAMEL OR ANOTHER PUP STOP IF NECESSARY TAKE LEAVE STOP GO TO WOLSEY HALL TELL LADY WOLSEY I SENT YOU STOP

That depressed him enough, but when he rushed to the Sopwith factory in Kingston, even they could not even provide him with a Camel or a Pup, new or old. Bloody April had bled dry even Sopwith's stock of Pups, and now they had geared their production lines to produce the Pup's replacement, the Camel.

"Give me a Camel then."

The elderly boffin in a white coat peered over his glasses. "Believe it or not, every Camel on the assembly line schedule has been assigned for weeks. Major Hawker is a friend of Tommy Sopwith, and he got the first production line Camel. The ferry pilot left two days ago. Perhaps it hasn't got to Hawker yet, but your chances of getting another Camel are less than my chances of seducing a chorus girl from *HMS Pinafore*."

Despite his anger, Lance conceded a small smile. The girls in that musical were famously beautiful. "That low huh?"

"Afraid so. Listen, we'll ask around the training squadrons and get you a Pup."

Lance shuddered. A training squadron meant ham-fisted trainee pilots and unmotivated mechanics and fitters, which led to wheezy engines, over-stressed bracing wires, and fabric and undercarriage repaired a dozen times. And to think he had joined Hawker to *improve* his chances of survival.

"There really isn't a Pup anywhere else? Bloody April felt bad from the sharp end, but surely Britain hasn't run out of aircraft."

The boffin shook his head. "No Pups available for love nor money. I know it looks bad, but once the Camels start arriving, they'll come fast. Same for the SE5s when they solve the strike. Come back in three days, and we'll have a Pup for you. Best we can do."

Lance left the Sopwith factory door intact. His rage had bled away, leaving a deep depression and lethargy that made it hard to put one foot in front of the other. He'd tasted nirvana with his flight in the SE5, then had it ripped away from him by striking civilians who didn't give a damn for the men fighting on their behalf. The sense of urgency and moral purpose that existed at the Front contrasted with the indolent avarice back in England. Not only would he be returning to fight the crack Circus and their upgraded Albatross D111 in an obsolete Pup, but in a tired, beaten-up training Pup. It was as good as a death sentence. But his will to fight against his fate had bled dry.

He slurped tea at a railway canteen and considered how to kill the three days before a Pup would be ready. Arthur had foreseen a delay and told him to take leave and go to Wolsey Hall. He blew out his cheeks. He'd never met Arthur's wife, and Arthur seldom mentioned her.

The thought of consorting with polite society made his palms sweaty. After Ma died when Lance was ten, Pa did not exactly fill the boys' days with etiquette lessons. No belching and no elbows on the table was about as far as Pa stretched. As an officer in the army, Lance learned to use cutlery starting from the outside and which way to pass the port decanter. All else was an arcane mystery. He would disgrace himself, and Lady Wolsey would think he was a colonial oik.

On the other hand, much as Lance hated to admit it, he owned a sneaking desire to see Arthur's home and wife, his other life. It felt like peeking under a blanket at things Arthur chose not to discuss, which made it mildly illicit and irresistible. Besides, orders were orders, right?

He caught a train to the station nearest to Wolsey Hall, which turned out to be Farnham in Surrey, and from there hailed a cab to take him to Wolsey Hall.

They arrived in early evening while the soft summer light still cast long shadows. The first clue came with massive stone pillars that flanked ornate iron gates, and a driveway that curved a mile through ordered woodlands and manicured lawns. When Lance stepped out of the taxi, he almost cricked his neck gawping at the palatial building. The hall loomed as an elegant behemoth, two stories of graceful arched windows stretching more than a hundred yards long. Rose flower beds, regimented in blocks of red, yellow and white, marched every yard of the walls. Their soft scent flowered the evening breeze, a feminine contrast to the military precision of their planting.

Lance knew Arthur as his pilot, a friend, and a commanding officer. But this huge mansion reminded him that Arthur also ruled as Lord Wolsey, head of one of the wealthiest and most powerful aristocratic families in England. Lance noticed for the first time the threadbare cuffs on his jacket. He picked at a loose thread and suspected Lady Wolsey would not be impressed by the riffraff on her doorstep.

He rang the bell and waited, palms sweaty.

An old flunkey opened the door, dressed in a long-tailed black coat with a starched white shirt and high collar. "Sir?"

"My name is Lance Fitch, and I am in Arthur's…I mean Lord Wolsey's squadron in France. He told me to come here and call on Lady Wolsey."

The man looked down his magnificent hooked Roman nose. "Lady Wolsey is not in residence, sir."

"Er, is she expected back soon?"

The man's gaze dropped to Lance's medals and then back up at him with more respect. "Sir, the official answer to that question is 'Her Ladyship does not confide in me.' But I lost a grandson in France, so for a fighting man like you I'll tell the truth. Her Ladyship will remain in London until next week."

Lance was ashamed of the wash of relief that flooded through him. The magnificent estate reminded him of the vast gulf between Arthur and himself. In France, Arthur might rank higher, but Lance walked with the long shadow of a leading ace. In England, he'd passed through a social filter where Arthur's title threw a monstrous shadow that withered Lance's away to nothing.

Resentment curdled his mood. He took the cab back to Farnham and rented a room in the Hound & Stag Hotel as night fell. Coming here had been a mistake. Everything about this trip to England had been a disaster.

8
Exenrude

16 May 1917.
England, Surrey, Farnham.

The next morning, he sat in a deserted breakfast room and fought the black dog of depression that weighed on him. He sat listlessly, buttering his toast as he pondered what to do in this strange land for the next two days while he waited for his replacement Pup.

He took a sip of his tea and wished he hadn't. He signalled to the waiter.

"Could I have proper cup of tea? This tastes like someone waved tea leaves in the general vicinity of tepid water. I know there is rationing, but the railway canteen in Kingston managed a decent cuppa."

The elderly, stick-thin waiter adjusted his thick glasses between forefinger and thumb, reminding Lance of his first teacher. "Sir, that is Earl Grey tea. In the pantheon of great teas, it ranks at the *very* top. I am not personally acquainted with the Kingston Railway café, but I might suggest that its tea, *very* fine though it undoubtedly is, might rank a *smidgen* lower." His tone inferred that smidgenplaced Lance's exemplar tea somewhere among pigeon droppings.

"How about you take five times the amount of this Earl Grey fella and plonk it in the teapot and pour boiling water on it? Then bring it to me."

"Earl Grey tea must *never* be made with boiling water sir. It bruises the leaves and scalds the bergamot oil. I am *disconsolate* that we cannot satisfy you sir. Perhaps you would like me to arrange transportation to the *Farnham Railway café?*"

127

Lance surrendered. "A glass of milk would be fine."

He sighed; he couldn't even win a skirmish with a waiter. Maybe Lance had got too used to the gunpowder strength Army tea? For sure, he felt more at home at war in France.

When Lance first landed in England in 1915, the capital city glowed with light, a fabled land of riches and culture with towering buildings and a reputation to match—the beating heart of the largest empire the world had ever known. For Will and Lance in those days of laughter and dizzy excitement, England the Motherland was a present they unwrapped a little more of every day. Now it felt foreign, cold-hearted, and bleak, grey of colour and soul.

A female voice shattered his contemplations. "Mr Fitch?" The cultured accent and pleasant timbre sounded like uplifting musical bells. Lance looked up and leapt to his feet in deference to the lady addressing him. Raven black hair, long and lustrous, framed a face too strong for conventional beauty, but her skin was luminous, and she'd shadowed and slanted her alluring eyes with captivating cosmetic artifice.

"Yes," he blurted out, a tongue-tied adolescent unable to prevent his eyes from feasting on her.

She had sheathed her body in a dress of deep purple, cut with a demure neckline but revealing a thrust of breast and flare of hip. Around her neck she wore a silver choker whorled with Celtic patterns. Lance judged her to be older than him but not by too much.

She offered a gloved hand. "I am Arthur's sister, Lady Exenrude, but please call me Megan."

The silver bangles on her wrists tinkled as Lance shook her hand, surprised by her masculine gesture. A thought occurred too late. Was he supposed to shake her hand or kiss it? He flushed, but she eased his embarrassment with a sweet smile.

"I'm Lance Fitch. Pleased to meet you. I did not know Arthur had a sister."

"Typical Arthur. He is so focused on the war. On the other hand, he has mentioned *you* to me, Mr. Fitch. May I join you at your table?"

"Delighted."

Remembering his manners, Lance pulled out a chair for her and caught a whiff of an exotic scent. She smoothed her dress underneath her as she settled into the seat.

"I thought I had better rescue you," she said. "A stranger with an unusual accent," she smiled to remove the sting of the words, "asking how he can find Wolsey Hall arouses suspicion that you are a spy. Such tittle-tattle spreads dreadfully fast around the village."

"Well, Lady Exenrude, thank you for the rescue." Lance flashed what he hoped was a winning smile.

"Megan please," she said, placing a hand on his, silver bracelets jangling. "And may I call you Lance? As such a vital member of Arthur's squadron, I feel I know you already." Her hand squeezed his in emphasis.

"Of course."

"I'm glad, Lance. May I ask what you were doing at Wolsey Hall?"

"Er, Arthur told me to call on Lady Wolsey, and arrange a few things to go from the estate to the wing in France."

"Then there is a slight complication. Lady Wolsey has gone to London and will only be back next week. I am sure Arthur would like you to stay at Wolsey Hall, but you will find it dreadfully boring by yourself. I can help organise the things to go to Arthur, but he would never forgive me if I permitted you stay at a hotel. My home is nearby. I can send my chauffeur Perkins round to pick you up at five o'clock. He can show you to your room, and then we could meet for dinner at seven?"

Megan's beseeching gaze and warm hand suggested her dearest wish would come true if he agreed. He capitulated with pleasure. Megan bestowed a last glowing smile as she left, her dress beguiling in its shifts as she swayed towards the exit.

~

At five o'clock a Rolls Royce pulled in front of the hotel, gleaming in black paint with silver fittings glistening in the pale sunlight. An immaculate chauffeur introduced himself in a distant manner as "Perkins, sir" and ushered Lance into the backseat of the automobile. Lance stepped inside with trepidation, frightened to scuff such perfection with his boots. The rich smell of finest leather cosseted him.

He wiped his palms on his trousers and kept telling himself that this was just a dinner with Arthur's sister, but the butterflies remained. Lance wanted to impress her with the nervous need of a giddy schoolboy, but the gleaming splendour of the Rolls Royce intimidated him.He did not belong in this world. Lance leaned forward to tell Perkins to turn back to the hotel, but as he did so, he remembered Megan's dark wide-open eyes and those kissable lips.

Kissable? An image of Heidi's cornflower-blue eyes and laughing face loomed in his mind. Was he being unfaithful? He had never heard from her since the day of the ambush. She could have died from typhoid or the murdering bandits, both of which had swept through the region like plagues as the war spread and law and order melted away. The postal service had shut down between German and British East Africa so no letters would ever go through. And three years of war had bought peace no closer. The carnage could drag on for five, ten more years. Pa was right. Much as Lance loved her, for his own sanity it was best to forget Heidi for the meantime.

He loosened his tie a tad and opened the window for some fresh air. Scents, heavy with blossom, flooded into the Rolls Royce. The car had left the town and entered a winding country lane, lined with hedgerows, and overshadowed with spreading branches and dappled leaves. Shards of sunlight danced underneath the canopy, bright as jewels in the gloom.

Kissable lips? His brow furrowed. This was Arthur's sister. If he tried to kiss her and made a fool of himself, she would complain to Arthur. That would be mighty embarrassing at best, and at worst fatal to their recently fragile friendship. He wouldn't risk that over a woman, any woman.

"Perkins," he said, "Take me—"

The car braked hard. Lance bounced off the front seats and swore. A frightened sheep baa-ed and scrambled across the lane and through the other side of the hedgerow. Damned stupid animals, sheep. They would not last a day in the wilds of Africa.

"Sorry sir, part and parcel of driving in the countryside."

Lance pushed himself back into the plush seating. One good thing about a Rolls, with so much padding it was hard to hurt yourself. He could do with some of that padding in the Pup.

"You were saying, sir?"

For a second, Lance did not remember. But when he did, a wave of stubbornness seized him. "Forget it, Perkins."

Lance would not be a sheep. He had faced down stampeding buffalo so close that their snot flecked his shirt. He'd charged the massed machine guns of the Hun, if you called stumbling through glutinous mud 'charging'. He'd duelled Richthofen. And he'd survived them all. Surely, he could manage a dinner with Arthur's sister?

All he had to do was remember his table manners and avoid kissing her. That's all. Besides, she probably thought he was a colonial oik, and was charming him only because he was from Arthur's Wing. She'd be horrified if he made a pass at her. So, he wouldn't. He could handle the situation. "I'm in control," he whispered to himself.

Megan's "home" didn't reassure him. Where Wolsey Hall exuded wealth and sophistication, Exenrude Keep projected rugged strength. Walls of rough stone blocks soared high, crowned with notched battlements. The Rolls rumbled over a drawbridge between thick chain links and into a courtyard where menacing arrow-slits kept watch.

Some homes whisper 'welcome'. This one flaunted a challenge, 'Enter, if you dare.'

Lance closed his jaw with a click and followed Perkins through an iron-banded and iron-studded timber gate set under a massive stone lintel, in which a hole gaped.

"What is the big hole for?" Lance asked.

"It's called a murder hole," Perkins said, "for pouring boiling oil on any unwanted guests battering the gate. Very useful on those wearing suits of armour, cooks them nicely."

Lance raised his eyebrows. The Evenrudes must have been a hospitable bunch. Hopefully Megan had moved with the times, although Lance noted Perkins had not used the past tense.

They continued into a gloomy interior and up a narrow, curved stone staircase. "Curved clockwise to disadvantage right-handed swordsmen attempting to fight their way upwards," Perkins explained.

Lance raised his eyebrows. All the comforts of home. Even his bedroom windows were glassed-in arrow-slits overlooking a garden. He didn't need Megan to make him feel like a colonial oik. Exenrude Keep did the job just fine by itself. It must have stood guard for over five hundred years. In Taveta, anything over ten years counted as ancient.

At seven o'clock, Lance presented himself downstairs for dinner, worried about the shabbiness of his uniform. It had cost what seemed an absurd amount of money when he received his commission, but now he worried he'd spent too little.

Perkins, transformed into an immaculate butler, ushered Lance into a hexagonal-shaped dining room panelled in dark oak with narrow arched windows. The large dining table in the centre mimicked both the room's dark oak and unusual hexagonal shape. A large candelabrum in the middle of the table cast a flickering light that pooled in the centre of the room but made no impression on the dim corners. Lance found the mystical ambiance unsettling.

Before he developed this line of thought, Perkins brought him a crystal goblet of warm mulled wine. Lance was sniffing the wine's rich spicy aroma, exotic and unfamiliar, when he heard a jingling behind him.

He turned and found a bewitching world of smoky eyes, smooth pale skin and curved burgundy lips, all framed by a cascade of hair that shimmered the shade of a moonless midnight. A purple velvet gown left her shoulders bare and hugged her curves.

All standing close to him. Unsettlingly close. But it seemed churlish to complain.

"I put cinnamon in the wine," Megan smiled. "Hoodoo practitioners say it is an essential magic ingredient to assist purification, luck, love, and money." Candlelight danced in her eyes and shadowed the smooth swell of her cleavage.

"Well, that covers the most important angles," Lance said, struggling to keep his eyes on hers. Hard not to look elsewhere given the riches on display, but also hard to stay with eyes locked on hers when they made his blood smoke.

"Exactly. To luck, love, and money." She toasted him with a knowing half-smile.

"You missed out purification," he said.

"Yes, I did, it seems boring compared to the rest."

"I take it hoodoo is like our witch doctor stuff in Africa?" Lance asked.

"Close. It is a form of magic practised in America, using a mixture of folklore from Africa, the Native Americans, and even Europe."

"Are you an expert?"

"Not at all. I just dabble in the unusual. Like you, Lance." She took his hand and led him to the table. Her perfume mingled with the cinnamon in a musky bouquet that made his senses reel.

"My, you do look handsome in uniform. Women love young men in uniform, such potency, so manly." She mocked him with a smile.

Lance struggled to respond in kind, but found his wits befuddled. She leaned forward as she sat, and the silver chain nestled in her cleavage drew Lance's eyes downwards to the smooth swell of her breasts.

He dragged his eyes back to her face to find her regarding him with amusement. "Do I pass muster, Lance?"

Lance flushed, flustered by her cool directness. "No. Not at all," he mumbled, trying to deny the direction of his gaze.

She arched her eyebrows. "No? Not at all? Well, I must say that you are the first to complain. You, sir, are not gallant!" She teased, "Perhaps those African girls spoil you, prancing around with naked breasts?"

Lance was dumbstruck. An English Lady, a real titled Lady, talking about naked breasts? A vicar blaspheming would have surprised him less. How should he respond to that? He took a deep gulp of the spicy wine.

Megan took pity on him. "So, tell me about Arthur's squadron, and what it is like in France now."

Back on more familiar territory, Lance rediscovered his dormant eloquence. Megan prompted him whenever he faltered, exclaimed in wonder and support, and drew from him layers of insight and emotion that Lance had never revealed even to himself during the long months of war. Whenever the flow of words faltered, Megan re-ignited them with questions, a warm touch, a refilled glass, and the curve of her lips.

Lance was unaware of Perkins as he served their meal. His whole focus swam in those smoky eyes. He would never have unburdened himself to another man in such a way. But with Megan the sharing seemed natural. She might be a woman, but she avoided any fluttering female awe, and showed an understanding and appreciation of a soldier's world during wartime. Never had he enjoyed such a discerning audience, one so in tune with him.

Then the words ran dry. The desire to talk evaporated, and he stumbled into silence. She stared at him, those dangerous burgundy lips moist and parted. His right hand stretched out of its own volition, and the back of his fingertips brushed the creamy inner curves of her breasts. Her eyes locked on his with no discernible change of expression. Only her breathing deepened, pushing her flesh against his fingers. Lance's hardness pulsed with every heartbeat.

She stood, her chair scraping the stone floor, and glided around the table, her hips swaying like a dancer to the tune of her silver bracelets. Those half-lidded eyes held his as she seized his head and tilted it back so that her mouth could swoop on his. Her tongue pushed deeper, questing and demanding. Lance rocked in his chair, hands holding the curve of her hips as he kissed her back with fervent passion. She pulled her mouth away from his, panting, and searched his eyes with hers.

For a fleeting second, he thought of Arthur. "Control," whispered a small voice in his head.

Megan bit his lower lip, feeding on it sensuously.

Control was over-rated.

He surged to his feet and pulled her compliant body closer as he kissed her again and again. Her cunning hips inflamed him, oscillating against him with urgent little thrusts. He clasped her taut buttocks in his hands, picked her up and pushed her onto the dark oak table. The gown rode up, leaving her bare legs pale in the gleaming candlelight, emerging from the folds of the dark velvet as they clasped themselves around Lance's waist. Her lips never left his for a moment, but her expert hands found his fly and freed him. She cooed into his mouth as she stroked him artfully. Lance lifted away the folds of gown bunched at her thighs, and with a delicious shock discovered her nakedness beneath. He moved his hands under her bare buttocks, gripped her cheeks, and thrust into her molten core.

"Yesss!" she hissed, triumphant, and arched her back to take even more of him. Slim arms locked behind his neck to help her ride his thrusts. Lance gave an answering groan, rumbling deep in his chest, as he drove into her with a primal need. Her silver bracelets jangled with each thrust. Hoarse cries of ecstasy spurred him on, faster and faster. Too soon he exploded into her clutching depths.

Afterwards they lay panting, sweat cooling in the musky scented air. Megan eased Lance away so she could stand, but held onto him for a few seconds with her head against his chest as her shaking legs steadied. Then she knelt in front of Lance and licked him clean as a mother cat might clean a kitten. Once again Lance was shocked, but revelled in the pure sensation. When she finished she rose, still clasping his tumescence in her left hand, smiled at his questioning look, blew out the candles, and whispered, "Come to my bedroom." Then she led him, her hand squeezing tight, along the dark corridors and up the winding stairs.

9
English Blood Will Flow in Streams

Next day – 17 May 1917.
France, Arras Sector, Roucourt Airfield, near Douai. Luftsreitkrafte, Jasta 11.

Lothar Richthofen chuckled as he landed behind his brother's plane at the *Jasta* 11 airfield at Roucourt. The bitter taste of gun-smoke fouled the back of his throat, but he did not care. Champagne would wash away the rankness. He taxied his plane towards the wooden hangars hidden in the trees, then switched off the bellowing Mercedes engine. The plane stopped shuddering and blissful peace reigned. He slumped in his harness, exhausted but elated.

Father would be pleased. He counted his sons' victories with the avidness of a pawnbroker revelling in his latest bargains. When he heard Lothar scored four kills, and Manfred three, all in one day, Father would dance a jig! Bloodthirsty old codger, as a Major in the Army should be. He'd probably come around for a celebratory lunch. Their airfield wasn't far from Lille where the old man served as the German commandant. Manfred might be the most famous Richthofen, but Father still outranked him.

Mother would be pleased too. Lothar knew he was Mother's favourite. Things came easy to Lothar, whether it was girls, riding, making small talk and friends. Manfred always had to work harder, but by God, did he work! If anyone, including Lothar, possessed twenty percent more talent in anything, then Manfred would push forty percent harder. Mother once teased Manfred that Lothar was better at attracting girls. Lothar laughed. Manfred's blue eyes glared at them both and that square jaw jutted. "One day I will change that," he said. Nowadays girls flooded Germany's most famous war hero with marriage proposals.

Lothar clicked his tongue in rueful acknowledgement. Marriage proposition or kills, Manfred was way ahead these days. In April, Lothar downed fifteen kills, a rate almost unprecedented. Yet he'd finished the month even further behind his brother, who scored twenty-two. Remarkable.

Lothar slipped off his leather helmet and ruffled his sweat-soaked hair. It might be freezing in the skies, but combat generated its own sweat. His aching neck clicked and grated as he stretched it, and he gingerly unwound his scarf from the tender flesh. The pilots' silk scarves were not an affectation—without one, the flying jacket chafed the neck raw from ceaseless turning of the head to keep a wary eye on your tail.

Schmettow's white and red Albatross landed, or rather collided with the earth, bouncing twice before careering down the airfield like a runaway horse. Lothar shook his head. 'Ham fisted' was a generous description of Schmettow's flying. Only a close friend would be that generous, and Schmettow possessed no friends. He did have huge feet, which splayed outwards like a duck as he walked and seemed to affect his flying co-ordination of stick and rudder pedals.

Lothar made it his mission to persuade Manfred to get rid of the foul-mouthed oaf, to lance the boil before Schmettow disgraced Manfred and *Jasta* 11. But Manfred did not listen. "I tell you, Lothar, the man may be crass and a poor pilot, but he is a prince at deflection shooting, and it is easier to teach someone to fly than to teach them to shoot." Lothar could not argue with that. Few men possessed that instantaneous understanding of how to lead the target so the bullets would go where the plane would be when the bullets arrived, not where it had been when you fired.

As a hunter on his father's estates, Lothar had learned deflection shooting with a shotgun and pheasant, but even so the sheer speed of his first air fight caught him by surprise. In the half seconds in which combat flying took place, a pause for conscious calculation meant a miss.

Manfred usually discarded pilots who did not score often, but sometimes he followed his instincts. As a new pilot Kurt Wolff had flown for six months without a kill, and the whole *Jasta* wondered why Manfred did not dump him. But once Wolff scored his first, Englishmen fell under his guns like ducks in a shoot. Since then, Wolff had bloomed under Manfred's tutelage into one of Germany's fastest scoring aces, and his late-blossoming success cemented Manfred's reputation as a *Menschenfänger*—a leader who, through sheer force of personality, could coax others to feats they thought impossible. Now Manfred seemed determined to repeat the trick with Schmettow, which meant the foul-mouthed oaf often flew with Manfred and Lothar. Despite Lothar's complaints.

Lothar climbed stiffly out of the cockpit. The Albatross seats cut off the circulation to his legs. His fitter steadied him. "*Danke*," Lothar said as he stamped his feet, trying to hasten away the pins and needles. He took a rag and wiped the oil and grease off his face. Mercedes engines were damn fine pieces of engineering, but the exposed tappets chucked a lot of oil over you.

He scowled as he saw Schmettow striding towards him. The black sheep had scored his first kill for the *Jasta* today, and that kill was spectacular. An agile Nieuport 17 dodged Manfred's guns like a low-flying snipe and turned across Schmettow's nose. Eighty percent of kills in the air came from little or no deflection shooting from behind the enemy. Schmettow fired a three-second burst at the ninety-degree deflection target.

Which disintegrated. A small black body fell from the wreckage, tumbling earthwards. Schmettow had made a harder shot than Manfred had missed. Right under Manfred's nose.

Lothar shook his head. Either Schmettow was lucky, or Manfred had pulled another Wolff-like rabbit from his magician's hat. Shame the rabbit was a black sheep.

Schmettow approached and clicked his heels. "*Ich gratuliere Ihnen, Leutnant.*" Somehow the polite words sounded mocking. Lothar stared at him. Schmettow's cropped blond hair capped an innocent face with pale blue eyes and long fair lashes like a girl. The man looked like a choirboy but behaved like a ruffian. Those eyes always appeared liquescent, about to fill with tears as if life constantly played unfair jokes on him. If eyes represented a window onto a man's soul, then God played a cosmic joke on this occasion. Lothar turned his back on Schmettow, spurning the congratulations, and handed his helmet and goggles to his ground crew.

He smiled as the pilots flocked to hero worship his brother.Hero worship was not so easy for a brother.Only Lothar knew Manfred chaffed about his lack of height, that he hid the size of his big nose in official photos by always facing the camera, and that women tongue-tied him. But Lothar did not begrudge the acclamation that went Manfred's way. You couldn't deny that his big brother deserved it. Manfred's three kills today had taken him to fifty-two—more than ten ahead of any other fighter pilot on earth…or in heaven or hell.

Manfred had been granted an audience next week in Berlin, with generals Hindenburg and Ludendorff, the "All Highest War Lords of Germany", as the press called them. Even the Kaiser invited Manfred to lunch, an unprecedented honour for a twenty-five-year-old pilot from a minor family of landed gentry. Albeit a pilot who General Ludendorff stated was worth a division of infantry.

Ever the showman, Manfred had been racing to reach fifty kills before he left for Berlin so he could dedicate that historic feat to the Kaiser in person. Thank God the British had co-operated today, or Manfred would have been in a foul mood.

Lothar strolled over to join the boisterous group. Manfred's blond hair spiked upwards, wet with sweat. He ran his hand backwards to slick the hair down and looked upwards at the sky that was already growing dark. Lothar could read his brother's mind like a book. Manfred was hoping to squeeze in one more flight, but it was a vain hope.

Moritz, Manfred's giant Danish hound, bounded up to his master, jumped onto his hind legs with his paws on his owner's flying coat, and slobbered all over him. Manfred laughed as he swung the giant dog around in a clumsy waltz before putting him down and fondling the torn ears where a spinning prop had once chopped them ragged.

Manfred's face was stern these days. His blue eyes burned even colder, and the strain chiselled new lines around the mouth. But the sternness softened as the young pilots crowded round him. "*Hast du nummer fünfzig abgeschossen?*" they clamoured. Manfred smiled and nodded, and the pilots cheered, competing to shake the *Rittmeister*'s hand in congratulations on his fiftieth kill.

It wasn't only the pilots who fawned on Manfred. The German High Command wanted to distract the public's attention from the horrendous casualty reports, so they had sent Professor Schultz from the *Kölnische Zeitung*, the *Cologne Gazette*, to report to the adoring public how Manfred Richthofen ruled the air in this most modern form of warfare. Schultz, a small pudgy man with moon glasses, hung around the pilots like a nodding sycophant.

As Lothar approached the celebrations, Schultz saw him and bounced over. "How many today, *Leutnant*?"

Lothar held up four fingers, smiling at Manfred as he did so. The latter slanted an eyebrow at the unspoken challenge. "Four! One more than me but you are not alone on the pedestal. Wolff got four too!"

The diminutive Wolff looked down at his feet like an embarrassed schoolboy. Lothar's smile slipped. Wolff had been the *Luftstreikrafte*'s top scorer in April with twenty-three against Manfred's twenty-two and Lothar's fifteen. Never mind catching Manfred, keeping up with Wolff was one tough challenge too.

Manfred waved a hand at his brother. "See, *Herr* Schultz, how little my pilots respect me. Today I shoot three enemy out of the sky. How many men have done that in one day? Not many, for sure less than the fingers on one hand. But the day I achieve this, the glory hounds of my squadron ensure I am not the top scorer in the *Luftstreikrafte*, or my *Jasta*. I am not even top scorer in my family!"

The roars of laughter from the pilots emboldened the reporter. "Some people say Lothar is an even better flyer than you," Schultz said. "Would you agree, *Rittmeister*?"

The sudden silence made Lothar smile. Even he would never have dared to voice such a thought in front of Manfred, but he enjoyed his brother's irritation at Schultz's presumption.

Manfred stared at the reporter with those gun-barrel blue eyes, and the latter shrivelled. Then Manfred relaxed, although his eyes remained cold. "Perhaps he is a more reckless flyer, Herr Schultz, but not a better shot!"

Lothar pulled a face in jest and mocked the local French hand gesture for *"comme ci, comme ça."* As he did so, he saw thunder build on Manfred's face. Hastily he added, "My brother is my inspiration. I learn everything from him." The other pilots laughed nervously. No-one wanted to be on the end of Richthofen's famed 'death stare'. When the pale-blue gun barrels turned your way, fears of disgrace, dishonour and dismemberment flooded your mind.

And if you thought that was an exaggeration, then you hadn't been on the receiving end...

~

Hans Schmettow responded to Richthofen's summons and strode up the stairs of the Chateau Roucourt two steps at a time. Each footfall of his gleaming cavalry boots clicked off the marble steps and echoed around the stone stairwell in a most satisfactory way. No doubt Richthofen wanted to congratulate him on his kill earlier today.

Hans knocked and entered the room, which must have been a library under previous management. Bookshelves lined one long wall, now crowded with four dozen silver cups that gleamed even in the dim light of the office. Maps covered the other walls, numerous black and red rings showing friendly and enemy airfields. Richthofen sat behind a heavy wooden desk, and the podgy reporter stood in front like a pupil receiving a dressing down from the headmaster. Hans suppressed a smirk. For once, someone else was receiving the tongue-lashing, and Hans would be accepting the congratulations. It made a pleasant change.

"At ease, *Leutnant*," Richthofen said. "Wait and say nothing until I have finished with *Herr* Schultz. Professor, no more wisecracks in public about my brother being a better flyer than me. After the war you may write what you like. However, while the war lasts, you will write what serves the war effort. When you write about my *Jasta*, I decide what serves best."

Hans stared over Richthofen's blond head while he waited his turn. His back ached from his rigid posture. "At ease" was a relative term in the Prussian army, and Hans had learned long ago not to take it literally.

Richthofen sprang from his desk and looked out the high window where dusk was turning into night. He clasped both hands behind his back. "*Herr* Schultz, there can only be one herd bull in a *Jasta*, and in *Jasta* 11 that is me. Lothar, like most younger brothers, does not want to acknowledge that fact. He does so right now because he has a far lesser score. While Lothar lives, he may score faster than me. But only because I am a sportsman, and he is a butcher."

"What's the difference?" Schultz muttered, his mouth sullen.

Hans admired the pressman's balls. It was a good question, and not one that Hans would have dared ask.

"When I get my first kill of the day, it satiates me for at least a quarter of an hour," Richthofen said. "It is enough. Of course, I kill more if I can, for the emperor. But my brother is a butcher. He kills one, and it sparks a lust in him for more. I have seen him shoot down his second before the first has hit the ground. So one day Lothar may overtake me, if he lives long enough. He is too reckless." Richthofen smiled but there was no warmth in it. "After all, you can be herd bull even if you do not cover the most mares, so long as everyone understands that you have the pick of the mares when you want them."

Hans struggled to keep his face blank. The man was a megalomaniac.

A knock on the door interrupted them. "*Kommen sie*," Richthofen said.

Oberleutnant Bodenschatz, Richthofen's adjutant, appeared around the door. "*Rittmeister*, your car leaves in five minutes for your appointment with General Thomsen."

"*Sehr gut*. Professor, tell my servant to give you a bottle of schnapps," Richthofen said. "You will need it, for you will write of our triumphs until late into the night. Tell the German people how my *Jasta* shot down the equivalent of a whole British squadron in a single day. Next month, I will form the first ever Hunting Group—*Jagdgeschwader*—of four *Jastas*, with four times the planes I command today. The German public should know of these things; it will take their mind off the food shortages. And the British must know of it, too. I want them to imagine with dread hearts what Richthofen can do when he has not ten but forty planes under his command. If my *Jasta* alone can shoot down eighty planes in a month, then my *Jagdgeschwader* will shoot down 250 a month."

"Why tell them this?" Schultz asked, "Are you not afraid they will then keep clear of your new formations?"

Richthofen looked pleased with himself. "My dear Schultz, I study the psyche of our enemies. The French air force will read it, and many will avoid our sector. That means that our troops can make their movements in the secrecy they need. But the British are brave to the point of stupidity. Such an article will make them keener to prove that they will not be cowed. They will send over even more planes. Their generals will say, 'Richthofen is here, there must be something special to hide.' And so they will send sacrificial lambs in their plodding planes to see what we are hiding. For us it is far better to have our customers coming to our own shop rather than having to look for them."

Hans tuned out the words as Richthofen droned on. He let his eyes flick over the shelves behind Richthofen, inwardly snorting at the dozens of small silver trophies the baron had awarded himself, one for each kill. *Hope he gets a thousand and bankrupts himself.*

Abruptly Hans realised Richthofen had finished his lecture to the reporter and was talking to him.

"*Leutnant*, today you again strafed an enemy pilot on the ground. Our troops would have certainly captured and interrogated that man. This is the second time I have seen you do this. Why?"

"*Rittmeister*, don't you always say we should turn the enemy into flaming coffins in the sky?"

Richthofen nodded, the blue eyes as encouraging as chips of ice in a Prussian blizzard. Hans fought to keep his voice steady.

"Then *Rittmeister*, what is the difference between flaming him at five thousand metres and shooting him on the ground? Either way he is dead."

"The difference, *Leutnant* Schmettow, is precisely five thousand metres," Richthofen snapped. "Valuable altitude that takes us fifteen minutes to regain. That is a quarter of our available combat flight time. There are two points you need to learn. First, our job is aerial supremacy over our sector. That means we need to keep the allied bombers and reconnaissance from flying over our lines, which we cannot do while we are at ground level strafing downed pilots.

"To keep air supremacy, we must erode their resources while husbanding our own. The British have unlimited access to raw materials from all over their empire, and their cursed naval blockade prevents us getting those same materials. You wasted patrol time, altitude, ammunition, and fuel by following the Englishman down and shooting him. And it was Lothar's kill, not yours. Were you hoping to claim it yourself?"

"*Nein!*" The charge shocked Hans. Did Richthofen think Hans was that stupid? But Hans could not confess his lust for killing. He cleared his throat. "My only intent was to confirm the claim, to make sure the enemy pilot was not faking."

Richthofen glowered at him. "Lothar shot off the Englishman's propeller. Could he have flapped his arms all the way home?"

Hans bowed his head. "I did not see that."

"Then keep your eyes open in future!"

Hans clicked his heels together so hard that the room rang with the sound. "*Jawohl, Rittmeister!*"

Richthofen eyed Hans with distaste and continued the lecture. "Also, a duel in the air is a fight between soldiers. When you machine gun a pilot who has landed on our side of the lines, you murder a captive who can give us valuable information. My *Jasta* does not murder prisoners. A man with your hunting experience should know the difference between hunting a wild boar in the forest and shooting a pig in a pen. It must not happen again, or I will post you out of this *Jasta. Verstehen?*"

Hans' face burned at the rebuke, made worse for being in front of the reporter. He did not trust himself to speak but clicked his heels together again. To avoid those eyes, he stared rigidly over Richthofen's head. Seconds ticked past. A fly buzzed in the accusing silence. A drop of sweat ran down his spine. He kept his face impassive, his body immobile at attention. Prussian Military Academies taught that at least.

Richthofen's voice softened. "*Gut*. If you have learned your lesson, we will not speak of this again. Tomorrow you hunt with me again."

Hans bowed. "*Danke, Rittmeister*, you honour me." He hoped his face did not give away his true feelings. Fucking asshole. Another day at flight school with the Brothers Richthofen.

Richthofen rose to shake Shultz's hand. "When I come back from Berlin, the blood of English pilots will flow in streams. We will make the Allies long for the days of April with nostalgia. By the end of summer, the British air force will no longer exist. Germany will rule the skies, and our armies will strike with surprise. We will smash our way to Paris and sweep the British into the sea."

Richthofen's unblinking gaze and the utter certainty of his voice were those of a zealot, and Professor Schultz looked awestruck by Richthofen's vision of final victory. No doubt he was already penning the purple prose in his mind. Hans looked down to hide his cynicism. Richthofen was one of those bastards beloved by the gods who could thrust a hand into a toilet bowl and come up holding a bar of chocolate. But gods were fickle and one fine day even Manfred Richthofen might end up clutching a turd.

10
Hard Stubborn Bastards

Next day – 18 May 1917.
England, Sopwith Factory, Kingston.

When Lance saw his replacement Pup on the airfield at Kingston, he shut his eyes.

"Sorry it's a bit tired, sir," the mechanic said, his voice as mournful as his thinning hair and straggling grey moustache.

"Tired?" Lance's vehemence made the man take a step back. "'Tired' implies it will get better with rest. This aircraft isn't tired, it's a wreck. I'll have to stick my arms out and flap them to get across the Channel in this."

The mechanic coughed. "She's not that bad, sir."

Lance walked around the aircraft. Its fabric had been repaired so often it resembled a patchwork quilt. Old oil stains streaked the underside of the nose. The wings sagged forlornly, and the plane squatted on bowed undercarriage. "Really? You want to try fly across twenty miles of stormy sea in this piece of junk?"

"It's this or nothing, sir. She's the only one we could get."

Unbelievable. The might of the British Empire reduced to this sorry piece of equipment. Bloody strikers! His fists clenched and he felt a nerve in his cheek twitching as he thought of the bastards comfortable at home. He had to tackle the Circus with this? His best hope was they died laughing. The rumbling in his guts intensified, and his cheek twitch went rapid fire.

Lance took a deep breath. Venting at the mechanic wasn't going to change anything. He inhaled slowly and unclenched his fists finger by finger. "You think she'll reach France?"

"I've seen worse manage it, sir." The mechanic rubbed his fingers with an oily rag, like a man desperate to wash his hands of the whole thing.

Lance stared at him. "You've seen worse? God help me."

~

But the gutsy old girl carried Lance across the Channel. He refuelled at Saint-Omer and reached Le Hameau airfield at dusk.

He circled overhead, drinking in the glory of the resplendent sunset—one last treat before he re-joined the world at war. A thin wedge of cirrus cloud rippled across a soft blue sky tinged with myriad shades from pale pink to a glowing orange. Like many of the best things in life, sunsets came free.

Strange to think that only yesterday he'd made love to Megan under the cherry trees in her garden. For two blissful days, they had interspersed long love sessions with hard bouts of horse riding. Megan put them both on large raw-boned hunters and led Lance into the rolling country. Lance considered himself a good horseman, but from the moment she challenged him to keep up and set her mount at a towering hedgerow, he realised she was out of his league. She wore a long skirt and mounted side-saddle yet rode like a trooper and vaulted the highest hedgerows. Her tight riding jacket emphasised her curves, and the frantic exercise and chill air flushed her cheeks and made her dark eyes flash. The bedroom romps and exhilarating outdoor gallops exhausted his body but rejuvenated his spirit. For once, nightmares of tumbling planes and flames did not invade his sleep.

This morning he'd woken in Exenrude Keep, swathed in white satin sheets and spooning warm buttocks, soft hair tickling his nose and filling it with her scent. Tonight, he'd sleep on a wooden cot under coarse serge blankets, surrounded by the stink of unwashed flying gear. Tomorrow, an unshaved batman would wake him with a rough shake and a cup of army tea strong enough to paint his teeth black.

He sighed and banked the Pup over the attractive village. Lance had been to Le Hameau before with 13 Squadron, and its bucolic surroundings made it his favourite airfield in France. He treasured the peaceful orchard on the far side of Filescamp Farm, where he could loaf between patrols, sprawled in a deck chair in dappled shade, munching apples and listening to the drowsy bees. Hidden from the noisy airfield by the orchard trees and a slight rise, he could dream of anything but war.

He turned into the wind and began his approach towards Filescamp Farm, a hotchpotch of moss-covered buildings surrounding a pond. He blipped the rotary engine off and on to lose height and drifted in to land, compensating for the sloppy controls of the tired training aircraft. The Pup's shadow ran far in front of him, then came closer and closer as he descended, merging on the blurred green grass as the wheels and tailskid kissed the ground.

He taxied the Pup with bursts of engine across the empty landing strip, towards a corrugated iron hangar where yellow light glowed behind canvas flaps. As he did so the engine skipped a beat, then another. The old girl was wheezing. But she'd got him here. That was something to celebrate. Not a lot, it must be said, but these days Lance was learning to be happy with less.

A huge figure emerged from the hangar, wiping a rag over oily fingers thick as screwdriver handles. Sergeant Major Smythe was hard to miss at six feet three inches tall with a barrel chest to match, and a handlebar moustache that curled upwards like the horns of a Cape buffalo. The man exuded competence and ruled with a rod of iron over the fitters, riggers, and mechanics. Lance cut the engine and jumped down from the cockpit, clutching the duffel bag he'd housed on his lap during the flight.

Smythe ran a hand along the loose bracing stays of the wings and frowned. "This is one sorry aeroplane, sah. Engine sounds rough, and the bracing wires, ailerons…" The sergeant major shook his head.

"Do what you can, Sergeant Major. I don't expect miracles."

"And you won't get them, sah. This plane is not fit to fly, never mind fight."

Lance's brusque tone closed the topic. "Listen, I didn't choose this decrepit piece of junk, but it's what the RFC gave me, so I'll be fighting in it. Anything new since I've been away?"

Smythe's lugubrious face brightened as though someone had flicked a switch. "Yes, sah! Come look at these."

Lance followed Smythe into the hangar and found two Nieuport 17 fighters parked by the entrance. The Nieuport, small and nimble like the Pup, had played a full part in defanging the Fokker Scourge, and many of the British and French aces flew them. But the new Albatross DIII utterly outclassed it. Then Lance noticed one of the Nieuports had a red spinner, and his eyes widened. "Albert Ball!"

"Indeed, sah. The man himself. Arrived this afternoon. Seems like a right gent if I may say so."

Lance had never met Britain's leading ace, but there wasn't a man alive he admired more. Even so, he did not understand Smythe's conspiratorial grin. Ball or no Ball, the Circus would massacre the wing if it went into battle in these obsolete planes.

"But even better, sah." Smythe motioned deeper into the gloomy hangar.

There lurked the long, lean shadow of an SE5. "You beauty!" Lance stepped closer, entranced all over again. He caressed the enormous engine cowling, the sleek fuselage. "I was told there were none available! 'Cos of a bloody strike."

"They say the prime minister told the workers two days ago they were aiding the enemy with their strikes, and if they did not start work chop-chop, he would replace them with women, and send them to the front. Hey presto, an SE5 arrived this afternoon."

Lance laughed. "Good on Lloyd George! That's my sort of politician. Tell you what, Sergeant Major, we'll bloody the Circus with this."

Smythe's teeth gleamed in the gloom, and he gestured at another shadow. "Captain Thompson feels the same about the Camels, sah."

"Thompson?" Lance knew him by reputation. A Canadian on a hot streak of kills in April, though still behind Lance's total of twenty-one. "Mmm," Lance murmured, disbelieving that anyone could love a plane more than the warlike SE5.

Smythe led the way to a squat and pugnacious looking biplane with a pronounced dihedral slant to the lower wings. A hump in front of the pilot housed the twin Vickers machine guns and had inspired the plane's name, but the Camel reminded Lance more of a bulldog with its blunt head, powerful shoulders, and short haunches. The rotary-engine Camel originated from the same Sopwith design stable as the Pup, though it traded the elegance of the latter for brute power and agility.

Next to it stood a two-seater monster rearing high off the ground with a square fuselage, massive wide wings, a huge engine cowling, and two big axe blade propellers.

"Bristol F2 fighter, sah!" Smythe proclaimed, patting its side like a lion tamer.

"Now that is a bare-knuckled bruiser of an aircraft," Lance muttered, but he didn't fancy having to haul that rugged monster around the sky. "Who are these for, Smythe?"

"Prototypes, sah. Compliments of Major Baring. He said General Trenchard will court-martial anyone who goes within five miles of the lines in one of these. Major Hawker is to choose which type he wants for the new wing."

"When do we get to test them, Smythe?"

"The others have flown them, sah. We'll get you up tomorrow morning first thing."

"Grand! Any idea where Major Wolsey is?"

"Heading for the orchard, sah, last time I saw him."

~

Lance sauntered over to the orchard but found it deserted. The sunset still lingered, so he sat in one of striped deck chairs and watched the last glow of the sunset fade away. In this deluged French summer such glorious sunsets were treasures worth attention.

It also delayed meeting Arthur, an event Lance was dreading. Megan had been emphatic. "For God's sake don't tell Arthur we are lovers. He gets very protective and jealous of men he thinks have designs on me."

The strategy of silence suited Lance. He didn't have a sister, but if he did, he would not be chuffed if someone slept with her the same day they met. But lovemaking with Megan hadn't seemed sordid at the time, and still didn't.

Lance hated dissembling, especially to Arthur. He dawdled a little longer in the deckchair, delaying the inevitable, until the whine of the small French mosquitoes drove him from the orchard towards the officers' Mess. In the darkness he took a deep breath, squared his shoulders, and pushed open the door.

~

Arthur sat alone, reading and smoking a cigar in a comfy-looking lounge chair. He smiled as Lance entered. "Welcome home." Arthur spread his arms to indicate the long and comfortable room with a brick fireplace. It had been a shambles last time Lance had seen it, with broken furniture littered everywhere from the previous squadron's farewell binge.

Now the mess anteroom boasted furnishings of a quality rare for the RFC in France. A piano gleamed in a corner, and a long mahogany bar with a gleaming brass foot rail filled one wall. Deep lounge chairs and low tables provided comfort, and a newfangled record player sat on a sideboard. Only a battered ping-pong table survived from the inherited furniture.

"My word," Lance said, "someone has waved a magic wand while I've been away."

Arthur laughed. "I threw money at the sergeant major, and he has been ransacking the local towns. How is my lady wife?"

Lance cleared his throat. He felt as though he had "Megan's lover" branded on his forehead, and his words sounded forced to his own ears.

"I never met her. She had left for a week in London before I got there."

Arthur frowned. "Damn. She never tells me when she stays at the London house. Ah well, sorry I sent you on a wild goose chase. So, what did you do?"

"Oh, just hung around the area, enjoyed the sights and some riding." His cheeks flamed with the unintended double entendre.

"Excellent! It is good to have you back."

"I met your sister."

Arthur stopped smiling. "Megan? What in hell's name did she want with you?"

Arthur's vehemence appeared to bear out Megan's advice. Lance shrugged. "Nothing much. She asked after you."

"That is all?"

Lance nodded, holding Arthur's gaze with an effort.

Arthur relaxed. "There are things I should warn you about Megan, old family history. If I do not conceive an heir, her son will inherit the Wolsey Estate. I reckon if the Germans shot me down, she would crack open the champagne in a heartbeat. I don't suppose she told you about—"

The door banged open, and two officers entered the mess. "Aha," Arthur said. "Captains Albert Ball and Brian Thompson, meet Lieutenant Lance Fitch."

Lance swivelled towards Albert Ball. Despite his massive reputation, the youngster was short and slight as a jockey. Intense eyes burned in a clean-shaven face under dark hair rebelliously longer than regulations.

Lance offered a hand. "Call me Lance."

Ball nodded a greeting and pulled a rag from his pocket to wipe his hands. "Sorry, wait a second…bit oily."

Lance smiled. "Don't worry." Ball was only twenty years old but eighteen months of war flying showed. Plum-coloured shadows haunted his eye sockets and a tic pulsed in his right cheek.

His fingers wiped clean, Ball offered his hand and a guarded smile. "Albert." The gaze was steady and the handshake quick and decisive.

Lance turned to greet Thompson, who sported a meticulously clipped ginger moustache above a square jaw ridged with muscle. Pale grey eyes met Lance's and then flicked away as if searching the room for hidden questions. "Mama Thompson christened me Brian, but anyone who wants to be my friend had better call me 'Thommo'," he announced in a confident voice with a strange transatlantic twang.

"Thommo it is," Lance said as they shook hands. The crushing grip shocked Lance and the small bones in his hand creaked with strain. He struggled to keep his face impassive and Thommo's grey eyes gleamed as he prolonged the handshake. What the hell!

At last, Thommo released him with a big smile and turned away to the bar and rang the bell to summon the steward. "A drink! What do you boys want? This round is on me."

Lance flexed his hand—no broken bones, but it wasn't for want of trying. He looked up to find Arthur laughing at him. Even Albert Ball wore a tight-lipped grin.

"What's so bloody funny?" Lance asked.

"He did the same to Albert and I, but we squealed so he let us go straight away," Arthur said. "I bet Thommo he couldn't make you squeal, so you got the extra treatment. Strong little bloke, isn't he? Even if he did lose the bet."

Lance wrung his hand. "That grip of his is a cheat—you can't fight back. But it'll only work once when you aren't expecting it. You might have warned me."

"And missed you trying to keep a poker face as he mangled your digits? Priceless!"

"Glad you found it funny. Infantile games. That's my flying and shooting hand. Wouldn't be any good in plaster."

"He's right," Albert Ball said.

"Relax, Lance," Arthur said. "No harm done. I was afraid you'd punch him if I didn't make it a joke."

The door at the far end of the Mess opened and a limping orderly appeared.

"Whisky," Thommo ordered. He drummed both hands on the wooden bar top while he waited, then downed the whisky in a single gulp and tapped the bar for a refill.

"Don't be so stingy," he said to the barman, and held three fingers against the glass to show the desired tot. Then whisky in hand he turned to his fellow pilots. "What did you all say you wanted?"

"Good evening, O'Reilly," Arthur said to the barman. "Shrapnel in your leg giving you gyp today?"

The orderly grimaced. "Some days are better than others, sir, thank you for asking. Your usual malt, sir?"

"If you would be so kind but serve these gentlemen first. Lemonade, Lance? Albert?"

Lance nodded.

"Same," Albert Ball said.

"Teetotallers, huh?" Thommo asked. "That saves my wallet. So, Lance, flown the new planes yet?"

"I flew the SE5 in England but not the others."

Thommo leaned forward conspiratorially, a man about to reveal the long-lost location of El Dorado. "Don't bother," he confided, "Sopwith Camels are the only choice that makes sense." He leaned back, hitched a boot on the foot rail, and punctuated his words with jabs of his whisky glass. "Give me a squadron of Camels, and I will knock down so many of those Circus crowd they'll dread the day they met Mama Thompson's boy. Two guns at last, side by side. And with the turning circle of the Camel, none of the Huns will be able to live with me."

Thommo's pale grey eyes raked the others, challenging them to disagree.

Arthur took a diplomatic sip of wine, and Albert Ball gave the Canadian a thoughtful glance. Lance bit back his immediate vehement response in defence of his beloved SE5, remembering his promise to Arthur to be diplomatic in the new wing.

"Perhaps we shouldn't close our minds to the SE5?" Lance said. "I haven't flown the Camel yet, but the SE5 also has two guns, is much faster, and I'm told it has a better ceiling and high-altitude performance."

"Rubbish," Thommo said. "Sure, the SE5 is good, but in an exceptional pilot's hands the Camel is the best. A killer."

"If you are in a dogfight maybe," Lance replied. "But first we have to catch the Huns, and that takes speed. Against the Pup, the Albatross pour on the power and run away from us, and the Camel isn't much faster. If you are at a tactical disadvantage over the Huns' side of the lines, you could dive away in an SE5. It'll be the fastest scout in the skies. You won't outrun the Albatross in a Camel."

"You'd pick a plane because it allows you to run away? Attack and shoot the bastards down, I say."

Lance fought his rising fury and attempted a neutral tone. "The SE5 can catch those high-flying Hun reconnaissance aircraft—"

"Bugger the two-seaters! Our job is to kill the Richthofen pilots." Thommo downed the remnants of his whisky and eased off the foot rail and onto his toes like a boxer re-entering the centre of the ring for another round. Even his short ginger-blond hair bristled.

Lance's diplomatic veneer vanished. "If you listened for once and—"

Arthur cut across him. "Albert? What do you think?"

Lance steamed while Albert Ball considered the question for a couple of seconds. "I fight the same way as Thommo. Attack and just scrap. It works for me, and the Camel is more like the Nieuport which I love, but even more manoeuvrable and with extra firepower and a bit more speed." Ball ran his fingers through his tangled black hair and left a smudge of oil on his forehead. "But the Camel is tricky for most pilots, and they'll like the speed of the SE5. For the wing and squadron operations I think it should be the SE5, but I'd like a Camel for my solo flights."

"That's a cop out," Thommo protested. "Don't be selfish. If you prefer the Camel, get the Camel for everybody. Don't sit on the fence, have the balls to commit."

Lance smiled to himself. Although usually diffident, Ball carried a notorious history of bluntness when provoked, one that had aggravated numerous superior officers.

Ball said nothing but turned his intense dark eyes on Thommo and waited. The two men locked stares for a second before Thommo's grey eyes flicked away. Lance put Thommo as five years older than Ball, but his aggression seemed brittle in the face of Ball's understated certainty.

The Canadian broke the deadlock with a laugh. "Mama Thompson always told me I had a big mouth. The balls remark was out of line. Sorry. But you should commit." He flashed a grin. When Thommo's chin jutted, it announced he would like to ram your words back down your throat. And if they didn't fit, too bad, he'd cram them in anyway. But when he laughed, his wide, lazy smile invited you to laugh with him as his best friend. It was one hell of a smile. You found yourself grinning back, even while you wondered why. But if the face was as changeable as summer storms, capable of moving from jutting jaw to beaming smile in the time of a lightning strike, the flatness in the pale grey eyes altered not a jot.

"I have committed," Albert Ball said. "The SE5 would be best for the wing even though I don't like it so much myself."

"Sweet Jesus! Why can't you all see the flaming obvious—get Camels and we will rule the sky."

"Listen chaps," Arthur said. "Major Hawker will be the one deciding, so why don't we hold our fire for then? In the meantime, I know a nice little estaminet down the road. What do you say to us adjourning there for dinner?"

"Darn good idea," Thommo said. "I'll get my coat."

Lance waited until Thommo exited before he spoke. "Why is he so bloody opinionated and obstinate?"

"For the same reason as you, and Albert." Arthur said. "Because if you weren't, none of you would be top aces. You're what you need to be to take on Richthofen's crew—hard, stubborn bastards."

11
Attack Everything!

Next day – 19 May 1917
France, Arras Sector, Le Hameau Airfield. RFC, 100 Wing.

Nerves fluttered in Lance's stomach as the sun burned off the early morning mist.

He was ready. The big wooden propeller ticked over in front of him as he completed his take-off checks. Test pilots at Sopwith had told him that thirty per cent of maiden Camel flights resulted in crashes. Tommy Sopwith had packed ninety per cent of the aircraft's weight into the first seven feet of the eighteen-foot plane, a unique front-loading ratio that gave it hair-trigger responses to the controls and some weird flight characteristics. The gyroscopic effect of the powerful rotary engine torquing the propeller shaft at 1,250 rpm exacerbated these quirks. "It's designed to do things no other aircraft will do," said the Sopwith test pilots, "and it does, for better and worse!"

Not only were Camel crashes more frequent than most, but also more fatal. Three hundred pounds of hot engine sat almost in the pilot's lap and a fuel tank nestled against his back. If the engine did not crush the pilot into a bloody mess in a crash, a ruptured fuel tank would baste him in petrol that would ignite when it touched the red-hot engine. In the unlikely event that neither of these apocalypses occurred, the machine gun butts would likely stove in the pilot's face. In short, Lance was looking forward to his first Camel flight with the sort of anticipation he normally reserved for gelding a stallion back on Taveta Farm.

But Lance needed to fly the Camel to earn credibility for his opinion that the SE5 would be the best aircraft for the new wing. So far Hawker had shown no sign of where his own preferences lay, but Lance knew he had already canvassed the others. Arthur had chosen the versatility of the big Bristol two-seater, and Albert Ball had given the same mixed message that he had expressed the night before in the officers' Mess. With Thommo so forceful for the Camel, Lance seemed alone as a strong advocate for the SE5.

As the ground crew swung him into the wind, he saw the others had come to watch the fun, standing beside the hangars in the weak dawn sunshine. The windsock hung limp, and the Camel's wheels had left tracks through the dew-laden grass. He listened one more time to the engine's raspy snarl, full of raw power and more threatening than the Pup's genteel purr. The nasty taste of the burned castor oil chucked off by the rotary engine already coated his throat and nose. He took a deep breath and opened the magnetos for good.

None of the warnings had prepared him for the reality.

The engine pulled like a chained typhoon, catapulting the Camel down the runway, swerving thirty degrees left. Lance eased on right rudder. The Camel ignored him and hurtled towards the line of hangars. Lance stomped on full opposite rudder as his tailskid lifted. His plane ceased veering left but refused to steer away from the hangars.

Christ! Can't go left, won't go right. The only way is up!

The dark mass of the hangar blocked his view as it loomed closer. Lance shut his eyes and pulled the Camel off the ground—and the nose shot towards the heavens. Whoa! He eased off the stick, but the nose still pointed far too high. The aircraft juddered a stall warning, and Lance heaved the stick forwards. The nose pitched down and picked up speed again, just in time for Lance to ease up the nose before he ploughed into the ground. Sweat trickled down his armpits. He'd been a heartbeat away from burying himself twice in the first thirty seconds.

He took the Camel up to eight thousand feet, where he had plenty of height to recover from a stall or spin, and played with the new fighter. He banked right without rudder and the wings banked, but the nose went left in a massive adverse yaw. *It'll fool the Huns no end, they'll think I'm going right when I go left.*

Next time he applied heavy right rudder before he banked, to correct the yaw and execute a classic banking turn. That was the plan. But the nose pitched down, and the next second the earth spun below Lance in a howling spiral as the plane flicked over and over like a falling autumn leaf. Castor oil sprayed his face, and his stomach heaved as he ricocheted around the cockpit. He shut off the petrol and applied full forward opposite stick and rudder. The world stopped revolving around him, but now the Camel was falling in an almost vertical dive with a nasty sideslip. The unusual combination left him dizzy and hanging against his harness. By the time he fought the nose level again he had lost four thousand sickening feet. His head swirled and bile flooded his mouth. *What a savage bitch!*

Lance turned the engine back on and climbed to eight thousand feet again. Through trial and error, he found the worst vices could be mastered by an experienced pilot, and even turned into virtues in a dogfight. He formed a grudging respect for the quirky plane that was like nothing he had ever flown. But it was exhausting to fly. The stick needed constant forward pressure or the nose would climb into a stall, and his legs ached from constant use of the rudders, which the plane more or less ignored while responding instantly to the elevators. Sometimes Lance felt the plane flew sideways. Trying to fly straight was like balancing an egg on the point of a needle, and he vowed never to turn right with engine on while under a thousand feet.

Pilots who wanted to be a dervish in a dogfight would love this plane like a mistress. The quirks that could kill you at low altitude could also be lifesavers with a Hun on your tail at more than six thousand feet. Any Albatross pilot insane enough to attempt following a Camel's contortions would find himself without wings. Now he understood why Thommo loved the Camel. It mirrored Thommo's own character: chippy, aggressive, and dangerous to anyone taking liberties, whether friend or foe.

Pilots such as Lance, who worshipped speed and height and a stable gun platform, would loathe the jittery Camel. The Camel might have been a lot better than a Pup, but it was a terrible alternative to the SE5. Hawker, as an engineer, would prefer reasoned logic to Thommo's emotional appeals, and Lance planned his pitch accordingly.

He finished his flight and taxied the Camel to the hangars. His ears buzzed with the waspish snarl of the rotary engine. As he climbed out, Hawker emerged from the hangar holding a rag that he offered to Lance. "Nice take off, Fitch! Here. The oil on your face tells me you found the secret to making a Camel turn!"

Lance took off his leather helmet, wiped his face with the dirty rag, and acknowledged the dig with a rueful smile. "That is one hell of a demanding plane, sir."

"Don't worry about it. I did the same for the take off and the spin. What do you think of her?"

Lance took a deep breath. "Thommo is right, with a skilled pilot she'll be a Hun killer in a dogfight. But she's slow compared to the Albatross or Pfalz."

"That's true, but that means pilots will have to shoot down all the Huns to come home because they can't run away."

Lance glanced at Hawker to see if he was joking, but there was no smile. Hawker wouldn't choose the Camel, surely?

Lance cleared his throat and hurried on with his assessment. "Also, the fuel tank is too small, so patrol time will be half an hour less on the Camel compared to the SE5. And her performance becomes very soggy above twelve thousand feet where the Albatross like to lurk." Lance paused. "It has to be the SE5 for me, sir."

Hawker rubbed his forehead, leaving a greasy streak. "All three planes are a dream compared to my DH2. I agree with Thommo that the Camel is a wonder..." Hawker paused and darted a look at Lance, "but all things considered the SE5 is my pick."

Lance couldn't prevent a broad smile from splitting his face.

Hawker smiled. "Had you worried there, eh, Fitch? But you'd better let me break the news to Thompson. I don't think he'll be happy."

Who knew? Hawker had a sense of humour after all.

"By the way, Fitch, HQ wants us to send up a patrol this afternoon. They know the wing is not yet active, but they are short of pilots and planes. Our new planes are not allowed near the lines, so we'll use our old planes for a patrol at 1600 hours. The patrol will be you and I, plus Forrester from my old squadron. He joined the wing this morning and brought his own DH2.

"And Major Wolsey recommended you for a flight commander. I'm not convinced. I reckon you are too much of a loner, but I'm willing to give you a chance. You lead this patrol and if you pass muster, I'll make you a flight commander. Remember—'Attack. Attack. Always attack.' Let's see what you can do, eh?"

The smile slipped from Lance's face. The last thing he wanted was to be a flight commander; it would curtail his freedom to fly when and where he wished. But he'd promised Arthur he would not antagonise Hawker, so he nodded and kept his mouth shut as Hawker left. It would be worth it when he took on the Huns in a SE5. He closed his eyes and repeated Francis' invocation—"They have sown the wind, and they shall reap the whirlwind."

~

At the afternoon patrol briefing, Hawker introduced 2nd Lieutenant Forrester, a lanky twenty-year-old with flaxen hair, more pimples than chin hair, and a confident smile. "He's an up-and-coming champ," Hawker said, ruffling Forrester's hair. "Seven kills in two months. Flies like a dream, and his shooting isn't bad. We'll see if we can get you another kill today, eh, Forrester?"

The pimply boy gave Hawker a look of hero worship and punished the air with a flurry of shadow boxing punches. Lance rolled his eyes. Another public schoolboy twit who thought of war as a sport. The Huns wouldn't roll over for a decrepit Pup and two DH2s. This patrol would be about survival rather than chalking up victories. Oh the irony, if Lance died just before he got the SE5. No, today's aim would be to stay alive.

But Hawker did not agree. "Attaboy, Forrester. Attack, always attack! Alright, Fitch, give us the patrol gen."

Lance tried to give the classical pre-patrol briefing that Arthur had coached into him. "HQ wants us to patrol from Arras south to Bapaume…" Lance stopped in disbelief as Forrester squeezed an enormous white spot on his cheek until it popped.

"Sorry," the teenager said, flushing a tender shade of red. Hawker suffered a coughing fit. Lance stared hard at Forrester, and then marginally less hard at Hawker, before resuming the brief.

After take-off, Lance led the flight up to twelve thousand feet for the planned patrol south of Arras. At this stage of a patrol with 13 Squadron, Lance's habit was to "lose" his companions. He operated better alone and found it irksome to fly as part of a flight, even when leading it.

But Arthur had anticipated his impulse. "Don't make an ass of me, again, after I recommended you. Stick to him like glue, or I will ground you when you return."

So, Lance kept a close eye on the two DH2 planes spread behind him in a V shape. A blue streamer fluttered from Hawker's struts, denoting his status as a squadron leader. Lance admired Hawker's determination to come on this patrol. The Pup might be outclassed, but Hawker's DH2 was positively antiquated. Forrester no doubt thought it was a game, and may the best man win, but Hawker understood the risk he was taking.

As they approached the front, Lance cleared his mind, and his eyes began a methodical quartering of the sky. The trick was not to stare; the eyes picked up small movements better from the peripheral vision. Bitter cold seeped through his flying coat and boots as they droned south through the light blue sky, dodging occasional clouds. The winds were strong and pushed them east deeper into Hunland, forcing Lance to correct course from time to time.

Below them, the trenches coiled like intertwined snakes as the old and new trenches merged and meshed in the chalky soil. South of Arras the soil changed often, and the snakes turned from chalk white to clay red or loam black. The old hands could navigate by the soil colours of the trenches, unlike up north where the trenches writhed in a uniform brown.

The patrol reached Bapaume and turned back north. Clouds were building now, solid white galleons scudding fast across the sky, pushed by that strong west wind. More hiding places for ambushers, friend or foe. Minutes later Lance saw two dark crosses flitting across the brown and green earth at six thousand feet over Achiet.

Proud to have noticed them before the great Hawker, Lance alerted the others by waggling his wings and stabbing his gloved hand at the enemy. He blocked the disc of the sun with his gloved thumb and searched the glare for long eye-watering seconds. Then he checked the nearby clouds above and below. The Huns often dangled two-seaters as bait for the unwary, but he saw nothing. He tightened his harness, then rolled the Pup into a plunging dive.

Wind whistled through the wires and the engine howled, and together they stirred Lance's hunting blood. He whooped as the British fighters plunged on their prey, falcons swooping on fat pigeons. The Huns, Roland two-seaters, fled into their own dive eastwards.

Lance's exhilaration faded quickly. The supposed pigeons dived as fast as the falcons. He smacked the cockpit rim in frustration. If he had an SE5… With an effort, he bridled his runaway thoughts. 'If'; the most useless word in the English language.

He looked behind to check the others were behind him. *How the—? It's raining Albatross!* His heart thumped, and his stomach clenched.

It didn't matter how he'd missed them. The Huns had played him as a sucker. He had seconds to decide. His eyes narrowed as he computed the distances. The Albatross would catch his flight before his flight caught the two Rolands. The Huns outnumbered them three to one with the wind blowing them deeper into Hunland. Best to run away to fight another day. Lance pulled hard out of the dive, swung away from the approaching Albatross, and fled for the Allied lines.

He looked around to check for the others. Forrester was with him, but Hawker was still diving on the Rolands. *Damnation! Didn't he see them, or doesn't he care?*

"Attack everything" was a fine motto that Hawker had made famous throughout the RFC, but this was beyond common sense. It could kill them all. But Lance couldn't abandon his major. It'd be cowardice in the face of the enemy. He swung east again, and the hammering of his heart was louder than the howling engine. Forrester turned with him. Lance sensed the youngster's big eyes looking across the narrow gap, and he dared not return the look. The boy was trusting him, and Lance was leading him into a fight against serious odds.

The Huns pounced. At the last possible moment, Lance turned hard into the attack. White tracer lines smoked past. Pursued by an avalanche of rainbow-hued Huns. The Pup rocked in the turbulence. Lance reefed into turns, the tightest he had ever made, muscles quivering as he threw the Pup around the sky, dodging the endless streams of tracers that searched for him. He turned and turned, skidded and dodged like a drunkard on roller skates.

An Albatross snarled towards him head-on and Lance accepted the challenge. He had no choice. To turn away was death. Twin lines of tracer flashed between his centre struts. His own single gun hammered back. Cordite bit at the back of his throat.

At the same time, a red and yellow Hun attacked from the side, guns flickering. *Ignore him, he's got the harder angle. With luck, he's a duff shot.* Lance hunched smaller in case Lady Luck did her usual lousy job.

Tracers slid towards him from front and left, their deadly web criss-crossing around him. *Tsk! Tsk! Tsk!* Bullets from the left stitched his wings. The holes smoked. Bullets from in front hammered into his engine with nasty thunks. He kept his finger on his trigger, the Pup shuddering with the recoil. The Albatross ahead reared up and fell away on one wing. Got him! Another burst from the left riveted Lance's petrol tank. Pungent fumes stung his nostrils. *Christ! If petrol gets on the engine, I'm a flamer!*

He shut the engine and ducked as the side attacker howled feet above his head. The silence of his dead engine tolled a death knell. Yet another Hun came at Lance from the side, deadly white fingers of tracer reaching for him. Lance was helpless without his engine. This was the end.

The Hun sheared away as Forrester fired at it from behind.

Lance's cheeks blew out. Saved by the pimply kid. *I owe you.*

Lance saw thick cloud a thousand feet below and half rolled his crippled plane into a dive. He twisted his neck to check pursuit.

Behind him, a twenty-foot banner of flame streaked the sky red and black. A DH2 on fire, no streamers. Forrester.

The boy had saved Lance, and his reward was a fiery death. A burning bundle jumped from the plane and tumbled earthwards. Lance vomited into his cockpit.

Even the Huns paused, transfixed by mutual horror.

As they hesitated, Lance escaped into the cloud. Clammy grey vapour blanketed the Pup and thick mist robbed him of his flying horizon, forcing him to rely on his other senses. With his engine dead, he flew by hearing. He eased the stick back until the howl of the wind through the wires faded to a muted whistle. Good flying sang true in the wires. A discordant moan through the rigging and a breeze on one cheek meant a sideslip, often a fatal precursor to a spin. Too little wind noise presaged a stall. He turned with careful bank and rudder until his compass swung onto a westward course as he glided through the eerie silent fog.

He burst into daylight without warning. It dazzled him, and he blinked against the glare as he searched the sky. The gaggle of Huns had vanished. It never ceased to amaze him how a crowded sky emptied like magic. Lancecalculated his glide to the British lines. Despite the strong wind pushing against him, he had enough altitude to cross without problems. His stomach, knotted since he first saw the Albatross, unclenched.

An aircraft burst from the cloud four hundred yards away. Sunlight glistened off the wet red fuselage as the white wings tilted, and the Albatross nosed towards the damaged Pup like a shark scenting blood.

~

Hans exulted when he noticed the Pup gliding towards British lines. An easy kill for his fifth, and one the ground troops could confirm. Five kills took him half-way to an ace. Fame beckoned.

He lined up behind the gliding plane and fired. The Pup skidded from the path of the bullets, and the Albatross overshot the gliding plane. Hans cursed; he'd forgotten how slow the Pup would be without an engine.

On the second pass Hans throttled back, almost to stall speed, and lined up the victim again. The Englander twisted around to watch him, trying to judge when Hans would open fire. Hans oscillated his gun sight across the Pup and imagined his enemy on the razor's edge of anticipation of his own death.

Hans caressed the triggers, scanning the face of the man staring back at him. *The Englander is too calm for my liking.* Hans triggered a split-second burst. The Englishman ducked as the tracers flashed past his head. *That's better!*

Minute adjustments of stick and rudder slid the sights onto the Pup again. Hans' thumb eased onto the triggers.

Before he could fire, bullets hammered into the Albatross from below. Startled, Hans thrust on full throttle and banked away. Who the hell was shooting at him from the German side of the lines? Holding the steep bank, he searched the ground and cursed. The German ground machine gunners, ignorant of deflection shooting, had hit his Albatross as they fired at the British plane just ahead of him.

Hans hauled the Albatross around for another attack, but the British pilot rammed his plane down among the shell holes in No-Man's-Land. The tail rose and cartwheeled the plane upside down onto its top wing.

Hans dived towards the crashed Pup. The Englishman wormed out of the upturned cockpit and lurched into a doomed run towards the British trenches a hundred metres away. Hans chortled at the man's panic, his stumbling lurch through the mud and his snatched glances over his shoulder. This was Hans' favourite game, the running rabbit. But all good things come to an end. He fixed the fleeing figure in the crosshairs of his sights. And fired.

Bullets stitched twin fountains of mud towards the target. The runner's arms hurled wide as he flew forwards. Hans soared into a climb, his scream of exultation matching the howl of Mercedes. *Kill number five! Eat that, all you Arschleckers in Jasta 11.*

~

Blood singing through his veins, Hans turned towards home. Five kilometres east, he saw two planes circling each other. He headed towards them, and found Manfred Richthofen duelling with a DH2 flying blue streamers.

The pair fought a remorseless battle, each trying to fly a tighter circle than the other to get on his opponent's tail. The British plane was nimbler, but the Albatross sported a more powerful engine. In the hands of these pilots, the planes looked matched in their turning circles. But Richthofen's extra power kept him higher, a crucial advantage. To get the Albatross in his sights, the Englishman would have to point his nose higher and thus lose speed. Then Richthofen would gain ground in the circle, bringing his sights closer to his opponent's tail.

Round and round went the duellists. Hans went dizzy just watching them. Whoever broke from the turn first would grant their opponent a fleeting but easy non-deflection shot. To break the circle against a good marksman invited death. Tracer flashed from both planes, but neither pilot won a killing opportunity.

Hans had no wish to join this duel. First, if this Englishman was skilful enough to give Richthofen trouble, he was too good for Hans. Second, ever since Boelcke had died in a mid-air collision with one of his own pilots, Richthofen preferred other pilots to keep out of his way. The baron's prey was his alone.

So, Hans stayed above the fray and enjoyed the show. He gave up counting the revolutions. Suddenly the DH2 reversed its turn. Richthofen fired and missed. The duellists still circled, but in the reverse direction.

The Englishman had to be running low on fuel and would have to break for home soon. Richthofen had every advantage, but the Englishman did not look worried. Hans saw him take one hand off the joystick and wave at his opponent. Hans smirked at the Englishman taking the piss out of Richthofen, even in an outclassed plane.

Still the duellists ratcheted into their circles, now less than a thousand metres above the ground, while the strong wind pushed them deeper into German territory with every turn.

Abruptly the English plane straightened and soared into a series of loops. They were crisp and tight and finished with the Englishman behind Richthofen. His gun hammered. Richthofen skidded inside the tracer lines.

Hans cackled in glee. Richthofen forbade his pilots from doing loops. "It's pretty flying that has no place in combat. It will get you killed while you hang on the top of the loop as a big fat target." Apparently Richthofen had forgotten to tell the Englishman.

While Richthofen finished his evasion, the Englishman ran for home. Hans, six hundred metres above and behind the pair, followed them as they raced westwards.

Richthofen's faster Albatross closed to within fifty metres as the Englishman zigged and zagged between the tracers like a will o' the wisp, as if its pilot was reading his pursuer's mind. Hunter and prey were now only thirty metres above the ground that blurred beneath the racing planes. Still Richthofen could not deliver the coup de grâce.

The front lines loomed. Soon Richthofen would have to give up the hunt or risk the British ground fire. His blood red Albatross closed even further until its propeller almost chewed the tail of the fleeing DH2. Tied together by invisible string the two planes raced towards No-Man's-Land—safety for the Englishman, danger for Richthofen.

Richthofen fired. A one second burst. The Englishman's head smashed forward. His plane's nose dropped and slammed into the ground in an explosion of mud and debris just two hundred metres from safety. The two red Albatross flashed over the wreckage and banked for home, unchallenged victors of the sky.

~

Lance watched Hawker's death from a shell hole in No-Man's-Land. When Lance fled from the strafing Albatross, he never saw the hole. He fell into it headfirst as he was looking back. The killing stream of bullets had thumped over him, a slap-slap-slap into the mud just over his head. He lay there, uncertain of what had happened, only the urgent hammering of his heart and the sucking pain in his winded lungs convinced him he still lived.

When he recovered sufficiently to claw himself to the lip of the crater, he was just in time to see Hawker's plane disintegrate into a welter of flying wood and metal, just a few hundred yards away from his refuge.

Lance slumped to the bottom of his shell hole, knee deep in stagnant mud. Many pilots said Hawker was the best flier in the RFC. If he couldn't take on the new Albatross, what chance did the rest have?

For the first time Lance noticed the stench. He looked around his shell hole. Rats chittered the far side, ignoring him as they feasted on a rotting corpse face down in the oozing mud. Frantic to escape, he scrambled out of the crater. As he did so a machine gun pounded from the German side of the lines. He leapt back into the hole as the bullets slapped into the mud above his head.

"Hey you! RFC man!" a voice bellowed at him from the British lines. "Wait there 'til dark and we'll come get you. Lie low. The Huns will shell your plane in a minute. Just hang on."

Lance sat in the puddle, shaking with the memory of Forrester's death, the falling bundle of flame as the boy burned his way to the ground. Lance clasped his head, trying to shake away the vision. Instead he saw Hamisi reaching out with bloody claws, his lidless eyes wide in their burning hell. He heard again the inhuman howls of agony and smelled the repulsive stench of cooked men. More than most, Lance knew Forrester's last moments.

He opened his eyes and focused on his hands. Blood smeared them, crusted under his fingernails. He scooped up mud to rub away the red stains and willed his hands to cease their shaking. But still they trembled.

He tried to reason away the shakes. Hawker had caused his own death by swaggering into this fight with everything—numbers, height, speed, machinery, firepower, and wind—against him. If Hawker had followed Lance in running for home, all of them might have lived to fight another day

Still his hands quivered. He slumped back helpless into his hole, liquid mud sloshing cold into his flying boots. The shriek of a shell split the sky. Lance cringed, expecting death. The blast swept over his head, but the pressure wave punched his ribcage and stabbed his eardrums.

A second shell struck, a third, now endless. Their separate explosions melded into one rolling fury, continuous thunder as the German batteries hunted the wrecked British airplane in No-Man's-land. Lance cowered as metal fragments moaned over him. Clods of mud spattered him.

The percussive thunder, the stench of explosives and the heaving earth unleashed the demons of Lance's shellshock. Great winds howled deep inside his skull. Icy whiteness sent tendrils to unshackle insanity. He curledup, a foetus in the fetid womb of the shell hole, hugging himself, eyes screwed shut, mumbling, "Please God, please God, please…"

He clutched at the remnants of his sanity and summoned the only help he knew—his hate. A flicker of flame fought against the clammy whiteness. He called on the ghosts of the fire-seared Hamisi, Will and his slithering brains, the torn meat that had been Sergeant Moss.

Still the artillery searched for him, a shrieking storm of shrapnel. Lance clenched his teeth and ground his jaw until it ached. The thoughts of retribution were dark and bloody, and he welcomed the hate with joy.

And then the barrage was over, the abrupt silence shocking.

He lay still while the last tendrils of clammy madness slithered back into their lair. He wiped the foul mud from his face and crawled to the lip of his crater. The barrage had obliterated his plane and churned the earth into a devil's playground of grotesque shapes. Smoke drifted, sour in his mouth, and his ears rang in the silence. He clenched his fists to stop his hands trembling.

Lance glowered eastwards at the empty sky. He'd recognised Richthofen's blood red Albatross as it wheeled away over his shell hole. Stoked by his hate, he swore new vows to the gods of revenge. Now he possessed, and was possessed by, his own quenchless feud against Richthofen and his murdering, ground-strafing pal with the white and red Albatross

When he looked down at his hands, they no longer shook.

1 2
Kill Bloody Richthofen!

Same day – 19 May 1917.
France, Saint-Omer. Royal Flying Corps HQ in
Western France.

Another sad day. Sometimes it seemed there was no end of sad days. Baring shut his eyes, took a deep breath, and replaced the phone on the hook with exaggerated care. He muttered a brief prayer for the departed and sidled into Boom Trenchard's office.

Boom scowled as he tamped tobacco into his pipe bowl. "What is it this time, Baring?" He lit a match.

"Hawker's dead, sir. Richthofen killed him earlier this afternoon."

The match in Boom's hand froze halfway to his pipe. Carefully, he shook the match until the flame went out. He placed the match in the ashtray and his head slumped to his chest, something Baring could not recall happening. A long silence ensued, until the large head lifted. "So, their man kills our man?"

"Looks that way, sir. Very Hector and Achilles."

"Eh?"

"Nothing, sir."

"What a disaster."

"I'm sure Major Hawker would concur, sir."

Boom did not register Baring's cynicism. "Was he shot down our side of the lines or theirs?"

"Theirs, sir."

"Damn and blast! Soon they will realise who they bagged, and their papers will trumpet it." The general sighed. "Well, small mercies, at least we had not announced his appointment so we can hush it up. Tell anybody who knows to keep their mouths shut about Hawker commanding a new anti-Richthofen unit. Shut, do y'hear! If it leaks that Richthofen killed him before he even formed the new wing, the RFC will be a laughingstock."

"I agree, sir. I'll make sure it does not leak."

Boom took a deep breath. "Hawker was a fine man." By Boom's standards that was a sentimental eulogy. "Who's the next best man for the job?"

"What about Arthur Wolsey himself? He was Hawker's first choice as a squadron leader, that says a lot."

Boom looked dubious. Baring knew the problem. Wolsey was many of the things that Boom disliked in his officers.

For starters, he was as aristocratic as they come. For five hundred years the Wolseys had ruled as one of England's most powerful noble families. Secondly, Arthur Wolsey wasn't regular army; he'd joined on the outset of war. Lastly, his fair hair, blue eyes and strong jaw, made him undeniably handsome. In Boom's view officers who were aristocratic, or non-regular army, or handsome, typically owned an inflated sense of self-worth. Wolsey possessed the first three of those attributes in spades, but without the self-importance.

"I know he's aristocracy, sir, and only a volunteer, but he's a good officer who understands military hierarchy. He's also an ace, not one of the top ones, but an experienced war flyer. His men love him, and he's as brave as a lion—one of the few majors who flies over the lines on a regular basis. He'd be a good choice, sir."

"I'm not convinced by Wolsey, and your last suggestion has turned out to be a disaster. I hope this one is better," Boom grumbled.

Baring almost choked on the unfairness of that comment, but years in the diplomatic corps had trained him well. "So do I, sir. So do I."

In Baring's experience Boom did not suffer from self-doubt, but the general's next words sounded as though he were seeking reassurance. "If their top man kills our top man on their first meeting, what chance is there of our new wing winning this battle?"

Baring rubbed his elbow as he considered. "Well, sir, two things give me cause for optimism. I am hopeful our new batch of planes will match or beat the Albatross. Also, Hawker was our first ever ace and famous for his VC and his flying skills. However, if we are brutally honest, he was past his best as a fighter pilot. He was at his zenith back in 1915 and 1916, and flying tactics have changed since those days. There are many more planes in the air, and the Hun tactics are more sophisticated. And war flying is a young man's game. Too much time at the front erodes the reactions and resilience of even the bravest of men, which Hawker certainly was. Based on the number of kills and the pace at which he scores them, Albert Ball is now our top ace, not Hawker."

"Bit bloody late telling me this now!"

"No, sir. We were looking for an inspirational wing commander who was an ace in his own right, not our top ace to duel theirs. Hawker fitted that first description as a leader, so too does Major Wolsey. Albert Ball is twenty years old and not wing commander material. We are lucky to have accomplished commanders like Shepard and Wolsey, and excellent individual fighter pilots like Ball. But nobody who combines both like Richthofen."

"The Germans seem to churn out a bloody conveyor belt of these people," Boom said. "Boelcke was their top ace and top tactics chap too, and he gave us no end of trouble in the Fokker Scourge. Then as soon as he dies, along comes Richthofen who turns out to be even better. Why don't we produce people who can do both?"

"Perhaps because Prussia has a tradition of regarding war as a science, whereas in England we see it as a game. Or it could be a coincidence. After all, Boelcke and Richthofen are only a sample of two. And we got Boelcke in the end."

"Got Boelcke? One of his own pilots flew into him! That's hardly getting him."

"Dead is dead, sir," Baring replied. "Does not matter how. If we can kill Richthofen, it is conceivable the Germans will find the conveyor belt ends."

Baring saw the glint coming back into his boss' eyes. Boom slammed his meaty paw onto his desk with a bang. The desk shivered and the paper trays jumped with fright.

"You're right, Baring. If we can't breed our own, we can take theirs away. That's the answer—kill bloody Richthofen! Get Wolsey here straightaway. I'll talk to him and see if I think he is the right man for the job."

Baring walked back to his office. The sun had come out while he was in Boom's office, and shadows from a pear tree danced on the wall across from the tall French windows. He stopped to admire the delicate blossoms as they nodded in the breeze. Last year the tree never bloomed and consequently produced no fruit. This year looked more hopeful.

~

"Come in!"

The sheer volume of Boom Trenchard's voice rattled the door, and Arthur entered the room with trepidation.

"Ah! Wolsey!" The general scowled at Arthur. "Baring has recommended you replace Hawker as commander of 100 Wing to hunt down and kill Richthofen. What do you think of that?"

Before Arthur could reply, Baring interceded: "How much did Hawker tell you before he died?"

"Not much, nothing more than the general has just mentioned."

Baring tapped a folder in his right hand. "100 Wing must ensure that Richthofen's pilots are not allowed to gain supremacy over their sector. We need to regain control of the air. Firstly, we must prevent the Huns' reconnaissance and gunnery aircraft from getting behind our lines. Secondly, we need control of the air for ten thousand yards behind *their* lines to aid our artillery efforts. Thirdly, we have to protect our own reconnaissance and bombing patrols deep behind Hun territory."

"For God's sake, Baring!" Boom snapped. "Stop repeating what I have just said. We have to kill the Richthofen buggers. Wolsey, what do you say?"

"I would be honoured to command 100 Wing, sir, if I were appointed."

"Humph." Boom lurched out of his chair and marched to the window where he gazed at the grey curtain of drizzle. "Hawker's death made us look bad. Their first choice shooting down our first choice before he even got his feet under the table."

Anger flooded Arthur. *Not half as bad as it made Hawker look. He's in the mud now.* He kept his mouth shut with an effort.

"The point is," Boom continued, still looking out the window, "we cannot afford another debacle. So, if you command this outfit, you won't be allowed to fly over the front lines."

The anger surged again. Hawker had been a fine man, and his death was a tragedy, not a debacle. "Then I cannot command 100 Wing, sir."

Boom pivoted, and his bushy eyebrows came together. "You would refuse an order?"

"Why, Major?" Baring intervened. "There are plenty of majors in charge of squadrons who never fly over the lines, some who never fly at all. And *you* would be commanding a wing, not just a squadron."

"Because you cannot lead the best pilots by sitting behind a desk. They need a leader who knows what they are going through, who knows the enemy. Richthofen does not sit behind a desk. Boelcke did not, and the best of our leaders do not—like Hawker. And if I pay the price for that, like Boelcke, like Hawker, then so be it."

"You could say," Baring countered, "that the same logic applies to infantry, and yet all infantry generals lead from the rear."

"Indeed they do, and how does their record stack up against Richthofen's?"

"You think you know better than the British army, young man?" Boom growled.

"No, sir. But fliers are not infantry, and I am not a general. As far as I know majors operate in the front line. If you want this idea to work, whoever leads it will have to lead in the air. And if you want the CO kept alive, give him a better plane than a DH2 or a Pup."

Arthur warmed to his theme. "And while we are discussing such things, the squadron leaders should not be pen pushers either. We need the best fighter pilots leading the squadrons in the air, whatever their age and their rank. Then buttress them with the best administrators on the ground so our aces are not wasting their time on paperwork."

Boom grunted. He opened a drawer, took out his pipe and matches, and lit the pipe with much puffing. Clouds of smoke rose and wreathed his face. "As of now, Wolsey, you are a lieutenant colonel (acting), and a flying one if you want. Baring, take Colonel Wolsey away before he upsets me. Give him everything he needs to make this a success. Get going!" Through the smoke, Arthur was not sure if there was a fierce grin or a grimace of disapproval.

The last exhortation rattled the windows, and Baring hustled Arthur out of the room and into his own office. "Congratulations on your promotion, well deserved." Baring's smile somehow managed to both praise Arthur and simultaneously pity him. "Right, let's get down to details. Which of the new prototype planes would you choose for your wing?"

Arthur pulled a face. "There is a strong debate about that. If it is alright with you, I would like to get back to you on that decision."

"All right but make it quick. Who do you want as the squadron commanders? Hawker wanted you, Grid Caldwell, and Raymond Collishaw of Naval 10 Squadron. The navy refused to give us Collishall, but we could get Grid from 60 Squadron if you want him."

Arthur sucked his teeth. "Shame about Collishaw and his Black Flight. They would be a great fit. But Albert Ball would be my first choice. I don't think he is a great tactician or even a good military officer, but he is a first-rate fighter pilot and an inspiration to everyone. If we can get someone to do the paperwork for him, he would be a great choice."

Baring rubbed his bald head. "Damned young to be a major."

"So keep him as a captain, just give him the role as a leader in the air."

The aide-de-camp looked dubious.

"It is what Richthofen does," Arthur said. "His leaders are the best air fighters, not the best officers."

Baring hesitated, then nodded. "It helps that Boom admires Ball. I'm sure he'll agree. All right, Albert Ball is one. Who do you want as the second?"

"I would like to give Lance Fitch the job."

"Fitch? A rising star as regards kills, but he has a poor reputation as a leader, I believe."

"He is the best shot I have seen in the air, and he understands Hun tactics better than anyone on our side—maybe better than some Huns, I daresay. He has hunted big game in Africa and knows how to stalk and kill."

"All good points, but he is only a lieutenant now. And from what I hear, not a popular one. From there to commanding a squadron with this elite outfit will be quite a jump. Grid Caldwell is a lot more senior and a lot more popular. He would be a great help to you as CO, whereas Fitch will be someone you have to invest a lot of time and effort on training."

Arthur took a deep breath and shook his head. "Grid is an outstanding officer, sir. He is brave, and a good pilot, but two things count against him. The most important is he cannot shoot for toffee. He flies so close to the enemy planes it seems harder for him to miss them than hit them, yet miss them he does. If we are challenging the best the Huns possess, we need pilots who can kill them."

"You'll need leaders too," Baring protested.

"Grid is an amazing leader on the ground, none better at boosting morale, but he lacks tactical skills in the air. He belongs to what you might call the Charge of the Light Brigade school of tactics, bull-in-a-china-shop brave but not very savvy. We will be fighting four *Jasta* who will fly together in a coordinated way. They will try to jump us at the time and place of their choosing so they outnumber us and hold a height advantage. It is critical we develop counter tactics. I would prefer we adopt the hunting ploys that Fitch uses for himself and adapt them for a squadron or a wing. That way we might outwit the Huns."

"Interesting idea, worth a try in the circumstances I suppose. We could promote Fitch to captain and tell him it is probationary until he proves he can handle the role. But as a quid pro quo I want you to appoint Thompson as your third commander."

Arthur squirmed. His instincts warned him against Thompson as a leader; he was too similar to Ball in his lack of tactics, and too dissimilar in his overt ambition.

Baring saw the hesitation and raised an eyebrow. "To be honest, Hawker did not choose Thompson. Boom and I did. The Canadians have been pouring in new pilots from their training programs back in Canada. So much so they want to form their own air force. We want to short-circuit their bid for independence by showing them they can have senior officers inside the RFC."

Arthur rubbed his forehead, wondering whether Richthofen had to worry whether his leaders were Prussians, Bavarians, or Saxons. He sighed and surrendered to the inevitable. Politics should not warp personnel decisions, but in truth Thompson's kill rate qualified the Canadian as a candidate under the logic Arthur had used for Albert Ball. Baring had approved Lance as a commander and that was more than Arthur had expected given the latter's reputation as an awkward bugger. Getting Lance was more important than not getting Thompson. "If that is your recommendation," he conceded.

"Anything else?"

"I would like to take Captain Clayton, my intelligence officer, and make him adjutant for the whole wing. It will take a heck of a lot of organisation to get three squadrons up and running, and organisation is Clayton's forte. He knows how I work, and he understands how the RFC's requisition system works too."

"A miracle worker then," Baring observed. "All right, I will make the posting orders." The aide-de-camp shook hands and ushered Arthur out. "The sooner you give me the names of the planes and other pilots you want, the sooner you'll get them. You'll have everything you need—trucks, living quarter plans, fitters, spare parts, etcetera—

within ten days. In two weeks, this outfit must be operational and taking on Richthofen. Haig wants—"

"Two weeks!"

"Haig will launch an offensive in early June. Without effective RFC reconnaissance and artillery spotting the troops will be charging into fully intact machine gun nests, barbed wire, and entrenched artillery. It will be a massacre. Thousands of soldiers' lives are at stake. Our pilots and observers are dying in droves trying to get Haig what he needs, and still we are failing. It's your job to change that, and fast."

Arthur blew out his cheeks. "Why not postpone the attack a few weeks? What difference does that make?"

Baring looked around, then pulled Arthur back into his office. "You did not hear this from me, but the French army has mutinied. The French are desperate to keep it hush-hush, and Haig needs to distract the Huns before they notice."

"Mutiny? Jesus Christ! If the French fold, we are all in trouble."

Baring turned brusque. "Not going to happen. We are all doing our bit to prevent it, and yours is to get this wing up into the air and fighting the Circus—in two weeks—without fail."

13
Jonah

Three days later – 22 May 1917
France, Arras Sector, Le Hameau Airfield. RFC, 100 Wing.

The office door slammed open, startling Clayton. A biting wind and a furious Wing Commander raged through the doorway. "Bloody bureaucrats!" Arthur snarled. Clayton clapped two hands on his desk in a vain attempt to stop the memos on his desk from swirling into a paper blizzard around the office.

Arthur jammed his sodden raincoat on the hook behind the door with such force that the coat ripped, then threw himself into his desk chair. "I wish we could focus on winning this blasted war without interfering busybodies tripping us up every day."

Clayton raised his eyebrows at the tantrum, decided discretion was the better part of valour, and remained silent. He had left 13 Squadron and re-joined his old boss just a day ago, and in that one day he had heard Arthur curse more than the preceding twelve months. Partly because Le Hameau's limited number of huts meant he and Arthur shared an office, and partly because, like most warriors, Arthur found fighting his own bureaucrats more demoralising than fighting the enemy.

Rain drummed on the tin roof as Arthur shook his head in disbelief. "It is such a simple concept. Get the finest aircraft plus the finest pilots and fight the Huns. Is it too much to ask that senior officers do not screw everything up?"

"That would be against a few hundred years of British army precedent," Clayton said. "Let me guess. Bum and

Eyeglass' surprise inspection concluded our fledgling wing was not shipshape?"

"That is Brigade Commander Higgins to you, Clayton. He is my direct superior while we are in the Arras Sector, and if he ever hears that nickname someone will get shot at dawn. God knows why he came here because there is nothing to inspect yet. But he demanded we stand in front of our aircraft for inspection—in the sodding rain. Then he bollocked Albert Ball because he had not rigged the machine gun on his Nieuport according to regulations. It never occurred to his tiny bureaucratic brain that Ball might be our leading ace precisely because he did *not* have his gun mounted as per a desk-wallah's regulations."

"I'm amazed Higgins even knew the business end of a machine gun, never mind its proper mounting. But what's the problem? Just say 'Aye aye, sir' and put it back the way it was the second he's gone."

"Before I could say that, Ball looked at him with utter disdain and said, 'Who is going to fight with this gun? Me or you?'"

Clayton could not help himself. He laughed so hard he had to bend over to catch his breath.

Arthur regarded him with a sour face. "Enjoying yourself?"

"I bet his monocle dropped and his eyeballs came out on stalks!"

"He told me to cashier Ball and send him back to Blighty to fly latrine brushes."

Clayton's laughter choked. "You're joking? Cashier Britain's leading ace? You talked him out of it, I assume?"

"He would not listen. I told him with all the diplomacy I could muster that putting our leading ace on bog duty might be in line with the British army's finest traditions of discipline, but would not help us defeat Richthofen's Circus. He answered that if Ball was still here in two days,

I would join the miscreant on latrine duties for insubordination."

"What the hell are you going to do?"

"Tell Boom Trenchard that if he does not overrule Higgins, then he needs someone else to run the wing. Of course, if Boom does overrule him, Higgins will dislike me even more."

"Can't make omelettes without breaking eggs, I suppose."

"Thank you for that earth-shattering insight."

The phone rang. Arthur frowned at it but answered. Clayton could hear the bellowing from the other side of the desk. Arthur held the phone away from his ear and raised his eyebrows at his adjutant. When the barrage ceased, Arthur said, "Yes, sir, understood, sir." He placed the phone back on the hook and put his head between his hands.

"I assume," Clayton said, "that was Boom Trenchard booming about us being behind schedule already?"

Arthur spoke through his hands, the words muffled. "Apparently if Gough's attack fails, the Germans attack the French, the French mutiny, and we lose the war it will all be our fault."

"Gosh, and I thought we were just humble insignificant cogs in the grand scheme of a world war. But no, we are the lynchpin. You did not bother mentioning we have not received either the planes or the pilots he promised us would arrive yesterday? Or about Higgins and Ball?"

Arthur sat upright and pulled a resigned face. "I learned as a child not to piss against the wind. Better to wait until the wind is in my favour."

"Boom at full force is more like a hurricane," Clayton agreed as he bent down to rescue the papers from the floor and handed them to Arthur. "If you used the paper-weights I gave you, your papers wouldn't fly everywhere every time someone enters the office."

Arthur threw the papers untidily into his in-tray. "I asked you to do the paperwork."

"Some things only you can sign. If that weren't the case, I'd have dealt with them."

Arthur grumbled as he rifled through the stack of documents, and Clayton limped over to a small primus stove to conjure up a pot of hot tea. Damp weather made the old bullet wound in his hip ache like the very devil. While he waited for the kettle to boil, he peered through the rivulets of water cascading down the windows. The branches of the orchard trees swayed and thrashed in the gale. Farm pigs, gloriously immune to the foul weather, snuffled between the fruit trees for windblown treasures.

Le Hameau was ten miles west of the key battlegrounds of Arras, and just eighteen miles farther east was the Circus base at Roucourt Airfield. Hameau airfield fitted the wing's needs—close enough to hound the Circus and large enough to house three squadrons. A motley mixture of hangars protected the planes, some old permanent wood and iron structures and a few of the massive Bessoneau hangars made of canvas. Aircrew and senior officers would sleep in Nissen huts, the ubiquitous half-barrel-shaped army accommodations made of corrugated steel. The rest of the wing would sleep in canvas tents.

Clayton poured steaming tea into two battered tin mugs with no handles, and exclaimed as he lifted the scalding cups. He hurried them over to Arthur's desk, spilling tea as he did so. He didn't bother wiping up the mess. The old school desk had been carved on by a hundred kids. A few extra ring stains would only add to its character.

Arthur rescued papers from the steaming puddle on the desk and frowned at Clayton. "These personnel files on Albert Ball and Thompson are turgid and uninformative, nothing about their personalities. I need to know if such a cast of strong characters can work as a team. Are these reports the best you can do?"

"What do you expect from the army, the insight of Fyodor Dostoevsky and the prose of Gibbons? Those are the Army personnel files you asked for, not my literary debut."

"Come on, man, channel your inner Fyodor," Arthur wheedled. "You fancy yourself as a student of human nature. You were with Ball in 60 Squadron for a while. What makes him tick?"

Clayton pulled a face and scratched his neck. "Ball is a conundrum. In the air he is this gutsy, fire-breathing Hun killer. No one in the RFC fights as often and as hard as Ball. Sometimes he flies five or six sorties a day in summer, double or triple what most pilots do. And on every one of those flights he attacks three, five, or ten Huns. When he lands, there are always bullet holes within a foot of the cockpit, sometimes inches. The type of holes where a pilot says, 'How in God's name did that miss me?' He's the only man in history to win three DSOs, and most pilots reckon he should have the Victoria Cross."

Clayton blew on his steaming tea, took a loud slurp, and sighed in appreciation. Arthur frowned at him. "You drink tea like an Irish navvy."

"You wouldn't talk to Fyodor that way."

"My humble apologies. You were telling me about Albert Ball."

Clayton extended his little finger and took an ostentatious sip of his tea. "My manners refined enough to win the war yet?"

Arthur scowled at him, and Clayton continued. "Yet on the ground our fire-breathing hero turns into an introvert who prefers the company of his vegetable patch to that of his fellow officers. If he's not tending his garden, he's in the hangars checking his engine or his guns. He shuns the officers' Mess, just like Fitch."

"So why is Ball so popular with the other officers, who despise Fitch for the same behaviour?"

"People see themselves in Ball. An ordinary bloke with no airs or graces, who uses extraordinary guts to get the job done. Compared to Fitch he is very English, and he isn't so vocal about wanting to kill his fellow human beings, even if they are German."

"Hmm. Baring thinks Ball may struggle to lead others. What is your view?"

"He won't be an inspirational talker or a cunning tactician, but if leadership by example means anything then he's a great leader. Right now, a lot of pilots don't believe in their heart of hearts that they can win against Richthofen and his crew. Ball is living proof you can do it and succeed.

"But if Ball had nine lives, he's used twelve. You will need to give him more frequent rest periods than the others, or he will break. Handle him as he deserves, and he will infuse the whole wing with courage and belief."

"Sounds just the man to tackle Richthofen," Arthur said. "Do not worry, I will give him all the leave he wants."

"No," Clayton said, dumping more papers into Arthur's in-tray. "You have to force him to take the rest he needs, not listen to what he says he wants."

Arthur picked up the pile of papers and moved them into his out-tray. "You handle the paperwork, Clayton."

"If you don't sign those papers, we won't receive the planes and pilots."

"I have seen you forge my signature before. Do it again. What do you know about Thompson?"

Clayton took the papers to his desk and stuck his tongue between his lips in concentration as he dashed off large sloppy signatures with élan. "He was in 60 Squadron after my time, though I've heard a bit about him. He sounds similar to Lance Fitch and Albert Ball in that he is a good shot and prefers to fly alone. Unlike those two, he is a feature at the officers' Mess and generous in buying rounds. Not as popular as Ball, but more popular than Fitch. He was one of the few RFC pilots to flourish in April and is not that far behind Fitch's twenty-one kills." Clayton shook his aching wrist. "Your signature is too long. I'll shorten it for you. Speed up the signing process."

"Be my guest. Is Thompson well connected?"

"Oh yes! My sources in London say our Canadian is plotting a glittering career in the air force after the war. An old society dame, Lady St Helier, has adopted him almost as a godson. She pulls strings for him with the likes of Churchill and the Secretary for Air, Lord Cecil. There is even scurrilous scuttlebutt," Clayton said with an interrogatory eyebrow, "that she wangled him a posting into our new elite wing as commander of a squadron?"

The drumming of the rain on the roof faltered and resumed five seconds later with a continuous hammering.

"Hailstones," Arthur sighed. "In May. Remember that wonderful spring of 1914? All sunshine and garden parties. Seems a long time ago. At least Thompson is another who will not take a backward step against the Huns. With Ball, Thompson, and Fitch we have a bloodthirsty crew."

Clayton grunted, seeing Arthur's deflection as confirmation that the innuendo about Thompson was true. "So were Blackbeard, Captain Kidd and Henry Morgan, and they all came to a sticky end. Aren't you worried you're appointing three buccaneering pirates as squadron commanders? You've been talking about developing new tactics, honing team spirit, and all that stuff. None of our likely lads are Nelson when it comes to strategy."

"Our first priority has to be good pilots who can shoot down Huns without getting shot down themselves. Hawker's unfortunate demise showed the truth of that. Team spirit and morale will follow if we have success in battle. And Fitch can develop the tactics. That man carries in his head the template of what the RFC's fighter tactics should be. I think he could be our Boelcke."

Clayton smudged one of his forgeries in surprise. "Are we speaking about the same Lance Fitch? The one who hates command responsibility and focuses only on his personal vendetta against Huns? Boelcke? Please! I don't dispute the success of Fitch's tactics in the air for himself, but as for sharing that knowledge, being part of a team, providing leadership—"

"He will be a duck to water, given the chance."

For a moment Clayton floundered for words. He was proud of having recruited Fitch, but could not remember a single instance of Fitch acting as a leader. Outside his rapport with Arthur in the FE2b, there was no indication that Fitch even knew what a team was. Now he was flying single-seater scouts, he flew resolutely on his own. Whether Fitch was nominally in command or part of a flight, he always disappeared from everyone else before they reached the front lines.

"Arthur, you've lost me. Fitch is not even a team player, never mind a team leader. You are doomed if you are relying on him as our Boelcke."

"Your problem is that you are a natural pessimist. Goethe may have been a German, but he had the rights of it: 'Treat a man as you wish him to be, and he will become that man.' You will see."

Clayton shrugged. "Care to wager a guinea on that?"

"Done. With three Hun-getters like these, and a supporting cast of good pilots and new planes, we can bloody Richthofen's crew. But we need to get our boys into the air soon before they start fighting each other."

~

"Speak of the devils," Clayton said as he heard raised voices. The door flew open with a spatter of lashing rain as three officers jostled into the hut, bringing with them the aroma of castor oil and soaked wool. They hung their sopping greatcoats and caps on the drunken-looking coat stand, where a minor lake formed around the base. Clayton lit the primus stove to reheat the battered tea kettle.

This would be interesting. The first test of Arthur as leader of 100 Wing, and of his much-desired teamwork. By the end of this meeting, someone would be spitting teeth over Arthur's choice of aircraft for the Wing. Clayton had a pretty good idea who that would be.

"Goddamn frog country," Thompson grumbled. "Call this spring? Mamma Thompson said never join the navy, and look where I am, surrounded by water. Don't suppose there's any coffee?"

"What do you think this is?" Clayton asked. "A Lyons Corner House? Tea or nowt."

"Brits and their goddamn tea. This being the navy, Clayton old fella, I don't mind a spot of grog in mine."

"No milk, no sugar, and no rum either since you ask. The army supply depots are reacting with their usual lightning pace," Clayton replied, thrusting hot tin mugs at the newcomers. Thompson and Albert Ball took theirs, exclaimed in pain and dropped them on Arthur's desk, spilling more tea on the desk.

"I don't care what it tastes like," Lance said, cupping his hands around the scalding mug and hunching his shoulders over it as though it was a comforting fire. "Just so long as it's hot."

"If it got any hotter," Thompson observed, blowing on his scorched fingers, "it'd set off those ammunition clips you're using as paperweights."

"Sit down, chaps," Arthur said. "We will start the meeting when the tea has thawed you."

"That'll be August then," Thompson muttered.

Silence reigned, broken by murmurs of appreciation as the tea warmed them. Clayton looked at the small band of damp men huddled around the wooden school table. They had the Herculean task of wresting control of the air from

Richthofen in less than a month. If they managed that, their names would be toasted in champagne. If they failed they would be just more forgettable names on forgotten tombstones.

Arthur put down his tin mug with a bang. "Excellent tea. Thank you, Clayton. Now to business. Welcome to the first official meeting of squadron commanders of 100 Wing. Haig and Boom have given us priority in the RFC for choosing pilots and aircraft. You three will command the squadrons. Ball, you will command 111 Squadron, Fitch 222 Squadron, and Thompson 333 Squadron, chosen alphabetically. Although squadron commanders are traditionally majors, you will be captains to begin with until you prove you can do the job. Then you will be promoted to major. Congratulations."

Albert Ball looked surprised, Thompson delighted, and Fitch deadpan. Each to their character, Clayton thought.

"The official objectives of 100 Wing are to control the air wherever HQ sends us," Arthur continued. "Unofficially, but direct from Boom Trenchard's mouth, we are to hound Richthofen and his Circus to death. And gentlemen, we have a ticking clock. Haig will soon launch a major assault. We must gain control of the air from the Huns before then, so none of their reconnaissance planes spot Haig's build-up of men and material in the attack area. Otherwise, it will be a bloodbath."

"When is this assault taking place?" Thompson asked.

"The exact date is secret, but soon. In about month, I'd guess."

"Jeezus!" Thompson exclaimed. "What are those goddamn brass hats drinking? They want us to clear the skies of Germany's best pilots who are flying the best fighter in the world today—in a month? When right now we have no pilots or planes?"

"That is the point of this meeting," Arthur said, "to sort out the planes and pilots. Hawker and I picked a few pilots, but you can choose the rest. Give me a list of the pilots you want in your squadron by 1700 hours today. Boom says he will get them here within two days. But it will take longer to obtain the planes. Boom can terrorise the rest of the RFC into giving us the pilots, but even he cannot manufacture new aircraft. The Bristols will be ready first, followed by the SE5, then the Camels."

"You're going with the Camels, of course," Thompson said. "A wing of thirty Camels, and we will rule the skies."

"Sure you need thirty others, Thommo?" Lance needled. "A few days ago, you said you could clear the skies with a squadron of twelve."

Thompson turned to Arthur, throwing his arms wide like a martyr. "Do I have to listen to this abuse?"

"Besides," Lance said, "Hawker already chose the SE5 for the wing."

Thompson blew a raspberry. "We only have your word for that. No-one else heard Hawker say he'd chosen the SE5s."

"Are you calling me—"

"Stop squabbling," Arthur said, rising from his chair to loom over them. "I have decided we will have one squadron of each. The planes have different strengths and weaknesses, so we will have flexibility to match every type of operation with the best plane for that task."

Thompson clapped his hands. "Bloody good, as you Brits say. I'll take the Camels and show the rest of you up."

"And who commands the Bristols?" Ball asked.

The pilots looked at each other.

"I know they are two-seaters, but they are excellent as fighters," Arthur said. "Also, they will be available first and HQ is desperate to have 100 Wing into the fight. Bristols will be the quickest way to do that. Who wants to be first to fight the Circus?"

"Fighting is one thing, winning is another," Lance said.

Ball shrugged. "I don't want the responsibility of another person in my plane. It's bad enough giving up my Nieuport for an SE5. I don't want something even bigger and clumsier."

Clayton watched, amused, as Arthur turned to Lance, his eyes pleading for support. But he was surprised to see Lance wavering, on the verge of acquiescing out of loyalty. Then Lance squared his shoulders. "No. Only SE5s for me. Their speed will be crucial."

Arthur chopped off further debate. "All right, here's my decision. Thompson, you get the Camels. Ball, the SE5s. And Fitch, the Bristols."

Thompson clapped and smirked at Lance. The latter's face was impassive.

Arthur silenced Thompson with a pointed finger. "A reminder: Boom will court martial anyone who takes a prototype near the lines. He wants to keep them hidden from the Huns until we can unleash them at squadron strength and give the Circus a real beating. So, if you go hunting across the front lines while we wait for new planes and pilots, you must use your old Pups or Nieuports." He looked hard at Thompson, who studied his fingernails, a picture of aggrieved innocence.

"I wanted to give the Camel a proper test without worrying about fuel," he said.

Clayton snorted. When the prototype planes had arrived, Arthur ordered Sergeant Major Smythe, head of the ground crews, to fuel them with only enough fuel for short test flights. Soon afterwards Thompson ordered his fitters to fill up the Camel. Smythe intervened and refused. Thompson's bawling attempt to pull rank on the huge sergeant major alerted Arthur, who reprimanded the Canadian.

"Anything else?" Arthur asked. "No? Good. Remember, I need your lists of pilots by 1700 hours today."

"Peary of the North Pole would be my choice," Thompson muttered as he left.

Lance hung back until the others had put on their coats and stepped back out into the driving rain. Clayton grimaced, anticipating a confrontation.

~

The leaving officers had pulled the door shut as they left, but the gale force wind slammed it open and howled through the office, causing a blizzard of paper and a volley of swearing. Clayton jammed it closed and shook off the water he shipped in the process. "Bloody weather," he said.

"Arthur," Lance said, "about —"

"I am sorry, but I have made the decision. You fly Bristols, at least to start with."

"No, it's not about that. It's about being a captain and squadron commander. I'd like to—"

"No need to thank me for your promotion," Arthur said, smug as a magician who'd produced a rabbit from a hat. "You deserve it, although I had to twist their arms."

Lance stood speechless. Clayton smiled. No doubt Lance was dumbstruck by his good fortune, the onetime outcast and rebel now a captain and soon to be a major.

"No," Lance said, his voice flat.

Clayton blinked. Arthur frowned. "What do you mean, no?"

"I can't lead a squadron. I'm a Jonah."

"A what?"

"Everything I touch when I am in charge turns into a disaster for other people. I am a jinx, like the guy in the Bible, Jonah, the one the whale swallowed."

Arthur took a deep breath, a parent dealing with a difficult child. "But I need you in that role, Lance. I need you to teach your tactics, the benefits of surprise, height, and speed, and how to attack out of the sun and clouds.

Boelcke and Richthofen have trained their pilots this way, but most RFC pilots don't have a clue. We won't beat the Huns by charging at them bull-headed every day and expecting to win because we are British and we are brave." Arthur rubbed his chin, "Besides, I fought damn hard to get you this promotion, and Boom has already approved it. It's a done deal."

Lance tried again. "Arthur, you make me feel like I'm letting you down. But I don't want responsibility for other people. They die when I'm in charge. I've caused enough deaths. No more."

"What deaths? I have known you since you joined the RFC, and I've not seen you responsible for other people's deaths."

"What about Hawker and Forrester?"

Arthur shook his head in exasperation. "That was Hawker's fault, not yours. You turned back, but he flew on. It was his choice to get into a fight in those circumstances, and still you did your best to help him."

Lance shook his head. "Hawker flies for two years without getting killed, earning a VC for charging into piles of Huns regularly. Then he flies one patrol when I am flight commander, and he dies. I got one of our greatest fliers killed." Lance was pleading now, desperate for Arthur to believe him. "Forrester saved my bacon, and the Huns roasted him alive. Before I joined the RFC, I got a whole platoon obliterated before I got them to the front lines. When I lead, bad things happen, and men always die. I'm a curse, a Jonah."

"You have never said anything about this before."

"It wasn't relevant."

"Well, it did not stop you accepting the role of flight commander in 13 Squadron," Arthur pointed out.

"You and I both know I didn't act as one. In my first few patrols I tried to be a proper leader, but my flight was too soft and too lazy. When I flew at 17,000 feet, they complained it was too cold. They'd rather the Huns ambush them than have a cold arse. Neither would they load their own ammunition even though it was their lives at stake if it jammed. On morning patrols half of them were hung over. If people can't be bothered to help themselves, I'll not waste my time. I won't nursemaid lazy incompetents. It hinders me from doing my job, which is killing Huns."

Arthur steepled his fingers and took a deep breath. "I understand your point of view, but in an elite wing the pilots will have more motivation and drive. A lot of the pilots in 13 Squadron joined the RFC to escape the trenches. They hoped it would safer. Ha! If only they had known! But in 100 Wing the pilots are volunteers for the most dangerous job in the RFC, fighting Richthofen every day. They may need help with tactics, but they will be tough and keen. We can build on that, with your help. I know you want to focus only on your revenge, but you have obligations to help the living, not just debts to the dead."

Lance frowned, but Arthur was relentless. "And to be truthful, you could be a better teacher. You assume others will accept that your ways are best, and so you never tell them the thinking behind your tactics. People learn better, follow better, when you explain things to them in terms they understand."

Lance's frown deepened. "Just as I said. I'm not a teacher, and I won't be a good leader."

Arthur passed his hand over his face. The two men stared at each other until Arthur broke the silence. "How did you learn to hunt?"

"By watching great hunters and copying their habits."

"Did they never talk? Did you not learn from listening to them?"

"Yes, I bloody well listened. I didn't start a debating society, which these guys do. I listened like a disciple to those who had been successful, and I copied them, and I practised like a zealot. My flight in 13 Squadron didn't listen, didn't watch and learn, and didn't practise. Losers, all of them."

"But in this wing," Arthur argued, "the best will want to get better. You are one of the RFC's most successful aces now, and they will be as keen as mustard to learn these hunting tricks that are so alien to us Brits. Even those who have hunted in England don't worry about being savaged by pheasants or rabbits. They've no experience of hunting dangerous animals. But if you never impart your knowledge, you waste it. Do not be such a loner."

"I *am* a loner. I won't take responsibility for anyone on the ground or in the air. I want to shoot down Huns. *That's* what I am good at."

"For God's sake, try it. You might surprise yourself at how good a teacher you can be. If you pass on your skills, a whole new crop of pilots will fly smarter and live longer. I believe you can become the British Boelcke."

"Bugger being Boelcke."

Clayton had never seen Lance change his mind once his face had that mulish look. Arthur might as well hand over that gold sovereign now.

Arthur threw up his hands, and the three of them sat in silence. Clayton looked at Lance more closely. There were new lines around the straight mouth that made it severe, and the bright green and tawny eyes had lost some lustre. A curious flatness sat in those eyes now, a deadening. Was it tiredness or something else? It almost looked like fear.

Arthur switched tack. He picked up a piece of paper from his desk and waved it at Lance. "This is translated from the *Cologne Gazette*'s interview with Manfred von Richthofen. Let me read it to you: 'I am proud to have brought down Hawker, the English Immelman... His machine gun now ornaments the entrance to my dwelling.'"

Clayton watched the blood drain from Lance's face. "The bastard, making Hawker a trophy, no better than a stag's head." Lance ripped the offending paper from Arthur's hands and tore it into shreds. "I'll kill the sick son of a bitch."

Clayton's lips twisted. For such a chivalrous man, Arthur could be manipulative when it suited him.

Lance took a deep breath and ran his hands over his face. "Arthur, I appreciate the honour of being part of this wing under you. But don't ask me to lead other people. I'll hunt down Richthofen with pleasure, but don't ask me to be a squadron commander."

Arthur refused to relent. "Even Albert Ball has agreed to be a squadron commander. God knows he hates leading others as much as you. If he can do it, why can't you?"

"Ask him. Maybe he hasn't had the bad experiences that have proved time and time again I'm a Jonah when in charge."

"I do not believe you are a Jonah, Lance—I know you too well."

"You do, do you? Well try this for size. Do you know German troops ambushed me in Africa while I was daydreaming about kissing a girl? They crippled my younger brother and burned my friend alive, after they shot his son. Do you know I got my brother and my company shredded by Hun artillery because I didn't have the guts to challenge my superiors and take my troops off the crossroads? My brother's wife wrote me a letter cursing me and calling me a Jonah, and she was right. I even got my mother…"

Lance stopped. He shut his eyes, blew out a gusting sigh, and squared his shoulders. "And now Hawker and Forrester prove it again. All these deaths on my watch, my conscience, Arthur. So now you know my history, get the hell off my case!"

Clayton winced. Lance had never revealed those stories. No wonder he was so bloodthirsty against the Huns.

Arthur held up his hands. "Calm down, Lance. I had no idea, and I am sorry. I was remiss in appointing you a squadron commander without checking with you, but I was not aware you had this…history…of bad luck. Tomorrow I will ask Baring for another squadron leader. But until the new chap arrives, I need your help to fill in as squadron commander. There are few planes or pilots at the moment anyway. As soon as the new squadron commander arrives you can step down. Will you do that for me?"

Lance shook his head.

Clayton spoke for the first time. "Lance, in this war we all have to do things we don't want to do. If you can't face leading men in battle, there's no point in trying to fake it. But help us get the wing up and running. Otherwise, a lot of infantry will die in Haig's attack."

Lance hesitated, and then nodded. "All right, but only until the new commander arrives. When we fly in squadrons against the Huns, I want to be flying SE5s under Ball."

Arthur stood and shook Lance's hand. "Thank you, Lance, I appreciate it."

Lance nodded and stalked out of the office stiff backed, every muscle proclaiming resentment at the compromise.

Clayton held out his palm to Arthur. "You owe me a sovereign."

"Eh?" As usual Arthur was slow to recall a losing bet.

"Goethe. Leader. Lance. Boelcke. You used these words together less than an hour ago, and I wagered you a sovereign that the word 'Lance' did not fit with the rest. Now he's just confirmed it. So, stop dragging your anchor. My sovereign coin please."

Arthur waved a hand in dismissal. "I do not recall saying he would be all that today. Give him time."

Clayton rolled his eyes. "Pay me before you fly against the Circus, will you? Just in case you don't come back."

Arthur stared at him. "Not funny, Clayton, not funny at all."

~

Lance sat on the cot in his hut, his head in his hands. What had he been thinking? He had almost told Arthur and Clayton the greatest secret in his life, one he had never told anyone, not even Pa. Especially not Pa. The rant at Arthur about being a Jonah had allowed old demons to surface; memories that Lance kept buried deep. Oceans deep.

Will's widow, Kathy, had been the one who named him a Jonah. Poisonous with her grief and rage, she'd thrown Will's death and Francis' crippling at him, and Ma's death too. Lance couldn't fault her reasoning…but not even Kathy knew how right she was about Ma. He shuddered as memories of her death, memories that he had locked away for over ten years, came flooding back.

He would not have noticed the snake if the red-brown scales had not glinted a warning in the early morning sun. The evil wedge-shaped head lay sunning itself on a flat stone by the drainpipe near the kitchen door. It seemed unaware of him, probably still sluggish from the night's chill. Lance could see only the head; the rest of it flowed back into the pipe.

He stayed motionless as his heart thudded inside his ribs like a small animal desperate to escape Should he call the grown-ups? But if he called, the snake might bite someone who came out of the kitchen door. Perhaps he should kill it himself? Plenty of snakes were not poisonous, and this one's head looked small—it might even be a baby. He bit his lip; he didn't want a reputation as a sissy.

A week ago, a bright green snake had dropped onto the veranda from an overhanging tree while the family took their afternoon tea. It had just missed Lance's lap, slapping his bare knee as it fell. He had lurched to his feet, slopped scalding tea over his shorts, and shrieked "Snake!" before running into the house.

Ma and Pa came inside to reassure him. Ma hugged him. "It's only a tree snake darling—it's harmless."

His brothers, Will and Francis, were as understanding as younger brothers always are. Several times a day, they would scream, "Snake!" and double over with laughter. Even Ma and Pa chuckled. Lance's face burned at the memory.

Two days ago, Pa had left home to take a client on a hunting safari. He knelt and looked into Lance's eyes. "You are ten now. That makes you the man of the family for the next few days. You'll look after your mother, yes?"

Pa had laughter in his voice, but Lance had squared his shoulders and stood taller. "I'll look after Ma."

"Good man! I knew I could rely on you." Stan Fitch put an arm around his wife and kissed her. "You'll be in good hands, Maria."

Ma smiled as Lance swelled with the trust they had placed in him.

Now Pa was still on safari, and a snake lurked just outside the kitchen where Ma was cooking. But if Lance called out a warning and the snake turned out to be harmless, there would be more scornful laughter from his brothers. Lance scowled. He looked at the snake again. It probably was harmless—it wasn't black like a mamba or hooded like a cobra. He could handle this.

A stick, about three feet long and thick, lay on the ground near him. He eased into a crouch and slowly picked it up. The snake did not move. He inched closer. The snake did not appear aware. How could it not hear his thudding heart? Quickly, before he could change his mind, he swung the stick down to pulp the sleeping head against the stone drain.

The rotten stick disintegrated as it hit, sending wood chips and white termites flying.

The snake's head whipped upwards, no more hurt than if he had hit it with a Christmas cracker. It unhinged its jaws to bare its fangs and hissed with rage. Lance stood open-mouthed, his feet rooted as four feet of reptile raged from the pipe. Its head reared back and flared into a cobra hood larger than his hand. The head jerked and something flew at him. He twisted away—too late. A splash of venom hit him across the bridge of his nose. Agony stabbed like a fishhook deep into his eyeballs as he shrieked in pain and fear. Spitting cobra!

Blinded, he tried to run but blundered in circles, then tripped and fell. Fangs stabbed into his ankle. He screeched and flailed his legs in horror. A high-pitched incoherent shout rang out beside him, a woman's war cry, and the snake was torn from his leg.

"Ma!"

His mother screamed again, this time in pain. But she lifted him and ran with his limp body in her arms. Men shouted at each other to kill the snake, their voices shrill with fear and loathing: "Nyoka! Kuua nyoka!"

Ma laid Lance on a table.

"Ma," he whimpered, grinding his knuckles into the searing agony in his eyes. "It burns…"

"Darling, I'll pour milk in them to dilute the venom."

She tried to move his hands from his eyes, but he resisted. Hands pulled Lance's fists from his face and held them against the table; others prised his clenched eyelids open and poured cool liquid into his eyes.

His mother's voice cut through the Swahili: "Lance. We're going to cut your leg to suck out the venom. Bite on this towel and try to hold still."

The fire in Lance's eyes was too intense for the words to sink in, and he bucked as a knife slashed above his ankle. A mouth sucked on his leg and then spat, sucked and spat, over and over. He whimpered into the gag. Then the sucking ceased and something drew tight around his leg. They took the towel from between his teeth.

"Eyes any better, darling?"

The fire still burned, and Lance kept his eyelids screwed tight. He wanted to tell Ma that he couldn't feel his feet anymore, but his lips and tongue were too numb and swollen to form the words. His breath sawed in his throat and invisible bands constricted his chest. Through his half-conscious state he heard the urgent whispers. "Memsahib, we must cut you and suck out the poison out of you now. We cannot wait so long."

"In a minute, Hamisi."

A cool hand rested on his brow. "Lance, relax now. You'll be fine, but you must rest."

He grunted and thrashed as the first convulsion seized him. The hands holding him tightened to keep him on the table. Every inch of his body was either numb or on fire. More spasms racked him as the poison coursed through his body. *It's too much!* He slipped into the welcome darkness, the only escape from the hellfire burning his eyes and convulsing his body.

~

When he recovered, days later, Lance wished he were dead.

"It's not your fault, Lance. It was bad luck the cobra was there, bad luck it bit you and Ma. Bad luck that Ma's heart didn't survive the shock from the venom. The only good luck is that you survived. Thank God for that at least."

Pa seemed to sense Lance's guilt, but even Pa did not know how well earned the guilt was. If he had not hit the snake, if he had been quicker to run, then Ma would still be alive and hugging them with her clean soapy smell and soft warmth. It should have been him who died, not Ma.

His eyes were raw as if sandpapered, and they burned with acid tears. The guilt hurt worse.

"Ma," he whispered later, alone in the silence of his room. "Ma, I'm so sorry. I was trying to protect you."

He never told anyone that he had hit the snake. That would be his secret forever, his private shameful burden.

Three days later, Lance laid out twelve dead snakes on the lawn with their heads cut off. Hamisi skinned them and hung the skins in the sun to dry. When Pa returned to the ranch house that afternoon, covered in dust from a day of checking the farm fences, he stopped at the sight.

"What's this?" Pa asked Hamisi.

"Bwana Lance, na kufa yote." Hamisi beamed with pride and pointed at Lance, who sat on the porch steps.

"That true, Lance—you killed them all?"

Lance nodded.

"Why?"

"I asked Hamisi why the snake killed Ma. He said it's the nature of snakes—that is why the devil gave them venom. So I killed all the snakes I could find, as revenge for Ma."

Pa scratched his neck. "You must've gone hunting in the long grass outside the garden. Who told you to take revenge?"

"No-one, Pa. Even the Bible says God threw snakes out of the Garden of Eden, and it says an eye for an eye, a tooth for a tooth. Snakes killed Ma. We should kill them all."

Pa opened his mouth, then shut it again. He rubbed his chin.

"Lance, one snake killed Maria. God knows I hate snakes as much as the next man, but you can't kill the entire snake population to get revenge for Ma."

"Why not?"

Pa sighed and squatted on his haunches, bringing his eyes level with Lance's.

"Your mother risked her life to save you, God bless her. If you hunt snakes like a fanatic in the long grass, sooner or later they will bite you again, and this time you might die."

"So what?"

Pa winced, then gripped Lance's arms in his strong hands. "How do you think Ma would feel if you died trying to revenge her? She died helping you to live. It would make her death in vain."

Lance looked at Pa, who held his gaze.

"Don't you think Ma would prefer that you help me bring up your brothers as she would have done? I can't do that without you."

Lance thought on that plea for a moment. Then he nodded. "All right, Pa. I'll only kill the snakes I find in the garden."

Pa pulled Lance into a strong hug, and the dust on his coat had made Lance's eyes water.

The banshee howl of a Camel flight taking off jerked Lance back into the present. The corrosive guilt of the day Ma died still seared him, as raw as ever. Lance forced himself to stand and looked in the small shaving mirror over the tin washstand. Wild eyes stared back at him. He splashed cold water from the jug onto his face. Time to lock the memories away again.

But Kathy was right, and Arthur was wrong—Lance was a Jonah when he was in charge. And this Jonah would not be responsible for any more deaths.

14
Liquorice Allsorts

Two days later – 24 May 1917
France, Arras Sector, Le Hameau Airfield. RFC, 100 Wing.

Lance threw up his hands in despair.

"God damn it!" Thommo said in exasperation. "We're good to go. We've got planes ready. Let's paste the Huns." The sun had set, and the gas lamps in Arthur's office lit the room in harsh yellow, throwing monster shadows on the wall as Thommo gesticulated.

"No," Arthur said. His tone was quiet but definitive.

Lance rubbed the back of his neck. "Come on, Arthur."

"No!" This rejection was louder. Arthur glared at them. Lance glared right back.

In the two days since Lance had agreed to take temporary command of the Bristol squadron, planes and pilots had poured into Le Hameau. Each dawn rose to the angry snarl of the rotary engine Camels and the growling roar of the Hispano-Suiza engined Bristols and SE5s. As the sun rose higher, the metallic hammering of machine gun testing joined the cacophony. Pilots, fitters, and mechanics familiarised themselves with each other and their new tools. The air of excitement grew as the squadrons moved closer to readiness.

But hitches with new aircraft and a new wing were inevitable. Lance rose every day eager as a bird dog on a hunt and ended each one cursing with frustration. He was not alone.

Lance's chair squeaked as he leaned forward. "Arthur, if you don't want to start formal patrols, at least let the three of us off the leash now. With our new planes, we can wrack up a score on behalf of the wing and get Boom and the generals off your back."

Arthur shook his head. "None of the new planes are going across the lines until I say so." He stared hard at each of his squadron leaders. "That goes for all of you. I want squadrons at full strength, the planes all tiptop, and the pilots fully familiar with their planes. The first squadron to manage that will be the first across the front lines."

Thommo crossed his arms, his eyes shadowed in the gloom. "I say my guys are ready now."

"Thommo, do not take offence, but your Camels are the least ready of the squadrons. Smythe tells me you want a hole cut in the centre of the top wing so you can get rid of the blind spot. He says he needs to confirm it will not weaken the wing too much. Also, I watch the landings and I listen in the officers' Mess, and your pilots are not confident in the Camel yet."

"Sure they are. They love the Camel, it's just a few negative types who moan."

"Name me a pilot who has mastered it?" Arthur challenged.

"Elliot Springs. He told me today that the Camel is the fastest way to a Victoria Cross. That's what I call confidence."

Clayton cleared his throat. "I think you will find the exact quote was a tad different. As I recall he said: 'This crate is the fastest way to a cross of some kind. Either victories galore and the Victoria Cross, or a visit to the Red Cross, or a grave under a wooden cross.' I would not call that a resounding vote of confidence."

Thommo gave Clayton a filthy look.

Lance could not resist. "I haven't met Springs yet, but I'd say he has the Camel pegged." Thommo gave Lance two fingers behind Arthur's back. Lance grinned back. He hadn't forgotten the Canadian's smirk when Arthur gave Lance the booby prize of commanding the Bristols.

Arthur changed the subject. "How are the Bristols doing?"

"We'd be ready but for the engine situation," Lance said. "The first batch of planes came with Hispano Suiza engines. Then Bristol ran out of Hispano engines because they're earmarked for the SE5. So they switched the Bristols to Rolls Royce Falcons engines. The pilots are happy because the Rolls has more horsepower and is more reliable, but it will take time to train the mechanics on the different engine and replace the Hispanos. When that's done, we'll be good to go."

Clayton snorted. "What a copper-bottomed foul up! They've known the SE5 and the Bristol were coming out together for a year and nobody noticed they'd be competing for the same engine? And Boom blames us for being in the doldrums?"

Arthur shrugged. "C'est la guerre. Let us focus on what we need to do, not what has gone wrong. Albert, how about the SE5s?"

Albert Ball had been quiet so far, but now he pulled a face as though he'd bitten into a garlic bulb. With his face, hands, and uniform streaked with oil and grease, he looked more like a mechanic than the British ace of aces. "It's a disaster. I'd rather keep my Nieuport 17."

Lance choked on his tea.

"And I told Boom Trenchard that when I saw him," Ball added.

"What?" Arthur, Clayton, and Lance said simultaneously.

"I told him I wanted to keep my Nieuport, and he said I could."

Lance wanted to scream. He'd soared on the wings of the SE5, revelled in its power and speed, gloried in its rugged functional beauty. Now Ball threatened to rip it from him and ruin the RFC's best chance to destroy the Albatross' supremacy. Albert Ball was Boom Trenchard's favourite pilot, and the SE5 was doomed if Ball pilloried it. Lance admired Ball beyond belief, but this was a disaster.

"Oh dear," Clayton said.

Arthur shut his eyes and ran a hand down his face.

"See?" Thommo said in a smug tone. "Told you Camels were the best choice."

"But Albert," Lance protested, "we agreed that if we junk the armour-plated seat and the hideous glass cage around the cockpit, we will save a lot of weight. The plane will be even faster, much more agile—even more so when we get the new two hundred horsepower engines in a month. That will unlock the potential of the airframe above fifteen thousand feet, and the SE5 will dominate the Albatross at every altitude."

Albert Ball did not look convinced. "I hope you are right, Lance. Boom said I could keep my Nieuport for my personal flights, but I must use the SE5 for squadron and flight operations when we are authorised to fly them."

Lance sagged in relief. Taking on the Circus in an agile but obsolete and underpowered Nieuport would be a death sentence for anyone but Ball.

"Good," Arthur said, relief making his voice scratchy. "We have work to do tomorrow. In the meantime, let us join the new pilots in the mess. I want you three to know the pilots in every squadron, so we can work together. I do not want small cliques and loners like we had in 13 Squadron." He looked at Lance.

Lance snorted. It wasn't his fault that the snobs from the public schools looked down on everyone else.

"Nothing like bonding at the bar!" Thommo said. "Let's go. First round is on me."

~

Lance sighed; bonding at the bar ranked among his favourite activities alongside visiting the sadistic army dentists. But though he would never admit it to anyone, he hadn't enjoyed being the pariah of 13 Squadron. He really ought to make the effort. Not to make friends, he would not make that mistake again, but to avoid being a pariah. It didn't seem too outrageous a goal.

Besides, unlike the class conscious 13 Squadron, this wing had enjoyable characters from the breadth of the British Empire and beyond. So much so that Clayton called the new wing the "Liquorice Allsorts" after a popular brand of mixed sweets. So Lance trailed after the others.

The officers' Mess was abuzz with the frenetic baying of young men busy impressing each other. Lance headed to where Rod Andrews, one of his Bristol pilots, held court to a wide circle of listeners. The Australian's broad shoulders, slicked back dark hair, and wide generous mouth gave him the air of a rugged lady-killer. Arthur had been elated when he poached Andrews. "What a cricket player! He bowls like the wind and bats like Jessop. When the Australians last played England, he won the match almost on his own. Thirteen wickets and a century in even time."

Lance had rolled his eyes at Clayton. The Aussie might be a sporting legend, but that would not cut any ice with the Huns. But when Lance tackled Andrews in a practice dogfight, he changed his mind. As a fighter pilot, the Australian was ballsy with an unorthodox flair. That unorthodoxy extended to his plane, where against all RFC regulations, he'd painted a small green and gold kangaroo on the side.

"G'evening, boss," Rod Andrews said. "Beer?"

"Lemonade, please," Lance answered.

"Yer can order that yerself, mate—it'd ruin my reputation. Here, let me introduce yer to my gunner, Fred Libby. Fred's a mustang rider, a genuine cowboy from Arizona."

"I already know Fred," Lance said, shaking the American's hand with real pleasure. Libby had volunteered for the Canadian army in 1914, years before America's recent entry into the war. The Yanks had threatened to pull his citizenship, but Libby went ahead anyway. That was a level of commitment to fighting the militaristic Junkers that Lance admired.

"Good to see you again, sir," Libby said, his grip strong and his smile wide under his thick bushy eyebrows and large nose.

"Forget the 'sir' rubbish." Lance turned to Andrews again. "Fred is the patron saint for us old FE2b gunners. He invented the gunstock that made the Lewis machine gun twenty times easier to aim. Terrific shot. You're a lucky man to have him."

"Don't I know it, mate. For the first time in this God forsaken war, my back feels safe. Look at the size of his arse—no bullet could get past that and hit me!"

Libby punched the Australian hard on the shoulder amidst the roars of laughter, but Rod Andrews did not even spill his beer.

"Oi, Fitch! Clayton! Come here!" Thommo bellowed at him from the other end of the bar, waving two glasses of champagne. "I said the first round was on me, and here it is."

Lance dreaded the Canadian's heavy drinking and equally heavy humour, but loath to rebuff Thommo's hospitality he meandered over to the bar. Thommo beamed at him and thrust the glass forward. Lance demurred and raised his glass of lemonade.

"Then that champagne must be for me. Awfully kind." A hand reached over Lance's shoulder and grabbed the glass.

Thommo glared at the newcomer. "Fitch, meet Elliot Springs, one of my Yankee pilots. You know he's mad because he volunteered for this war before America joined. Springs, for a man with a rich daddy who owns half the cotton mills in Carolina, you sure sponge a lot. You are a louche."

Springs carried the face and build of an unsuccessful middleweight boxer, with a broken nose and scar tissue across his cheekbones giving him a rugged, lived-in visage. But at Thommo's insult it split into a beaming gap-toothed grin. "Sure am, boss, but only 'cos my father keeps me on a tight allowance."

Thommo snorted. "When the RFC was training this kid in London, he rented a house in Berkeley Square, complete with butler and chef. He threw parties every night. Some allowance. The butler would come in carrying a tray of poached trout, whole with tail and head. Springs would lob the fish at his Yank pals, for them to catch in their mouths like performing seals. It impressed the English gals to no end, they said they'd never seen anything like it!"

"I'm not sure they meant it as a compliment," Clayton murmured.

"'Course they did," Springs declared. He staggered off his bar stool, swaying with the effort of staying upright, then seized a wine bucket and banged on it until the Mess quieted. "A toast! A toast!" He raised his glass. "To London girls, the most wonderful, accommodating, jolly girls in the whole world!"

"I reckon," rumbled a deep voice in a Devonian burr, "that the farmer girls in Devon would give those city slickers a run for their money."

"Wha? Who said that?" Springs demanded, weaving through the crowd until he bumped into a man monolith.

Bob Weston was Lance's idea of an archetypal Anglo-Saxon yeoman. The farmer's blond thatch and affable face topped six feet and three inches of rough-hewn muscle and a dray horse's depth of chest and weight of limb. When Lance first watched him take off in a SE5, he had the vivid impression that Weston was riding the plane rather than sitting in the cockpit.

Springs craned his neck upwards. "You, huh?"

Weston smiled amiably. "To girls," he toasted.

Springs' unannounced roundhouse punch bounced off the massive farmer's granite jaw. Weston blinked. His uppercut in reply only travelled six inches but sent the American crashing to the floor in spectacular style.

"Camels to the rescue!" Thommo cried, downing his drink and rolling up his sleeves before barging his way towards Weston.

Somewhere en route, Thommo realised he was on his own, and the Canadian's charge on the man-mountain from Devon turned into a solicitous enquiry into Spring's health. Weston grabbed Springs under the armpits and hoisted him onto a bar stool like a puppet and placed another glass of champagne in the American's hand.

Springs swayed on the stool and shook his wobbly head in admiration. "Never been punsshed so hard in my life! A man who punssh like that should be treasured." Then he handed Thommo his glass and slid like a sack onto the floor, out cold.

"Drinks for everyone!" Thommo hollered, then shook Weston's hand. "I used to be a boxer, lightweight of course, but I recognise a damn good punch." He demonstrated an uppercut. "See, lads, comes from the waist and shoulder, not the arm. Eh, Weston?"

Weston examined his own ham-like fist dubiously. "I don't know. I just hit people and it seems to work."

Clayton saluted Weston as the Bristol and Camel pilots pushed to get their drinks. "Good to see old-fashioned bonding between pugilistic connoisseurs."

"Huh?" Weston said.

"This isn't like the stuffy mess in 13 Squadron," Lance said to Clayton, "I enjoy this place. It's like theatre."

"As far as Arthur's bonding goes," Clayton murmured, "I think the evening has gone jolly well. Fewer fisticuffs than a Glasgow pub on a Monday night."

~

26 May 1917

Two days later, Arthur winced as Lance slammed his fist onto the rickety table that served as Arthur's desk. Even Clayton, waiting not so patiently behind Lance, jumped. Arthur sighed. English subordinates often erred on the side of being obsequious yes-men, but colonials seemed to regard superiors as someone to be bullied.

Lance glared at Arthur, who remained seated. "The Bristols are almost ready to fly, and you promised I'd not be the squadron commander when that happened! I just want to be in Ball's squadron flying an SE5 and killing Huns."

"And *you* promised to remain the squadron commander until I got a replacement," Arthur replied. "So, keep your word. And do *not* slam my desk!"

"When is that going to bloody happen?"

"You are out of order, Captain Fitch." Arthur surged to his feet. "Tread carefully. You are already on Boom Trenchard's blacklist for rejecting your promotion. For some strange reason, he does not think the RFC revolves around what Lance Fitch wants."

Lance shrugged. "I'm not looking for a career in the army. Why should I care what Boom thinks?"

"Because thanks to you, I am on that same blacklist for recommending you."

"Why do you care? You don't want an army career either."

"God, you are dense sometimes," Arthur said. "In case it has escaped your notice, the war has been going for three

Arthur smiled and shook his stunned adjutant's hand. "These days I can even get a clodhopper captain like you promoted to major. Congratulations."

"Goodness gracious me. Do you have photographs of Boom in compromising positions?"

"Tsk, tsk—you do yourself a disfavour. No matter how good our pilots and planes are, if we are not in the right place we cannot prevent the Circus winning control of the air. So, this wing must be the most mobile in the RFC. Wherever Richthofen and his crew go, we need to follow them, two days behind at most. If we cannot find a suitable airfield in the right location, we will use meadows and live in tents. As wing adjutant, you will oversee 450 personnel—administrators, fitters, riggers, armourers, and drivers. Not to mention forty aircraft and sixty pilots and observers, plus a transport fleet of trucks, trailers, cars, and motorcycles. HQ agreed it would take a major to handle the logistics challenge." Arthur leaned back in his chair and stretched his legs before taking another puff.

"I'm flattered HQ rates my talents so highly," Clayton said.

"They do not. I said they agreed that the wing adjutant should be a major. They almost had a fit when I suggested that major should be you."

"I am indebted to your noble worthiness, Lord Wolsey."

"Sometimes, Clayton, you are total twit. Why would I ever put myself out for you? I may have mentioned to HQ that whoever took the job must be expendable. I promised them that if the person in charge of this logistical and intelligence nightmare failed, I would fire him. Mysteriously the flood of well-connected volunteers for this nice safe role in the new prestigious wing evaporated, and HQ deemed you ideal."

"Aha! There had to be a sting in the tail."

"I knew you would understand," Arthur said, flicking ash into the base of a fired shell-casing that he used as his ash-tray. "But with Sergeant Major Smythe to do the real work, there is a remote chance you might succeed."

"Perish the thought. Hercules had it easier with the Augean stables."

"Do not be so dramatic. There is one more small detail—"

"A trifling one, I'm sure."

"Absolutely trifling," Arthur confirmed. "I want an orchestra."

Clayton's clipboard slipped out of his hand, and papers fluttered over the floor. Arthur blew smoke rings as Clayton collected the skittish papers.

At last Clayton straightened up, red faced. "Excuse me, I misheard. I thought you said you wanted an orchestra."

"I did."

"Would this be any orchestra in particular, say the London Symphony Orchestra? Or perhaps your tastes lean more to the Royal Philharmonic Society?"

"No, no, just a common and garden orchestra."

"Pray do tell, how common and how garden?"

"Well, pretty common since the players need also to be mechanics, riggers, fitters, chefs, drivers, whatever."

"I see…actually, I don't see at all. What the hell are you talking about?"

"For 100 Wing to bond in the skies it needs to bond in the officers' Mess. These pilots will fight the enemy's elite several times a day. Many will die, and the stress will be enormous. I want to keep their morale high when they are passing time in the Mess on rainy days, or long winter evenings after a tough day's flying. Something that helps them celebrate their victories or help mourn their friends. The only thing I can think of is an orchestra. So, you will contact other squadrons, and offer to swap our fitters, mechanics, armourers, with any of theirs who can play an instrument—always provided they are competent at their primary job. You can use my private booze supplies to bribe anyone reluctant to trade their personnel."

Clayton was silent for a while.

"Well?" Arthur raised his eyebrows.

Clayton sighed. "'See the world,' they said, 'Join the army.' Now I am a musical impresario and a juggler of men, machinery and munitions, but like a hero in Greek tragedy, inevitably doomed to failure and public crucifixion."

"Do not get carried away, old man, it will just be a private court martial, I expect. Then shot at dawn on a cold and misty morning with no one around. I doubt it will even make the pages of the *Times*. By the way, if Albert Ball tells you he plays the violin, take it with a pinch of salt. He plays like a cat being strangled. That gave me the idea. If people were listening to his caterwauling, they must be desperate for music, or something that passes for it… So, Major, earn your new rank and get going on that orchestra if you please." Arthur stubbed out his cigar.

Clayton shrugged into his raincoat as if in a dream and left the office, still looking stunned. Arthur smiled as he fingered the coins in his pocket. Clayton had forgotten to collect his guinea.

~

Lance splashed through the rain towards the officers' Mess, his chin hunched inside the turned-up collar of his trench-coat. Rain pattered on his peaked officer's cap, and he sneezed as cold rivulets ran down his neck. Bloody weather, bloody Arthur. He pushed open the door and shook himself like a wet Labrador. Lance took stock as he shook out his coat and cap and hung them on wooden pegs beside the door.

A new officer, tall and clean shaven, was playing the piano and singing in a rich baritone.

Greensleeves was all my joy.
Greensleeves was my delight,
Greensleeves was my heart of gold,
And who but my lady Greensleeves.

Despite himself, Lance hummed along with the tune. The man was good.

Albert Ball and Thommo lounged over the piano, the former with his eyes closed and a dreamy expression, no doubt thinking of a girl in England. Thommo joined in the next chorus, which diminished the quality of the performance. Lance stopped humming. A third person, a junior lieutenant from the single pip adorning his shoulder epaulets, stood at the bar, hunched over his drink with his back to Lance.

The haunting old English love song reminded Lance of Megan. She'd sent him a letter saying she was trying to get over to France for a visit. He pulled a face. He had no idea how a civilian woman could get near to Le Hameau, but if anyone could it was Megan with her money, influence and force of character. Maybe she meant Paris, but getting leave for Paris would be difficult. And once the new planes were ready, getting any leave at all would be impossible. He pushed her out of his mind. A meeting was a nice dream, but that's all it was.

The song finished, and Ball introduced the singer. "Lance Fitch, meet Daddy Heath, one of my new pilots, so called because he is thirty and acts like an adult most of the time."

"I can't help the adult bit," Daddy said. "I have two kids and have to act mature for them. Besides, I was an accountant before the war, so I'm supposed to be boring."

Daddy shook hands with Lance, who registered the pleasant open face and relaxed smile.

"It *is* old for the RFC. What made you volunteer?" Lance asked.

"I'm too old to tromp in puddles in the trenches, collecting lice, but I want to do my duty. Although I'd like to get home in one piece. I have a beautiful wife and two daughters I dote on. So, you won't find me volunteering for balloon busting or anything suicidal like that, but I will do my bit when I am in the air."

"Don't listen to his modesty," Ball said. "He's got eight kills already."

"Not my fault," Daddy smiled. "Fly long enough and pump enough bullets into the air and sooner or later a Hun will fly into them."

"Oi, Warbaby! Come say hello," Ball said.

The skeletal teenager wandered over from the bar, carrying a lemonade. Lance stared. The minimum age for joining up was seventeen, but damned if this boy looked a day over fifteen. Not only was he baby-faced, he looked consumptive in his frailty. But his handshake was strong and dark eyes bored into Lance's.

"Lieutenant Harmison," Ball introduced, "christened 'Warbaby' by his previous squadron after his tenth kill. He's almost as keen to kill Huns as you, Lance."

"Pleased to meet you, sir," the newcomer said in a flat Northern accent.

Over drinks, Lance squeezed conversation out of Warbaby. Durham was his hometown, and the lad spoke in an unemotional monotone of backbreaking hours spent down mines for little pay. His father and two elder brothers had signed up for the infantry on the day war broke out.

"They thought it'd be better than t'mines," Warbaby said, his dark forelock hanging over his pinched face. "T'were wrong. All three died same day on t'Somme. So, I joined the RFC. As Bunyan says in *Pilgrim's Progress*—

'We are come to revenge the quarrel of the many that thou hast slain of the pilgrims.'"

Ball looked startled. Lance felt oddly protective. He could appreciate a good revenge quest.

15
If You Were the Only Girl in the World

Two days later – 28 May 1917
France, Arras Sector, Le Hameau Airfield. RFC, 100 Wing.

Lance, frozen and frustrated, landed his Pup at dusk. He'd had time to kill as the Bristol squadron mechanics installed the new Rolls Royce engines, and he'd wanted to fly his Pup and bag some Huns. But it had taken two more days for Smythe to get 'Frankenstein' into the air, and Lance's maiden flight with the clapped-out monstrosity had not been a success.

"Frankenstein needs a kick up the arse," he told Smythe as he wiped castor oil off his face. "I found a Rumpler at sixteen thousand feet, but this clapped out machine wouldn't get past fourteen." The Pup's official ceiling was seventeen thousand, but Lance could only grind his teeth as the Hun had sailed serenely two thousand feet above him.

Smythe fingered the loose wire rigging. "This was taut when you left, sah. I checked it myself. This plane is falling apart, too much warp and flex. I recommend we retire it, sah. It ain't safe to fly, never mind throw around in a dogfight."

"It may not be safe, but it's all I have," Lance said. "The engine was the real problem today—missing beats and low on power. Also, it's chucking so much castor oil into my face there has to be a leak. It makes me gag, and it's giving me the runs."

"The mechanics have rebuilt the engine twice, sah. From scratch."

"Make it three times, starting now. I'll join the mechanics after supper. This time, they'd better get it working."

Smythe's magnificent moustache bristled, and he eyed Lance like a Cape buffalo about to launch into a thundering charge.

Lance wasn't intimidated. He'd faced the real thing. "Don't pull that face, it makes you look constipated." Then he strode away quickly just in case Smythe lost control and used his six-foot-high and four-foot-wide frame. After all, when Lance had faced buffalo he always had a Rigby .416 rifle to hand.

He heard a wooden crate splinter behind him. It had his sympathy. A size sixteen army boot powered by Smythe's powerful thighs would pack a mean punch, almost as much as the Rigby. But Smythe would cool down by the time Lance finished supper.

Hopefully.

Lance's brusque mood worsened when Clayton told him that Albert Ball and Thommo had both knocked down a Hun in their Nieuports. For a second, he fantasised about stealing one of their Nieuports for a flight, but the ground crews wouldn't let him. And neither would Ball or Thommo lend him their aircraft. He wouldn't in their shoes, either.

After a quick shower, he stomped into the officers' Mess to find it empty except for Ball and three of his new pilots. They clustered around the bar with their squadron commander, although the latter was drinking only lemonade. A record played on the newfangled gramophone, and George Robey's rich voice filled the room.

There would be such wonderful things to do
If you were the only girl in the world
And I were the only boy.

Lance joined the others at the bar and Ball did the introductions.

"Cyril Crowe, a founding father of the RFC on his third flying tour of France."

Crowe smiled as he shook hands. "Because Ball is twenty, he thinks I am ancient at twenty-three." Lance noted the steady eyes, neat moustache, immaculate uniform, and firm handshake.

Ball waved at a tall willowy youngster with a long face and heavy nose. "Cecil Lewis, a literary type who loves quoting poets and dead Romans but sports a Military Cross."

Lance could not resist. "Forgive me for asking, but you seem very young to have an MC?"

Albert Ball's face twitched with what might have been amusement. "Believe it or not, he's been in the RFC since 1915, even though he's younger than me."

Cecil Lewis flushed bright red and petted the Irish wolfhound that sat at his feet.

"A pilot in 1915?" Lance asked, "Strewth, how old were you then?"

Lewis looked up from his dog and gave a smile of rare charm. "Er, let's just say that being six-foot-three helped fool the recruiters over my age. One minute I was at school making model aeroplanes, the next I was flying Moranes against the Fokkers. Surreal!"

"Last but not least," Ball said. "Henry Meintjes. He's a colonial from Africa, just like you, but with better manners. In fact, he is so posh we call him 'Duke'. Was with me in 60 Squadron. Star man."

"Delighted to meet you," Duke said with a warm smile and firm handshake. He turned out to be from South Africa, a long way from Taveta, but soon the two of them were swapping their memories of Africa.

Too soon the door to the Mess banged open. "C'mon, guys," Thommo said, "I've found my wallet. Dinner on me at the café in Le Hameau."

Crowe and Cecil Lewis drained their drinks and collected their caps. Duke Meintjes gave Lance a regretful glance. "I said I'd go. See you tomorrow."

"Ah, Lance," Thommo said. "Hear you had bad luck with your plane." He smirked. "I'll buy you a consolation drink."

"Thanks, but I'll pass. I need to help fix my engine."

"Suit yourself. What about you, Albert?"

Albert Ball shook his head. "Thanks for the offer, but I want to write to my girl tonight."

"C'mon," Thommo cajoled. "There are waitresses at the café who'll help take your mind off home. Mama Thompson always says a girl in the hand is better than two in the bush."

Ball demurred, and Thommo exited in disgust with the newcomers in tow.

The record ended, and the needle hissed on the turntable. Ball wandered to the gramophone and put on a different record—*Thank God for My Garden.* He gave Lance a shy smile. "This song reminds me of my girl back in England."

"What's her name?"

"Flora, but I call her Bobs." Ball pulled a creased and dog-eared photo from his wallet and passed it to Lance. The young girl was gorgeous, even frozen on battered black and white paper.

"You're a lucky man."

"I know. Have you got a girl?"

"Sort of. She's trying to get over here to visit."

"Good luck." Ball put the photo away. "Funny. I haven't shown that photo to anyone else. Maybe I trust you because you aren't a gossip like all the rest. I've been watching you. You are serious about this war, like me."

Lance nodded. "I am. I've got personal scores to settle with the Germans. Speaking of which, you are the most successful of us all, and I'd like to pick your brains sometime."

Ball searched his eyes. "I want to write letters now while the others are away and I've got use of the gramophone. But if you want to talk, I'm in the hangars at 0600 hours most mornings sorting ammunition."

Lance left the mess as elated as if he had arranged a date with the best-looking girl in town.

An hour later he was less happy. Frankenstein was dead.

The mechanics' attempt to extract full power from the rotary engine resulted in a loud explosion, a shower of castor oil, and an engine casing fractured by metal fatigue. Lance and Smythe glared at each other.

"Sah, I told you the engine couldn't take more," the Sergeant Major said, his jaw muscles grinding. The mechanics edged away, finding other tasks further away in the hangar.

Copious amounts of oil blotched the Sergeant Major's face and overalls, and his face was suffused a choleric shade of red. His hair was mussed with the force of the explosion and one end of his handlebar moustache bent downwards mournfully. Lance suspected he himself must look the same—minus the damaged 'tache of course.

A chuckle escaped Lance. At first he wasn't sure what it was, but then the mirth bubbled out. His mouth opened wide, and laughter poured out until it bent him over, and he had to clutch his knees for support. When Smythe glowered menacingly in return, it only made Lance laugh harder until tears ran down his cheeks. Eventually, a deep rumble came from the Sergeant Major. When the dam broke, Smythe's booming guffaws and Lance's belly laughter soared into the cavernous gloom around the lamp-lit hangar.

Next day – 29 May 1917

"C'mon Arthur!" Lance wheedled. "Frankenstein went kaput last night. Let me fly an SE5 across the front lines."

"No, no, and a hundred times, no." Arthur did not even look up from the paperwork on his desk.

"Why ground me?"

"I am not grounding you. I'm following Trenchard's orders. You know 'orders', right? Those things that are meant to be obeyed."

Lance glared at Arthur. "What the hell am I supposed to do? Hang around the airfield picking my nose while Albert Ball and Thommo increase their score? Let me fly an SE5 over the lines, for God's sake. This is insane."

Arthur's friendly blue eyes grew frosty. He picked up the phone handset and held it out towards Lance. "Be my guest, tell Boom Trenchard."

Lance's eyebrows went up. "He'd speak to me?"

"No. He'd bellow *at* you. Then he'd post you to Blighty to a training squadron." Arthur offered the phone again. "Call him or shut up!"

"He wouldn't find out if I flew an SE5 across the front lines if you didn't tell him."

"Lance, stop being a blithering idiot. You think no one will spot an SE5? Especially when you shoot down a Hun? Now get out of here. You could, of course, help others get their planes ready."

Lance stomped out of the office. Pilots and ground crew avoided that thunderous scowl, and even Cecil Lewis' Irish wolfhound slunk out of his way. Smart dog. The compulsion to kick something was overpowering.

An hour later a spotty French youth, too young to be mobilised into the Army, drew up outside the airfield on a back-firing motorbike to hand deliver a scented letter addressed to Lance. Megan's flowery script announced her arrival in the Belfort Hotel in Amiens and invited Lance to join her whenever he could. Lance inhaled the scent one more time and then hid the letter in his breast pocket. Megan was a magician; her timing was uncanny. A day ago, he'd have said 'no'—he had Huns to kill. Now he was planeless, she was a saviour.

He asked Arthur for a night's leave, his face burning as he stammered about looking for spare parts in Amiens. Arthur interrupted him before he could complete his lie.

"Go! When Haig starts his attack our chances for leave will be rarer than snowflakes in hell, and you are a giant pain in the posterior moping around here. For the love of God, go!"

~

30 May 1917
France, Town of Amiens, Hotel Belfort.

The next morning Lance woke in heaven. A heaven of a soft feather bed and fluffy pillows with the delicious aroma of bacon and eggs. Megan had ordered a breakfast delivered to their hotel room, and now she sat with him, naked and with her slim legs curled under her, as he ate.

"This is quite possibly the best hotel stay of my life," he said as he wiped the plate clean with the remaining chunk of the fried bread.

"Possibly?" Megan pinched him.

"Ouch! Definitely!"

'That's better," Megan said as she wiped egg off his lips with her thumb. "Are you sure you've had enough?"

"Enough of you? Never! You take me to a world away from war." He pulled her closer to kiss her. She smiled his reward and groped his groin under the bunched sheets as their slippery tongues duelled. They had made love in the night, but he hardened again.

She pulled away. "Enough food, silly? You may be ready for loving but I'm not. You'll have to wait. Tell me how you and Arthur met."

Megan reached over to remove the tray, her breasts brushing his arm. He cupped their soft warmth, but she slapped his hand away. "Behave, or you'll spill the tray."

He peeked at his watch. Only an hour until he had to leave. She snuggled up to Lance and threw one long leg possessively over him, apparently content to lie there for a moment.

A strand of her long black hair tickled his nose, and he puffed it away. Dried lavender scented the spacious hotel suite, and a radiator ticked in the corner, keeping the room warm enough that Megan could lie on top of the sheets. Not something that would be possible in the draughty huts at Le Hameau, with their rough serge blankets and the smell of castor oil and sweaty flying clothes.

He stroked her hip. Love making with Megan was a voyage into new-found lands. Lance was no virgin. The Du Plessis twins, big-boned pillow-breasted Afrikaner girls from the neighbouring farm, had used him as a stud horse when they felt randy. The sisters would toss their blond braids and whinny their pleasure as they mated, but loving was not part of their repertoire. Mrs Hetherington, the English teacher near Taveta sadly widowed too young, introduced him to a softer style of romance. Then Heidi had kissed him, and he had forsaken all others, even though their most ardent sessions ended only with kisses and clothed fondles.

But Lance had never met a sensualist as skilled as Megan. She enrolled caressing silk chemise and stinging leather whips, tickling-soft feathers and sharp-pointed hatpins, ice-chilled champagne and guttering-hot wax, blindfolds like midnight and candles' flickering light, all accompanied by the rhythmic jangling of her silver bracelets and the husky-voiced urgings of a harlot.

She interrupted his thoughts by prodding him with a finger. "I'm waiting. How did you and Arthur become friends? Your personalities and backgrounds are so different."

Lance sighed. The sooner he gave her what she wanted, the sooner he might get what he desired. "When you share one plane and it is kill or be killed against the Huns, the only thing that matters is whether you can rely on your crewmate. Does he have the guts and the skills needed for us to live? And when you find that rare person, someone you can trust literally with your life, it creates a bond that transcends everything. Arthur and I found that bond our first flight together, but we didn't relax into true friendship until we were shot down in our pyjamas."

"You went to war in your pyjamas?"

"When you are on dawn patrol you have to turn up dressed to fly until you are officially told the patrol is cancelled. But when it is obvious the weather is too bad to fly, pilots just pull their flying coat on top of their pyjamas so that when the patrol is cancelled, they can go straight back to bed. On this day the rain was lashing down, and we were sure our patrol would be washed out, so we did the usual. But a strong weather front was pushing the storm away, and the Germans had launched a surprise attack. HQ told us to take off immediately, rain or no rain. We had no time to change, so we ran for our planes still in our pyjamas."

She snorted with laughter. "How little us women at home know of the strong and bold warriors who hold our nation's hopes. Perhaps it is better this way."

"Mmm. It was brass monkeys freezing on patrol until 'Archie', that's what we call the German anti-aircraft fire, shot through our fuel line. Fortunately, we had enough height to glide to our side of the lines and land in a field next to an artillery regiment. Our teeth were chattering, so they dragged us into a dugout which was so warm and stuffy we stopped shivering and started sweating. They gave us rum in a pint glass. A pint of rum! I'd never even had a sip of rum up to then."

"What a sheltered life you led, Lance."

"Before I met you, anyway. We tried not to take off our flying coats and reveal what was underneath, but Arthur caved when the sweat ran down his face in streams."

Lance giggled at the memory.

"What!" Megan exclaimed, sitting up so abruptly that her breasts bounced. "You never giggle!"

"Imagine the scene. A dark enclosed dugout twenty feet below the muddy trenches, lit by gas lamps, with a bunch of macho, muddy and unshaved soldiers knocking back rum. Then Lord Arthur Wolsey strips off his coat and stands there drinking in his muddy sheepskin flying boots and—ta-da!—natty black silk pyjamas embroidered with red and gold Chinese dragons!" Lance chuckled. "I had a coughing fit trying not to laugh. Arthur pretended the RFC always went to war like that. He came across as such an upper-class twit!"

"What about your pyjamas, darling? Tartan? Paisley?"

"Very boring. White long johns and a rugby jersey. Safe to say our garb provoked a lot of comments about fliers being crazy! Anyway, to prove we were manly fliers we had to drink extra hard. When the squadron tender arrived to pick us up, our hosts gave us another pint of rum to see us home, and we polished that off on the way back. When we reached the airfield, the driver poured us out of the tender." Lance shook his head at the memory. "That was the first and last time I ever got drunk, and somehow it broke down the barriers between us."

"They do say alcohol is a great social equaliser."

"Lady Exenrude, are you being snobbish?"

"Of course! I can't believe I am in bed with a man who doesn't have monogrammed silk pyjamas with dragons. It's an absolute first for me, darling. Although," she murmured, stroking his leg, "I rather like you in your birthday suit myself. Why don't we ring the bracelets again before you go?"

He looked at his watch. Enough time. Thank God for small mercies.

Since Hawker's death he suffered two new re-occurring nightmares. Forrester consumed in flames, reaching to pull Lance into the pyre with burnt claws, and Lance rooted in front of Hawker's plane as it crashed, helpless as it hurtled towards him until the still churning propeller chopped into his flesh.

Night after night he wrestled these dreams of fire and blood. They stole his sleep and sapped his energy. When he looked in the mirror in the mornings, a haggard man of forty glared back.

Which was a blessed relief.

Because he didn't feel a day under seventy.

But look on the bright side. It was his only chance to learn what he'd look like at forty, because sure as hell he wasn't going to live long enough to attain those distant hills.

Lance reached for her warmth, her soft curves, her smooth skin, her musky scent. Only she could banish his chilling dreams. Only she made him feel young, invincible and inexhaustible instead of ancient, beaten and burned out. When Megan welcomed him inside, when she crooned her husky love song, when the bracelets jangled, then the world turned in a different orbit.

~

Next day – 31 May 1917

"For he's a jolly good fellow," roared the pilots of 100 Wing, and Clayton laughed as Albert Ball flushed to the roots of his unruly hair. The man at the centre of the celebrations looked as though he would rather be alone with his vegetable patch.

Ball's kill three days ago had been his fortieth, a unique achievement in the RFC, and one that took him past Guynemer, the French Ace of Aces, as the highest scoring Allied airman. Now he was second only to Richthofen among pilots of any nation, and that by a mere dozen.

"It is the perfect excuse for our first official shindig," Arthur had said, "and our last before we tackle the Circus. Clayton, I want you to organise the best damn party any of the pilots have experienced. You will find some crates in the hangars that may help."

Clayton hailed from an aristocrat family, albeit a minor one compared to the Wolsey Estates, but even his mouth hung open as he supervised the unpacking of the mysterious crates. The Wolsey Family crest, a rampant lion with crossed axes, embossed the silverware, the long-stemmed crystal glasses, and the embroidered tablecloths of the finest Flemish linen. When one crate yielded vintage brandies and wines that cost a fortune, Clayton could no longer stay silent. "Arthur, this is casting pearls before swine. Honestly, no one here will appreciate this stuff. It's sacrilegious to waste your family's cellar like this."

Arthur waved a dismissive hand. "Much better that pilots fighting for their king and country get to drink it than the fat politicians and ancient snobs who I have to entertain at Wolsey Hall. I want 100 Wing to feel they are the RFC's finest warriors and appreciated as such."

So, Clayton turned the shabby mess dining room into a miniature banquet hall. Tables shimmered with pristine white tablecloths. Flames from magnificent candelabras reflected on the silver wine buckets loaded with champagne bottles, and crystal decanters glowed with ruby coloured wines of impeccable vintage.

"Hell of a way to fight a war!" said Lance, "Why did we never have this in 13 Squadron?"

Clayton shrugged. "Ask Arthur. I think he's inspired by this elite concept. Got his Lordship's leadership juices going. He may not have been enough of a slave-driver to challenge 13 Squadron out of their determined mediocrity, but I think he will come into his own surrounded by a crew of self-motivated warriors."

Lance shrugged. "Who cares why? It makes a colonial oik like me feel special."

"Bonzer piss up," Andrews agreed. "I could get used to this living like a lord."

"Don't get too used to it," Clayton warned. "When the war is over, you'll be back to your Aussie hovel. By the way, have you met Ball's latest recruit, Rhys-Davids? He's over there talking to Elliot Springs. Odd pairing—one teetotaller and one lush. Let's rescue the poor lad."

Rhys-Davids possessed much of the same dark good looks as Ball, but was even younger. By reputation he fought like Ball, attacking the Huns wherever he found them without regard for odds or tactics. Those angelic looks must bely a bloodthirsty hankering for glory.

There the comparisons ended. Clayton knew from the personnel files that Ball had gone to a grammar school and his father was a plumber, while both Rhys-Davids' parents were professors specialising in Indian languages and Buddhism. Rhys-Davids himself was an Etonian who had given up his classics scholarship at Oxford University to join the RFC. He and the spindly Cecil Lewis had hit it off, and would hobnob in the mess spouting poetry at each other and quoting Euripides.

"Did you know Springs read philosophy at Princeton?" Rhys-Davids asked, sounding impressed. "Philosophy means 'love of wisdom' in Greek, so he must be a wise man."

Clayton almost choked on his champagne. Springs looked at the boy as if wondering whether Rhys-Davids was taking the piss, but the youngster's face shone with earnest interest.

"So, Springs, care to share any of your great wisdom?" Clayton asked, one eyebrow cocked.

The American sighed. "My personal philosophy is that in this war it is our solemn duty to enjoy as many willing women and bottles of wine as possible, while we are still alive."

"Hardly Plato," Rhys-Davids said, sounding disappointed.

Springs smirked. "My philosophy is more Epicurean with large dollops of Dionysus."

"I don't want to be a killjoy," Lance said, "but you might stay alive longer if you cut down on the—"

Springs interrupted. "I fly worse when I'm on booze withdrawal."

"I'll drink to that," Andrews said, tilting his glass.

Lance snorted. "As if you'd ever tried."

Springs shrugged. "There speaks a born warrior. Sadly for the rest of us, to keep a relative sanity in this insane war, alcohol is not only a crutch but a food staple. Besides, you are lucky enough to be flying the SE5 and not that castor oil–throwing monstrosity, the Camel. Without the binding effect of brandy on my bowels, I could never get off the toilet to wage war with the Hun."

"Mate," Andrews said, "it's a good job you're flying Camels, or you'd be bung-full of shit."

That set Springs off on a fit of giggles. Clayton rolled his eyes at Rhys-Davids and the two of them drifted off, disappointed in their search for pearls from the Princeton School of Philosophy. "Springs seems to have rather loose morals around women and wine," Rhys-Davids said.

Clayton made a mental note to introduce the young Etonian to anyone who would lead him into sin. It would be a shame for him to die a virgin.

"Ding ding." Leefe Robinson, the new squadron commander of the Bristol Fighters of 222 Squadron, rang a wine bucket with a fork. He had arrived earlier that day, and Lance had handed over command of the Bristols with obvious relief. Then Lance had transferred to Ball's SE5 squadron as per Lance's agreement with Arthur.

Leefe Robinson possessed saturnine good looks with a small moustache, pointy ears, and a face that crinkled with a sense of playful mischief and vibrant good humour. Despite his fame as the first pilot to down a Zeppelin airship bombing London, and winning a Victoria Cross as a result, he displayed no airs or graces and had pitched into the party. "Gentlemen, I launch the Champagne Challenge. If anyone can beat me at this game, I pay for their bottle of champagne."

He vaulted over the bar and grabbed a bottle of chilled champagne from the barman. Then he seized a large carving knife and decapitated the top of the bottleneck with a neat stroke. He lay flat on his back on the floor and balanced the bottle on his forehead with great care. "If I use my hands or spill a drop of this precious elixir while getting to my feet," he announced, "drinks for the rest of the night are on me." The pilots cheered at the prospect, but soon lapsed into disbelieving silence as Leefe Robinson wriggled and squirmed from his back to his feet without using his hands, all the while balancing the open bottle on his forehead like a seal in a circus act. True to his word, he did not spill a drop of champagne.

Wild applause broke out. "Any challengers?" the new squadron commander asked.

Rod Andrews took off his jacket. "Anything a Pom can do with booze, an Aussie can do better!"

Two shattered bottles and some good-natured jeering later, Andrews surrendered. Elliot Springs weaved to the front of the crowd as the next challenger. Clayton grimaced—this would be another criminal waste of good champagne. He fell back on his Indian Army experiences to divert the cyclone of destruction before the pilots could devastate the newly gentrified mess. "Ahoy," he shouted. "All aboard for a game of Hodson's Horse Steeplechasing."

"What the hell is that?" asked Leefe Robinson.

"It's an old Bengal Lancer's game for young reprobates with more energy than brains. Each squadron will put forward a team of five members, who will relay-race around the Mess walls without touching the floor. The winner is the first team to complete this circuit."

Leefe Robinson was not the only one who looked baffled. "And how the heck do we get around the Mess without touching the floor?"

"Use your imagination, old man. It's not for me to do your navigation for you. But a quick look tells me that rearrangement of the furniture would allow a start across the sofa; a tough stretch along the curtain rail over the door; an easy run along a couple of tables; then up to the picture rails again; along the mantelpiece over the fire, and a final swing on the curtains to make it back home onto the sofa."

"Strewth!" Leefe Robinson exclaimed, his small moustache twitching in delight, "I like it!"

Ball shook his head at the juvenile antics and took his leave. Thompson pulled an imaginary train cord. "Choo Choo Chooooo! The Camels are coming."

Lance grinned at the Canadian. "No chance, mate—Ball's Bulls will leave you in the dust."

Clayton shook his head in wonder. Lance playing games in the Mess, with Thompson no less. Who'd have thought it?

The game began in a storm of cheers and jeers as the participants stumbled their way around, learning the intricacies of the unfamiliar contest. The Brisfits disposed of the Camel with ease, the latter team being handicapped by Thompson and Elliot Springs, whose transatlantic enthusiasm exceeded their capabilities.

Clayton watched the horseplay while perched in a safe corner with his own bottle. He took a delicate sip of his red wine and rolled the results around his palate. It caressed his taste buds, gamey and velvety at the same time. Marvellous stuff. He'd rescued several bottles of Clos Vougeot 1865, a legendary Burgundy year, from Arthur's crates. Too good for philistines. It needed someone who could appreciate the finer things in life. He held his glass to the light and drank in the deep ruby colour that sparkled in the candlelight. A piece of wine history from an era before Bismarck had even unified Germany. He inhaled and closed his eyes in pleasure at the gloriously intense scent. While the human race could produce such beauty, surely there must still be hope for civilisation?

A drunkard weaved past and knocked Clayton's table. He clutched the bottle protectively to his chest. "Hooligan," Clayton muttered.

In the final, Rod Andrews powered the Brisfits into an early lead, but Duke Meintjies clawed back most of the gap in the penultimate round. The last hand-off saw Lance a mere five yards behind Leefe Robinson. The curtain rail was Leefe Robinson's weakness, and his slow hand over hand allowed Lance to catch him. As they raced across the table a swift ankle tap by Lance sent Leefe Robinson crashing face first onto the table. Lance gleefully leapfrogged him. Leefe Robinson, a growing bump on his forehead, started his dogged circuit again as the Brisfits bayed their disapproval at Lance's underhand tactics.

But when Lance swung down from the mantelpiece to land on the ledge over the fireplace, Thompson sloshed red wine on the smooth stone. The treachery caught Lance by surprise and his feet slid away from under him. He overbalanced and arms flailing, slipped off the fireplace to land catlike on the floor. Lance wasted no time in recriminations. He sprinted back to the start and resumed his chase of Leefe Robinson, who seemed groggy from the effects of Lance's earlier ankle tap. Even so the lead was too large.

Leefe Robinson was well ahead when he tiptoed with exaggerated care across the still treacherous fireplace, and swung on the curtain to the sofa that was the finishing line. As he landed, he yanked the curtain from the rail. "Oops! Sooooo sorry old boy!" he said, turning to taunt his pursuer. "My, that is a big leap from the fireplace to the sofa. No one would blame the Balls-ups for not finishing the course."

The mess rocked in delirium, with the chants of "Brisfits, Brisfits" drowning out the angry remonstrations of Ball's Bulls about two-seater chicanery. Lance eyed the gap and shook his head.

Leefe Robinson extended his hand: "Here, let me help you." The fickle watchers now cheered his good sportsman-ship and urged Lance to jump.

Lance took a take-off run and almost made it. He landed one foot on the arm of the sofa and frantically grabbed for Leefe Robinson's extended hand to prevent him from toppling backwards. As Lance did so, Leefe Robinson withdrew his hand and thumbed his nose at his pursuer. Lance windmilled his arms, but gravity was too strong, and he fell backwards, cracking his head against the wooden floor.

Leefe Robinson revived the stunned Lance by pouring ice cold champagne on his face. "Ashes to ashes, dust to dust," Leefe Robinson intoned. "If Richthofen doesn't get you, Leefe Robinson must!"

"God, that hurt! I can't believe I fell for that."

"Me neither," Robinson said with glee. "It's clear you never went to an English public school. If you had, you would not be such a poor trusting sap. No hard feelings, Fitch old man?"

"No hard feelings," Lance wheezed, still on his back, "Here, help me up."

Leefe Robinson solicitously took Lance's outstretched hand. But Lance snapped his foot into the standing man's stomach and pulled hard on the helping arm, launching Robinson over Lance's prone body and into a back-first crash landing on a sofa. He thudded into the seat with a twang of springs and a cloud of dust. The two men looked at each other for a second, and then burst into laughter.

"Absolutely dastardly," Leefe Robinson shouted as he detached the sharp end of a wire coil from his trousers. "You, sir, are a credit to your school, wherever it may have been!"

Clayton, draped over the bar, gave the official verdict: "I hereby declare the Brisfits the inaugural champions. Free drinks for the Brisfits!" More cheers, and the officers thronged the bar.

As the Brisfits jostled for refills, the windows flooded with garish red light. The pilots rushed outside, expecting a night attack by Hun bombers, but found only Albert Ball. He had stuck a burning flare into the ground and was playing his violin by the flickering light.

Clayton would never forget that sight until the end of his days. The slim, serious Ball, a silhouette backlit by the red glare, sawing away at the violin. Schubert's Unfinished Symphony—"Very unfinished in this version," Clayton muttered—soared high as drunken pilots cavorted like dervishes amongst the darkness and the smoky red light.

Clayton stood in the darkness, swaying as he watched the bacchanal. What a night! He'd delivered the 'best damn party' that Arthur had demanded, and then some. He should feel proud, but the alcohol made him maudlin, and without warning his mood turned ugly.

Soon 100 Wing would enter the fray. How would they fare against the cream of Richthofen's men? He looked around the young men cavorting in the firelight whose frenetic cheerfulness seemed tinged with fear.

How many of them were wonderingwho would be alive for the next party?

~

A sorry crew gathered for breakfast the following morning. Clayton wasn't immune. He nibbled a piece of toast as the stench of bacon turned his stomach. That second bottle of Clos Vougeot had seemed an excellent decision at the time. And it probably was. The problem was the third, the one he could not remember opening. When he saw the empty bottle beside his bed, his brain denied the evidence. The sour taste in his mouth and the marching band stomping round his skull said otherwise. It appeared he did not suffer alone. The clink of cutlery against plates was the only sound.

Until Leefe Robinson bounced into the morgue.

"Grand party!" He spooned himself a large helping of porridge and looked around at the human wreckage around him. "Well folks, I am proud to announce that not only are the Brisfits the Hodson's Horse Champions, but we are also the first squadron ready to fight the Huns. I have Arthur's permission to launch 100 Wing's first formal flight across the front lines tomorrow."

"Hooray," Thommo muttered, stirring his porridge with the enthusiasm of the hung over. "Bully for you."

"Thank you, kind sir." Leefe Robinson smiled as he slathered marmalade thickly over his toast, his appetite unperturbed by either a hangover or Thompson's cynicism.

Clayton watched with slitted and jealous eyes as his head throbbed. Leefe Robinson had downed enough champagne to float a battleship—the man must be indestructible.

16
A Bloody Nose

Next day – 2 June 1917
France, Arras Sector, Le Hameau Airfield. RFC, 100 Wing.

The big day dawned—how would the Bristols fare?

Lance huddled with Arthur, both burrowed into their greatcoats against the damp chill. The sun rose but failed to burn through the thin mist clinging to the fields. Weather reports showed the sky clear above five hundred feet although there would be low-lying fog on the German side. The whole wing turned out of their beds to wave Leefe Robinson's Brisfits off with a mixed feeling of excitement and apprehension.

HQ had thrown the Bristols a challenging first operation—a patrol over the town of Arras, Richthofen's backyard. A head-on confrontation with the Circus seemed preordained. The pilots left on the ground hummed with suppressed excitement. "Lucky sods," said a voice, "Wish I was going with them…first of 100 Wing to give the Circus a bloody nose."

Lance wandered towards where the Bristols loomed through the thin mist. The big planes looked warlike, crouched high off the ground with massive wings and giant two-bladed props set low in their long-snouted radiators. A streamlined fuselage flowed into the smooth ellipse of the tail, giving the plane a rakish air. He found Leefe Robinson tying a silk stocking to his starboard struts, just below the red streamers that denoted his status as commander.

"Lucky charm from a lady friend?" Lance asked.

"I figure Lady Luck would prefer silk stockings to a rabbit foot."

"Came to wish you luck," Lance said.

"Thanks. Appreciate it." Leefe Robinson pulled on his leather flying helmet and buckled it with shaking hands. He saw Lance looking at his hands and smiled crookedly. "When you've won a Victoria Cross everyone thinks you are a nerveless hero. There's pressure to behave that way. But I'm nervous as hell." He held out his trembling hands. "Last time I was over enemy lines was as an observer in 1915, and I collected an armful of shrapnel. Now I'm leading men against the Circus. I don't want to let anyone down."

Lance clapped him on the arm. "I've been across the lines a hundred times or more, and I still get nerves. Part of the job. You've got damn good planes. Just keep your eyes peeled, and we'll share a drink when you get back."

He gave what he hoped was a reassuring smile and strode away. Lance had never thought about it before, but for sure the pressure of living up to the legends of VC winners must weigh on a man.

He stopped by Rod Andrews and Fred Libby, ready for the usual repartee between the Aussie and his American gunner. To his surprise, they were taciturn and grim faced.

"I'd wish you luck," Lance said, "but I know the devil looks after his own."

Andrews just grunted. Lance turned to Libby and jerked a thumb at the Australian. "What's wrong with Grumpy, you hidden his booze supply?"

Libby gave only a ghost of a smile. "We're going over at 4,000 feet."

Lance frowned, out of words. Andrews saw it and nodded grimly. Lance grimaced. "Break a leg," was all he could say as they climbed into their plane.

One by one, the Bristols' engines coughed into action and settled into their thunderous roar, shredding the remnants of mist into swirling wisps. Propeller-wash lashed the onlookers as the Bristols swung into the wind with bursts of power. The gunners crouched, facing backwards, backs hunched against the prop-wash, working their rear facing guns on the new Scarf ring mountings. The pilots waggled the ailerons and rudder to test them, then waved away the ground crews and taxied onto the runway. Leefe Robinson, his commander's red streamers fluttering from his wing struts, gave the watchers a flamboyant salute. He opened his throttle, the big Rolls Royce engine bellowed, and he led the six machines over the hedgerow eastwards. Their growl faded and left the airfield hushed.

"They look good," Arthur muttered, beating his hands together to keep them warm.

Lance grunted, but not in agreement. "Leefe Robinson's tactics are daft. He plans to patrol at four thousand feet—not low enough for surprise or high enough for tactical advantage."

"I will not overrule a squadron commander leading the flight," Arthur retorted. "It is their mission, their choice, their lives. End of story. Besides, Leefe Robinson is a Victoria Cross winner."

"A VC says he's brave, not always the same thing as being a smart leader. He has never fought against these Albatross and the new Hun tactics. It's one thing shooting down a big gasbag like a Zeppelin over London at night, and quite another taking on Richthofen and his crew. All credit to him for the first, I could not have done it, but it's not relevant on the Western Front today."

Arthur reddened. "If you wanted a say in Bristol tactics, you should have taken the squadron commander role. You would be leading them right now, in the manner you want. But you refused, so do me a favour, shut up and wish them luck."

Lance blinked under the attack. "I don't believe in luck. Practice and training are better."

"Ha! You believe in your own bad luck, so you should at least be consistent and believe in good luck too."

Lance opened his mouth to respond but found no suitable retort. He blew into his cupped hands, and his breath smoked in the dawn chill.

~

Same day.
Arras Sector near Douai, Roucourt Airfield. Jasta 11.

Fog squatted over Roucourt airfield as the pilots of *Jasta* 11, wrapped in their flying coats against the damp of the early dawn, sat around the outdoor breakfast table. Hans Schmettow burped spicy sausage, sat back in his chair with a sigh of satisfaction, and crossed his legs at the ankles. Say one thing about *Jasta* 11, they ate well. While pilots in other *Jastas* choked down ersatz coffee, powdered milk, and gristly sausages, Richthofen's men enjoyed the real stuff; a minor miracle in the third year of Britain's all-encompassing naval blockade. That prig, Adjutant Bodenschatz, had his uses. He bartered the luxuries from the army supply commissar in exchange for signed photographs of Manfred Richthofen. Those bastards in the commissar had adding machines in place of hearts, and they knew the cult of the baron was so strong back in Germany that such photos were better than cash.

Hans pulled up his collar of wolf's fur and snuggled lower into his flying jacket, glad for the prospect of a day off. No one would fly in this soup. The fog muffled the sounds of the airfield: the hammering of tools on the engines, the bellowing of engines being warmed up, and the shouts of the fitters and mechanics. A surreal world washed pallid white as the sun struggled to penetrate the haze. Just like the early morning gatherings in the hunting lodges back home in eastern Prussia.

He tuned out Richthofen as the man blathered about meeting Kaiser Wilhelm, dinner at the palace, how gracious the Empress had been, blah blah... Then a toady asked Richthofen about the hunting, and the conversation took a more interesting turn.

"The hunting?" Richthofen repeated in a tone of deep satisfaction, "Superb. The Prince of Pless invited me to his estate, the last place in Europe with bison. We—"

The shrill clamour of the phone shattered the tranquillity. Bodenschatz, the adjutant, leapt to pick up the phone linked to the forward observers on the front lines. Hans could not imagine a less martial noise, yet the phone was the clarion call that sounded the charge for *Jasta* 11.

Bodenschatz slammed the phone down and shouted at Richthofen: "Six British two-seaters heading this way between one and two thousand metres."

Richthofen had snapped to his feet on the first ring. Now he grabbed his gloves and helmet.

"Festner, Simon, Schmettow, fly with me. If the British are up, it must be clear above this fog."

The named pilots grabbed their gear and ran for their planes, which the mechanics had been fussing over since dawn.

By the time Hans vaulted into the cockpit, the ground crew had the engine running. He took a quick glance at the gauges—all fine. His crewman fastened his safety harness, gave his screen a last rub to wipe the moisture away, and whisked away his chocks.

Hans' palms were wet with sweat. He'd never flown in mist. A vision flashed through his mind: his plane smashed into smithereens against the ground, his broken body and sightless eyes staring into the sky.

Richthofen was already taxiing. Hans motioned away the ground crew and pushed the throttle open. The flicking propeller accelerated into a brown blur, and the Mercedes engine pulled him forwards with a throaty roar. He stuck his head out of the side of the cockpit to see better through the murk, but the prop-wash buffeted his face and sent rivulets of water running across his goggles. His wheels lurched over the grass, and the airframe creaked and rattled until the Albatross lifted off the ground. The green blur beneath him vanished into white nothingness. Moisture streaked off his windshield as he climbed into the mist. He groped upwards through the blindness, his nerves stretched to breaking as his imagination played its tricks.

At one hundred metres, the Albatross burst into a weak sunshine, filtered through a morning haze but no less welcome for that. Hans sucked in deep breaths of relief and swung after the other red-hued planes climbing westwards towards Arras.

There they found the intruders, six specks sliding towards them on a diagonal path. Richthofen continued climbing until they were above the enemy. Hans squinted at the unfamiliar silhouette with big square wings and a long snout. Bodenschatz had briefed the JG1 pilots that the British were coming out with new aircraft, rumoured to be formidable.

Fear nagged him. The superiority of the Albatross over the British aircraft helped to compensate for Hans' lack of flying skill, and his superior marksmanship did the rest. But if the British produced new planes as good as the Albatross—or God forbid even better—Hans would struggle to survive, never mind bag the kills he desperately needed to impress Richthofen. Kills were the currency Richthofen dealt in, and if the necessary payments were not forthcoming, he would be as ruthless as a Berlin loan-shark.

The Englishmen tightened their formation into a circle, the so-called "ring-a-ring-a-roses"—an old British two-seater tactic using interlocking fields of fire from the rear gunners to protect each plane. This formation was hard to break if flown with skill and conviction, and it took guts to press home an attack into the storm of crossfire. Hans took a deep breath. With Richthofen assessing him, he couldn't afford any cock-ups today.

Guns hammered ahead of him as Richthofen tested his guns. Hans did the same and the sulphurous reek of gunpowder sparked his confidence. Richthofen's gloved hand gave the axe chopping gesture for attack, and he rolled his Albatross into a plunging dive on their prey, his pilotsfollowing in arrowhead formation. Hans' slipstream shrieked like the Valkyries in his ears and adrenaline surged through his body. He screamed into the howling wind. *Tod oder Ruhm! Death or Glory!*

The Albatross slashed through the English formation, attacking with such ferocity that the British planes scattered like a flock of pigeons hunted by sparrow hawks. Hans' guns pounded, and his tracers criss-crossed the return fire from the rear gunner. The enemy missed while Hans' tracers streaked into the fuselage of the British plane—yet it flew onwards. Hans overshot and pulled up in a soaring dive to regain height for another attack.

Only Richthofen had disabled a victim on the first pass. His victim skidded downwards, trailing thin grey smoke, and Richthofen swooped to deliver the coup de grâce. The other Albatross harried the British, keeping them from reforming. Hans pursued one with gritted teeth and closed to fifty metres. He would get a *verdammt* kill today. His target twisted and turned out of the way each time Hans was about to press the trigger. Sweat ran into his eyes as he threw his heavy fighter after the enemy. At last, he saw his chance when the big plane turned across him. His thumb tightened on his gun triggers as his sights floated onto the enemy. Before he could fire, tracers from the rear gunner slashed at Hans' face. He flinched and stomped on the rudder bar to skid away from the bullets. Hans dived underneath his supposed prey without firing, so close he saw the yellow kangaroo painted on the fuselage.

He pulled up into a steep climb, his mouth as dry as a desert. Hans had smelled the phosphorous—which meant the bullets had passed within a metre. He puffed his cheeks. Best to challenge a plane with a less dangerous gunner.

He took stock of the situation. The enemy planes were still deep behind German lines. One of them fluttered erratically downwards while Festner followed it, guns flickering. The remaining four were running for home, isolated from each other. Leutnant Simon harried one. Richthofen had reappeared and was chasing another. Hans turned away from the plane with the accurate gunner and dived on the remaining Englishman. This one had red pennants fluttering from its struts, the British sign of a commander. As Hans chased the enemy, he saw the gunner beating at his gun with his gloved fist.

His guns must have jammed. A wolfish glee filled Hans. With no rear gun to worry about, Hans closed to within twenty metres. The gunner looked up, and his assault on the jammed gun became frenzied. Hans touched his rudder bar to line the sight's crosshairs on the gunner. His twin machine guns pounded. Tracer lines speared into the gunner, who jerked in the hail of bullets until he collapsed into the cockpit. Hans pulled back on his stick a fraction to allow for the deflection and fired another short burst. His bullets missed the pilot but punched into the engine cowling. The enemy propeller slowed and windmilled to a stop. Hans overshot his quarry and reefed around in a tight turn so he could flame the bastard before he landed.

But the British pilot intuited Hans' intent and dropped the nose of the aircraft into an almost vertical dive. This new British plane dived like a brick, and Hans lost ground as he followed more cautiously. The Englishman pulled out of his headlong dive and flared into a hasty crash landing. An undercarriage sheared off and a wheel bounded across the mud. Wings crumpled into matchsticks as the big plane slewed sideways, trailing wreckage.

"Yes!" Hans screamed to the heavens, clenching his fist and pounding the cockpit rim with glee. Kill number seven! He dropped his plane lower to strafe the wreck. He deserved a treat. The pilot had struggled free and was pulling the limp gunner from the plane. As Hans soared lower, the pilot stopped and looked up. He didn't run, just stood there staring at his executioner. Hans licked his lips and placed the crosshairs on the man.

A shadow loomed in the corner of his eye.

He jerked his joystick into a steep turn as he screwed his head backwards to see who was behind him. Richthofen! The *Rittmeister* signalled Hans to fall in, and he obeyed without hesitation. Thank God he had seen the shadow before he opened fire. Richthofen had reamed him a new asshole the last time he had caught Hans strafing a downed enemy.

A few hundred metres away a black pillar of smoke rose from the flaming wreck of another Englishman. It must be Richthofen's second kill of the day. This had been another massacre—the new British planes were as useless as their old ones.

The killing glow spread through Hans' belly like the finest cognac. His seventh kill! Hans nodded in reluctant admiration at Richthofen's genius. Other *Jasta* would never have attacked with such ferocity and broken the enemy defensive circle. Kills came thick and fast around Richthofen, and if Hans kept licking the megalomaniac's ass and stayed in the *Jasta*, he'd have his ten kills and an Iron Cross in no time.

~

Lance's guts coiled in knots at the sorry scene. Two battle-torn Bristols sagged on the airfield, the other four were wrecks in Hunland. He blew out his cheeks. The maths was easy enough. Good planes plus good men minus bad tactics equalled eight men gone west, two badly wounded, and only two men untouched. The very smallest of consolations was that he couldn't blame himself for this tragedy.

One of the surviving planes was a write-off. Its riddled undercarriage had crumpled on landing and the propeller chopped itself to splinters against the ground. The top-left wing hung askew, and the fuselage lay broken in half, the rear part lying ten feet from the rest. Long streaks of blood smeared the fuselage where Pike and Griffiths had been lifted from their riddled plane and stretchered to hospital. Lance liked Pike. Only last night they had shared a lemonade while the young Canadian rhapsodised about his home city of Montreal.

The second Bristol, crewed by the Australian Rod Andrews and the American Libby, was hardly in better shape. Pinpricks of daylight showed through the bullet holes riddling the wings and fuselage.

What a fiasco. 100 Wing's first official patrol and the Circus, their supposed prey, had inflicted more than eighty percent casualties.

Arthur conducted the postmortem inside his office. Andrews had been at the front since 1916 as both observer and pilot, and counted as a battle-hardened veteran. He was usually among the most happy-go-lucky of men, but now his anger made his Australian twang even more noticeable.

"It's not the bloody planes. But we need to fly them like fighters, with the advantage of a rear gunner. I'd be happy to take on those red bastards again tomorrow in this crate. But Leefe Robinson got everything wrong. We went over too low, and our formation was too defensive. And the other poor bastards all had their machine guns jam."

Clayton handed Andrews a tumbler full of whisky. He knocked it back like water. When Clayton offered to refill it Andrews nodded, but could not hold the glass steady enough. The Australian frowned and grasped the glass with both hands, concentrating as the glass rattled against Clayton's bottle. Andrews threw down the whisky in one shot again, but at least acknowledged the spirit with an appreciative sigh as he held out the glass for more. The others said nothing. They had all suffered post-combat shock at some stage.

"Look mate," Andrews continued, "I liked Leefe Robinson, but these Huns were smart and aggressive as hell. That bugger Richthofen was one, an all-red plane. His mates were good too. They dived out of the sun, broke our circle straight away. The red bastard got Lechler on the first pass. Another Albatross, white and red, was a helluva good shooter—I saw him down Leefe Robinson." Andrews took another swig, paused, and took a longer one that emptied the glass.

"White and red, you say?" Lance asked. "I know that one—he strafed me on the ground the day Hawker died. Sounds like I have another bone to pick with that bastard."

"He may be a bastard, but he can shoot. Which is more than most of our guys could say. Looked like a lot of them suffered jammed guns, and I know why. The armourers told Leefe Robinson that the Lewis guns were jamming in training 'cos the oil was freezing at high altitude. So he told them not to oil the guns, so there wouldn't be anything to freeze."

"What!" Lance exclaimed. "That's insane. The guns would jam in seconds without lubrication—at any height!"

"That they did. Libby and I kept our guns oiled and they worked fine."

"Bloody amateur hour," Lance muttered.

"Carry on, Andrews," Arthur said.

"Well, that's about it, sir. After the Huns broke our circle, I dived for home, jinking all the way in a hell of a funk and praying. Libby did a grand job keeping the buggers off our tail."

The howl of an SE5 Hispano Suiza engine on full throttle blasted over their heads. Led by Arthur, they jostled out of the office to investigate. An SE5 was disappearing over the poplar trees on the airstrip boundary as Sergeant Major Smythe marched towards them. He came to full attention, made a magnificent salute, and announced, "Sah! Mr Ball. Taken an SE5, sah."

The officers looked around. None of them had noticed Ball's departure from the debriefing.

"The devil he has," Arthur swore, "and taken off crosswind to boot. Did he say where he was going?"

"Yes, sah. To kill Huns. Furious he was, sah."

"Sergeant Major. Your ground crew has express orders to prevent any SE5s from taking off with enough fuel to go over the lines. Why are your men not enforcing my orders?"

"It's Mr Ball, sah. They won't go against his wishes."

Thompson made a noise like kettle steaming. "Well, they bloody well go against mine! I tried to go over the lines in my Camel and the bastards removed the rocking lever so the engine wouldn't start. Why do they stop me and let Ball go?"

"They love Mr Ball, sah."

Lance hid a smile. Ask Smythe a question, and you always got a direct answer. Thompson went puce and turned to Arthur. "Don't know why Ball always gets special rights," he grumbled. "It should be a level playing field. He gets all the chances for glory."

Clayton took Thompson by the arm and pulled him away from Arthur, who was glaring at the Canadian. "Thommo, it's precisely because Ball does not care for glory," he said, "that others give it to him. When General Trenchard gives you a personal aircraft and personal permission to undertake solo missions whenever you like, as he has done with Ball, then you can tick off your wing commander about unequal treatment. In the meantime, why don't you button it?"

Thompson shook off Clayton's hand. "Don't patronise me. We'll see who's the best when I get my Camels over the lines." He stalked away, his back rigid.

Arthur was still staring after the SE5. "I can see Thompson's point that Ball enjoys special treatment from Boom, and from the mechanics, but there again Ball is unique. He is just…Albert Ball. While we talk, he acts."

Lance nodded. The quiet unassuming overachiever inspired the whole RFC. But the RFC possessed a plethora of brave men. Ball offered something more—the indomitable arrogance of a true warrior. A warrior willing and capable of taking on all comers, focused more on killing challengers than on his own survival. Ball epitomised the belief not that he could win, but that he *would* win whatever the odds.

"We are not going to take this lying down," Arthur said, his voice taut with anger. "In two days, I want all the Bristols we have left armed with Mills bombs, and as many SE5s and Camels as are ready. We will bomb and strafe Richthofen's airfield at dawn. I will lead the raid myself in an SE5. Get organising." Arthur made shooing motions at Andrews and Smythe but nodded for Lance to stay.

Arthur waited until the others had left and spoke without preamble. "Lance. I want you to take command of the Bristols. You refused before, but this massacre changes things."

"No."

"Damn it, man, I need you leading them. This will tear the guts out of the Bristol squadron. They need you."

"Give it to Andrews. He's earned it the hard way, and he's got good ideas."

Arthur's lips thinned in anger. "All right, Lance, you are forcing me to say this. What would you have done differently than Leefe Robinson?"

"Number one—oil the guns. Number two—use the Bristols as fighters instead of going into a defensive circle. Number three—go over at twelve thousand feet to prevent the Huns bouncing us out of the sun with the advantage of height."

"How many survivors if they did it your way?"

Lance shrugged. "It isn't a precise science, but six of us against four Albatross, I'd like to think we'd lose none."

"So, is it fair to say that if you had not dodged command and if you had led this patrol, then eight men might still be with us now instead of dead or captured?"

"Whoa, Arthur!" Clayton interrupted. "You're punching below the belt."

The wing commander swung on his adjutant. "Am I? Lance thinks bad things happen when he's responsible for people. Well, reflect on this, Lance. We lost eight men today, who might be alive if you had not ducked responsibility."

There were white spots on Lance's cheeks. "You bastard! Don't lay those deaths at my door. I didn't appoint Leefe Robinson, you did."

"You are right, I did. I take the blame for thinking a VC holder would be competent, and I am taking my mistake to heart. I do not stick my head in the sand, say things are obvious, and then refuse to be part of solutions to the problem. It is time you stood up and became a leader, not just a critic."

Arthur stabbed his finger into Lance's chest. "You too carry blame, whether you want to admit it or not. There are sins of omission as well as sins of commission. Now you can rectify your mistake and take over that squadron."

Lance turned from Arthur's accusing stare, but it did not help. The pitiful tableau of wrecked planes only added weight to his friend's charge. He turned back to Arthur. "No. I won't be a squadron commander. We've been through this."

"I thought you might possess the decency to reconsider in the circumstances. Your guilt is a luxury 100 Wing can't afford."

"Give the squadron to Andrews, he deserves it."

"Lance, stop running from command. This whole sad episode shows bad things can happen in war when other people are responsible, not just when 'Jonah' Fitch is in charge."

Lance shook his head. "It's true I would have done most things differently. But when you're a Jonah, fate finds different ways to kill. You'll hear no more opinions from me on tactics, daft or otherwise. I won't be responsible for other people."

Lance stomped out of the office.

Arthur turned everything back to front. When Lance blamed himself, Arthur didn't agree. When Lance held himself blameless, Arthur pointed the finger. Seemed blame attached itself to Lance whenever folk died, all that varied was the accuser.

Arguing with Arthur was like raiding honey from a beehive. When the swarm of words came at you, some always got through your defences. And God, did they sting!

Why were Leefe Robinson's boneheaded tactics Lance's fault? Leefe Robinson and Hawker shared much in common; both vanquished heroes had won the Victoria Cross; both simple-minded tacticians had led men to needless deaths; both possessed too much courage and too little cunning.

But who was Lance to point fingers at anyone else? God knows enough corpses trailed his conscience like rotten fish. *Damn Arthur. Damn them all. I am not my brothers' keeper. I'm here to kill Huns, not babysit. Bugger everything and everyone else.*

17
Seven Peals of Thunder

>   Next day – 3 June 1917
>   France, Saint-Omer, RFC HQ.

"Baring!" The windows rattled at RFC HQ. Baring winced. He knew the problem. Boom Trenchard was copied in on 100 Wing's combat reports, and he had just read about their ignominious failure yesterday. Time for Baring to earn his keep and protect Wolsey and his fliers from the wrath of Boom. Many RFC pilots would choose a shelling from the Huns before a verbal volley from Boom.

To make matters worse, today the Germans were trumpeting their capture of the famous Leefe Robinson. He hoped that Boom had not heard that bit yet. Just in case, Baring sidled into Boom's office on his toes, ready for a quick escape. Missiles were known to fly in this office.

"What a sodding disaster! Give Wolsey a Victoria Cross winner, and he gets the man shot down on his first flight by the very people he's supposed to be hunting! First Hawker, and now Robinson. Bloody useless!"

"Well, sir, Ball scored two kills the same day, so he improved the net score. But indeed, the losses are disappointing."

"Disappointing?" Boom slammed his meaty fist on his desk, which rocked under the impact. "I promised Haig and the politicians parity in the air if they got us these new planes. They gave the RFC top priority for scarce material and factory production over the rest of the army and even the navy. And now? We look bloody stupid for making promises we can't deliver, and they look stupid for believing us. The politicos never forgive if you give their opposition a stick to beat them with. The next time we beg for priority, they will take great delight in putting the RFC at the back of the waiting line." The general shut his eyes for a few seconds and composed himself with a deep breath. "At least Ball did some damage. If we had ten Albert Balls, Richthofen's bloody Circus would perform their next act in hell. Still think Wolsey's the right man for the job?"

"I believe so, sir. I have here a plan he is hatching to bomb Richthofen's airfield. He's burning to get revenge."

As Boom read the plan, his face softened. "I like it. Shows guts. Takes a beating, gets right back into the ring. Good man. Approved. If we can't shoot the bugger down, bomb him while he's on his early morning khazi with his pants down. Tell Wolsey I need his outfit to shoot down more Huns than they have losses."

"I'm pretty sure Wolsey knows the plan, sir, and is endeavouring to execute it to the best of his abilities. It's possible we may be asking too much of 100 Wing at this stage."

"Bollocks, Baring. I won't stand for defeatism. Haig and Gough will launch their attack sometime inside the next ten days. The RFC can be the difference between a glorious success and a bloody failure. 100 Wing will put planes in the air to support that attack whatever the cost! If the pilots die but the ground attack breaks through, General Haig and the Prime Minister will count it a good trade. Now get out of here and tell Wolsey to kill that bloody Richthofen!"

Baring exited, but not before slipping more papers onto Boom's desk in such a way they nudged Boom's favourite pipe under his inbox, where he would not find it for a few frustrating hours.

~

Two days later – 5 June 1917
France, Arras Sector, Balleul Airfield. RFC, 100 Wing.

"Here is our new base," Arthur said, and braced himself for the inevitable reaction.

He and his senior officers stood on a wooden walkway that connected the new 100 Wing HQ buildings and stared morosely over their new airfield. The buildings themselves, the offices, the dining Mess and anteroom, and a shower block, were wooden shacks, separated by mud that made the walkways a blessing. To the west, a watery evening sun silhouetted a church tower and its attendant cemetery that sprawled around it. Northwards, the forbidding wall of the large local asylum loomed over some hangars. Farmland stretched away south and east, where an arrowhead of birds winged their way homewards. A chill breeze made Arthur shiver

"You call this an airfield?" Thompson asked. "It's wetlands surrounded by a graveyard and a lunatic asylum. Which is what it is good for, loonies and corpses. If a bureaucratic genius wanted to pick somewhere with no redeeming features as an airstrip, he would have chosen this place."

Arthur pulled a face. There was some truth to the remark. Unlike the bucolic countryside of their old home at Le Hameau, Bailleul was large, crowded and noisy, a typical military garrison town. Even worse, its airfields were prone to flooding.

"Be reasonable," Arthur said. "It is difficult to find an airfield at short notice opposite the Circus and large enough for three squadrons."

Arthur's original plan to attack the Circus had been altered when spies reported that the Circus had moved from the Roucourt airfield in the Arras sector, to Courtrai in the Ypres sector. HQ went into full-scale panic mode.

Did the Circus' move to that area mean the Germans had sniffed out the British plan to attack near Ypres? Either way, HQ must block German aerial reconnaissance around Ypres to hide the British build-up of men and artillery. The order for 100 Wing to follow the Circus to Ypres went out within twenty minutes of Haig hearing the news.

Clayton's new ground organisation excelled, and within two days the planes, pilots and ground crews had moved to Bailleul Aerodrome, just thirty-five miles from the new Circus base in Courtrai.

In fact, Bailleul was three separate airfields situated close together.

Clayton pointed to the church. "The Bristols will be based on the Town Aerodrome," he told Rod Andrews, the newly installed commander of the Bristols.

Andrews raised his eyebrows. "Perfect," he declared, "landings and take-offs over the cemetery, so if anyone crashes their remains will be into the ground faster than a dingo down a rabbit hole."

"Thommo, your Camels are on Asylum Aerodrome" Clayton said.

"Appropriate," Thompson said. "Camel jockeys have to be lunatics."

"I'm afraid," Clayton continued as he turned to Albert Ball, "that the SE5s have the short straw. You and your pilots will be housed in tents on the East aerodrome." Ball's mouth twisted as though he was sucking a sour lemon. He looked at Lance, stood beside him. Lance shrugged at his squadron commander. "The landing strip looks fine, higher than the others," he said

"Gentlemen, please, restrain your enthusiasm," Clayton muttered.

"Enough," Arthur declared. "You are officers in the RFC, not trade union officials choosing your next holiday camp. Come into my office."

Thompson threw his cigarette into the mud where it sizzled and died.

They traipsed into the office, which was bare except for packing cases, a plank which served as a desk, and a scattering of three-legged farm chairs. Their boots clunked on the creaky floorboards and trailed wet footprints and mud.

"Sit down," Arthur said. He moved behind his 'desk' but remained standing, leaning forward with his knuckles on the plank. He stared around them, holding each of their eyes for several seconds. "In thirty-six hours, Haig will launch his attack at Ypres. And at the same time, we will bomb the bejesus out of the Circus."

The effect of the announcement was everything Arthur had hoped. His officers sat bolt upright. He continued. "Now we've finished moving, Clayton is gathering intelligence and photos on the Circus' new location. When we have that information, we will plan the attack in more detail. In the meantime, get your squadrons ready for a dawn attack in two days.

"One more thing. I want to agree to some distinctive markings for 100 Wing so the Circus will always recognise us, especially after this attack. I want us to be in their faces every time they fly and for them to realise we are dedicated to their destruction."

"Why?" Albert Ball asked.

"Fitch once told me a story that stuck in my mind. Tell them your poacher story, Fitch." Arthur saw Lance wince at the use of his surname. Good. Since Lance had turned down command again, Arthur had not once used his first name. Lance should understand how seriously aggravated Arthur was by that refusal.

Fitch shook his head. "That story is not relevant."

"And I say it is. Tell them. That's an order."

Fitch squirmed in his chair. "We had an elephant poacher around our farm and—"

"Do we have to listen to this?" Thompson said. "How are elephants relevant to the Hun air force? I need a drink."

"Carry on, Fitch," Arthur said. "I'm interested in anything that gives us a potential edge on the Circus."

Thompson scowled and Arthur glared back until the Canadian's pale grey eyes dropped. Fitch smiled faintly at the interplay and continued. "Poachers shoot elephants with poisoned arrows, and the poor beasts suffer days of agony before they fall. The poachers cut out their tusks before the elephants are dead. It is cruel and wasteful killing, so we would capture the poachers and hand them in to the authorities. One time we were tracking a particularly canny poacher when—"

"Can we at least have the short version?" Thompson interrupted.

Arthur braced for the worst, as Lance narrowed his eyes and gave Thompson one of his tawny-eyed stares but kept his voice even. "We see this little old guy running into a belt of trees, and we gallop after him. I'm in the lead, and bam! My horse goes down as though pole axed, and I fly over his head. The cunning old man put telegraph wire between two trees at shin height and lured us into a trap. I was lucky. The poacher had stretched a second wire further up the trail, but this one at neck height. If I hadn't got caught in that first trip wire, I would have literally lost my head. Anyway, it knocked me out for a minute, and so we camped there that night. The next morning when I woke up, there was a poisoned arrow, broken in half, stuck into the ground between us. The poacher showed he could kill us if he wished, and that hunters could also be the hunted."

"Why didn't he kill you?" Clayton asked.

"That would have put the whole King's Rifles after him. He just wanted us to back off."

"And did you?"

"Of course," Lance admitted. "He was out of our league. He'd snuck into a camp of white hunters, Maasai trackers and hunting dogs, and planted an arrow right in the centre of the camp. That's a mighty dangerous man."

"So much for the great white hunters of Africa," Thompson interrupted. "What's your point, Fitch? I've got a whisky with my name on it and—"

"The point is the poachers' ambush and message made us less keen to hunt poachers and more cautious when we did. A lot more of them escaped as a result."

"Exactly!" Arthur said. "If the Circus feel we are always hunting them, it will make them think twice. They will be less aggressive and less effective."

"Makes sense," Ball said.

Thompson shrugged. "No skin off my nose."

"She's a beauty," Andrews drawled.

Arthur had no idea what that meant but took it as agreement. "Clayton, what can we do that Boom will allow? He does not like squadrons having individual markings," Arthur asked.

"Well, I once saw blue and white chequerboard cowlings on a night-fighting squadron back in England. They were distinctive, but the RFC must have approved them. If we stick to khaki paint with these chequerboard cowlings, it should be noticeable to the Circus but simple enough not to upset Boom. And if it does, we can argue a precedent."

"Let's do it," Arthur decided. "I want the Circus to sense our hot breath on their necks every time they take to the air."

~

Two days later – 7 June 1917
Belgium, Ypres Sector, Bailleul Airfield. RFC, 100 Wing.

Lance chewed his lower lip. Arthur was rolling the dice with this attack, and his wager bet with their lives. The luminous hands on Lance's watch showed almost 0300 hours as the pilots huddled outside their new officers' Mess. Many of them clutched steaming mugs of tea, their hands cupped around the warmth. The occasional loud bray of nervous laughter betrayed the tension in the air.

At dawn, 100 Wing would navigate thirty miles in near darkness to the Circus airfields, attack the hornet's nest, then fight their way back against the prevailing wind, pursued by vengeful Albatross with full fuel tanks and stocked ammunition belts. But if 100 Wing caught the Circus on the ground, a good strafing attack and some Mills bombs should cripple them for a week. A week in which Haig would launch his great offensive.

Lance smiled sourly. "With the balls of a bull and the brains of a gnat," one of the pilots had muttered when they heard the plan. Lance didn't agree. Momentum was vital, and 100 Wing had been slipping in sloppy mud and falling flat on their faces. This attack, if it succeeded, would change that dynamic. 'If it succeeded'—that bastard word 'if' again.

And if not? Well, most likely that would be someone else's problem. The dead don't carry worries. He hoped.

HQ had synchronised 100 Wing's dawn raid to support an infantry assault to capture Messines Ridge. Clayton had briefed the pilots. The British army would attack at Ypres to draw the German's attention away from the disintegrating French forces, but taking Messines Ridge was a necessary precursor. Messines Ridge, perched three hundred feet above the flat Flanders plain, was a lookout from which the Germans could see any gathering of material or troops miles behind the British front line. If the Huns held onto Messines Ridge there could be no surprise attack at Ypres, and many thousands would die.

"So," Clayton concluded the briefing, "taking that bloody ridge will be damn hard, but Haig has put two thousand artillery guns on a ten-mile front. That's a gun every seven yards, and we will pound them every day with half a million shells. The more spotting aircraft we can get over their lines, the more accurate that artillery fire will be. Our job is to keep the Circus away from those spotter aircraft by wiping them out on the ground. Also, our sappers have dug under the Hun trenches and planted over one million tonnes of high explosive. The ground attack will start when those mines blow at 0300 hours. 100 Wing will take off to attack the Circus at first light at 0500 hours."

A sound like wind sighing through grass rippled through the men as they exhaled in disbelief. Characteristically Thompson voiced his thoughts first. "One million tonnes! Jesus! Gives a whole new meaning to blowing them sky high."

"Precisely," Clayton said in a satisfied tone. "As General Plummer said, 'We may or may not make history with the attack, but we shall certainly re-arrange the geography.'"

Now the pilots kept vigil outside the Mess, waiting for the greatest explosion in the history of mankind. Most nights the front lines were lit by green and white flares and filled with the crump of shellfire. Tonight, sepulchral calm reigned, and the low moon reflected silver in pools of standing water between the huts. The pilots talked in muted tones, stamping their feet to stay warm. Lance looked at his luminous watch, faint in the dark. He frowned, convinced that at least fifteen minutes had passed since he looked at it last. He checked with Clayton, but the adjutant's watch showed the same time. Lance shrugged in disbelief and Clayton grinned, his face pale in the moonlight. "Always the way before an attack, time crawls."

The appointed hour for the attack came...and went. "The greatest dud in history," opined a hushed voice. "Maybe the Huns discovered the mines and—"

A searing flash of red ripped apart the eastern horizon. Pillars of crimson fire heaved the earth hundreds of feet high, while hell boiled out from underneath. For long seconds, the earth's crust hung suspended in the eerie flash. The image seared on Lance's retina. Then the red bloom faded and night rushed back, spots dancing in his eyes.

BOOM! The shockwave slapped his eardrums and reverberated in his bones. He staggered as the ground rippled, his senses reeling. When the world ceased shaking, he planted his feet wide like a man who'd lost faith in the earth's solidity, took a deep breath, and looked around. The other officers gawped into the renewed blackness, wide-eyed and slack-jawed.

An awed voice, disembodied in the darkness, wondered aloud. "We're ten miles away. What would *that* have felt like in the Hun trenches?"

Seconds later the British barrage opened fire. Thousands of heavy guns hurling hundreds of tonnes of high explosive, an orchestrated rolling barrage of percussive detonation. The rumbling thunder of continuous heavy shelling, the ongoing lightning flashes on the horizon—in previous great assaults lesser barrages had inspired awe. But this time, after the bass profundo of the mine explosions, the guns were yapping poodles.

"As John Bunyan prophesied, the seven peals of thunder have spoken," Warbaby intoned as he stared towards Messines, teeth gleaming in a manic smile. "Destruction is with us."

"I never had Bunyan pegged as someone who undersold fire and brimstone, but I may have to reconsider," Clayton murmured. "I almost feel sorry for the Huns. Half a million shells from the sky above, and a million tonnes from the earth beneath them."

"Then the bastards shouldn't have started the war," Lance said.

"I rather think the Kaiser started the war, not them. They are just cannon fodder like us."

"Keep your sympathy for those who deserve it, like our lads," Lance snapped. The mine explosion fed his memories of the barrage that had killed Will, the same barrage that first sent the terrifying white roar tumbling through his mind. Now that white surf threatened to suck him into madness once again. Desperately he searched for his hatred. When he found it, he let the thoughts of revenge for Francis, Hamisi, Will, Hawker, and Leefe Robinson all flare into his guts and up into his mind. He stoked the flames of hate until they scoured clear the mist of insanity. Then he held on tight to that loathing, that deep lust for revenge. He welcomed the pain as his clenched fists cut his nails into his palms.

Clayton broke the silence. "Well, the first wave of troops should be going over the top right now. Bless 'em and good luck. You lot are due to take off forty minutes before sunrise, so 0500 sharp."

The pilots broke up, chattering with excitement, their adrenalin stoked. Their confidence was now as palpable as their doubts had been.

This would be the first time that Lance would fly across the lines as part of a large formation, the first time he would rely on others to help him stay alive. The strangeness of such dependence had been troubling him, but now he caught their new mood of confidence. 100 Wing would bring fire to the Circus.

Lance looked at his watch again—an hour and a half before take-off. The bombardment and his adrenalin would not allow any sleep. He headed to the hangars to check his ammunition one more time. Anything to distract his mind from the worries that gnawed at him like a hungry jackal feasting on a bloody carcass.

~

When Lance entered the huge, tented hangar, he found fitters and mechanics swarming around the planes, preparing them for the attack. Hurricane lamps hissed from every available hook, and giant shadows leapt against the canvas walls as ground crew scurried between the aircraft. Shouts echoed, the voices urgent and demanding.

Lance grabbed a bucket of rounds, an ammunition checking clamp, and an empty galvanised bucket from his armourer. Albert Ball sat on a stool in the far corner, beside his SE5 with its distinctive blue spinner, surrounded by ammunition belts and three tin buckets. Lance strolled over. The harsh glare of the gas lamps etched deeper the exhaustion lines on Ball's face, and his round-shouldered stoop as he laboured over the ammunition completed the look of a man closer to forty than twenty.

Ball looked up when Lance's shadow fell over him. Long locks of black hair flopped over the squadron commander's forehead. "Hello, Lance. Care to join me? We never found time for that chat. Now would be good. It'll take our mind off what's coming."

"Good idea."

Lance sat on a stool and began checking his own .303 cartridges. His armourer and Lance had both checked the belts once already, but another check often threw up at least one duff. A slight bulge in the metal jacket, not discernible to the naked eye, would prevent the cartridge from sitting precisely in the clamp. If it didn't fit the clamp, it would jam a machine gun. Ball's reject bucket contained half a dozen cartridges, and, as Lance joined him, he tossed another into the bucket which welcomed it with a loud clang.

Lance kicked off the discussion with a question that had dogged him for a while. "Albert, how are you so successful when you attack large formations? You often nailed one and sometimes more, and then escaped despite flying that old tortoise of a Nieuport 17. How the devil do you do it?"

Ball chuckled. "I call it my Mad Dog theory. The more Huns in a formation, the less alert they are for solitary aircraft. The pilots think only large formations will dare attack them. And if a single aircraft does attack them, they all chase that one plane. That sucks them into the same small space, and they risk colliding. They must watch out for each other as well as me. That gives me the advantage. Every plane is an enemy for me, so I don't worry about colliding. I make that fear of collision even worse for them by flying like a mad dog. It's too unpredictable, and it takes their stomach for a fight away. So much so, I'm more confident attacking eight planes than three."

"What happens if you meet a Hun who is pretending to be mad too?"

Ball shook his head. "Oh, no—I'm not pretending, old man. I *am* prepared to ram the buggers. If you don't one hundred per cent mean it, they sense it and don't get unnerved."

Lance struggled to understand. His fingers carried on sorting ammunition while his mind worked on the problem. There was silence for a while with the occasional clang as the two men flung cartridges into their respective buckets.

"Albert, you're not the mad sort. What unlocks that madness? If you're not pretending, how do you…summon it?"

"Fear." Ball saw his incomprehension. "When I see a big formation of Huns, I am afraid. Then I get angry that I am afraid. I channel that fear into the Mad Dog fighting rage."

It clicked in Lance's mind like tumblers in a lock, and he sat back with a small smile. Ball saw the recognition. "You understand, don't you? You've used the same technique?"

Lance nodded. "Sort of. Listen, I've told no one this, and I'd appreciate it if you kept it under your hat. When I was in the poor bloody infantry the Hun artillery caught my platoon in a barrage that blew my brother and my men to pieces. God knows how I survived. I had a bad case of shell shock and was a basket case for months. Rage pulled me through the shellshock, a rage for revenge. When I'm most afraid, I fight like a berserker to keep the insanity away."

"Mine isn't revenge, but I use my anger the same way—to override the fear. We're alike, you and I." Ball looked pleased. "It's good to have someone who understands."

"That's true," Lance agreed. The two of them shared the bond of utter dedication to the art of air fighting. An obsessive dedication that even Arthur and Clayton could not under-stand. The others were too balanced, too sane to comprehend the all-consuming drive. Thommo had a focus on being a famous ace, but Albert Ball and Lance alone possessed total tunnel vision on killing Huns.

Now that Lance had opened the confessional gates with Albert Ball, he wanted to share more. "Our rage, it sustains us in the air. But how do you cope with the quiet times? I find those the worst."

Albert Ball grimaced. "Me too. When I'm back on the ground, I shake like a leaf. For me it's easier to do six patrols a day than sit here and think. That only leaves the nights, and I'm so tired even the nightmares are exhausted!" Ball's slim shoulders squared, and he sat upright. "I can only do it because I trust in God. If He wants me to make it through this war, I will. And if He does not, then I won't. Belief in God, love of my woman, and 'Mad Dog' tactics—these are the things that keep me alive." Ball's serious face cracked with a self-mocking smile. "And my mother's lucky fruitcake. I never fly without some. Keeps hunger pangs away too!"

Lance returned the smile. "Quite a mix of religion, love, and superstition. I envy you for your belief in God and love of a good woman. Revenge is my only sustenance. It seems thin gruel at times."

Lance finished a belt of ammunition for the Vickers, and Ball passed him an empty Lewis gun drum for loading. Lance said nothing, still digesting what he had heard. The two men continued their work in companionable silence.

Halfway through loading the Lewis drum, Ball spoke again. "Do you understand women?"

Lance laughed. "I've had a few girlfriends, but I can't claim to understand them. Not sure any man does."

"Isn't that the truth? When I joined the RFC, I was afraid I would die a virgin. Making love to a woman became the most important thing in the world. And once I'd done it, I needed to do it again and again...while I could, before I die. I loved each one of them, but I loved the next girl even more. Until I met Thelma, and then I wanted to settle down in a house and live a peaceful life with her."

"Hang on. The other night you said your girl was called Flora."

"You interrupted me. I loved Thelma, and could not wait to see her when I got leave. But then I met Flora, and I loved her even more and I'm engaged to her. But how can you be certain you've found the right girl? Is Flora the one for me, or might I find someone else even better on my next leave?"

"If God wills it," Lance joked, but Ball didn't laugh.

"My father gets angry with me for 'leading those girls astray' as he calls it, but I can't help myself. Dad hasn't a clue what it's like to fly every day with your nerves shredded, knowing you might soon be dead meat. Women are so warm and comforting—they take my mind off the war. Nothing else does. Am I a bad person for loving so many women? Is my dad right?"

"Phew! That's a lot of questions, and I'm not sure I'm qualified to answer any of them. What I do think is that these girls are choosing to be with you, so you shouldn't blame yourself. Besides, you aren't the only soldier doing such a thing. Whether Flora is the one for you—why not let time tell you the answer? How often have you met her?"

"Around six times."

Lance shrugged. "Don't think you can know the answer after a mere six meetings. See how your next leave goes. As for your dad—well, I'm sure he means well, but he can't understand our lives, so it isn't fair for him to judge. I agree with you that the act of loving is the only antidote to the carnage. We live so close to death every day, maybe God compensates by giving us a compulsion to do the thing that creates life."

"You've hit the nail on the head!" Ball waved a cartridge in one hand to punctuate his words. "I thought you might understand. Every time I shoot down a Hun, I rejoice because I am doing my bit to win the war, but sometimes at night, I worry I am murderer. I must have killed over fifty men. Who in history has personally killed people on a scale like that? Can't be many. In peacetime I would be a mass murderer, but in war I'm a hero. It's a sick secret burden to carry in a dark corner of your soul. I talk to God, but it's hard to get an answer. Loving women keeps me sane back in England among those politicians and conscription dodgers."

"I understand. With death sitting on our shoulder, there's a special sweetness to making love."

"By Jove, Fitch, you are right. Glad I talked to you." Ball was ebullient. "Know anything about vegetable gardens? My peas are struggling, and I haven't a clue why."

"Er, no. I know nothing about gardening."

"Shame. Sure?"

"Sadly sure," Lance said. "Gardening is almost as big a mystery to me as girls." He straightened his back. "I think we have enough ammunition to wage war on the Huns now. Breakfast should be ready in the mess by now."

Ball smiled. "It will taste extra good knowing that we'll be serving the Huns bombs with their sausages in a few hours."

~

After breakfast, Lance joined the others for a last briefing in the anteroom, where all the furniture had been pushed against the walls. Many of the pilots lit cigarettes, their puffs quick and jerky. The low ceiling trapped the smoke, and a throat-scratching fug hung in the air. Lance welcomed the swirl of fresh air every time the door opened and more pilots pushed inside, joshing loudly, keeping the demons at bay with bravado.

Clayton and Arthur stood at the far end, in front of a map and numerous enlarged photos. Extra gas lamps helped illuminate the wall and cast a harsh light on their faces.

"Ladies and gentlemen," Clayton said. The excited murmurs died away, leaving only a few hacking coughs. "This morning, you will be visiting Marckebeeke Aerodrome. His Majesty's finest landscape artists have lovingly captured this sylvan scene." Clayton tapped the enlarged reconnaissance photos pinned to the wall. The men pushed closer to see the details.

"First, we will deliver the early morning paper to the Baron and his butler who are with *Jasta* 11, living the good life next to the Chateau de Bethune. After that delivery, you will wake the pretty milkmaids of *Jasta* 4 next door, located in the shabby farmhouse to the north. When you finish there, you might care to visit *Jasta* 10. They are on the south side, hidden the other side of the railway marshalling yard, like unwanted bastards. For your ease and convenience, I have arranged for your welcoming committees to wear colour coding. *Jasta* 11 are red Albatross—attack them first. *Jasta* 4 are the Albatross milkmaids dressed in pale brown with black diagonal stripes—attack them second. The unwanted bastards of *Jasta* 10 are silver and yellow Pfalzes—if you have time and the inclination, drop in on them too."

Clayton dropped his jaunty tone and raised his voice. "All of you—pay attention!"

He waited until even the coughs subsided. "You have one fly in the ointment on this pleasure jaunt. We don't know where *Jasta* 6 are hiding. So, you can assume that less than five minutes after you knock on the Circus' door, *Jasta* 6 will sneak up behind you to pick your pockets. Be warned, gentlemen! No matter how attractive your dance partner is, you must leave the party when Wing Commander Wolsey signals your departure time with a green flare."

Arthur took a pace forward and took over the briefing. "The object is to cripple the Circus for the duration of the ground attack on Messines Ridge, but without unnecessary losses on our side. I want discipline, not glory hogs doing their own thing. The Bristols bomb first and Captain Andrews will fire a red flare to launch the attack. I will fire a green flare to signal the end of the attack. If anyone attacks early or does not disengage on the signal, I will court-martial you so fast your feet will not touch the ground between here and lavatory duty at Skegness. Assuming the Huns have not killed you first."

"Aw, Christ!" Rod Andrews said, "Not Skegness! I'd rather do the bog cleaning in Berlin."

Arthur acknowledged the tension-breaking laughter with a thin smile and motioned for Clayton to continue.

"We are still not at full strength, but we are taking every battle-ready plane we have. There will be five

Bristols and four Camels all loaded with Mills bombs. The Bristols, led by Andrews, will be the navigators and lead planes. Wing Commander Wolsey will lead nine SE5s in three flights. He will lead A Flight himself, Ball B Flight, and Fitch C Flight. The SE5s will provide high cover for the bombing and strafing planes in case any Germans are in the air already. If there are undamaged planes after the Bristols and Camels have finished bombing and strafing, A and B flights will act as an extra strafing attack. Fitch's C Flight will stay high as protection for rest of you in case *Jasta* 6 gate-crash the party. The invitation for the Baron's Summer Ball is for 0500 hours sharp. Please tell your social secretaries there is no need to RSVP. Enjoy the party, gentlemen!"

Lance's lips twisted but he did not join the laughter. Typical English. They took fun events like cricket seriously and made fun of things like war. But the tightness in his throat and the thumping of his heartbeat would be afflicting every man on the raid. For when the tracers started smoking in the dawn light, no-one would be laughing.

18
Reap the Whirlwind

Same day – 7 June 1917
Belgium, Ypres Sector, Bailleul Airfield. RFC, 100 Wing.

Lance paused by the darker shadow that was his SE5 and drank in the beauty of the stars like a man taking his last sip of cool water before heading into the desert.

If 100 Wing lost the advantage of surprise, they would be attacking massed machine guns defending the airfield as well as the might of Richthofen's four elite *Jasta*. And then the wreckage of 100 Wing would litter the Ypres mud.

Theirs' not to reason why,
Theirs' but to do and die:
Into the valley of Death
Rode the six hundred.

Lance worked saliva round his mouth. They weren't six hundred men on this attack, but as for the rest, Tennyson might have the rights of it. Hopefully not. Lance would settle for being an unsung winner rather than a lauded loser. Losers were losers, and the dead were dead. No amount of words would change those facts.

A hint of dawn smudged the faint edges of the horizon as Lance clambered into the cockpit. He methodically worked his way through the pre-flight checks, shivering despite his woollen underwear and sheepskin flying coat.

Lance's mechanic, Digby, showed as a dark blur in front of the SE5's long snout. "Contact!"

Lance switched on and sang out, "Contact." Digby's silhouette raised both hands to the upper propeller and yanked the huge wooden blade down and around to kick-start the engine. It caught first time, and Lance closed the radiator shutters to warm the engine and flicked the pressure selector to the air pump. The machine thrummed with life, vibrating on high idle, only hinting at the raucous power of the Hispano-Suiza engine. *Oil, air pressure, water temperature—all fine. Mags good at one thousand rpm. Open radiator shutters.* Lance waggled the ailerons and rudder to check them and waved for the mechanics to remove the triangular wooden chocks holding the wheels in place. They scurried underneath the wings and scuttled hunchbacked out of the way, then ran to the rear to turn the SE5 towards the take-off strip. Lance opened the throttle partway. The engine responded with a throaty roar that always comforted him, and the plane bumped across the field.

He swung his SE5 into the wind, confirmed that the two other SE5s in his flight were behind him, and opened the throttle to the limit. The dark ground blurred beneath him and the plane rattled, until at fifty miles per hour the wheels separated from the earth and birthed the smooth miracle of flight. Lance held the nose down to gain speed, and then pulled the square snout above the pink pencil line of the dawn, up into the lead-grey sky. The fighter, exhausts flickering angry red, juddered with the strain and clawed its way towards the faint stars glimmering among the ghost shadows of the clouds.

The SE5s rendezvoused at 3,000 feet before climbing up to the cloud ceiling, which looked to be about 5,000. Any higher and the shepherding SE5s would not see their flock below. Thommo's Camels and Rod Andrews' Bristol fighters would cross the lines at low altitude but well clear of the direct route to the enemy aerodrome, so the ground watchers could not guess their target. Once behind the lines, the attack would swing onto a course to intercept the River Lys and follow it eastwards to Markebeecke.

Darkness ruled at ground level, even the tortured snakes of the trenches were invisible. Lance followed the prearranged compass course, until with the rising dawn, he glimpsed the silver glint of water and turned eastwards along the River Lys. Turning in his cockpit, he grunted in satisfaction as he noted Weston and Rhys-Davids tucked either side behind him. For the first time he could recall, a flight tagging along did not feel like a millstone. The muscular and earthy farmer and the slight and intellectual Etonian were chalk and cheese, but both were good men in a battle.

Lance searched the lightening sky above him. Nothing. Below, long shadows appeared on the ground as the low sun cast oblique rays on the earth. He checked his harness and slipped into his hunting ritual.

Lance imagined himself a stalking leopard: the flare of nostril checking the scents of the bush, the prick of ear interpreting the sounds, the faint ruffle of fur on flank signalling the wind direction, the sensitive paw pads avoiding sticks that might crack. His conscious mind was still, but his senses were heightened—a hunter's focus.

He searched below and made out the Bristols flitting above the ground. Ahead of them a tall chimney pointed high into the dawn sky, its shadow elongated—Pottelberg Factory, the main navigation feature that Clayton had highlighted. Lance traced the spidery line of the railway leading from the factory, looking for the *Jasta* 10 airstrip. And there it was! Lance checked the south bank of the river, looking for the airfields of *Jasta* 4 and 11.

Where the hell are they? Clayton said they used a castle as their Mess. Lance grew anxious as he searched in vain. But then Rod Andrews's red flare lit up the gloom—attack!

White tracer lines flickered from the ground close to a little wood. Lance followed the tracer and saw the Bristols attacking, and everything snapped into focus—a chateau close to a farmhouse, and a cluster of hangars between the woods and the river.

Three Albatrosses of *Jasta* 11 were already rolling along their airstrip, tail wheels lifting as they desperately tried to get into the air. *By God, we've caught their dawn patrol with their pants down!* The Bristols dropped their bombs and explosions flared among the shadows. One explosion flipped the wing of an Albatross and sent it into a fiery cartwheel. Thompson's Camels whipped over the wood and machine gunned the remaining Huns from behind before they could lift off the runway. One skittered sideways, its undercarriage collapsed, and it ploughed its own grave through the turf. The other caught fire, a flaming meteor careening along the runway, until it caught its wheels in the railway tracks and somersaulted like a Catherine wheel firework.

Jasta 11's hangars and aircraft burned with leaping flames, but the untouched rows of *Jasta* 4 Albatrosses remained as a juicy target, though one defended by machine gunners who were now filling the air with the deadly white lines of tracer bullets. Not only that, but *Jasta* 6 should be on the way by now.

Lance willed Arthur to fire the green flare, but the lure of *Jasta* 4's untouched planes was too strong. Arthur led his and Ball's flights down towards the targets and they flew into a storm of bullets. One plane staggered and disintegrated into a fireball, another jerked and snap rolled into the ground. Arthur and Ball, their red leader streamers making them easy to identify, emerged miraculously through the fire, the only attackers to destroy any of the parked planes. The following pilots were too busy jinking for their lives, and they shot wide. Arthur pulled up at the end of his strafing run, and banked round, obviously to assess the damage and the remaining targets. When he swung around for another strafing attack, Lance unleashed a torrent of curses.

Lance scanned the sky—still no sign of *Jasta* 6. There wasn't much point in providing high cover if the ground fire shot down Arthur and Ball's flights before *Jasta* 6 even arrived, so Lance led his flight down in a curving dive to ambush the defending machine gunners from behind. They never saw C Flight before Lance fired his Vickers. Bullets kicked chunks of turf and flesh into the air, catapulting bodies out of the machine gun emplacement like a giant threshing machine.

As he flashed past his savaged target, the remaining machine gunners hunted him for revenge. Tracer lines crisscrossed in front of his face. He winced as wood splinters flew from the centre struts and hunkered down in his seat, kicking the rudder bar, skidding side to side in erratic patterns. An SE5 flying in the opposite direction rocketed past him so close he flinched. A greasy pillar of black smoke marked a burning Albatross. Lance swerved to barrel through the stinking smoke, seeking a few seconds of cover from the relentless machine gun fire. It worked, but the acrid fumes stung his eyes and tears blurred his sight.

At last, he cleared the airfield and climbed above the enemy fire and into clean air. He wiped his forehead with the back of his leather gauntlet and took a deep breath. That had been worse than his most terrifying dogfight. He looked back. Multiple funeral pyres marked the line of parked enemy planes—his attack had freed Arthur and Ball's flights to do their business. A green flare soared, and Lance laughed with relief.

A vague hint of a shadow flickered in the far corner of his peripheral vision. Instantly, he flung his plane into a hard left bank. As he did so, something plucked the right shoulder of his flying coat and bullets stitched across the fuselage behind him, ripping gashes in the fabric with a noise like a thousand angry bees. An Albatross with black and white chevrons rocketed past Lance. *Jasta 6!*

Lace took a deep breath. Now 100 Wing faced a long slog home against the wind and Huns.

They fought a running rear-guard action against the angry hornet swarm of Albatross and Pfalz, whose repeated attacks splintered the wing's cohesiveness. Planes fought their way east in dribs and drabs as best they could.

Lance lost his flight in the maelstrom, and he ran for home alone. But many of *Jasta* 6 had a height advantage. They used it to gain speed in the dive and catch him, forcing him to turn and engage in short savage dogfights before turning tail again. That's when the SE5's speed counted, and Lance revelled in the fleetness of his new mount. He settled into a pattern—running when he could and fighting when he had to—nursing his fuel and ammunition like a miser.

As he drew near to the Allied lines, he saw two Albatross attacking a lone SE5, whose engine smoked a grey trail. The lone SE5 wallowed helplessly as the Huns closed in for the kill. Lance checked his own tail. His pursuers had lost enthusiasm in the face of the SE5's superior speed and had abandoned their chase.

As a yellow Albatross painted with black chevrons lined up the crippled SE5, Lance closed from behind to fifty feet and triggered a short burst from both guns. Tracer stabbed into the pilot's back. The plane half-rolled into the ground, its wreckage catapulting across the sodden ground. *From Hell's heart, I'll stab at you.* The other German tried a fancy loop to escape. Lance riddled the petrol tank at the top of the loop, and the fiery Albatross fluttered downwards like a giant ember. *Perdition's flames.*

Lance noticed the red commander's streamers on the SE5 for the first time. Arthur waved a gloved hand in thanks. But the thanks were premature. They were still flying low on the German side of the lines. The Hun ground troops, who had held their fire while their planes were savaging Arthur, now opened fire with a vengeance.

They had an easy target. Arthur needed to nurse his damaged engine across the lines and evasive manoeuvres were not an option.

Lance swore. He reefed around in a tight turn to dive under and ahead of Arthur's plane. A mass of grey infantry fired at Lance, fireflies of rifle and machine gun fire flickered bright against the mud. He pointed his SE5 in their direction and depressed both triggers, weaving his nose from side to side to hose them with his own machine gun fire.

His Lewis drum gun ran out of ammunition first, then the belt-fed Vickers. Now he could only draw fire away from Arthur. He had one Lewis drum left but by the time he changed the drum, it would be too late.

He twisted to look back. Bugger!Arthur and his helpless plane still had a long way to go.Lance couldmock-attack the Germans from the British direction. The Huns wouldn't know he was out of ammo. He might keep a few heads down and sure as hell he'd attract Hun fire. Every bastard ducking or firing at Lance was one less firing at Arthur, whose crippled plane made for the easier target.

It was a good plan. But putting it to practice took a bit of doing. His mind said "turn", but his hands on the controls wanted no part of the plan. He gnawed his cheek, welcoming the pain. Best get it over with fool! He clenched the joystick until his bones ached and willed the turn back into the maelstrom.

As he crossed the lines, he jinked left and right, right again, nearly impaling himself on a burst of gunfire. Steel slashed through his left wing. He squeezed his sphincter tight and flew even lower until it seemed his wheels must catch in the rolls of barbed wire. Images streaked below; barren mud, twisting trenches, field-grey uniforms, coal scuttle helmets, flashes of upturned faces—all a blur.

When he reached Arthur, he banked hard for home, wing tips trailing the mud, to repeat the low-level lunacy over the gun-bristling earth. Blood pounded in his ears, louder than the guns that hunted him. Thousands of muzzle flashes hypnotized him. His toes clenched inside his flying boots. A round spanged off the breech of his Vickers gun. His shoulders hunched. Sweat dripped. *Please God...*

When he crossed the British lines in tandem with Arthur, the British troops waved their caps in delight as the smoking fighter sputtered over them to safety.

Lance was too drained to share the jubilation. Protective as a mother hen, he escorted Arthur while his friend nursed his crippled plane back to Bailleul.

Lance landed behind him. When he shut the throttle, his ears rang from the engine roar and the pounding machine guns. He slumped in the cockpit for a second or two, drawing huge lungfuls of air. His mechanic, Digby, looked at him with concern and shouted something, but Lance could not hear. He pulled off his goggles and helmet and lurched out of the cockpit with Digby's help.

Arthur strode to meet him, fair hair tousled, open features creased with strain and black gunpowder. Lance had seen that face a hundred times after air fights, always a sight that brought a smile to his face. Lance extended his hand for a shake in their usual ritual, but Arthur brushed past it and folded him into a bear hug. The two men slapped each other on the back, awkward in their flying suits and sheepskin boots.

When they broke apart, they walked towards the wing office, passing Rod Andrews, who had gathered his pilots and gunners around him in a semicircle.

"Yer a magnificent bunch of bastards, you beauties," Andrews was saying to his men. "Last week we took an old-fashioned licking from the Huns. Today we handed one out. From now on, we dish out the punishment, and the bastard Huns will regret taking on the Bristol Misfits."

The Bristol crews, faces flushed with a joy that had seemed impossible a few days ago, cheered him to a man. Andrews spotted Arthur and Lance and could not resist adding, "And if they ask nicely, we might leave some of the Circus for the rest of the wing!"

Lance flipped him a casual two-fingered salute. "Let me know the next time you lot need a nursemaid, always delighted to help."

The Misfits jeered, then followed them to the office where Clayton had already started the debriefing.

"How did we do, Clayton? How many did we lose?" Arthur asked with a face that dreaded the answer.

Clayton looked up from his scribbling and his face broke into a rare unreserved smile. "Damn well, I'd say. Sounds as though we scuppered two-thirds of *Jasta* 11 and *Jasta* 4 on the ground. Then in the air the Camels got two taking off. Ball got one on his way home. All those confirmed. So, say three kills in the air and twelve planes destroyed on the ground. Not too shabby for two hours' work!"

"Lance got a couple of Albatross. I can confirm them and so can the troops. But what about our losses?"

"Two of the SE5s went down in the attack you led, Parker and Treadwell. Those were our only dead. One Brisfit and two Camels crashed on landing, but the crews are safe. Rhys-Davids landed just on our side of the lines. He's all right other than an ankle sprain, but his plane is a write off. Everyone else accounted for, lots of damaged planes but nothing terminal."

Arthur shook a baffled head. "Only two dead? How in blazes did we suffer so few casualties?"

"Well, far be it for me to blow your trumpet for you, but I'd say the wing had a smidgen of luck, a bucket load of skill, and good planes, pilots, and leadership. Mix well and serve up a beating for the Circus."

~

Same day.
Belgium, Ypres Sector, Marckebeeke Airfield, *Jagdgeschwader* (JG) 1.

Lothar von Richthofen gagged as the smell of burnt meat blew back over Marckebeeke airfield. He looked down on the line of bodies laid out in a row, his cap doffed in his hands as he paid respect to the dead. These bodies were just the ground crew. Klugerman and Low, the pilots taking off when the attack came, lay as charred flesh at the far end of the airstrip. Schweinsteiger was also dead but at least not cooked.

The British must pay for this.

The sheer physical volume of the attack had shaken Lothar—the deep howl of the attacking engines and the thud of the bombs still reverberated in his chest and bones. For the first time he had sympathy for the whingeing of the ground troops—the enemy planes were a damn sight more intimidating from the ground than when you were up in the air. The thundering roar of the two-seaters was the first sign, the almost instantaneous percussion of their bombs the next. Lothar and the other pilots had scattered from the breakfast table like a flock of pigeons, pursued by the manic howl of the engines and the chatter of the diving attackers' machine guns.

Fortunately, the enemy had focused on the hangars and planes rather than the officers' Mess tent, where the pilots had breakfast. Some pilots ran to the machine gun nests to take on the attackers. Not Lothar. It would be a stupid way to die. Germany could replace the planes in days, but aces were more precious. He watched from the safety of a slit trench as the attackers savaged their airfield. When they droned away, they left a hellscape of crackling planes and hangars, bodies, and the cries of the wounded. A pall of black smoke hung in the air like a banner of doom.

Manfred surveyed the field, hands on hips. "*Scheissen!* Most of our planes—wrecks."

If he'd been grovelling in the slit trench, he didn't show it. His habitual deerskin trousers and knitted sweater seemed incongruently elegant against the carnage, and they were pristine. Unlike Lothar who had mud in some undignified places. Manfred's eyes turned haunted. "Moritz? Where is he?" He turned to Lothar, who shrugged. Manfred ran towards his quarters, calling for his dog.

Lothar walked over to the body of his fitter. Klose looked unmarked; his fair hair ruffled in the breeze, and someone had folded his hands across his chest. Yet the ground beneath the body was soaked dark with Klose's blood. A metal splinter had opened his femoral artery and bled him to death while the British strafed the airfield. He had been morose man but a painstaking craftsman—Lothar's plane had always been impeccable.

Manfred's voice from behind made Lothar jump. "Your fitter?"

Lothar nodded and said nothing.

Manfred added, "I am sorry."

"Be sorry for him, not for me. Is Moritz alright?"

Manfred snorted. "He is not a brave dog. He was whimpering under my cot." His voice softened. "But thank God he is safe. He means more to me than almost anything."

Lothar nodded. "No harm, Manfred, if you paid your respects for the dead ground crew. The men prefer not to come too far below a dog in your concerns."

Manfred's head jerked round and his eyes were hard, but then he nodded. "I will do as you suggest. But more importantly, this attack shows the game has changed. We can no longer rely on blundering amateur British fliers. They targeted us and knew where our planes were even though we moved here only a few days ago. Good planning and good execution. So, we are facing new tactics and new planes. The big two-seaters we encountered the other day, and two new types of fighter."

Manfred walked along the line of dead, noting their faces. When he reached the end, he turned and held a long salute to the fallen. Then the brothers strode towards the hangars where Adjutant Bodenshatz was bellowing orders amidst the smoke and flames.

"Did you notice all the aircraft had blue and white chequers?" Lothar asked. "Perhaps they are the new anti-Richthofen outfit we have been hearing rumours about?"

Manfred rubbed a hand across his blond stubble. "Must be. Tell the *Jasta* heads to meet in half an hour with reports of what they need to get us back into the air as soon as possible. Never known the *verdammt* English to get out of bed so early. From now on, we will post a dawn patrol over the airfield before sunrise. It's a waste of fuel and pilot's flying time because I don't think the British will dare do it again, but we can't take the risk."

Lothar nodded. "It's the first time we've had to react to what they are doing. We need to wipe them out before they kill more pilots. Planes come and go, but good pilots take half a year."

Manfred grunted, but he was staring into the sky towards the lines, his lips compressed into a thin line. "Perhaps we have grown complacent with our easy victories? Now with new planes and new tactics, the British grow insolent. If their new planes are better than the Albatross, we may lose technical superiority, but we can retain numerical superiority in air fights. From now on we fly at *Jasta* strength as a minimum. We will swarm all over small groups of British, and smash them." Manfred turned, his blue eyes cold, and smacked an emphatic fist into his hand. "We will burn them from the sky."

19
Nine Lives

Two days later — 9 June 1917
Belgium, Ypres Sector, Bailleul Airfield. RFC, 100 Wing.

Lance's sinuses and eardrums throbbed, and every swallow made him wince. He had landed from a high-altitude patrol just minutes ago, and needles stabbed his fingers and toes as circulation returned. Flights in the oxygen-starved air at eighteen thousand feet always resulted in a splitting headache, and exhaustion so extreme it took a conscious effort to shuffle one foot ahead of the other. He longed to curl up on his camp bed and nurse his thumping head, but he had to write his flight report first.

Clayton was alone in the office, reading briefing papers. "Bloody brilliant!" he said to Lance. "The Messines mine killed ten thousand Hun troops, and after our raid took out the Circus, the RFC kept sixty gunnery observation planes over the battle. With their help, our artillery took out eighty per cent of the Hun guns. As a result, our army captured all their objectives around Messines Ridge within twelve hours. Now the high ground around Ypres is in our hands. Since I've been in France, this attack by the army is the first to succeed as planned." Clayton rubbed his hands together in glee and carried on reading the paper.

Lance squinted and rubbed his brow above the bridge of his nose where the throbbing was worst. Maybe there was a lot to be happy about, but he could not find the energy. He slumped onto a wooden three-legged chair opposite Clayton's desk. It creaked and protested, just like his muscles.

Since 100 Wing's raid, the RFC had blanketed the sky around Ypres. With the German ground forces blinded by their loss of the only high ground around Ypres, the British army had already started the build-up of men and munitions opposite Passchendaele Ridge, where they would make the main attack. Now only German reconnaissance aircraft could betray that build up, and Trenchard had put up a barrier of aircraft to prevent such a loss of secrecy.

Front and centre flew 100 Wing. From dawn to dusk their patrols hung in the sky ten thousand yards to either side of Passchendaele. Every day they manned the barricades, and every day the Germans battered at the doors at every level, but the *Luftstreitkräfte* had lost their cutting edge. While Richthofen and his Circus waited for replacement aircraft, 100 Wing pressed home their advantage. Plenty of Germans were keen to fight, but the agility of the Camels and the speed of the SE5 startled the German fighters and two-seaters alike. Now Albatross and Pfalz pilots fought on equal terms at best, and their losses mounted. Hanover and Roland reconnaissance two-seaters resorted to hiding in the gloaming, sneaking high-level reconnaissance flights at sunrise and dusk.

"Apparently they heard the mine explosion in London," Clayton said. "The papers say it's the largest in history. The politicians are claiming credit, and our generals are basking in praise. Would you believe a small portion of the glory has even filtered through to 100 Wing?"

"Clayton, please calm down and let me finish my patrol report. I want to go to bed."

"Bed? The sun hasn't even set. This, my dear chap, is worth getting excited over. If the army carries on like this, we might actually win the war this decade!"

"Don't hold your breath. I don't think the Huns have turned into patsies overnight." Lance rose. "Listen, do me a favour. Write up a report for me, will you? Forty-minute patrol at eighteen thousand feet from Plugstreet Wood to Mount Sorrel. Nothing." Lance yawned and his eardrums popped, releasing some of the pain and pressure.

Clayton leaned back in his chair and looked at Lance with a curious expression, "You're the one who always talks about ending the war and going home. How come you aren't excited?"

"I've got a frigging headache."

"Aha, say no more. Altitude-itis. Consider your report done, in masterful prose to boot. Haste ye to bed my good man."

"Not so fast," Arthur said as he entered the office. "Lance, you are just the man I need. I want your help to persuade Ball to go on leave."

Lance slumped back onto the chair with a deep sigh. "Leave? 100 Wing has only just started operations."

"True, but Ball has been out here for six months straight and is near breaking point."

Lance shrugged. "He's been knocking the Huns down like bowling pins since he got the SE5, so I assumed he was fine. Mind you I seldom see him—he's flying every single hour of daylight."

"He is taking ridiculous risks. Listen to these." Arthur shuffled the sheets of combat reports in his hands. "The day after the raid on the Circus, he attacked six Albatross and shot down one, got shot up by the rest but got home okay. Later the same day, he attacked a two-seater and chased it so low that the Hun anti-aircraft gunners pasted him. They shot up his SE5 so badly he had to land with no elevators. God knows how he managed that."

Lance smiled tiredly. "I saw that landing. When he climbed out, his face was covered with castor oil. Fuming he was! The SE5 wasn't fit to fly, so he climbed straight into his Nieuport to give the Huns payback. What a man."

Arthur nodded. "The following day he attacked eight Albatross and shot one down, but the Huns riddled his plane and he crash-landed. He made it to our side of the lines—just. The mechanics told me the windscreen had four bullet holes through it and his cockpit mirror was shattered. A hell of a lot of bullets must have missed him by inches."

"When he came here to make his report," Clayton added, "he was shaking like a leaf—his hands, his knees, even his lips. He was in the worst shape I have ever seen him. Took him ten minutes before he could talk."

Arthur sighed. "I told him to take a breather, but he took off again in his Nieuport and shot down another Hun. He's shot down six Huns in three days, but he's destroying himself." Arthur collapsed into his chair with a sigh and steepled his fingers. "Sheer willpower is keeping him going, but if he carries on like this, we will lose him for sure."

"So, send him on leave," Lance said, pinching his nose shut and blowing hard, trying to ease his pressure headache. "What's this got to do with me? I need my bed."

"The problem is," Arthur said, "he's obsessed with scoring more kills than Guynemer, the French ace. Right now Ball is ahead, but not by much. He told me he will kick up a fuss with Boom Trenchard if we try to send him on leave. And Boom always backs Ball. I hope you can convince Ball to take two weeks' leave. You might be the only person close enough to him that he will listen."

"Hmph—close is relative. He's closer to his violin and veggie patch. I didn't notice anything unusual about him this morning. He doesn't need advice from me."

"He's all right in the morning before he flies," Clayton said. "But forty minutes ago when he landed, he was shaking like a man with a high fever."

"Hell, we all get the shakes. Arthur, you know that as well as anyone. I don't want Ball to think I'm poking my nose into his private affairs."

Arthur just looked at him. And waited. Lance glared back. Talk about the devil and the deep blue sea. If Lance didn't capitulate there would be more words, and Arthur used words like binding ropes—you ended up tied in knots. Lance would get to his bed faster by talking to Albert Ball. "All right, I'll try."

~

Lance found Albert Ball by his garden. The late summer sun shone soft and mellow, and the evening birdsong was at full throttle. Bloody birds always sounded so fricking happy. Albert looked up as Lance's long shadow fell on him.

"Hello, Lance. Are you sure you know nothing about plants? Look," Albert held up a green bedraggled mess, "my green peas were growing nicely, four inches high, and now there are only a few stalks left. What the heck happened?"

Now that Lance looked closer, he noticed that Albert's eyes were deeper in their sockets than usual. That was true of all the pilots, and Albert's eyes still burned with their usual intensity, but his hands, which had been steady this morning, trembled.

Albert saw the direction of Lance's gaze and hastily dug the offending hands into the soil, plucking at some roots. Oil and black gunpowder smeared across Albert's face, and his tangled dark hair lay lank with sweat and grime. He reeked of stale sweat, gunpowder and castor oil. This was a man who needed a good wash, a good barber, and a good rest.

Lance squatted by the little vegetable bed. "I know nothing about plants, but I do read animal tracks. See that cloven hoof print? I'd say a goat has eaten your peas, and seeing as Thommo's squadron seems to have picked up a goat as a mascot, I'd venture Bessie the mascot is your offender."

Albert looked impressed. "You are a bit of a Sherlock Holmes. So how do I stop her?"

Lance shrugged. "Put barbed wire around your patch."

"No! This veggie patch takes my mind off war, I don't want barbed wire around it."

"Get a dog that hates goats. Cecil Lewis' Irish wolfhound ought to scare off Bessie."

"Now you're talking." Albert stood and put his hands in his pocket as he smiled at Lance. For a second Lance glimpsed the teenager that Albert might have been without the war, and he found himself grinning back. Then he remembered his golden rule, and crushed the feeling of companionship.

"Listen, Albert, I'm supposed to approach you subtly, but since I'm not good at being subtle, I'll be blunt. Arthur thinks your nerves are shot and you need a break. He wants you to take two weeks' leave. I agree, it would be good for you."

Albert looked at him askance. "That *is* blunt talk. No doubt my nerves are shaky, but nobody has dared say it except you."

"There's no shame in it. It's the same as being out of breath at the end of a four-hundred-yard sprint. Your body needs a break. The way you fight, your body *and* mind need frequent breaks. You English pretend you don't have nerves, but everybody gets in a funk from continuous fighting. You've done six months. You need to rest and recharge."

Albert scratched his head, leaving earth clinging to his hair. "Then Guynemer will get ahead of me again."

"He'll be ahead of you forever if you get yourself killed. Guynemer is human too. He'll need to go on leave as often as you. Listen, Albert, you've used all your nine lives in the last three days alone. Go to England, see Flora for a week or two, come back refreshed."

Albert sighed. "It's a rotten business, this war. I shall be glad when it's over. I'm so tired, tired in every way." He took his hands out of his pockets and studied them as they shook. "But I'm also afraid. Afraid that if I stop, I won't be able to force myself back into the air again. Each time I come back, I find it harder to force myself into my plane. It's easier to fly all day every day and have no time to think. Half of me wants to go on killing Germans as fast as I can, so I can be the ace of aces. The other half wants to go back to England, make a home with Flora, have children and live a normal life."

Lance shrugged. "Hard to reconcile those two ideas."

"You're a fat lot of help, Sherlock."

"Well, I understand the nerves and the tiredness, but can't say I've ever had the dream of kids and a cottage. Or of wanting to be the top ace."

Albert glanced at him. "You will get the top ace fever someday. Once you get a sniff of it, the fever grips you. At first, you are just doing your bit for the war. But the higher your score gets, the more you obsess over it. You take more risks. Your kills come faster and faster, and you suffer from a strange combination of invincibility and resignation. When you are in the air you feel invincible. Yet when you are on the ground, doubts eat at you until you are sure you cannot possibly survive this bloody war. Don't ask me how you get two such opposite ideas in your head, but you do."

"So go on leave and enjoy Flora. Get your head back on right, then come back and knock down more Huns. Want help with planting those seeds?"

Albert gave him a handful and together they inserted the tiny seeds into the moistened earth, working together in silence. The simple act was soothing, and for the first time Lance understood Albert's hobby.

When they finished planting the seeds, dusk had almost turned into darkness. Albert watered the soil from a small can and patted down the damp soil over the new plantings.

"Maybe you're right. I got shaken up yesterday. I swear the Hun tried to ram me. He was as mad as me, and it gave *me* the shakes. No one likes tangling with a mad dog, not even me." Albert shook his head, his eyes a million miles away and harrowed by the recollection. Then he brightened. "And I do want to see Flora again. I'll take some leave next week. Damn the rain, my onion bulbs are looking soggy, and my marrows are mildewing."

"Good man, the leave will do you good. What the heck are marrows?"

For the first time Lance heard Albert laugh, really laugh, a plain old happy-to-be-alive laugh. When had Lance last laughed like that? He couldn't remember. Albert's peal of mirth came from the belly, uninhibited and gleeful, and his teeth gleamed in the dusk. "Sherlock doesn't know what marrows are!"

20
Fountains of Versailles

Two days later — 11 June 1917
Belgium, Ypres Sector, Bailleul Airfield. RFC, 100 Wing.

Lance shook his head. "I won't let this chap kidnap me and fly me to Versailles." He pointed into the morning blue sky, which stretched unblemished by even a puff of cloud as far as the eye could see. "With no clouds, the Hun high altitude reconnaissance planes will be up in force. I need to be up there."

The little moustachioed Frenchman in his kepi hopped in agitation and appealed to Arthur. *"Mon colonel! Capitaine Fitch doit m'accompagner immédiatement pour que le General Pétain peut lui accorde la Croix de Guerre en personne. En personne!"*

Lance took a sip of his sugary tea. He woke earlier than he needed to every morning, so he could enjoy a quiet cup of tea before the day subsumed him. Arthur's summons had interrupted Lance's ritual, and his irritation rode him like a burr. "My mother told me never to accept lifts from strangers, and I don't trust my life to other pilots."

The little Frenchman's pointed, and waxed moustache wiggled in indignation. *"Je suis un très bon aviateur. J'ai volé ici juscu'ici sans problème."*

Lance ignored him. "Listen, Arthur, I got a letter two months ago telling me the French had awarded me a gong. That's all I know. Now that we're busy killing Huns, I don't have time to go to Versailles."

"According to this—" Clayton waved a letter written in French and embossed with enough red wax seal to sign a peace treaty—"GeneralPetain wants to pin the Croix de Guerre medal on your chest personally, to show the eternal gratitude of the French nation to this bold foreign aviator risking all to defend France and kill the foul Boche. And he wants to do it today."

"*Immédiatement!*" the Frenchman crowed, gusting garlic over Lance and pointing his finger upwards like an exclamation point.

"Clayton, tell him if he points that finger up my nose again, I'll break it. No way am I being piloted to Versailles in that clapped out two-seater."

Arthur looked dubious. "Lance is right. The high-altitude Huns will come over in droves, and Lance is our best high-level hunter. On the other hand, the letter *is* signed by Petain. Who outranks even Trenchard by a very long way."

"*Oui! General Pétain. Commandant Suprême de l'Armée Française!*" The finger rose, but the Frenchman caught it halfway and hid his hand behind his back.

"Over my dead body," Lance said.

~

Now Lance was kicking his heels in a long corridor of Versailles Palace. With nothing else to do, he strode the length of the corridor counting arched windows that stretched forty feet high. Seventeen. Then he counted mirrors. He gave up at three hundred and fifty.Everywhere Lance looked, he leered back at himself, scruffy and unkempt in his crumpled uniform. He was out of place—a mangy cur in a poodle parlour.

Lance sighed and looked out through an enormous window at the gushing fountains—perfect flying weather.

He could be killing Huns. His feet ached and hunger gnawed his belly.

The French bantam, his moustache twitching with his righteous victory, had flown him to an airfield outside Paris and delivered him to a haughty uniformed chauffeur who drove at breakneck speed along the tree-lined roads to Versailles. The urgency bewildered Lance, even more so when he found himself in limbo on arrival.

A flunky, dressed in enough gold braid for several generals but still manifestly a flunky in this gilded palace, clicked down the corridor. Lance turned to him in expectation, but the flunkey walked past him without a glance. Lance ran to catch him and grabbed his arm. "Please, Monsieur, *je, moi...*" Lance pointed at himself. "*Moi* want...ah, damn, what's the word? *Retournez? A mon squadron immédiatement, si vous plait.*"

The flunkey drowned Lance in a torrent of French and waved his hands in the grandiloquent French manner. At the end he glared at Lance.

Lance refused to be intimidated. "*Moi. Vroom vroom. Retournez a Ypres, tout suite!*"

The man looked down his long nose and shrugged. "Pff!" he snorted with Gallic contempt before striding away.

Lance scratched his head. He considered an escape, but settled for gawking at the gold statues of half-clad women. They held aloft, with serene ease, massive candelabras that Weston, the muscle-bulging Devon farmer, would have struggled to lift.

At last, Lance was ushered into a massive hall full of dignitaries. A long flowery babble of French introduced him to General Pétain, the French commander-in-chief on the Western Front. The legendary "Lion of Verdun" pinned a bronze medal with crossed swords on Lance, and fixed him with a piercing gaze from inquisitorial blue eyes above a ferocious moustache. "*Merci, mon brave,*" he said with conviction and a crushing handshake.

Oddly, this thanks felt more sincere than any Lance had won from the British Army. Perhaps because the British fought for ideals while the French were fighting for their land, to prevent Prussian boots from trampling their fields. A memory of Fitch Farm burning in the night, ash coating his skin, flashed through his mind. The French and him had this in common.

Nevertheless, this had been a day wasted on collecting a meaningless bauble while Hun planes soared in the wide blue with cameras clicking.

~

The flunkies ushered Lance into a car which drove off, heading who knew where? He leaned forward. "Bailleul?"

The chauffeur deflected Lance's questions with a shrug, and the car swept him onwards. An hour later, as dusk was dying, Lance recognised the landmarks of central Paris. He gave the driver a volley of abuse in English, but the man ignored him, and Lance steamed in frustration. If he'd kept his revolver, he'd have held it to the kidnapper's head.

The car dropped him in front of a hotel so discrete it possessed no name on the facade. As he departed, the chauffeur passed Lance his bag and left his hand out for a tip. Lance growled and the man fled. The whole day had been a charade, a total waste of time.

An obsequious manager oiled him to the top floor, nattering in incomprehensible machine-gun-fire French. They reached a pair of large double doors, which the manager opened wide with a flourish and a look of envy. "*Entrez, Monsieur.*"

A huge luxurious suite basked in front of him, lit in a soft golden glow by a mass of flickering candles. In the shadows at the far end, against a long French window, stood a female silhouette. Lance frowned. Did the French provide a woman to go with the Croix de Guerre? The idea seemed excessive, even for the French. He opened his mouth to explain it was all a mistake, but then the woman swayed into the flickering candlelight.

His breath checked in his throat. She walked on naked feet like a pagan queen, her black mane crowned with a glinting silver coronet. A white toga-style gown left her shoulders and arms bare but clung to her curves in all the places a good gown should. And shouldn't. Candle flames fractured and danced in her eyes, and her musky scent whispered promises. Her lips curved with amusement, not ashamed to show she was aware of her effect. Lust surged through him, raw and elemental as a stag in rut.

"Good God!" was all he could say.

"Trust me, darling, God has little to do with it," Lady Megan Exenrude said with a smile, her voice husky.

"Megan! You're like a genie from a bottle, appearing when I least expect. Did you set up this whole thing?"

"Me? Heavens no! The Croix de Guerre is all your doing." Megan ran a finger over the medal on its green and red striped ribbon. "It looks gorgeous on you." She took his arm and led him to a bottle of champagne chilling in an ice bucket, popped the cork with an expert twist and poured two glasses. "I heard Philippe Pétain would award you a medal in person, and I pulled a few strings to kidnap you after the ceremony. Philippe is a sweetie and was happy to oblige, and here we are."

"Philippe? A sweetie? The man has just shot a boatload of deserters!"

"Then I'm sure they deserved it."

Lance eyed her. "The rumour mill says when Pétain's staff need to find him they have to call the houses of all his mistresses."

"You aren't jealous, are you?" she asked in delight. "Philippe is *charmant*,but when I have a handsome young war hero like you, what would I want with an old man like that? Even if he is a general." She toasted Lance, batting her eyelashes: "To Captain Fitch, aviator extraordinaire and saviour of France!"

They chinked glasses, smiling at each other. The champagne was too bitter for him, but he drained the glass in one swift gulp, swept her into his arms, and threw them both on the huge bed. He forced himself to hold back his raging lust and gazed down at her face, her ripe lips curving in welcome below the brown eyes, deep enough to drown in. A slim arm slid around his neck and her bracelets jangled, awaking memories of long ecstatic nights.

The words slid from him without volition. "God, you are beautiful."

Megan laughed, and her hips oscillated against his groin. "Mmm, someone is glad to see me."

His self-control burst and he kissed her hard, their tongues duelling, still cool from the champagne.

~

The following morning, Lance woke at dawn and clambered out of bed, naked, to gaze through the high arched windows overlooking the Arc de Triomphe. The glow of a new dawn touched the ornate grey rooftops and lit the ubiquitous red brick chimney pots and pale pink church spires. He rubbed his arms against the morning chill and felt the goose bumps on his flesh. It felt wrong, luxuriating in bed in Paris, while the war rumbled onwards.

"Come back to bed," Megan said, her voice throaty. He sat on the bed and stroked her lustrous hair that gleamed in the golden light through the window.

"Megan, I can't take time off for these off-the-cuff liaisons. There's a war on, and I'm needed."

She stirred, languorous, and his eyes lingered on the way her soft curves shape-shifted under the bedclothes. "All the more reason, Lance, to make the most of such moments while we can. Besides, I didn't get you the time off, GeneralPétain did. He wanted to award you the medal. I just ensured that your one night off in Paris took place with me instead of with some floozy from the theatre."

"Why do you make all this effort to see me?"

"Is it so wrong to want to have time with my man?"

"Is that what I am—your man? All your noble birth, your money, and your influence, and you waste yourself on a second-rate army captain from a third-rate colony?"

Megan cupped his face with a pale hand. "I'll do my own judging, thank you, Lance Fitch. Perhaps you'll understand when you reach my age. Besides, I would point out that having one of the Allies' leading aces and a decorated war hero as your man can't be that bad. The 'Ace from Africa' the papers in England are calling you. The downside of the war hero is that any day he may die and disappear forever. So don't judge, just enjoy what is on offer while you can. Now come to bed."

She threw the sheets open for him, and he slid in beside her. He welcomed her warmth, and his arms closed around her, stroking the satin smooth skin of her back.

Her voice was muffled against his chest. "How's Arthur?"

"Fine. Keeps pestering me though. He thinks I would make a good squadron commander and won't take no for an answer."

She sat up, her dark hair tousled. "And neither should he. You would be a fine leader, better than Arthur even."

He laughed, and she scowled. "I'm serious. You may think I'm just a woman and know nothing about men at war. But I know when the world is being torn apart, hard men want to be led by even harder men with certainty in their heart. Arthur is a good man, a much better leader in peace than a hard man like you. But men want tough leaders in war."

She leaned forward, her breasts falling free from the sheets. "Stop looking at my breasts and look into my eyes. You are a natural war leader whether you like it or not. Be that leader!"

"Alright, alright, relax. I'll think about it." Lance exhaled. "But for now, I'd rather pretend that the war doesn't exist. Can we do that?"

Megan raised herself and straddled his body. Her voice turned husky.

"What are your favourite things in Paris so far? Do you like the views?"

"From where I'm lying, the view of Paris is unbeatable."

"Or is it the food?" She cupped her right breast and offered it to his mouth.

"The food is amazing." Lance lapped at her rising nipples.

"Maybe the wine?" She pulled her breasts away and swirled her tongue deep into his mouth. They kissed, soft at first but with urgency as their hunger built.

"Or is it the women?" she cooed, gyrating artfully so he slid inside her warmth.

"Definitely the women."

"Are you sure? What about the music?" Her bracelets jangled to the rhythm of her hips.

"Now that you mention it," he managed, his voice ragged, "the music is pretty good too."

"Really Lance, you need to make up your mind." She unsheathed him, and her fingers trailed up and down his turgid shaft. "We haven't even mentioned the Eiffel Tower…
and the gushing fountains of Versailles."

"Damn you, witch!" He grabbed her, rolled on top of her, scissored her legs apart, and drove into her with every ounce of the pent-up lust in his loins. Her laughter echoed around the room, dancing with the dust motes floating in the dawn glow.

~

By the time a different chauffeur dropped Lance at Bailleul at noon, grim grey clouds had clamped down to three hundred feet. There would be no flying.

Lance did not feel social and headed for the hut that served as the wing anteroom, on which a wag had painted "Xanadu" in large capitals, with "did Kubla Khan a stately pleasure-dome decree" in smaller letters underneath. There Lance settled into a comfy chair with a lemonade to finish one of the books Arthur had given him a few days ago. A short read and then maybe a catnap to recuperate from the strenuous night with Megan.

Lance had accepted the books from Arthur as if they were poisoned chalices. Both books were by the famous Rudyard Kipling and inside their fly leaves Arthur had written: "To my good friend Lance Fitch, read & learn!" Subtle as a sledgehammer. Arthur was losing patience. Good. Maybe he would give up soon.

But Lance read the books.

He had already finished *The Second Jungle Book,* and enjoyed it despite Arthur's heavy-handed underlining. How dumb did he think Lance was? Some lines Arthur had underlined twice in case Lance failed to work it out for himself:

Now this is the Law of the Jungle—as old and as true as the sky;

And the Wolf that shall keep it may prosper, but the Wolf that shall break it must die…

For the strength of the Pack is the Wolf, and the strength of the Wolf is the Pack.

To Lance's relief, the second book—the *Just So Stories*—did not contain any underlining. He was engrossed in the tale of "How the Leopard got its spots" when Clayton and Arthur walked into the anteroom.

"Ha!" Clayton said. "Our Gallic hero returns, looking haggard, I must say. Being fêted by the frogs must be exhausting. Wine and dine, women and song, followed by a hangover and post-coital tristesse I imagine?"

Lance started. How did Clayton know, or was he guessing? The man had a nose for guilt like a hyena sniffing for blood. Lance hastily schooled his face, but he was too late. Clayton's eyes glinted. "Ha! I recognise that shifty look. I do believe some damsel—"

"Lance," Arthur interrupted, oblivious to the interplay, "you are actually reading one of the books I gave you? How do you like it?"

"*The Jungle Book* stories were great stuff—ripping yarns. And the *Just So Stories* may be even better."

"That's it? Ripping yarn? Has it taught you anything? Did you think about the bits I underlined for you?"

"What underlining?" Lance asked innocently. "I learned a lot about India."

Arthur glowered. Lance smirked.

"Give Ball the bloody books," Arthur growled. "See if he learns more than you."

"I haven't finished this book yet, but I'll give him *The Jungle Book* tonight, so he can read it on leave."

Clayton peered over Lance's shoulder at the chapter heading. "Aha, 'How the Leopard got his spots'. Very apt, as we want to know if you will change your spots, and take over 111 Squadron when Albert Ball goes on leave in two days. My esteemed colleague here thinks you will accept the job. I think he is delusional, and I have bet the monstrous sum of a guinea coin that you will flee from the responsibility."

"Is that what you want to know?" Lance asked in a reasonable tone, then grabbed Clayton's nose in a vicelike grip between thumb and forefinger. "A well-read man like you should remember it was insatiable curiosity that got the elephant child his long trunk. And that real leopards never change their spots."

"Ow! Led go, you are hurtig be."

Lance released him, and Clayton fingered his nose to check it remained in one piece. "Dastardly trick. It took many centuries of careful breeding to get such an aristocratic nose, and now you damage it in an instant."

"Then don't stick your aristocratic nose into my business."

"My, we are touchy today. Methinks the horse wants water after all, but resents being led to it."

"Clayton," Lance said, his voice rising, "Sometimes you talk absolute rot."

"Sometimes?" Arthur said, before turning to Lance. "So, I can count on you to take command of the squadron while Ball is away?"

"No."

A flush of red suffused Arthur's face. "God, you are an infuriating man."

Lance shrugged. "Leopards don't change their spots."

Clayton held his hand out to Arthur. "A guinea coin if you please."

Arthur scowled blackly at him and strode away with an exclamation of disgust.

21
Polygon Wood

13 June 1917
Belgium, Ypres Sector, Bailleul Airfield. RFC, 100 Wing.

The following evening, Lance looked up from his book as Clayton bounced into the Mess. "Bad news, chaps," Clayton announced. Heads turned as the pilots waited on tenterhooks. "HQ has cancelled the last patrol of the day due to the bad weather." Cheers, followed by jeers for the adjutant, rang out across the Mess. Clayton grinned as he left, waving off the abuse. The volume of chat soared, and a crowd formed around the bar.

Lance collapsed into a sagging armchair. Thunder grumbled in the distance. Energy leached out of him as he sat there with his eyes shut. He'd done three patrols today and it took a physical toll, but part of the lassitude came as the subconscious relaxed and switched off Man's ingrained fight-or-flight survival mechanism. Mind and body unwound their knots of worry, knowing he would not die today.

He felt a touch on his shoulder and looked round into the smiling face of Albert Ball. "Thanks for the book." Albert patted his jacket side-pocket. "I'll take it on leave with me. By the way I ran into Charles Guynemer yesterday in Hazebrouck. He told me your medal award is the talk of the French military circles."

"Don't know why. They give out the Croix de Guerre like confetti. Not like your Legion of Honour."

"Well, Guynemer was most impressed that the great Pétain awarded it in person. Signal honour apparently."

Lance flushed and changed the subject. Megan's pull must be greater than he had realised. "Thought you'd gone on leave today."

"Tomorrow. In fact, I am just going to pack my stuff, so I can depart early tomorrow. Flora will meet me in England. I can't wait."

"Give her a kiss for me."

"Certainly not! I'm keeping them all for myself." Albert clapped him on the shoulder once more and sauntered out of the Mess looking more relaxed than Lance could remember.

Lance went back to the *Just So Stories*. Soon Kipling's prose lulled him into a magical world far away from France. *'You are making my spots ache,' said Painted Jaguar, 'and besides, I didn't want your advice at all.'*

Lance jumped as the Mess door slammed open to Clayton's bellows. "Change of plan by HQ! All hands to repel borders. 111 Squadron, grab your flying gear and be at the office in two minutes for a briefing."

Lance leaned his head back and closed his eyes in disbelief. Around him cursing pilots lumbered to their feet. They'd relaxed their mental defences. Now they had to crank themselves up to fight again—no easy task.

Lance ran for his coat, gloves and goggles. He did not need to run, but it psyched him back into a hunting mind-set. War flying while lethargic was a sure way to die.

Outside the office Arthur started the briefing. "Sorry, chaps. Artillery spotters just reported ten to twelve scarlet Albatrosses over Poelcapelle, north of Passchendaele. The Circus sniffing around the army's build-up for the Passchendaele attack has sent HQ into a tailspin. They want a squadron up, whatever the weather."

"How can spotters see plane colours in this weather?" Lance asked.

Arthur shrugged. "Ours not to reason why. HQ is in full panic mode and not in the mood for a rational debate. They want a full squadron to split into three patrols—one over Passchendaele, one north at Poelcapelle, and one south at Polygon Wood. Prevent any aircraft crossing our lines. Clayton, show Ball the map?"

Lance's brain churned while Ball conferred with Clayton. If the spotters were correct, this would be the first direct confrontation with the Circus since 100 Wing had shredded their airfield. While the Circus licked their wounds and replaced their aircraft, 100 Wing had pruned the lesser *Jastas* of the German air force. Every kill gave the pilots increased confidence in their planes and each other. Now they believed they could bloody the Circus in the air.

"We've only got eleven serviceable aircraft, so I'll take A Flight and cover Poelcapelle," Ball said. "Lance Fitch will take B Flight and Passchendaele, and Cyril Crowe and C Flight will handle Polygon Wood."

Worry niggled at Lance. The Circus' successful ambush on Hawker and Lance was still a raw wound to his hunting pride. He shook his head. "It doesn't ring true. Richthofen never fights without all the advantages on his side, and he's skilled at concealment in clouds. Now he's flaunting himself to ground observers. The cunning bastard has a trap up his sleeve. Just because ten planes allow themselves to be seen doesn't mean there aren't others lurking. If just one other of the Circus *Jasta* is up there, hidden in all that cloud, isolated flights of four planes will get mauled in a hurry by twenty enemy."

"The squadron commander decides patrol tactics," Arthur said, "and you are not the commander, Lance." A mean smile played on Arthur's lips. Too late, Lance recalled his oath to Arthur—*You'll hear no more opinions from me on tactics, daft or otherwise.* Arthur was within his rights but damn, it was hard to stay silent when every hunting instinct was screaming a warning.

Ball, still studying the map, missed the by-play between Arthur and Lance. He looked up and shrugged at Lance. "Hard to keep together as a squadron in this weather—easier to split and then we don't have to worry about colliding. Besides the patrol zones are close to each other."

Lance gritted his teeth and kept his mouth shut.

Ambushes would spring shut at close quarters in this tumultuous sky. If clouds separated the line of sight between the patrols three miles apart, the Huns could wipe out one flight while the other two remained blissfully ignorant, parading their beat like the guards at Buckingham palace.

Two things were for sure—there would be no shortage of clouds or Huns on this patrol.

~

Albert Ball led the squadron aloft at 1730 hours, weaving upwards between the angry black clouds. Lance's doubts dropped away with the powerful growl of his Hispano engine. Eleven SE5s dipped and swayed in the air currents around him, flown by the best fighter pilots in the British Empire, between them more than a hundred kills. Pride and élan surged through him.

As they crossed the lines, he turned his eyes upwards, searching past the towering cumulous clouds for any ominous black dots. No enemy, but still plenty to worry him. The sky seethed like a devil's playground with cloud mountains, valleys, and ravines shape-shifting constantly. Such dark cumulonimbus clouds, pregnant with wind shear and sometimes lightning, could rip a plane apart in a heartbeat. The squadron threaded their way through the clearer air, engines thundering defiance against nature's threats. With so much moisture in the air, Lance's goggles kept misting, and he pulled them down. The slipstream buffeted his eyes, but he could see better without the goggles once he hunched lower for more protection from his small windscreen.

When they reached Passchendaele, Ball turned north to Poelcapelle, followed by the under strength A Flight—the vengeful Warbaby and the steady Daddy Heath. Seconds later a silver-blue Albatross burst from the clouds nearest to A Flight. Apparently surprised at seeing the British formation, it dived back into thick cloud. Warbaby pursued it and disappeared into the murk. Lance cursed Warbaby's stupidity, certain that the Albatross was bait for a trap.

Lance wanted to send one of his four aircraft to strengthen A Flight, now reduced to just two planes, but had no clue how to explain that to his pilots. Besides Ball was not waiting. He'd already headed north with Daddy Heath.

C Flight under Cyril Crowe turned south to Polygon Wood, leaving Lance's flight alone over Passchendaele. Lance looked back to confirm that his flight was in a proper V formation. Weston gave him a thumbs-up from his left. On his right flank swayed the SE5s of the lanky teenager Cecil Lewis, and behind him Rhys-Davids, the classics scholar from Eton. Lance had ordered them to keep close, a part of his brain marvelling at his own hypocrisy after having ignored that same order so many times in his own career.

He took his flight up to ten thousand feet, sliding close under a large cloud so nobody could jump them. The turbulence trapped under the cloud jolted his plane, but it was preferable to being ambushed.

To the north a red flare burst bright in the gloom. Ball must have sighted the enemy. Lance squinted into the murky haze. The two distant SE5s dived on six dots below them. Tracer sparkled as the formations clashed. A firefly glowed and fell, leaving a finger of black smoke as a tombstone. Then a cavalcade of dots materialised from the clouds above the dogfight and plummeted to join the swirling planes.

Richthofen's ambush!

Lance swore. His duty was to hold the patrol lines at Passchendaele. If the Huns detected Haig's preparations, they would wreak carnage. The British army had lost 60,000 men in one day assaulting alerted Hun defences at the Somme. But Albert Ball and Daddy Heath were odds on to die if Lance did not aid them. Lance twisted on the horns of the dilemma, conscious of precious seconds ticking away.

His brain ached. This was why Lance had avoided being a squadron commander. Damned if he did, damned if he didn't. The only certainty? More guilt.

Five Sopwith Triplanes materialised through the cloud, startling Lance. Their leader nosed closer to investigate and waved when he recognised the SE5s. Lance returned the greeting, grateful to recognise the black planes. Outside of 100 Wing and Guynemer's elite French Stork Squadron, no Allied flight boasted more kills than No. 10 Naval Squadron's Black Flight.The triplanes, whose three wings gifted them enviable lift and high-altitude performance, climbed even higher and settled into a broad patrol loop over Passchendaele, dodging around the dirty grey clouds.

That was the excuse Lance needed. The Black Flight could hold the fort against reconnaissance aircraft over Passchendaele.

A hunting hawk unleashed, Lance turned his flight north on full throttle to help his friends. The wind screamed through his wires, the engine howled, and the plane bucketed as he dived towards the battle. But to Lance, his SE5 was crawling.

Ahead the distant ballet played out, graceful and deadly. A plane spun earthwards out of control until swallowed by thick cloud. Lance strained to see whether the falling plane was British or German, but the distance was still too great.

He drew closer, close enough to count four slender Pfalz and nine Albatross, all harrying two square snouted SE5. Both Ball and Heath were alive!

Lance hunched forward in his cockpit and willed more speed from his mount. An Albatross fastened on the tail of one of the British planes, firing short bursts of tracer. The SE5 rolled tiredly onto its back and spiralled downwards into dense cloud. Lance ground his teeth and swerved towards the killer. But the Hun was too canny. His blood-red Albatross dived towards the thick cloud cover. The other Huns slid after him like the body of a snake following the head.

The sole surviving SE5 chased after the dozen Huns until the cloud swallowed them. Only Ball was that crazy. Sure enough, when the thwarted plane turned back to join them, Lance saw the blue spinner of Albert Ball. Thank God his friend was all right.

Then guilt hit like a punch to the stomach. Daddy Heath's greatest fear had come to pass—his children would grow up fatherless. Lance's vision misted for a second. He set his jaw. Blubbing over spilt milk wouldn't change anything.

Richthofen had run away, despite having numerical superiority, because he was at a height disadvantage in a crowded sky. That showed he placed more priority on altitude than numbers. Lance agreed with him. With height came speed, and with speed all things became possible. Lance respected the cool calculation of the German leader.

Ball drew up next to Lance, only fifty feet away, smiled, and gave a wave of thanks. Unlike most pilots, Ball wore no goggles and the black gunpowder streaked across his face made him look like a mischievous schoolboy. An unaccustomed rush of affection flooded Lance, the second surge of emotion in a few minutes. He cursed and willed himself to focus. He motioned for Ball to take charge of the flight, but the latter shook his head and fell back into the V formation. Small mercies. Lance had expected Ball to charge off on his own.

Lance turned south after the Circus, towards Polygon Wood where Crowe's flight would be on patrol. At least two of the Circus *Jasta* were up, maybe more, so they outnumbered C Flight three to one at best. Lance threaded his flight between the dangerous dark thunderclouds as they climbed.

As B Flight closed on Polygon Wood, they burst from a corridor of cloud into a three-mile-wide fishbowl of clear air surrounded by towering cumulus on three sides and bottomed by the dark earth.

A massive dogfight raged in the fishbowl below them, the largest Lance had ever seen. Crimson Albatrosses nosed everywhere like voracious sharks in a feeding frenzy, hunting darting Sopwith Triplanes and square wing tipped SE5s. White tracer lines crisscrossed the sky and a column of vertical black smoke hung suspended in the centre, shredding as planes zoomed through it.

His stomach muscles clenched—this was a gladiatorial arena for the gods—and he half-rolled into a diving attack. The SE5s plunged into the mêlée, firing short bursts they carved through the bedlam, dodging collisions as much as bullets, but splintering Hun formations. When their speed from the dive bled away, B Flight were themselves fragmented, and soon fighting for their lives against superior numbers.

Two Albatross charged Lance head on. His gut clenched as he sighted on the nose of the lead plane. Two hundred yards. One hundred. Flame flickered from the Albatrosses' gun muzzles. Tracers seemed to aim straight for Lance but smoked wide. His nose wrinkled at the stench. He held his breath until the bead sight on his Vickers obscured the Albatross pilot. Then he thumbed the twin triggers. The SE5 shook as the machine guns pounded and shell casings cascaded. A puff of black smoke broke from the lead Albatross, which swerved wildly—straight into his comrade.

The two melded Albatross hurtled at him. A crumpled red wing filled his vision, beads of moisture glinting on red paint.He yanked back on the stick and flung his other arm across his face, waiting to die in embrace with his enemies.

Nothing.

Lance opened his eyes. And breathed. *How did we miss?* He blew a hasty kiss of thanks to Lady Luck.

Bullets stitched his top wing. He ducked. A central bracing wire twanged. *Fickle bitch. Give her a kiss and get bullets in return.*

He kicked the SE5 into a gut-wrenching spin. Opposite rudder, straighten, and dive away as if the hounds of hell howled behind him. Which, when he looked behind, they were. Three Albatross. Tracers stitched his left wing. Lance chopped the throttle and half-rolled into an inverted dive, praying that the wings would hold. Debris from the cockpit floor whipped his cheeks. His vision clouded, and his guts tried to heave out of his mouth. He'd swear he heard the wooden ribs of the wings groan as they flexed under the strain.

But no rattle of machine guns.

He twisted round. None of the three Huns dared follow the foolhardy manoeuvre in their more fragile Albatross. He sagged with relief and blessed his SE5 as he eased gingerly out of the headlong dive.

Alone for precious seconds, he gulped in frigid breaths. His heart ceased skittering against his ribcage like a cornered bat and slowed into a sonorous beat. Still alive. So far…

He lurked near a cloak of dirty grey cloud and took stock of the fight while he changed his Lewis drum. The dark thunderclouds were rolling in, compressing the fishbowl. Inside the shrinking arena the sheer weight of Hun numbers was overpowering the British, forcing them lower. Soon they would be trapped between the voracious Hun predators and the earth. It was too late now for any German reconnaissance aircraft, so the SE5s could honourably flee.

Lance fumbled for his flare gun and fired the signal for home into the centre of fishbowl. The green flare reflected garishly from the massed slate-grey clouds as it drifted lower.

The surviving SE5s disengaged and fled, saved by their speed and the fading light. Lance could not count them in the indistinct light as their shadows flitted through the gloaming, but of one thing he was certain—there were too few.

Above him two British Triplanes soared upwards, trying to use their incomparable lift to escape. A highflying Albatross dived on them as they climbed. Tracers streaked both ways. One Triplane took a tracer in the tank and exploded. The flash seared Lance's retinas. When his sight returned, all the planes had disappeared. He flew in a small cone of empty sky, surrounded by brooding thunderclouds in an ominous bruised sky. He took a deep breath and turned homewards.

There would be more empty chairs in the Mess tonight, but if he found any Hun bastards alone in the murk, he still had enough fuel and ammunition to make them pay.

~

"*Schreckliches Wetter!*" Lothar von Richthofen swore. He was alone in a sky with many hostile planes not to mention the threatening weather. Turbulence buffeted his plane, making it rattle and jar as if he were flying over rocks instead of air. He picked his way eastwards between the threatening masses, desperate to land at Marckebeecke before darkness set.

Huge forbidding clouds squatted across the sky, lit by occasional flashes of forked lightning. Towering grey thunderheads soared high, looking as solid and impenetrable as castles, and the passageways between them were plunging ravines snaking between rock faces.

This was JG1'sfirst day in the air since the humiliating raid that had destroyed their planes on the ground. With the blue and white nosed enemy in mind, Manfred had dinned his instructions into the ears of the Circus pilots—*Stick together at all costs! Fight in a Jasta-sized pack at minimum! Never alone, never singly!*

The heavy clouds had hindered formation flying. Lothar found it nerve-racking as planes materialised and vanished like magic, often before he identified them as friend or foe. But the bulk of experienced *Jasta* 11 pilots managed to stick together and reaped the rewards. Six times they picked off isolated British aircraft alone in the cloud-filled void. Even better that several of the victims were the blue and white nosed SE5s that had raided them.

But the last dogfight with British Triplanes and SE5s had swirled the *Jasta* cohesion like wind with autumn leaves. One minute the air was full of planes, tracers and black smoke, and the next Lothar was alone in the sky among canyons of menacing grey cloud.

He searched the sky carefully. The new SE5s were fast, and this blue-nosed outfit were tough and determined. Even the ones JG1 had shot down had fought with heart and skill. For the first time since Lothar joined *Jasta* 11, they were fighting a skilled foe with weaponry as good as or better than theirs. The easy pickings of April were over. Some of the lambs had turned into wolves…but as today proved JG1 could still handle them. Lothar grunted with satisfaction

A red flare exploded a kilometre away and made him twitch—the British signal for attacking the enemy. He squinted around the grey amphitheatre surrounding him but saw nothing at first. Then the lean pike-like silhouette of an SE5 barrelled out of the gloom at him.

He turned into the attack—too late. Fire already flickered from SE5 guns. Lothar threw his Albatross into a steep left bank. Bullets struck his engine block, a metallic drumming that made the plane shiver. The Mercedes engine coughed as the Englishman howled over the Albatross, so close Lothar saw a strip of torn fabric fluttering from the lower wing. Prop-wash battered the German plane and Lothar fought for control.

His engine died. The sudden silence rang in his ears as a death knell.

Lothar swivelled his neck to watch the Englishman, who swooped around to deliver the coup de grâce. Another blue and white bastard—a damned good one and keen for a kill.

Lothar pushed his stick forward and plunged for the nearest cover, an ominous grey storm cloud. Better to risk the storm and having his wings ripped off than be roasted alive. As the Albatross dived, the shriek of the wind through his bracing wires sounded louder without the usual howl of the engine.

Tracers sparkled in the gloom as they flicked past his left wingtip. Lightning flashed in response. Spots danced in his eyes. Lothar kicked the rudder, skidding in the direction from where the tracer came. Sure enough, the Englishman corrected his next burst right as the Albatross skidded left. Lothar glanced back.

The mad son of a bitch was following him into the storm.

Lothar had no choice if he wanted to live, but this Englishman must be rabid for a kill to take such a risk.

The Albatross plunged into the gloom with tracers flashing past the wings. Cool vapour enveloped him and beaded on his goggles. He banked hard so the madman would not run into him in the blindness.

Then he was at the mercy of the storm. A giant invisible hand plucked the plane and tossed it where it willed. The plane juddered and creaked under the violent wind shear. His stomach surged into his throat as the invisible force of the savage winds flipped his plane hundreds of feet up or down—he had no idea which. He tasted blood. He'd bitten his tongue when the plane jolted. With nothing solid to fix his eyes on, he could not orientate himself. His altimeter was useless, jerking round the dial. If the clouds extended to ground level, he would be a dead man.

He rode his gliding plane through the cloying grey mist, his crotch and armpits pooled with sweat as he waited for a building or tree to rear up and kill him. His tongue mumbled unfamiliar words as he prayed to the God he had not spoken to for a long time. Perhaps too long?

But no, the cloud spat the Albatross out into a chasm of clear air. For a second, he was confused by the clouds below him and the ground above—he was upside down! Yet his senses in the cloud had told him he was flying level. He rolled the Albatross the right way up, and followed the canyon of clear air as it turned and twisted between the clouds, clenching his teeth as the plane jolted in the turbulence, and praying that his luck would hold to ground level.

Which it did.

The cloud base had sunk to a hundred metres above the ground, but Lothar's seam of clear air allowed him glide towards the ground with good visibility. He picked out a flat-looking grass field and hoped the ground was not too uneven. As he landed, the undercarriage rattled and creaked, but the plane rumbled to a stop over the rough grass without mishap.

Lothar sagged back in his seat and tilted his head back to let the fresh rain slap onto his upturned face. He clambered stiffly from his cockpit and pulled off his leather helmet and goggles to inspect the damage to his engine.

As he did so, an inverted SE5 spun out of the cloud just a hundred metres above the ground.

Lothar understood flying. The laws of physics bow to no one. He knew when gravity would kill even a good pilot. In this case the cloud was too low, the ground too close, and the plane upside down at the wrong angle. This funeral was a certainty.

The Englishman fought it. He tried the only hope, the only prayer, that he had left—the one trick that might allow him to live if some miracle bent those immutable laws of gravity for a few seconds.

He pushed on full power and flew upside down, just metres from death. The engine screamed its protest and the inverted nose lifted skywards. For the first time it looked as though the Englishman just might cheat his fate, and Lothar willed the nose of the man's plane to rise higher still.

As the plane howled over him, Lothar saw the pilot's gloved hands working throttle and stick inside the cockpit. The world slowed as Lothar's empathy yoked him to the pilot in the cockpit, who must have known the situation was desperate but fought for his slim chance.

Lothar would never forget the image. The khaki plane outlined against the grey clouds, the pale face of the pilot, the silver rods of rain. This man was not an enemy now; he fought that implacable foe of all pilots—gravity.

The inverted carburettor choked and the engine cut. Inexorably the nose dropped. The SE5 sailed out of sight behind a row of trees. Lothar held his breath, waiting for the inevitable. It came with a thud, then splintering and grinding noises. Then silence.

Lothar ran, frantic but clumsy in his flying boots. The heavy mud clung to his boots and soon he slowed to a gasping walk. The crash was at least two fields away in a populated area. Someone would help the flier long before Lothar reached the crash site. Perhaps he should stay with his plane and wait for troops to arrive, so he could organise a message to the *Jasta* to send a mechanic? But curiosity drove him onwards.

When he reached the crash, he found three farmers, caps in hand, standing around a young woman kneeling on the sodden ground. She was cradling the unmarked head of the pilot, but vivid red blood streaked her grey smock. She looked up with tears in her eyes and whispered at Lothar. His French was not great, but he understood the gist—the pilot had been alive when they pulled him from the crash but died moments later. Lothar nodded his understanding to the woman, not just the words but also her sense of loss. She had rescued a handsome young man, and he had died in her arms. His crushed chest was still, and his wide-open eyes filled with rain as they stared blankly into the weeping grey clouds.

"*Excusez moi*," Lothar muttered at the Frenchwoman as he reached into the dead pilot's pockets to find identification. He found a small book in the side-pocket. Inside the flyleaf was an inscription. Lothar mouthed the words, trying to remember his schoolboy English. It wasn't hard. Most of the words were similar. "To my good friend Lance Fitch, read & learn!"

Lothar rocked back on his heels. He recognised the name. The one the British papers called the "Ace from Africa." The Englander ace had shot down Lothar, but now Lothar was the real winner of the duel, courtesy of the weather gods and a badly designed English carburettor.

Pride flushed through him. Manfred had killed the great Hawker, Schmettow had shot down the famous Leefe Robinson, and now Lothar had duelled with the Ace from Africa and was the sole survivor. Lucky? *Ja*, for sure. But dead was dead and alive was alive. Those were the facts and there was no changing them. The Richthofen brothers and their *Jasta* were cutting a swathe through the British aces. Soon the British would have no worthy champions left.

~

An SE5 staggered over the airfield periphery and the officers of 100 Wing, huddled by the wing offices on the Town field aerodrome, whooped in joy. Then the cheers tailed away. White smoke trailed from the sputtering engine and the left wing flew low. The plane struggled over the poplar trees and wobbled towards its landing. The fire bell rang out, its notes jarring Clayton's already jangled nerves. Ground staff boiled from the hangars, carrying buckets of water and sand. A tall figure stuck out high in the cockpit. Disappointment stabbed Clayton. Of the missing pilots, only Cecil Lewis was that tall.

When the plane was ten feet from landing it was caught by a savage gust. The right wing flipped upwards even further. A sigh like autumn leaves ran through the watchers. But Cecil Lewis corrected and crunched into his landing, the plane bounding in big kangaroo hops as it careered along the grass. Clayton released his breath. Now only seven were still missing. *"Only" seven, for Chrissakes!*

Clayton looked at his watch again. 2015 hours, and darkness crawling inwards. It had been two and a half hours since the eleven SE5s took off—close to the maximum combat fuel endurance for the plane.

Still missing were the experienced Cyril Crowe, Lance's fellow Blackie Duke Meintjes, Daddy Heath, Warbaby, the young Etonian Rhys-Davids, and worst of all, both Albert Ball and Lance Fitch. Creases of dark worry haunted Arthur's face in the poor light as he muttered to himself. Clayton wasn't sure if it was prayers or curses.

"That's the last of them," Thompson surmised. "What a cock up. Told you SE5s would be found wanting in a dogfight. Ball and Fitch didn't want to listen to me, and now…" He shrugged and strolled away.

Clayton turned after Thompson, but Arthur caught his arm. Clayton tried to rip his arm free, but Arthur was too strong.

"Leave him, it's not worth it."

"Arsehole," Clayton said, shrugging off Arthur's hand. "Him, not you." He turned his face again towards the front lines where the darkening sky lay empty. Sheet lightning flared and thunder rumbled. A few drops of rain fell.

Other pilots drifted away from the vigil. Clayton could not fault Thompson's gloomy prediction that they had seen the last arrival, only his insensitivity.

The patrol had been a catastrophe. Those who had survived told of ambushes by the Circus and fighting against overwhelming odds in a chaotic sky. Richthofen and his men had extracted a crippling toll—sixty per cent losses from the cream of British aces flying the newest planes in the Allied arsenal.

God knew the deaths of Hawker and Leefe Robinson had been bad for RFC morale, but if Albert Ball and Lance Fitch died on the same day, it would send tremors throughout the RFC and the whole British Empire.

Only Rod Andrews remained standing on the airfield with Clayton and Arthur, as the last of the light leached from the stormy sky. The Australian was clutching a full glass of whisky in each hand and a bottle under one arm. Clayton eyed him.

"What?" Andrews asked. "I have faith in Ball and Fitch. They'll need this when they arrive. And if they don't make it, God knows I'll need it."

Clayton nodded. His mind wouldn't grasp that Lance might be dead, and it switched to military matters. "I'm not sure 100 Wing can survive this," he said to Arthur. "After Hawker and Leefe Robinson and now this, the generals may disband us. Enough senior officers hate the whole concept. Hell, even Boom doesn't like it!"

Arthur turned his anguished face to Clayton. "Bugger the generals. I'm more worried about Lance. And Albert Ball. And the others of course."

Clayton cocked his head. The faint drone of another engine wafted to his ears. At first he thought he was imagining things, but then Andrews thrust a glass of whisky towards the sky and screamed. "You beauty!"

The sound of a spluttering Hispano Suiza engine grew louder. An SE5 flitted like a bat at dusk towards the airfield boundary, indistinct in the gloom but undeniable. As the plane approached the sixty-foot poplars edging the graveyard, the engine sucked dry…died…coughed…then died for good. Out of fuel. The nose of the plane dropped.

"Can he make it over the trees?" Clayton whispered.

In the silence Clayton heard Andrews's gulp as he downed a slug of whisky. The smoky tang of the Scotch floated Clayton's way. He could do with one himself, his mouth was puckered dry.

"Who is it?" Arthur asked in a constricted voice.

"Can't tell," Andrews croaked.

The top of the poplars thrashed in the squalls, clawing at the sinking plane as it approached. The SE5 lurched as the branches brushed its undercarriage, and the plane teetered on the knife-edge of a stall. Clayton's breath caught. To make it all this way and…

The pilot caught the stall, pushed the nose down, and side-slipped into an immaculate three-point landing despite the treacherous gusting cross-wind. It had to be Albert Ball or Lance—no one else could have made that landing appear so easy.

Arthur led the run towards the plane before it even trundled to a halt at the far end of the field. Clayton and Andrews followed, the former handicapped by his gimpy leg and the latter by his concern not to spill too much whisky. When Clayton reached the plane, Arthur was hugging the pilot whose back was to Clayton. Lance or Albert Ball? Clayton stumbled to a stop, suddenly afraid.

The pilot turned. Their eyes met. Clayton sighed, gave a small half smile, and offered his hand. "Guess the devil looks after his own."

"That he does." Lance's teeth showed white in the gloom, and their handshake was firm.

"Outta the way, Adj," Andrews demanded. "Medical officer here." The big Australian proffered a whisky to Lance, who swallowed it in one gulp and doubled over coughing.

"That's the stuff!" Andrews said.

"Who's missing?" Lance wheezed.

Arthur told him the roll call in a low voice.

Lance closed his eyes, his grim face stained with gunpowder and castor oil. "Ball? Six?" asked Lance, his voice cracked in disbelief.

"It may get better," Arthur said. "Weston thinks he saw Rhys-Davids' plane in a field on our side of the Lines. Cecil Lewis saw Ball heading into a dark cloud in pursuit of a Hun right at the end of the patrol. Everyone else is a mystery."

"Not Albert Ball," Lance murmured. "Can't be. There's not a Hun alive who could nail him."

Arthur coughed. "No point in waiting here any longer. Let's go into the office and call around—find out if any others have landed elsewhere."

Andrews held up the other glass of whisky. "In my whole life," he said, "this was the only drink I *didn't* want." He saluted the dark sky with his glass. "To Albert Ball—a real stud." The whisky vanished down his throat, and he turned away.

22
Legacy

15 June 1917
Belgium, Ypres Sector, Bailleul Airfield. RFC, 100 Wing.

The weather was biblical the following morning. Storm-driven rain drummed against the windows and roofs, while squalls of wind thrashed the trees. Clayton gazed out the window as the pilots sat in the officers' Mess and talked in low voices. Pellets of rain machine gunned the puddles outside, and the spiteful wind moaned under the doors. The room reeked of soggy wool uniforms, stale cigarette smoke, and sunken hopes. Yet Clayton's spirits rose through the morning with a steady drip of better news.

Rhys-Davids was unharmed from his crash-landing and retained his ebullience despite having been outclassed by a red Albatross with a green ring around the fuselage. "Kurt Wolff," Clayton told him. "One of the top aces in the Circus, supposedly the baron's protégé."

"That so? Well, he was most tiresome and plonked my engine good and proper. Had me stony. No idea why he let me go. Must have been out of ammo."

Cyril Crowe had landed out of fuel at the Naval 8 Aerodrome nearby and cadged a lift to Bailleul. He was unwounded but still shaking from having the goggles shot off his face. He sat in the officers' Mess staring into space, no doubt reflecting on the difference an inch made.

Daddy Heath had also made it back to British lines. Bullets had smashed his leg and knocked him unconscious, but he woke up to find his plane in a spin over Hunland. Determined to see his family, he fought the massive loss of blood to reach the British lines and crash land. Now he was in hospital with a lower leg that needed amputation, but the doctors rated his odds of survival as good.

Perversely Clayton found himself relieved by the news that Daddy Heath would not fly again. A wooden leg below the knee might not be much fun, but Daddy's chances of future survival as a pilot would have been miniscule. His nerves had been going, and at his age that was no surprise. At least this way, he would spend the rest of the war warm in bed with his wife, and could watch his beautiful daughters grow up. If anyone deserved that, Clayton reckoned, Daddy Heath did.

Duke Meintjes, the South African, had crash-landed and was in hospital with a severe wrist wound. His time at the front was finished. He would be shipped back to England when he was well enough.

But by lunch, gloom and depression settled on the Mess again like the low scudding clouds, despite the news of the four additional survivors.

For there was no word of Ball.

Also, Daddy Heath had confirmed Warbaby's death— shot down in flames by the silver blue Albatross that had lured him out of formation. "Must have been a good pilot to best Warbaby," Lance said.

"Colour scheme sounds like Werner Voss," Clayton said. "A pilot captured by 61 Squadron said that Voss is even better than Manfred Richthofen as a pure fighter pilot."

Lance's eyebrows raised in disbelief. "I saw Richthofen fight Hawker. I doubt there's better. Hawker did all the fancy stuff like loops, but Richthofen did the simple things mighty well."

The phone rang and Clayton snatched it to answer, hoping it heralded news of Ball. He felt the gaze of the others searing his back, but the caller was Baring asking for news. Clayton told Baring there were four more survivors. Over the phone he heard Baring relaying the good news to Boom Trenchard, and Boom's response. "Never mind the others Baring—what about Ball? He's worth ten of the others. Find out about Ball, man!"

~

The next day the sun beamed in a clear blue sky. As Lance walked past Albert Ball's little garden on the way to breakfast, he noticed the onion bulbs perking up under the summer sun. It reminded him of Albert's dreams of life with Flora, and his throat tightened. He rubbed his eyes and dried his hand on the rough serge of his jacket, angry with himself for infringing his own rules. How often did he have to learn the same lesson—let anyone close and the bastard dies on you.

He remembered Albert's small smile when he had given Albert *The Second Jungle Book* and passed on Arthur's message. "Thanks. I'll read the book with pleasure, but tell Arthur I'm too old a dog to learn new tricks. You should be a leader—tactics is more your bag than mine."

"Old dog? You're a whippersnapper of twenty!"

Albert looked at the ground. "Inside I feel as old as the hills, Lance. I shall be glad when this is all over."

"Hey, snap out of it. You go on leave tomorrow, and soon you will be with Flora."

The sparkle returned to Albert's eyes, and he nodded. "You're right. Remember, you promised to water my veggie patch while I am away. No slacking, eh?"

Lance considered trying to keep the garden alive as a tribute to Albert Ball. Then he clamped down on the thought. He stamped the budding plants flat and kicked earth over them until no trace of them remained.

Lance wanted to lead the SE5 survivors out on a patrol—"To get back on the horse again"—but the SE5s were still too damaged. The Camels and Brisfits took over

111 Squadron's patrol schedule, which meant double time for them. Lance envied them. Flying would keep them too busy to indulge in depressing thoughts.

That afternoon, the Germans trumpeted the death of Albert Ball, killed by their Lothar von Richthofen. Lance dismissed the Lothar von Richthofen part as propaganda. A single Hun couldn't bring down Albert—not even the Red Baron himself, and certainly not his little brother.

After the last patrol of the day pilots and fitters moped around the mess and airfields. Arthur decreed a singalong for the night. "Anything to get the mopey buggers out of their blues. Time the band earned their dues."

At dinner the empty chairs weighed on the living, and only the clink of cutlery disturbed the heavy silence. Funny how people always sat in the same place at the dinner table. Maybe it gave them a feeling of an ordered world. So now a definable ghost filled each empty chair, and that ghost would leave only when a new man sat there, laughing and joking. In this way players had their exits and their entrances, and all the while you watched miraculously untouched.

For today anyway.

~

After dinner, the wing orchestra filed into the Mess. The musicians were nervous, coughing as they warmed up their instruments. At last, they launched into a jaunty tune. The pilots were slow into their stride, forgetful for a few heartbeats that Daddy Heath would not be leading the vocals. Eventually Rod Andrews's rough voice took up the refrain, then others joined in, all with more gusto than timing. By the time the chorus started the pilots were baying in full throat and the traditional riotous RFC wake was under way. The officers stood with arms linked and swayed to the tune, but the copious amounts of alcohol already consumed made the sway more of a discombobulated stagger. A rousing finale finished with the chorus.

What's the use of worrying?
It never was worthwhile, so
Pack up your troubles in your old kit-bag,
And smile, smile, smile.

As the swaying lines splintered, Elliot Springs tripped and brought his part of the line crashing to the ground in a giggling heap. Lance watched from a safe distance, propped up against the wall and nursing an untouched champagne.

Clayton rang the side of a champagne bucket with a knife to get attention. "Avast there! Silence, please! Gentlemen, the wing commander."

"Thank you, Major Clayton," Arthur said. "Men, I have here a message from General Trenchard. It says: 'Albert Ball was not only perhaps the most inspired pilot we have ever had, but the most modest and engaging character. His squadron, and indeed all the squadrons, must feel this terribly.' The general has nominated Ball for the Victoria Cross—an award as well deserved as any in history."

Applause crashed out. Bellows of "Hear, hear!" and a spontaneous chorus of "He's a jolly good fellow" rang out. Lance did not join the singers. Albert should have received the award long ago. When he was alive.

Arthur held up his hands for silence. "Lieutenant Cecil Lewis would like to recite Stevenson's 'Requiem' in tribute." The tall youngster shuffled to the centre, looking bashful, but when he opened his mouth, the words emerged haunting and beautiful.

Under the wide and starry sky,

Dig the grave and let me lie.
Gladly did I live and gladly die,
And I laid me down with a will.
This be the verse you 'grave for me:
Here he lies where he long'd to be;
Home is the sailor, home from the sea,
And the hunter home from the hill.

The last notes died, and the pilots observed a minute's silent remembrance. There was not a single cough or cleared throat, only the rumble of artillery in the distance. Outside the horizon bubbled with flash and flame, but only flickers penetrated through the cloth-covered windows into the cocoon of the Mess.

For the first time since his brother Will died, tears trickled down Lance's undamaged cheek. Lance remembered Pa's words when Lance was racking great sobs over Ma's grave.

"Lance," Pa had whispered, his arms around his son, "crying at someone's death is selfish. You are not crying for them but for pity of yourself that you must live without them. When you do that, you dishonour them. You should thank God that they lived and celebrate your good fortune to have enjoyed them in your life." Lance had suppressed his sobs, but even young as he was, he'd suspected that Pa's words were more for himself than his son.

Arthur signalled, and the band launched into a rousing marching song.

It's a long way to Tipperary, it's a long way to go, the pilots bellowed. They had paid their tribute, done their grieving, and now, to survive, the pilots must forget.

~

By midnight, the party was sinking to its natural end. Lance walked outside, away from the warm fug of cigarette smoke and alcohol fumes, and into the clean air.

He looked up at the stars. As always, his insignificance against the night sky humbled him. Those pricks of light against the black silk mourning shroud of the moonless night offered him hope. An irrational faith that a faint element of God's radiance still shone on the face of mankind in this inchoate world.

Smelling cigar smoke, Lance looked round, irritated by the intrusion on his thoughts, but he relaxed when he saw Arthur.

"I can't say I agree with that bit about gladly dying," Lance rasped. "The Grim Reaper will need to haul me in me kicking and screaming."

"Poetic licence, old chap. I dare say none of us want to shuffle off this mortal coil."

Arthur puffed on his cigar and the tip lit his face in a red glow. They stood there for long moments in the easy silence that only old friends share.

"Hard to believe, isn't it?" Arthur said. "The best of us gone, and so early in the fight."

Lance grunted in the darkness. It might have been agreement.

"What will be his legacy?" Arthur asked.

Lance rubbed his cheek. He had not considered legacies much. In Africa people died, and the world moved on without fanfare. Legacies were grand things for grand people with time to dwell on non-essential things. He turned it over in his mind while Arthur puffed on his cigar.

"Inspirational bravery, great fighter and good friend," Lance offered.

Arthur nodded in the gloom.

"No," Lance corrected himself, "he left more than that." He scratched his nose as he considered how to phrase the unfamiliar thoughts. "When I was a boy, I rode on the engineer's platform of one of the first trains in East Africa. The steam chuffed and the wheels clanked, and all the animals ran from it as it chugged through the plains. Even the rhinos ran. I remember one trotting away, his armoured backside oscillating like a fat old washerwoman's." Lance smiled at the recollection.

"Only one thing stood its ground against this clanking, gargantuan intruder. A crusty old buffalo bull, spattered with dried mud from a good wallow and covered with white tickbirds. He stood across the train tracks and refused to budge as the train approached. The driver blew the horn—'whooohee, whooohee!' I jumped, but the buffalo refused to budge, just stared at us, his wet muzzle flaring with dislike, big evil-looking horns and mean pink eyes hard with hate. The driver jammed on the brake lever and we juddered to a halt fifty feet away, with the buffalo's horns lowered and its haunches hunched for a counter charge. That buffalo was so bloody-minded it couldn't conceive of losing such a battle, even against an iron monster ten times its size. I've never forgotten him.

"That's what Ball gave the RFC. Not just inspirational bravery, but also inspirational belief he would prevail against the Huns no matter their superior planes or superior odds. The way he projected that belief and backed it up with kills in Bloody April, made Ball unique."

Arthur took a draw on his cigar. He let it out with slow satisfaction. "Great answer, Lance." A long pause ensued as both communed with their thoughts.

"Could he have left behind even more?" Arthur asked. "Did he leave behind teachings or tactics that others might use to fight better? Something like Boelcke's *Dicta*?"

Lance shifted out of the way of a waft of cigar smoke, wrinkling his nose in distaste.

"Nope, no dictums. To fight Ball's way would be suicide for ninety-nine pilots out of hundred. If anything, we should use his death to teach people not to fight that way."

"You fight alone, like him."

"No. I fight nothing like him. He waded into bucketfuls of Huns and started bar-room brawls. I sneak up and stab them in the back, one at a time if possible."

"And if you die, what will be your legacy?"

Lance looked askance at Arthur. "Why would I want a legacy?"

"Everyone should leave a legacy. Some say you die three times. Once the actual death. The second, when the last person who remembers you dies. And the third death occurs the last time someone speaks your name. Men will be speaking of Boelke's tactics and Ball's bravery in a hundred years. You could leave a legacy if you could teach pilots to fight like you."

"You mean be a devious bastard of a backstabbing assassin? It's hard work. Any fool can start a bar-room brawl. It doesn't take more than guts. That's why so many Englishmen do this reckless Charge of the Light Brigade thing. It comes easier to the Brit's amateur ethos than hatching new tactics, and training, and being seen to be trying. To fight my way, you must spend hours learning and honing hunting techniques, then hours more perfecting your shooting. Monotonous mind-numbing practice so everything is second nature under pressure. Few are prepared to do that. Certainly, no-one has asked me to train them. So no, there won't be a legacy from me."

"Shame."

"Other than a lot of dead Huns. That'll be my legacy to my brothers and Hamisi, Hawker, Leefe Robinson, Albert Ball, and the others."

"You might find a legacy to the living is more fulfilling than paying debts to the dead. You could offer to train others. Maybe you are too intimidating for them to approach you, too standoffish?"

There was more silence. This time Lance broke it. "Arthur, you're aggravating me. I don't like the way you are trying to herd me like a sheep. So, before you say anything else and make me change my mind again..." Lance took a deep breath, and the words came out in a rush. "I want to lead 111 Squadron. On two conditions."

Arthur took a long draw on his cigar, held the smoke in for a while, and then exhaled a series of perfect smoke rings. He regarded the rings with the satisfaction of a magician performing his favourite act. "Which are?" he asked.

Lance folded his arms across his chest. "If I can't cope mentally, or if I don't think I'm doing a good job, then you let me go back to being a simple pilot. No questions asked. No attempts by you to change my mind. And if *you* think I'm doing a bad job, you return me to pilot any time."

"Deal." Arthur took another deep puff of his cigar. "What changed your mind?"

"You think the Circus flaunting themselves over Polygon Wood was an accident?"

"I do not know," Arthur said with a frown. "I have not thought about it."

"Well, I have. We hurt Richthofen with our raid on his airfield. He worked out we were a threat to his Circus. That big dogfight over Polygon wasn't about reconnaissance—he lured us up into an ambush where he had every advantage. The baron is one cunning bastard."

"That seems a very convoluted thought process. Have you been reading too much of that nasty Italian chap, Machiavelli?"

Lance snorted. "I learned from leopards, who make nasty Italians look like your maiden aunt. My godfather, Frederick Selous, said man-eating leopards are the most cunning and ruthless killers that stalk this earth, and to hunt them you need to think like them. Richthofen is the most cunning and ruthless killer in the sky, so I try to get into his mind-set."

Arthur flicked ash off his cigar. "Bit beyond me. You might be giving Richthofen too much credit. Yesterday could be a fluke, just bad luck."

Lance grabbed Arthur by both arms and shook him. "Wake up, Arthur! There's nothing fluky about our losses. During Bloody April we blamed our inferior equipment. Now we can't use that excuse anymore, our planes are as good or better than the Huns'. Yet since we got the new planes, we've twice lost over half a squadron and their leader. On a single patrol. Twice in two weeks. Even a Jonah doesn't think that's bad luck. That's a pattern, Arthur!" Lance searched Arthur's eyes, looking for comprehension.

Arthur took a step back, breaking Lance's grip. "Steady, Lance, you are not supposed to manhandle your superior officer!" He rubbed his arm. "You yourself said Hawker and Leefe Robinson used dumb tactics. So perhaps our losses are due to bad tactics, but we do not have to attribute a leopard-like cunning to Richthofen."

"Two sides of the same coin. He's clever, and we're dumb. Deadly combination."

"Maybe," Arthur conceded. "Anyway, I am glad you are over your Jonah complex."

Lance shook his head. "I still worry that I'm cursed. I'm not sure I can handle more deaths on my conscience, Arthur. It slayed me having to choose that day over Passchendaele between helping Ball or protecting the lines. If Ball had died then, I'd have blamed myself and…"

His voice trailed off, and he stared into the Stygian gloom of the night sky. Heavy cloud had now obscured the heavens and he could not see a single star. Arthur stood silent beside him, the tip of his cigar glowing red.

Lance gave a gusty sigh and looked at his untouched glass of warm champagne. "Hawker, Leefe Robinson, and now Albert Ball were brave and popular leaders who deserved their Victoria Crosses. But their brainless tactics caused men to die who should have lived. We need to become smarter. To beat the Circus on a consistent basis, we need better tactics, better training, better discipline."

Lance squared his shoulders and drained the champagne glass in one throw, grimacing at the warm bitter taste. "I think I can do better than those brave but foolhardy men, even if I am a Jonah."

A waiter appeared in the doorway of the Mess, brandishing an ice bucket with an open bottle of champagne. Arthur motioned him over and filled both their glasses. Lance demurred but Arthur overruled him. "Lesson number one, Lance, drink champagne cold and fresh, not warm and flat. A toast—to Albert Ball, and Richthofen's fall."

Lance still found the first sip bitter, but the second slipped down better.

Arthur slapped him on the back. "You are a new man, Lance, from teetotal loner to alcoholic leader. Congratulations! Did you ever imagine you would be drinking champagne and leading a squadron?"

"Never." Lance looked dubiously at his glass. "I don't enjoy either."

"War is hell," Arthur said. "When you tell your grandchildren about your part in the great war to end all wars, you can wax lyrical over your battles against champagne and promotion."

Lance was on the verge of an angry retort when he glanced up and noticed Arthur's familiar lopsided smile, and he couldn't help but smile in return. "Aristocratic bastard," he said.

"Stroppy colonial oik."

Arthur produced a cigar, cropped it, and thrust it at Lance. "Time you smoked a good cigar. Draw on it to light it."

A match flared in the darkness and flame glowed around the tip of the cigar. Lance drew in, nothing happened at first, and then an acrid cloud of smoke surged into his lungs, rasping the back of his throat and causing him to cough convulsively. "Gargh!" he spluttered. "You like this?"

"Lesson number two, do not inhale a cigar. Great cigars are like leadership. It is an acquired taste, but when you get the hang of it, you will revel in it." Arthur blew a perfect smoke ring.

Lance drew on his cigar it with great caution, gagged a little, and coughed out a ragged plume of smoke. "Then I may never get the hang of leadership." Butterflies fluttered in his stomach. The prospect of taking responsibility for others made him as nervous as the prospect of fighting Richthofen's Circus.

"They say war is a great teacher." Arthur's gentle smile challenged Lance.

Lance grimaced. "If one survives. Richthofen and the Circus are cutthroat teachers."

He tossed the cigar into the darkness. As it hit the ground a shower of embers scattered and glowed.

Historical Notes

The creation of the elite 100 Wing is, in my opinion, the biggest single liberty I have taken with history. As indicated in the book, Trenchard opposed the creation of elites within the RFC. The famed 56 Squadron became a de facto elite only through the personal recruitment efforts of its commanding officer, Major Bloomfield, some of whose ideas I pinched for Arthur, such as the orchestra comprising fitters and mechanics and other non-flying personnel. So successful did 56 Squadron become that Richthofen himself apparently referred to it as the "anti-Richthofen squadron" even though it never under-took that role.

The rest of the history in this book is as accurate as I can make it, but where smaller historical facts have clashed with the needs of the story, I have altered small details and dates. Dates of major events such as Messines Ridge are accurate, but I have taken liberties with smaller items. Such liberties include:

- The exact arrival dates of types of aircraft in France.
- For example, the SE5a started operational war flying with 56 Squadron on 22 April 1917, not on 2 June as in my story.
- Leefe Robinson and Albert Ball's final flights took place in April and May 1917 respectively, not in June as in my story. The descriptions of their losing battles are

broadly accurate, although my scenes do contain fictitious characters.
- I have ignored the fact that Manfred von Richthofen took leave from France during May 1917.
- By far the longest liberty I have taken with dates is the death of Lanoe Hawker, who died as described but in November 1916, not May 1917.

This book is the first in a series whose primary intent is—to quote Lance—the telling of "ripping yarns" based around Arthurian legends and the air war of 1916–1918, rather than providing a history as such.

One of the delights of researching this period is the many brilliant histories written by the likes of Alex Revell, Peter Hart, Ian Mackersey, Jon Guttman, Peter Kilduff, and Mike O'Connor. For those who love their history pure, these authors are far more accurate and exhaustive than I could ever hope to be.

One of the major historical figures in this book who was not killed but who will play no part in 100 Wing going forward is Leefe Robinson. Two months after being shot down, the British authorities discovered that he was a prisoner of war. Always a free spirit, Leefe Robinson made several attempts to escape but was always recaptured. As a result, he suffered more brutality than most from a prison camp commander known as "The Beast of Holzminden." This left him in frail health, and although he returned to England for Christmas in 1918, he died on December 31 of influenza.

His grave lies at Harrow Weald Cemetery in Stanmore, Greater London, a one-minute walk from the Miller & Carter steakhouse, which until recently was called "The Leefe Robinson V.C." and displayed memorabilia of his

Zeppelin airship kill, the first to be shot down over England.

A fifteen-minute drive away is the Royal Air Force Museum at Hendon Airfield, which is a real slice of aviation history. Between 1862 and 1968, it saw some of the earliest balloon flights; the first man to fly the Channel, Louis Bleriot, gave flying lessons there; in 1912, under the name London Aerodrome, it held the first aerial Derby race watched by 500,000 spectators; and in 1940 pilots stationed there saw action in the Battle of Britain. At the time of writing TripAdvisor ranks this the 31st of 1,568 things to do in London, with 75% of visitors rating it as "excellent". It is free too. (Since writing this, the COVID epidemic may have altered what is still open and what is closed.)

Leefe Robinson's trick of standing up from a prone position without spilling any champagne was not in fact his. It was Major Baring's signature party trick and became legendary throughout the RFC. However, there was little room in that scene for yet another character so I gave the parlour trick to Leefe Robinson, who I think would have appreciated the gift.

Maurice Baring was variously a diplomat, journalist, novelist, poet, critic, linguist, Russian scholar, and travel writer—a character in an age of characters. He came from the Barings banking family, the son of a baron, and worked in the diplomatic corps and as a journalist in Russia before the war. Educated at Eton and Cambridge he was widely read and erudite, and often credited with introducing Chekhov to Western European audiences. When war broke out the forty-year-old became an officer. His famous partnership with Trenchard did not start well, with the latter thinking Baring was rich, indolent, and overly literary. Yet soon both the low and the high sang his praises. Aircrew loved the way he softened Boom Trenchard's hard edges. When he considered Boom had been overly harsh to men at the front, Baring made a point of telling the recipients that he would hide Boom's favourite pipe to punish him. General Foch said, "There never was a staff officer in any country, in any nation, in any century like Major Maurice Baring." Trenchard himself wrote that Baring was "the most unselfish man I have ever met or am likely to meet". After the war Baring wrote more than fifty books including *Flying Corps Headquarters 1914–1918*, which was hailed as one of the outstanding great war books. I leave you with one of the many anecdotes about a man who refused to take anything, including war, too seriously. When asked to spell his name he would recite "B for Beastly, A for Apple, R for Rotten, I for England, N for Nothing, G for God."

Albert Ball in real life was everything and more than I painted in the book. If anything, he was even more of a loner, but in the first half of 1917 he stood as a beacon in the hearts of the British public and the minds of the pilots as the leading ace of the RFC. He described his "Mad Dog" approach in letters, and it is no surprise that for some months before his death contemporaries described him as "a bundle of nerves". His brother, also a pilot, said he "may have looked alright... but he was mentally and physically spent." Just before he died he wrote to Flora that he had "such a dream. Oh! Such a topper. War was over and we all came home. You met me at the station and we had such a topping time."

However, his womanising became so well known that the *London Evening Standard* dared call him a modern Romeo in an age that frowned on promiscuity. In one instance he proposed marriage while dressed in full uniform regalia, including a sword. Notwithstanding this peccadillo, his comrades in arms admired him whole heartedly, and often commented on his "lack of side", modesty, and keenness to tackle the Hun, along with his garden and eccentric violin-playing in his pyjamas by the light of a flare.

His disastrous last flight is somewhat as described in this book. As in my book, history shows eleven SE5a of 56 Squadron took off that day, including Albert Ball, Cyril Crowe, Cecil Lewis, Duke Mentjies, and Arthur Rhys-Davids. Only five returned and the fates of the above named were as described. Warbaby Harmison and Daddy Heath are fictional. Ball did die in the arms of a young Frenchwoman, Cecile Deloffre, although Lothar was not present.

For some years, confusion reigned over the exact circumstances of Albert Ball's death. The Germans claimed Lothar von Richthofen shot him down, but this seems to have been propaganda. It is doubtful Lothar believed it, since although he made a kill that day he wrote in his claim that it was a Sopwith Triplane—not easily confused with an SE5. However, it does seem that Ball exchanged shots with Lothar just before crashing that day. Cyril Crowe reported that Ball fired two red flares and chased a Hun into cloud. Crowe tried to follow but lost them. Whether Lothar was that pursued plane or not is unknown, but during frantic fighting with 56 Squadron the German's plane was hit in the engine, forcing an emergency landing. It is now generally accepted that Ball spun into the ground, disorientated by heavy clouds and probably exhausted after nearly three hours of intense fighting.

The Germans buried him in their own cemetery at the nearby village of Annoeullin with full military honours. His grave still lies there. After the war Ball's father purchased the field his son crashed into and erected a headstone that you can visit today. (Mike O'Connor's *Airfields and Airmen* series will help you find it.) The headstone concludes: "one of England's famous airmen who fell on this spot, fighting gloriously… Aged 20 years."

But I will give the last word on Ball's last battle to Cecil Lewis, who wrote in *Sagittarius Rising* a typically lyrical description of an air fight. The famous playwright George Bernard Shaw wrote of Lewis: "This prince of pilots...is a master of words and a bit of a poet." Read and judge for yourself.

The last SE5, pressed by two Huns, plunges and wheels, gun-jammed, like a snipe over marshes, darts lower, finds refuge in the ground mist, and disappears. Now lowering clouds darken the evening. Below flashes of gunfire stab the veil of the gathering dusk. The fight is over! The battlefield shows no signs. In the pellucid sky, serene mountains mass and move unceasingly. Here where the guns rattled and death plucked the spirits of the valiant, this thing is now as if it had never been! The sky is busy with night, passive, superb, unheeding.

No surprise that Cecil Lewis went on to co-found the British Broadcasting Corporation (BBC) and to enjoy a glittering career as writer, producer and director, even winning an Oscar in 1938.

In Flanders the sodden battle-blasted landscape is now peaceful, sometimes deceptively so. Two of the British mines at Messines did not detonate. Over time their exact locations were lost, and an electric tower was unwittingly built over one of the mines. In 1955 the tower suffered a lightning strike, and the resulting explosion left a crater 100 feet deep and 300 feet wide. The exact position of the remaining mine is unknown, but if you like living dangerously you can visit its approximate location in Ploegsteert, Belgium.

The attack on Messines Ridge and the subsequent battles of Pilkem Ridge and Passchendaele did divert German attention and resources away from the fragile, mutinous French Army. The Germans lost the opportunity to smash through the French lines and isolate the British Army. General Petain's energetic cauterising of the mutiny involved 3,427 court martials, 2,878 sentences of hard labour, and 629 death sentences. On the other hand, he promised the French troops more leave, better food and an end to French grand offensives until the Americans troops arrived.

On the German side, my brutal Captain Peters of the Schutztruppe is fictitious, but if readers find the Hamisi burning episode at the start of this book overly brutal, they should know the Schutztruppewere more than capable of such things. In Africa the Germans often used natives used as slaves, and when the slaves dared rebel the German commanding general in South-West Africa approved the genocide of the entire Herero tribe. He wrote, "I believe the nation as such should be annihilated." The governor came across as a bleeding-heart liberal in comparison—"I do not concur with those fanatics who want to see the Herero destroyed altogether…I would consider such a move a grave mistake from an economic point of view. We need the Herero as cattle breeders…and especially as labourers." Back home in Germany the official publication of the German Army general staff, *Der Kampf*, celebrated the "extermination of the Herero nation".

The German Government offered $1 billion in compensation in 2021, an offer that was refused 'as too little and too late'. The Shutztruppe's brutal suppression of the Maji Maji rebellion in 1905 in German East Africa is briefly mentioned in this book, and although there was no official policy of genocide the number of native deaths exceeded even those in the South-West.

Against this background, you might think it would be impossible for a German colonial officer in East Africa to be summoned back to Germany, be found guilty of excessive brutality to the natives, and have his commission and pension taken away. But a man named Carl Peters managed it. In a place and time of much brutality he stood out. The locals called him "Bloody Hands" and the German press named him "Hangman Peters". He might have been the only point of agreement between the natives and Germans.

To escape criminal prosecution, he fled Germany. However, by 1914 the militaristic Junker ethos had routed the liberals in Germany. The small matter of murdering natives on a whim was no longer an outrage, and Kaiser Wilhelm invited him back by personal decree. Even more tellingly, twenty years later another personal decree—this time by Adolf Hitler—declared him a national hero and a movie of his exploits followed. I felt my villain and Carl Peters deserved to share such a surname.

On a more uplifting note, Oswald Boelcke gets only a passing mention in my book, but seems to have been one of the most remarkable of the aces on either side, not just as a military man but as a human being. When he died he led all aces in the world with forty kills, but more important to him than kills were his "cubs", whom he trained in his innovative tactics as outlined in "Dicta Boelke". Air Vice Marshal "Johnnie" Johnson, the top-scoring British ace of World War 2, wrote in his seminal history of air fighting, *Full Circle*, that "the modest Oswald Boelcke was one of the greatest air fighters…and his teachings were followed long after his death." Manfred von Richthofen, whom Johnson ranked as the greatest air fighter of WW1, said of his mentor—"I am after all only a combat pilot, but Boelcke, he was a hero."

But if the number of Boelcke's kills were no longer unique by the end of the war, his degree of personal popularity among those who met him certainly was. Manfred wrote in his autobiography, *The Red Battle Flyer*, that "It is a strange thing that everybody who met Boelcke imagined that he alone was his true friend. I have made the acquaintance of about forty men, each of whom imagined that he alone was Boelcke's intimate. Each imagined that he had the monopoly of Boelcke's affections. Men whose names were unknown to Boelcke believed that he was particularly fond of them. This is a curious phenomenon which I have never noticed in anyone else. Boelcke had not a personal enemy."

Even the enemy respected him. His courtesy to those he shot down—at least those who lived—was such that one said his encounter with Boelcke was "the greatest memory of my life, even though it turned out badly for me". As a result of a letter back to England written by a downed pilot Boelcke visited in hospital, a British paper called him a "Gentleman pilot". This when British papers more often painted the Germans as the brutal and savage "Huns". The British pilots dropped a wreath on his aerodrome after his death with the words, "To the memory of Captain Boelcke, a brave and chivalrous foe." In my reading across two World Wars, only one other person seems to have had such respect across friend and foe, and that was the "Desert Fox" of the Afrika Corps in WW2, Erwin Rommel. Today a German Air Force Wing still carries Boelcke's name.

Another remarkable character was Erwin Bohme—the same Erwin Bohme who helped rescue Lance from the brutality of Captain Otto Peters. Whilst those actions are fictitious, Erwin is not. When Boelcke died after a mid-air collision with his best friend, that friend was Erwin Bohme. Afterwards Manfred von Richthofen, among others, had to talk the inconsolable Erwin out of committing suicide. Erwin subsequently took command of *Jasta* Boelcke and remained one of Manfred's closest friends. By April 1917 these two men were the only founding members of Boelcke's *Jasta* still alive.

Erwin was in German East Africa in 1914, although I took the liberty of stretching his stay a few months to include him in the story. He had been one of Germany's premier mountain climbers, the only non-Swiss member of the Swiss Alpinist's guild—a tribute to his popularity as well as skill. Growing bored of Switzerland, he decided to go to Africa. To get there he walked from Berne, Switzerland, to catch a ship in Genoa, doing a solo climb of the Matterhorn on the way—as one does. He worked in Tanganyika (which in another quirk of essential history is my country of birth and early life) from 1910–1914, helping build cable car and railway tracks. Aged 36 when war broke out, he returned to Germany, and the rest you know. Unlike Leefe Robinson and Oswald Boelke, Erwin will surface again in the series when Lance meets his one-time saviour in the air. Another link between the two, Lance's teenage love, Heidi, will also reappear later in the series.

For the rest of the cast, some mystery needs to remain. At the very end of the series it will be clear who is historical and who fictitious—and where they are fictitious, who I used as inspiration for my character. Where my characters were real people, I have often used their own words as reported by themselves or others. Where this is not possible, I have endeavoured to stay true to their known character. Where I could not find a real character to fit the tale, rather than warp historical characters, I used fictional names and felt free to embellish their stories as my muse took me—as the Hollywood captions of today say, "inspired by a true story".

Acknowledgements

To my friends; Judy Weber for valiantly motivating me after she gamely waded through a stodgy first draft, and Jan Chojecki and Alex Lorenz, my most reliable and enthusiastic beta readers.

And to Peter Hart, Oral Historian of the Imperial War Museum and author of two of the most readable histories on WW1 aviation [*Aces Falling* and *Bloody April*], who on a blustery day at the Shuttleworth Air Show in England, responded to my tentative outline with enthusiasm. He won't remember the encouragement he gave a stranger, but to have the thumbs up from such an authority pushed me towards my first words on paper.

About Atmosphere Press

Atmosphere Press is an independent, full-service publisher for excellent books in all genres and for all audiences. Learn more about what we do at atmospherepress.com.

We encourage you to check out some of Atmosphere's latest releases, which are available at Amazon.com and via order from your local bookstore:

Among the Alcoves, a novel by Andrew Mitin
Family Crystals, a novel by Amber Vonda
The Truth About Elves, a novel by Ekta R. Garg
How to be Dead—A Love Story, by Laurel Schmidt
Waiting Impatiently, a novel by Andrew H. Housley
A Journey's Promise: The Helio Series, by Johnny Hall
Taint: A Novel, by Janey Kelley
New Shores, a novel by Ciaran McLarnon
Murder at the Olympiad, a novel by James Gilbert
The World Turned Upside Down, a novel by Steven Mendel
Dolly: The Reno Story, a novel by Fern Hammer

Author Biography

Iain Stewart was born and raised in East Africa. Time spent at Kenton College in Nairobi, Fettes College in Edinburgh, and Christ's College, Cambridge was usually enjoyable and often educational. His feeble qualifications as an author of this tale include a childhood fascination with *The Romance of King Arthur*, and obtaining his pilot's license at seventeen. Armed with these, he ventured forth to fly Tiger Moth biplanes and pretended to be Biggles. Who was basically Lancelot in goggles. However, earning a crust at HSBC for over twenty years delayed this book. Nowadays, he staves off reality by living in Miami.

If you've enjoyed the book, an honest comment on Amazon would be awesome. If you don't like writing comments or reviews, then taking a second just to give the book the number of stars you think it deserves would be most appreciated. This link will take you there.

https://www.amazon.com/review/create-review?&asin=B09V6B1Z6C

Printed in Great Britain
by Amazon